By Karin McQuillan
Published by Ballantine Books:

DEADLY SAFARI
ELEPHANTS' GRAVEYARD
THE CHEETAH CHASE

THE CHEETAH CHASE

Karin McQuillan

BALLANTINE BOOKS • NEW YORK

Copyright © 1994 by Karin McQuillan
Foreword copyright © 1994 by Paul G. Irwin

All rights reserved under International and Pan-American Copyright Conventions. Published in the United States by Ballantine Books, a division of Random House, Inc., New York, and simultaneously in Canada by Random House of Canada Limited, Toronto.

Library of Congress Catalog Card Number: 93-47125

ISBN 0-345-39780-0

Manufactured in the United States of America

First Hardcover Editon: August 1994
First Mass Market Edition: September 1995

10 9 8 7 6 5 4 3 2 1

To John

FOREWORD

CHEETAHS ARE EXCEPTIONAL animals. Capable of blinding speed, far more social than we ever imagined, quick to bond to humans when they are young, difficult to study in the field—the mysteries about these beautiful cats seem almost endless. One reality, unfortunately, is that the cheetah is in danger of disappearing from the face of the earth.

In many ways the cheetah, more than any other animal, represents quintessentially the sub-Saharan area of the African continent. Since the turn of the century this region has been plundered for its riches. Its people and its wildlife have been decimated, its beauty defaced, and its resources stripped—while the true character of the "Dark Continent" has remained an enigma to all who would seek to understand her.

Like the cheetah, Africa doesn't fit into any easy category. Sublime in her beauty, breathtaking in scope, Africa looms larger than possible in real life. Ostensibly peaceful, but dramatically violent in all aspects—from weather to the daily struggle for life—the true Africa eludes us. From past exploitation by colonists to the current corruption by her own leaders, this continent continues to struggle to survive in a world that seems hell-bent on destroying the essence of that which is necessary for her soul.

Karin McQuillan's *The Cheetah Chase* is a supremely entertaining fiction. And more. McQuillan fully captures the mystery and appeal of the cheetah and the concurrent mystery and paradox that is Africa. As President of the Humane Society of the United States, I have, through our international arm (Humane Society International), been actively involved in efforts to protect African wildlife for over twenty years. Ms. McQuillan's book is of particular interest, as the HSUS is currently supporting a critical program in Namibia to protect that country's remaining cheetahs.

It is the contention of the HSUS, however, that until we begin to value animals like the cheetah for their intrinsic worth—and not for their fur or as unique specimens in a zoo—then all of the special creatures on this earth will remain in jeopardy.

This, too, is a theme of Karin McQuillan's novel—and in her depiction of native African wildlife, she dramatizes the HSUS's fundamental principle: *all* life is unique and worthy of our efforts to ensure its place on this earth.

—Paul G. Irwin
President,
The Humane Society
of the United States

ACKNOWLEDGMENTS

THANK YOU TO Victor Kabiru, of Kerr and Downey Safaris, for many hours of pleasure observing cheetah in Kenya's national parks. Stuart Wells, at the National Zoo in Washington, D.C., was tremendously helpful, explaining the zoo's cheetah reproduction project, taking me backstage at the cheetah compound, and providing me with a foot-thick pile of reference material.

Thanks, too, to Laura Leibensperger of Harvard University's Museum of Comparative Zoology, for her unstinting help in teaching me about scorpions. Harvard University was generous in giving me access to their zoology and anthropology libraries.

Teresa Telecky, at the Humane Society of the United States, helped with material on the wild pet trade. For the material on Saudi hunting, I relied on Mary Ann Weaver's article in *The New Yorker* (December 14, 1992), "Hunting with the Sheikhs," and Sandra Mackey's fascinating book, *The Saudis: Inside the Desert Kingdom.*

I would also like to thank my wonderfully supportive editor at Ballantine, Joe Blades.

1

I WAS IN the cheetah barn grooming Gin, lulling myself into a state of silken reverie, when she perked her ears toward the house, grew taut in every sinew, and took off. I ran after her in time to see her black-tipped tail disappear behind the house. I rounded the corner, and for a moment I thought Nick Hunter was on his back, roughhousing with the cheetah, a favorite game. Then I noticed that Gin was still, and only Nick was moving. He was thrashing about as if in intense pain. Gin chirped in distress. Her brother, Tonic, came racing around the corner of the house.

"Wynn!" I bellowed. "Quick!"

I could hear running footsteps in the kitchen, and thanked God that Wynn was a former nurse, confident as a child that she would make everything better. I dropped to the ground, cradled Nick's dark, elegant head on my thighs, and felt his brow. It was frighteningly cold, yet slick with sweat. His long, tan hands clutched at the dust. Gin sniffed Nick's face and chirped, the birdlike cheetah distress call. Nick's eyes were open, but he didn't look at us. A froth of saliva gathered at the corner of his mouth as he labored for breath. Tonic sniffed Nick's face and backed off, chirping. My own breath seemed stopped in my chest.

Wynn burst through the door and crouched beside me, her face set and intense. She touched his cheek, picked up his right hand and examined it closely. It was bluish, swollen to the size of a grapefruit.

Nick's sister Viv and her husband Roger Porter were

1

right behind Wynn, both dressed for their country weekend as if they'd stepped from a whiskey ad in *Vanity Fair*.

"What is it?" Viv's eyes were two big O's of fear. "A snake?"

A chill ran through me. A snake. I'd been running safaris in Kenya almost three years now and had never had to deal with snakebite. Viv and Nick were born here, grew up on a big farm west of Mount Kenya. I seemed to remember a story of both brother and sister stumbling upon a viper as children, Nick saving his older sister and being bitten.

"I don't see a double puncture," Wynn said. Nick had a bit of gauze taped to one finger, protecting a cut. His other fingers were unmarked.

Gin pushed her tawny head closer to see what Wynn was doing, and wriggled in protest when I pulled her away. I knelt down and hugged her long, thin torso. I could feel the cheetah's heart beating rapidly against my chest. Tonic was nowhere to be seen. He must have run off in fright.

"Nick! What bit you?" Viv shouted, her voice panicky. He didn't answer, didn't even turn toward her.

Wynn raced back to the kitchen to pull the antivenin kit from the fridge. I followed her and went for the shortwave radio.

"What are you doing?" she asked.

"Calling the flying doctors."

"Right."

She ran outside. I explained the situation tersely to the dispatcher, and followed. Roger had found a big stick and was circling the outhouse, poking at the foundation, eyes raking the ground.

Wynn knelt in the dust and kissed Nick's brow. "Nicky, I'm here. We have antivenin. You'll be okay." With the rapid, experienced movements of a nurse—her job before coming to Kenya—she filled the hypodermic.

Viv caught her wrist. "Wynn, don't."

Wynn paused, hypodermic pointing at the sky.

"He's allergic to antivenin. He never told you? He was

2

bitten when we were kids. He . . ." Viv's voice trailed off at the sight of Wynn's face.

At that moment I realized that Nick was going to die. The nearest clinic was Isiolo, the nearest hospital Nairobi. The flying doctors couldn't get here in time, and we had no way to get anywhere.

Isiolo, several hours drive from here, was the only thing passing for a town in this vast region north of Mount Kenya. Beyond Nick and Wynn's house, scrub desert stretched out in a rolling wilderness that kept on until it hit the Sahara. The Hunters had chosen this land as a refuge of solitude and peace, with only cheetah and oryx, lion and kudu, as neighbors. Their plane was their link to civilization, and right now the plane was out of commission, being overhauled down at Wilson Airport in Nairobi.

Nick's breathing grew more labored and his legs and arms began to twitch and jump. The full horror of our situation pressed in on me. We had no way to get Nick out in time. Roger and Viv had come up on a commercial flight as far as Isiolo, and my boyfriend, Striker, had flown the Hunters and me up in his four-seater, spent the night and flown back to Mount Kenya after breakfast.

We didn't even have a car at the moment. Kaji, the Hunters' assistant, had taken it for a desert drive; there was a lone female cheetah she'd been watching closely, as part of a research project. We didn't expect her back until after lunch. Every way I looked, we were hours from help. Nick's life was ebbing away in minutes, not hours.

Wynn took Nick's pulse. Her usually laughing face was grim, deep lines of pain etched from brow to chin. "No pulse. He has no pulse. We have to counteract this venom," Wynn said, her eyes fixed on Viv's. "Do you remember what happened to him as a kid?"

"I'm not sure. He was seven and I was eleven. I remember Mother saying the cure was worse than the bite. They almost thought they'd lost him." Viv's eyes filled with tears.

"If only we knew what bit him," I said, "we could weigh the risks."

"I don't see a snake track anywhere." Roger's voice

3

came out rough and jerky. "And I can practically tell where an ant walked, in this dust." He circled the wooden loo, poking with his stick at the foundation stones.

"Look inside," Viv said. "That loo always made me nervous."

Roger opened the door gingerly with the stick, staying out of a direct line of fire in case a spitting cobra was inside. They can spit nine feet with deadly accuracy; their saliva blinds you. Roger looked in from the side and scrabbled at something on the floor with his stick. "There's a dead scorpion in here. A big one."

I went over to look. A black lobster-shaped insect as long as a man's thumb lay in the doorway. A few legs were broken off and the abdomen was crushed, but its deadly curled tail was intact. "Nick must have stomped on it after it bit him."

Roger gingerly picked up the black horror by a front pincer. One of the segmented legs dropped off. It was a nightmare out of the mists of time, born when all the continents were one big happy island called Pangaea. I hated the creature, wanted to pulverize it, make it disappear as if it had never existed. Roger must have been feeling something similar, for with a curse he hurled it into the desert. It caught on a bush and hung there like a deadly fruit.

Nick's breathing grew more labored. Before our eyes, his face, chest, both his hands, every patch of skin we could see, turned the blue of veins. The hackles rose on Gin's back, and I shivered as goose flesh stood up along my arms.

"His blood isn't carrying oxygen anymore," Wynn said. "We've got to try this." She inserted the needle. Nick's whole arm jerked, but she had a solid grip on his biceps and was able to push in the plunger.

She wiped his wet brow. I inwardly prayed, Don't let him die, don't let him die. The twitches in his legs ceased. I felt a moment of hope. Nick couldn't die. Then his body stiffened, his skin turning purple-black. His heels drummed on the ground in a rapid senseless rhythm. It was a sound of doom. Green spittle frothed at his mouth. Viv began to sob. I gripped Wynn's shoulder. It was hard as a rock.

"Nick," Wynn called. That's all she said. Just that one word, but it carried all the pain in the world. Nick, I love you. Nick, you're dying. Nick, don't go. Nick, I can't live without you. Nick. Please. Don't go. Nick, I love you. Nick: goodbye. It was the sound of someone's heart being torn open.

Nick Hunter self-destructed before our eyes. It was agonizing to watch. Gin whimpered and crawled forward. I had to turn my head away. Then the frantic sound of Nick's breathing stopped, bam, like a light switched off forever. Viv's sobs couldn't hide the silence.

Roger and I looked at each other in shock. Is this the way it happens? One minute you're alive, and the next you're dead? The whole thing didn't take ten minutes. I realized my mouth was hanging open, and closed it. I opened it again to speak, but found nothing to say. Gin whimpered and inched forward on her belly until her nose touched Nick's arm. Wynn tried and tried to revive him mouth-to-mouth, until we had to pull her off. Gin slunk away. By the time we heard the approaching whine of the flying doctors' plane, there was only a corpse for them to carry back to Nairobi.

2

I FELT LIKE rubble left behind after an explosion.

Wynn returned to Nairobi with the flying doctors and Nick's body; Striker was going to pick up the Porters and me around four. After Wynn left, I fell apart. I cried nonstop for an hour, cried for Nick, for Wynn, for myself. It felt so wrong. How could he be snatched away without a moment's warning? Crying that hard left me sick and dazed. I went to the kitchen and stuck my head under the pump. I could hear Viv sobbing in her room. From the sound of a bottle clinking against the slate-topped bar, Roger was still in the living room, drinking steadily. I didn't want to talk to him, so I slipped out of the house. I thought I'd finish grooming Gin: it might soothe her, and it would certainly soothe me.

As soon as I stepped out on the porch, I sensed something was wrong. There was Tonic, lying in the shade all by himself. The two cubs usually stayed within a few feet of each other, and if they were lying down, liked to be in body contact.

Feeling uneasy, I walked to the cheetah barn, calling, "Gin." No sign of her. Tonic followed me, giving his high-pitched distress chirp. I fought down my rising alarm. I went into the barn's shadowy interior. "G-in!" Nothing. Around the barn and the house. Had she snuck inside the house? I went back in.

Roger was on the couch, finishing off his whiskey and soda. Ever the gentleman, he got up when I entered. "Hullo, Jazz. Been outside?"

Roger Porter was a big man, with a hefty bone structure

and a middle-age paunch. He was looking uncharacteristically wilted at the moment, with a decidedly reddish hue to his tan face, but that might have been from the heat. Living in mile-high Nairobi, he wasn't used to the desert in August. He didn't show any outward signs of being the least drunk.

"I can't find Gin," I told him.

"She's not in here," he replied. "What can I offer you?"

"Nothing, thanks."

He went to the bar and added two fingers of whiskey to his glass, a short spray of soda, and an ice cube from a bowl. "No ice bucket, I'm afraid."

"You seem to be managing."

"I have the misfortune of having been born with a hollow leg," he said. "I've been trying to drink myself into oblivion, but it's not working." He whooshed the ice around and raised his glass. "Cheers." He took a big drink. "I say, may I ask you a favor? It would be very kind of you to look in on Viv."

"Sure." I listened: she seemed to have stopped crying. I went down the hallway and quietly knocked at her door.

"Yes. Come in," said a weak voice.

The blinds were drawn, but the afternoon sun had found a chink, and dust motes swam in a beam of sun that cut through the dim room. Viv was lying on her back, staring up at the ceiling.

"Roger?" Viv's voice quavered.

I quickly glanced around the room. No cheetah. "It's me, Jazz. Sorry to barge in. Can I get you anything?"

"Thank you. That's kind of you, but I don't think so. I'm all right." Her voice was weak, as if her throat hurt from crying, and she looked terrible. Her eyes were almost swollen shut and mascara was smeared under them in a raccoon's mask.

"A cold drink? Or a compress for your eyes?" I offered.

"A compress? That would be lovely, if you could manage it."

I got her set, and continued my search of the house. It didn't take long. I hated to bother Kaji, but I was worried about the missing cub. Kaji had returned from the bush

7

shortly after Wynn left with Nick's body, and I'd had to break the news to her. She'd reacted with disbelief and then cries of protest and grief. We'd talked only a few minutes—what was there to say?—and then each of us had crawled into our rooms like wounded animals.

I knocked on her door. "Kaji?"

She opened it immediately, took one look at my face and asked, "What's happened?"

She was in her usual outfit: khaki chinos and a slouchy olive sweater, despite the eighty-five-degree heat. Kaji's skin was a smooth medium-chestnut. Her face was bony enough to be interesting, framed by the neat dome of her hair. Right now she looked drawn, years older than her age of twenty-five.

"I can't find Gin. Tonic is lying alone on the porch."

Kaji didn't waste time asking me if I'd checked here or there. "I didn't see her when I got back." She headed for the front door and I followed. "I should have realized something was wrong."

Nick had been the cub's favorite person. When he was home, she liked to follow him around. She and her brother were orphans. Nick and Wynn had found them chirping next to the skinned carcass of their mother when they were only bits of spotted gray fluff, one month old. Somehow they'd managed to keep them alive. Now Gin and Tonic were sleek youngsters, almost a year old, at the age when their mother would be teaching them how to hunt. They wouldn't be mature enough to survive on their own for another six months at least.

"She was the first one to get to Nick. Tonic took one sniff of Nick and ran, but Gin stuck with him the whole time."

Kaji clicked her tongue with annoyance. "I should have looked for her."

"Let's hope she's hiding somewhere close by."

We checked out the cheetah barn again, even looking into open boxes in the storeroom. Tonic trailed us, chirping anxiously. He poked his head into the boxes, too.

"Where's your sister?" I asked him. "How come you let her run off alone?"

8

He looked at me with his clear amber eyes and chirped.

Kaji held her hands together as if in prayer and pressed them against her lips, thinking. "There's that big silver thorn near the airstrip where they like to lie sometimes."

The acacias and thorn trees in the nearby scrub were all leafless at this time of year, and shade was scarce. We hopped in Kaji's Land Cruiser and drove the short way to what we called the airstrip: a flat runway where the brush had been cleared and a wind sock erected. There was no sign of the cheetah.

"This is bad," I said, thinking of the inexperienced cub all by herself for the first time. Thinking of lions.

A pride of lions had moved into the area last month, drawn by the abundance of game around a marsh on the Hunters' property. For some reason, lions treat cheetah like an implacable foe, systematically searching for cheetah cubs and killing them with a single bite to the throat. It doesn't make sense: cheetahs pose no competition for lions—in fact, the lazy king of beasts steals the cheetah's kills, forcing the lighter cat to expend twice as much energy for a bite of food. The problem was frightening, because the game parks were full of lions, and cheetahs were losing ninety percent of their cubs. That's why private reserves like the Hunters' were crucial to cheetah survival. There weren't many of them.

Kaji and the Hunters had been carrying on a lively debate over what to do about the pride. Nick argued that they shouldn't interfere with the natural order on their land. Kaji countered that cheetahs are close to extinction and lions are not. Now it would be up to Wynn to decide.

"Gin can run faster than a lion, can't she?" I asked Kaji.

"Only if she sees it first."

Lions are short sprinters. They rely on stealth to creep up on a victim undetected. Would Gin know enough to avoid thick scrub, where a lion could surprise her? Or would she head for the shade, right into danger?

"If a lion gets her . . ." Kaji didn't finish the sentence.

"We'd better find her first. Do you think you can track her?" I asked Kaji.

She lifted her chin. "I'll have to."

We got back in the car. This time I took the wheel, so Kaji could stick her head out the window and study the ground. I ever so slowly circled the house and barn. It hadn't rained since the spring, and the ground was covered with a fine dust that took prints well. Too well.

There wasn't six inches of ground that wasn't covered by tracks, one on top of another: the deep furrows of zebras in single file, the sharp points of the impala's delicate hoof, the dinner plate tracks of elephant. It took a sharp eye to pick out the cub's prints on top of the confused pattern, and I had to keep to a crawl. Fifteen minutes passed. And another fifteen. Sweat started to trickle down my back.

Would Kaji be able to do this? She knew a lot about the bush, but most of it she'd picked up the last few years. Her tracking skills were nothing compared to the local Samburu people, herders in this semi-desert, who grew up observing the wild animals and their signs all around them. Kaji grew up as a city girl in Nairobi.

Most kids in Nairobi never venture farther than the city zoo, where the favorite attraction is a chimpanzee that smokes cigarettes. They know nothing about the wilds, and could care less. Kaji was unique, especially for a woman. Her parents' house was only a short walk from Nairobi National Park, and she and her brother had spent all their free time there, illegally sneaking in on foot. Her father had encouraged it, thinking that animals were safer company than the street kids and loafers. I wonder if he regretted that decision now, when college-educated Kaji had thrown over a white-collar career to be the foster mom to two cheetah cubs.

The Hunters hired her so that instead of being house pets, the cubs could spend most of their waking hours in the bush. The challenge was to teach them the lessons they'd naturally learn from following their mother, so they'd be able to return to the wild when they were old enough. Meanwhile, Kaji and the car were always there as a refuge if a lion or hyena got too close.

"I got it! It's Gin's print. Very recent." Kaji's voice rose in triumph.

10

I hopped out of the car and walked around to study the track. Cheetah have the round four-toed pad of a cat, but their claws don't retract, so the track has a doglike look. "Great. Now, we've got to stay with it."

The next two hours were long, hot, and frustrating. We lost the track twice on rocky ground and it took ages to find it again. We drove and called, and Tonic trotted alongside, adding his chirp to our cries. Gin had followed an erratic course, winding among the scrub, now trotting, now making a short burst of speed after a bird or a lizard, now slowing to a walk. What worried us were the numerous pug marks of lions, including ones ominously recent.

To add to our misery, Kaji had half a dead impala in the back of the car, which attracted a horde of flies. She'd stolen it from a hyena on her morning drive, to use in a hunting lesson for the cubs. Blood-gorged flies bumped and buzzed against my sweaty arms and face until I wanted to scream. "These flies are driving me crazy," I said. "Should we take a break, and give the impala to Tonic?"

"I hate to waste it. I was going to tie it on the car and race down the airstrip, give them the experience of running after their supper."

"So let's do it for Tonic now. It won't take long. I just won't be able to go as fast on this rough ground."

"Okay. Let me tie it on and get in back. Wait until we get to a long flat bit, where you can pick up some speed," Kaji directed me. "Start slow and easy. When Tonic starts to chase it, I'll yell. You hit the accelerator and go as fast as you feel safe. I want him to realize he has to run full out if he wants to eat."

Cheetahs do not instinctively know how to catch antelope. It's not easy, not even for the fastest animal in the world. Playing tag with your sister is different from catching a gazelle at sixty miles per hour, or picking out a vulnerable wildebeest calf from a stampeding herd and bringing it down. In the wild the cubs would observe their mother and practice on small wounded game she'd get for them. With all that, hunting is still so difficult, they often go hungry after Mom kicks them out to raise a new litter. Hunger is the final teacher.

11

Kaji tied a rope to the back of the Cruiser and to the leg of the carcass. Tonic approached the impala and swatted it with his foot. Kaji got in the back, waited for him to give it a tentative lick, then signaled for me to start up. I slowly accelerated, circled around a rocky spine, and came to a fairly clear level area.

"Is he following?" I glanced in the rearview mirror, and could see for myself Tonic's sweet round face jogging up and down on those long elegant legs, with his black-tipped tail floating behind.

"Yeah, he's definitely interested. Get into third if you can."

I reached a bone-jarring forty miles an hour, the steering wheel vibrating like crazy under my hands, and Kaji threw out the meat.

"This is great! He's really moving," she yelled. "He's closing the gap!"

"Hooray!" I felt a surge of adrenaline. A patch of dense bushes with tiny hard-looking leaves was coming up on the right. I readied myself for Kaji's shout to stop.

"There's a lion!" Kaji yelled.

"Oh, shit!" As we whizzed past I quickly looked right and glimpsed two lionesses rousing themselves from their midday snooze among the bushes. One of them had her nose raised in a sniff, and the other was on her feet and bounding toward Tonic with a low growl. *"No!"* I yelled.

Tonic spurted into top gear, flying at sixty mph past my windshield. He crossed his legs under him, then stretched full out, covering fifteen feet with each leap. It was so beautiful it took my breath away. Those lionesses would never catch him.

Kaji peered out the back hatch. I could hear a lion growling. "Stop, stop," Kaji yelled. "She's being dragged."

I stopped the car and put my head through the roof hatch to watch. The first lioness had jumped on the impala's back and gripped its neck in her powerful jaws. The second lioness was only seconds behind. She reached the carcass in a muscular sprint, seized it by the throat and held on, growling at her sister. They were nose to nose, their jaws only inches apart, muscular tails lashing the air. The first one laid back her ears and snarled. Blood matted her chin. She had an impressive set of teeth, but so did the second lioness.

"Look at those thin bellies. They must be hungry." Kaji couldn't help sounding interested. She was fascinated by every scrap of animal behavior.

One lioness growled deep in her throat. The sound raised the hairs on my neck. The other one didn't budge, except for the flick of one ear, bothered by flies. They were matching their wills. Neither one could eat, but neither wanted to be the first to let go. This was going to take longer than a few minutes.

I looked at my watch. "Now we have two cubs to find."

"This is bad. I'm also worried about my adult female: today I saw her nipples are swelling, so she's pregnant. It's the newborn cubs the lions really go after."

"She's pregnant already? Too bad." Kaji must have been disappointed.

In addition to working with Gin and Tonic, Kaji had a personal goal of gathering data on cheetah reproduction; that's why she'd been following this lone female so assiduously. A female without cubs was either newly pregnant or soon would be. Kaji had hoped to be there if and when males came courting. Very little was known about male-female interaction. No one had ever seen cheetahs mate. That information was vital to save cheetahs from the big E: extinction.

With parks providing no safety to them, thanks to the lions, and the intense population pressure, many people were expecting cheetahs to soon be wiped out, or close to it, in Kenya. That's one reason Nick and Wynn and Kaji were making such efforts to return the cubs to the wild. Every cheetah was precious. There were only ten thousand left in the world, less than the number of people living in a big Nairobi housing development.

For other endangered animals, zoos could function as a last refuge. Not for cheetahs. With rare exceptions, they wouldn't breed in captivity.

The problem, scientists discovered, was that cheetahs

13

suffered a devastating calamity ten thousand years ago Every cheetah on earth was killed, except for a single pregnant female. We don't know how it happened, or how she survived, but the proof is there: all cheetahs are as closely related as Siamese twins—hardly any genetic variety. As a result, their sperm count is so low, it's a wonder they can reproduce at all. Many matings are unproductive. But zoos can't even get their cheetahs to try, and that's where Kaji got her idea for her research.

We needed desperately to learn the social interactions that triggered mating, so that zookeepers could reproduce the proper conditions. Do males need to fight for the female? Should the two sexes be kept apart? Or do males need to have a territory that the female moves into and out of at will? Until we learned the answers, zoos would be helpless to stave off full extinction.

Kaji was hoping that once she got some interesting data on her own, she'd be able to win funding for a long-term project, get together a staff, go out there and spend the time necessary to find the answers. Wynn and Nick believed in Kaji's research, and were proud to support it. For all three of them, saving the cheetah had become a mission.

One of the lionesses tried to pull the impala out of her sister's grip. Her sleek muscles bunched powerfully under her tawny hide, but the sister growled and held on. Two pairs of yellow eyes glowed balefully at each other.

Meanwhile, Gin and Tonic were alone among the rest of the pride. I looked at my watch again. Chances were, the rest of the lion pride was scattered around in small groups in this corner of their territory. What would happen if Gin and Tonic ran into another lioness waking up from her nap feeling grouchy? Kaji and I were not doing a good job of being Mother.

"I've got to break this up," I said. "Let me try moving forward a few feet."

I eased forward. Neither one let go, but the sleeker lioness shifted her grip to a haunch, and no longer nose to nose, they tore hunks off the carcass with gusto. In a few minutes the impala was gone.

I drove slowly, while Kaji and I hung out the windows, looking for the cheetahs' tracks.

"I've got one on this side," Kaji said. She pointed. "To the left of this black thorn. It's Tonic."

"You can tell by his print?" I was impressed.

"It's a bit wider than Gin's, and he has longer claws. I'll show you when we get back."

We drove on, passing a family herd of Grevy's zebra and a few scattered giraffe.

Kaji straightened and rubbed her neck. "Listen. There's a car ahead."

"Got it."

"Let's see who it is."

I headed toward the noise of an idling motor, feeling nervous about bandits but embarrassed to show it. Nick and Wynn's place was miles from the main road, far enough north of the Samburu Game Reserve to be out of the radius of even the most enthusiastic tourist. You could drive around on their land for weeks and never see anyone but the occasional Samburu kid herding goats or cattle. Somali bandits, the *shifta*, had raided nearby tribes for centuries—but since clan warfare erupted a few years ago, they were crossing Kenya's northeast border in greater and greater numbers, armed with automatic weapons and a savage readiness to kill animal or human, whatever was unlucky enough to cross their path.

So I was initially relieved when we rounded a dense clump of white thorns and there was another normal Land Cruiser, no bandits, with Tonic on the roof. He was nose down and haunches up, peering into the open hatch.

"There he is!" Kaji shouted.

"Is he terrorizing people?" But even as the words left my mouth, I noticed the upstretched hand with a sandwich luring him into the car. Tonic delicately took it, swallowed it whole, and jumped into the Cruiser, looking for more.

3

I PULLED UP next to them. Three men turned toward us, looking none too pleased. The unsmiling driver wore a Cincinnati Reds cap. Next to him in front was a handsome white man, with a forthright nose, lean ruddy cheeks that had seen a lot of sun, and a big, white-toothed smile.

He gave me a handshake with a callused palm. "Gerry Weller."

He had on a well-worn tan shirt rolled up to the elbows, and a beat-up old safari hat over curly brown hair, but there was something about him—his voice maybe, with its confident tone that said money to me, or at least worldly success on his own terms. Our eyes met for an instant with mutual curiosity.

"I'm Jazz Jasper, and this is Marianne Kanja—Kaji for short. I see you've met Tonic." The cheetah was in the backseat, nosing at the remains of a packed lunch, half in the lap of an enormous black man.

"This is a visitor from the big city," Gerry Weller said, indicating the man in the backseat, "William Mutani." He did not bother to introduce the driver.

Mutani's neck bulged over the buttoned collar of his white shirt. Like the British colonials who had preceded him as Kenya's elite, he was obviously keeping up standards in the bush. He pushed Tonic off his lap. He even wore a striped tie, held in place with a diamond-studded gold clip. I looked back at his face, and realized I knew who he was. Mutani owned a glittering chain of opulent restaurants, nightclubs, and hotels, and was always making the papers, posed with high government figures at the

16

opening of his latest entertainment palace or some charity event.

I resisted suggesting he loosen his collar and tie. "Pleased to meet you. I had dinner at the Buckingham Court just last week. It's a beautiful place."

"I'm glad you liked it. It's been a big success." Mutani had a tenor voice, unexpected in a man his size.

"The food was excellent. I run a safari company, and I'll definitely bring my next group of tourists there." If the tourist trade would only pick up, and I managed to stay in business. I wondered if the poor economic climate was threatening Mutani, also. Despite his claims of success, the restaurant had been half empty on a Saturday night.

"Next time you come, you must ask for me. If I'm there, you shall be my guest, and if not, the host will give you the best table."

"That's very kind of you. What brings you out to Samburu country?"

Mutani patted Tonic's rump. "This cheetah is yours? We were wondering about it being so tame."

But how had they known Tonic was tame? Even wild cheetahs sometimes jump on a stationary car. They like vantage points. I doubted that Mutani would have dared offer a wild cheetah his sandwich.

"I guess you could say he belongs to Wynn Hunter, whose land you're on now, but we don't think of anyone as owning Tonic. Do we, baby?" The young cheetah looked up at his name, and with a graceful leap was back up on their roof, then over to our Land Cruiser. He looked at us with calm, honeyed yellow eyes, and hopped down to his favorite driving spot, Kaji's lap.

"His hunting lesson today was interrupted by a couple of lions," Kaji added. Tonic rubbed his head against her chin, eyes half closed.

"You two seemed quite unperturbed about a cheetah jumping into your car."

"Oh, I've been ricocheting around this corner of the world for a long time. I've picked up a lot of experience with animals," Gerry said, flashing another smile. "It'd

17

take a lot more than an overgrown cheetah cub to get me going."

"Do you know if Mrs. Hunter might be willing to sell?" Mutani asked. "If approached properly, of course."

I ran my hand along Tonic's sleek flank. "For what purpose?" I couldn't stop a slight edge from creeping into my voice.

"Just curious. I know someone who wants one." Mutani measured Tonic with his eyes, strangely devoid of pleasure. "Cheetahs are hard to get hold of these days."

"Also illegal."

"That depends on how you get one, doesn't it?" Gerry drawled with a lopsided smile. "Kenya has strict laws, but if you manage to avoid customs inspection . . . Big cats are completely legal as pets in most states in America."

"You're kidding."

"You can keep an endangered animal in your basement, if that's how you get your kicks."

"Are you sure? I can hardly believe that."

Gerry gave a half smile, not interested in arguing. Our eyes met again and he held my gaze an instant too long. He obviously knew he was an attractive man.

"And what do you do?" I asked.

"I'm with Kenarabia Oil. This may look like far bush to you, but I've been way northeast the last few months, next to Somalia, and let me tell you, it's paradise in Kenya."

"We're an island of sanity and order in the midst of chaos," Mutani said.

"Absolutely," I agreed. "Kenya deserves a lot of credit. Did you see many refugees?"

"Somalia is emptying out. Kenya is going to be overrun, if the Somalis don't cut this clan warfare crap."

"What brings you down to this region? Not oil?"

Gerry laughed. His eyes were light blue, the exact color of the washed-out desert sky. "You sound worried. Wouldn't you want oil on your friends' property? They'd be millionaires."

"On their property? Sure. Next door? Not really: they'd get to live in an oil field instead of a magnificent wilderness." I noticed Gerry staring at my lips as I spoke.

18

"Well, don't worry. There's no oil anywhere near here. I'm a certified geologist, and you can trust me."

"Are you staying at the park? This is a long drive." Mutani and Weller made an odd couple, and I still couldn't make sense of their popping up here.

Gerry hitched his head southward. "Yeah, I'm at the Crocodile Lodge. Beautiful place, right on the river. Nice pool, good chef, armed guards. A nice place to relax, unwind for a few days, before heading back to the hellhole near the border."

"Are you checking out the competition at Crocodile Lodge, Mr. Mutani?"

"No, no, I am up for the day, and my friend, Gerry," Mutani inched forward with effort to lean out the window, "was kind enough to offer to lend me his car and his driver. And as you see, I convinced him to also lend me himself. I met Nick Hunter recently and thought we'd drop in for a visit, give our drive a destination. They sound like an interesting couple. Nick is a journalist, and his wife, in development?"

"Yeah. She's working on a reforestry project through the Office of Conservation and Rural Development."

"Excellent." Mutani nodded. "Most impressive. Are you heading to their house now? We will follow you."

"I'm afraid this isn't the best time for a social call." I hesitated, reluctant to say the words. "There's been a tragic accident. This morning. Nick Hunter was bitten by a scorpion."

"Did he have to go to Isiolo?" Gerry Weller asked.

"He's dead."

"Dead? From a scorpion bite?" Weller was taken aback. "Those things hurt like hell, but they can't kill you. A child, yes, but not a grown man."

"I don't know. He died right in front of us."

"I'm sorry." Gerry's mobile mouth turned down with sympathy. "What a terrible—Is there anything we can do to help?"

"The flying doctors came, and Wynn's already left with the body. He's going to be buried in Karen, in a family plot." Karen was a wealthy white suburb in the Ngong

Hills, southwest of Nairobi, named after Karen Blixen. Nick hated the suburb, but Wynn didn't see any point in making a fuss over his gravesite.

I glanced at Kaji, who had checked out of the conversation a while ago. She was looking sadly out her window, leaning her head on Tonic.

"I'll give Wynn your condolences, and pass along the message about help," I told the two men.

"Thank you." Mutani extracted a maroon leather card case from his pocket. He handed me a card printed on thick paper. "Please. Let me know when they are having the funeral. I would like to pay my respects."

"Sure."

Finding Gin turned out to be a lot harder than finding her brother, but then it was really Gerry Weller and William Mutani we'd found. We went back to where we'd last seen her track, and with a lot of trouble found it again. Almost immediately we lost it over some rocky ground. When we found it, to our dismay, the track led into an area of thick scrub, where we spent the next hour tracking back and forth, with visibility of only a few feet. This was no place for a cheetah to hang out—too much cover for lions, too many places to be ambushed. A mature cheetah would have avoided this area and gone to the slope of the hill, where it was open enough to easily spot both danger and prey and use its speed to advantage.

There were lions all over the place. We passed another lioness, snoozing under a bush, her ears flicking flies away, and then ten minutes later a male and female together, zonked out on their sides. Tonic started to tremble. He dove for the window, but Kaji grabbed him.

"It's a mating couple," Kaji told Tonic. "They're not interested in you."

We couldn't take the time to stop. Too bad. You're sure to see a mating when there's a lion couple by itself like that. They mate over and over for thirty-six hours, first at five-minute intervals, then twenty, then an hour. Each mating only takes a minute, but it must be a hell of a minute to judge from their roars at climax, and the way they collapse afterward.

20

"Well, at least those two are busy," I said. "Unless Gin runs right over them, they won't bother with her."

"This isn't getting us anywhere," Kaji said. "Either she's cowering under a bush somewhere, where we'll never spot her, or she was lucky enough to get out of this area alive."

"Okay, let's climb. We can use our binoculars to look for her. I'll drive to that high spot. You know—where we get a big view."

It took a good while to labor up the steep, eroded hill. This was greater kudu habitat, and sure enough, we spotted a male browsing. He was five feet at the shoulder with magnificent spiral horns.

"Stop!" Kaji said. "Just for a moment." She turned to me. "I love kudu. They're my favorite antelope." For the first time since she'd learned of Nick's death, her eyes lost their dazed look and took on their usual expression of alert interest, nonjudgmental and receptive. I loved to watch Kaji watch animals.

She was absolutely besotted with this wilderness. I worried if Nick's death would mean the end of her job. There was no question that Wynn would keep Kaji on as long as Wynn stayed here—but how long would that be, all alone, constantly reminded of Nick's absence? When I got divorced—my husband walked out on me to marry a pregnant grad student of his—I'd fled not only my house, but my career and the entire continent. Admittedly that was extreme, but Nick's death would inevitably lead to changes. Death always did.

"What are your thoughts for the future, Kaji?"

She kept her eyes on the kudu as she answered. "I'll stay here as long as Wynn wants me. I'll tell you one thing: I'm not going back to Nairobi, live at home and have my mother after me all day long to get married." Kaji made a rude noise.

I smiled in sympathy. "Does she have someone particular in mind?"

Kaji snorted. "Yes, of course, the son of one of her church friends. His qualifications are that he's the right tribe and has an office job. He's a bullshit artist, he already has two children with a girlfriend—who he regularly beats up when he's drunk, which is most weekends. But that doesn't matter. Those are considered normal male weaknesses." She shook her head. "You know, I'm twenty-five, and I've had only one really nice boyfriend? And now, with the AIDS epidemic . . . and forget about asking one of these Romeos to use a condom. That's why I'd rather be up here."

"It's scary." I felt bad for her. "Still—men always seem hopeless, and then you meet the right person and everything changes." Why did words of consolation sound so idiotic?

Kaji looked serious. "If Wynn leaves, I really don't know what I'll do. There are hundreds of college graduates competing for every miserable little job, and the boss always expects you to sleep with him for the privilege of working there." She shook her head. "I prefer four-footed animals."

The wind must have shifted, because the kudu put its head up and stared right at us. It didn't move, unsure if we posed a danger or not.

"What about going to grad school?" I asked Kaji. "That way you could continue your field work on cheetahs."

"I would love that, but who has the money? Maybe I'll go to one of Mutani's casinos, win a fortune, and buy this place." She grinned. "I'll keep working for wildlife somehow. I'm an optimist."

"You'll succeed, one way or another. If you decide to apply to schools in the States, let me know. I have contacts that might help you get a grant." Having been an academic all those years must be useful for something.

The kudu resumed browsing, and I resumed driving. We reached the crest of the hill. I parked and we slowly and carefully covered the landscape with our binoculars. Tonic jumped out and scanned the terrain as if helping out. I saw a dozen or more giraffe hanging out in some trees, only their necks poking above the tops. To our south, the house and outbuildings cast sharp mid-afternoon shadows. Beyond them was a magnificent herd of Grevy's zebra, big as horses. Their many fine black and white stripes blended into silver at this distance.

In the other direction, a long line of oryx headed single file toward the marsh, the only source of water in the dry season for a hundred miles. There were also a lot of elephants scattered like huge boulders along the edge of the marsh. It was that little curve of green that made the Hunters' property such a wildlife gem in the midst of the desert. In the Serengeti plains, a single female cheetah needs a gigantic range—eight hundred square kilometers—because she has to follow the rains. Here, thanks to a permanent spring that fed the marsh, the cheetahs had good hunting year-round, and needed only a fraction of that much land.

"Kaji, look at this." I'd known something had brought Mutani and Weller this far from the park. On the other side of the marsh, just outside the Hunters' boundary, was a large tented camp, a number of vehicles, and men in scattered groups of one and two and three.

"Can you make out what's going on?" I asked Kaji. "See those tripods? Are they filming?"

I'd seen camera crews in the highlands when they filmed *Out of Africa,* and they didn't spread out like this. They might have used multiple cameras to get different angles, but you could always tell the center of the action. This scene was all activity and no center.

Kaji steadied her elbows on the roof of the car. "I think I see yellow ribbons."

"Yellow ribbons?"

"Yes. You know. Surveying ribbons."

A feeling of dread clutched my chest. "Somehow I don't think Weller and Mutani were completely open with us."

"You can't expect someone to tell you if they're looking for oil."

"Oil, around here?"

Kaji shrugged. We both watched the tiny figures of men with their matchstick tripods.

Kaji said, "Maybe they were coming over to approach Nick and Wynn about surveying their land. I knew there had to be an important reason to bring Mutani into the bush."

"Me, too. And this desire to go to the funeral of a man he barely knows."

Our conversation was ended by the sound of a complaining chirp, and there was Gin, trotting up to us with an accusing look on her face. Tonic jumped out of the car and bowled her over. They tumbled about, rubbing, batting, and licking each other. Then it was Kaji's and my turn to be greeted. We headed home, skirting the area thick with scrub and lions. The cheetahs loped along behind the car until they got tired and jumped on top to ride the rest of the way.

When we got back, before heading into the house I went behind the outhouse and looked for the broken body of the scorpion that had killed Nick. It was easy to spot, still hanging in the bush where Roger had flung it. I hesitated to touch it. The one scorpion I'd seen before in Kenya—a dead one killed by my friend Mikki's pet mongoose—hadn't looked so horrible. It had been much smaller and a golden tan, well-camouflaged for desert sand.

I steeled myself and picked up the scorpion in two fingers. The carapace felt like brittle leather. Even half crushed, legs missing, the curved tail looked poised to strike. So Gerry Weller was certain these couldn't kill. Maybe it would be a good idea to have an entomologist look at it. I carried the scorpion gingerly into the house.

4

STRIKER HAS AN old clawfoot tub big enough to hold two. He started the water going, put in a dollop of lemon-scented bubble bath, and lit the fat candle on the windowsill. I turned off the overhead light. Instantly the room was dark and mysterious and perfumed. I got undressed as Striker slipped into the living room to put on a Billie Holiday record. He came back with two glasses of white wine. He'd also paused to take off his clothes, and I watched him approach with pleasure, admiring his long legs and broad chest. In a certain mood, primates can be as beautiful as any great cat.

Striker bent down and kissed my breast as a sweet hello, and we slipped into the warm water, facing each other, leaning against each end of the tub with our legs entangled. Billie sang about missing Georgia, and her melancholy longing washed over me like a healing spring. I'd talked myself out about Nick during the plane ride from Samburu, and now the fist of pain I'd been carrying around all day began to melt. I took a sip of cool wine, closed my eyes and slipped lower in the water. Striker took my foot underwater and began to massage it. His hands felt wonderful, firm and gentle.

"Mmmmm. Keep that up forever, will you?"

"For you my love, anything."

That's the only thing we said for about ten minutes. Striker finished my other foot; I finished my wine and put down the glass. Billie was singing "All of Me." Striker slipped down to my end of the tub and put his arms around me. I reached for his lips and we kissed, a floating kiss that started in a pool of gentle love and sadness, then swept us into the current and whirled us away.

Striker slipped under me and into me, and I floated above him. Each thrust sent me higher and deeper, until I was dissolved in a warm darkness of sensation, no longer able to tell who was Striker and who was me, who started what rhythm and who was responding, swirling together until we were one. Then I started to build to a climax, and Striker was with me, as if he could feel every nuance of my body in his, as if his soul was inside me, experiencing with me everything he was doing. An indescribable feeling of pleasure began in my toes, then suffused into my thighs, my pelvis, my universe. Striker moved to match it, to urge it on. Then it exploded, a geyser of sensation lifting me high, higher, then tossing me forward into a gentle current that washed me onto a blissful shore.

Striker pulled out and we nestled and nuzzled and nibbled for a while, then he led me out into the current again, in a totally different way. He kissed my breasts until I had a small, sweet climax, and as I reached the peak, he slipped into me again. This time was hot and hard and fast. I could feel his urgency and I fed it, moving this way and that until it burst into a high flame. I half opened my eyes, and watched his face in the candlelight. He came, roaring aloud, and we both laughed, ringing round laughs of pleasure, delight, and love.

Later we made dinner, then sat out on his back deck, with all the house lights out, facing the deeper black of the forest around us. The sky above was brilliant with stars. I thought of Nick. We listened to the chorus of peepers. Without warning, screeches tore into the night's peace: a baboon troop roused from sleep, probably by a hunting leopard. The noise set off a hyrax, a small creature cuddly as a rabbit, whose terrifying screams seem to emanate from Hell. Silence fell again, but was soon interrupted by the steady ripping and chewing of a bushbuck cropping the rough grass on the hillside below us.

A breeze rustled the trees, and I heard a fast-paced boom, boom, boom that I didn't recognize. "Striker, is that a drum? Can you hear it?"

"I hear it every night when the wind comes down the mountain. They keep it up until midnight weekdays, till two on Friday and Saturday."

"Oh, God." Now I could hear the whine of electric instruments, or perhaps the imitation electric instruments of a synthesizer. "You can hear the nightclub all the way down here?"

"I can't stand this. Let's go inside."

I followed Striker into the house. He flopped down on one of his beat-up old leather couches and stretched his legs out in front. His mouth was a hard, angry line. "I've never seen anything go up as fast as this fucking Mountain Refuge Convention Complex. Like a mushroom on a pile of shit."

I felt so awful for Striker. His cabin on Mount Kenya was his own piece of paradise, as personal and perfect for him as a second skin. A relaxed clutter of magazines and books shared the tables and shelf space with odd twists of driftwood and seashells collected on long-ago beach holidays. On the walls were a fine collection of two-foot gourds decorated with intricate beadwork, which the Maasai make to hold their food supply—blood and milk from their life-giving cattle. Everything in the house had a personal meaning, and outside, all was unspoiled nature. Until now.

Striker stared in front of him, seeing nothing but his black thoughts. "That Mutani is a slick bastard."

"How did he get away with it?"

Striker rubbed his fingers together, sign language for moolah. In other words, he'd bribed the development agency.

I sat down next to him. "Where is he getting the money? And why build it at all? Business has been terrible. It's not just Jazz Jasper Safaris: all the tours and hotels have been under-booked for the past year. And he's building another hotel-casino complex on Limuru Road that's only half finished."

"He's coating the entire country with sleazy resorts that no one wants. People come to Kenya to see real animals, not his plastic menagerie."

27

"Did I tell you I saw Mutani today?" I described the odd meeting with Mutani and Gerry Weller, and Kaji's conjecture that they were prospecting for oil in Samburu Province.

"It doesn't surprise me. Mutani is well-connected. He gets a sniff of every pie before the public even knows there's dough around, and believe me, he gets a cut whenever he wants it. All the ministers are involved in real estate speculation; Mutani makes sure they get their bribe up front, plus a piece of the action; they make sure Mutani has a free hand. He brings in the foreign dough. That's why he doesn't care if there are tourists to come to his casino or not: he and his government patrons have made their money before the doors open."

Striker fell into a morose silence. Sounds of the rock band floated in through the big screened windows. "This is grotesque." He got up. "Let's go to bed."

I stood at the bathroom door while he brushed his teeth. "Maybe you can give the manager a little gift for a little silence."

Striker grimaced at the mirror. "I have. It lasts a few days and then goes back. I can't very well put him on retainer."

"There must be something you can do."

Striker's hazel eyes looked dark in the mirror. "I talked to Nick about it. He suggested I take a world cruise and forget it."

"Oh, that's constructive."

"More seriously, he was going to do a piece on how this fucking project got on the fast track in the first place. He was trying to find out Mutani's foreign backers."

Hearing Nick's name gave me a bleak feeling of loss. "Had he come up with anything?"

"Yeah. He thought there was oil money behind it." Striker spat into the sink with more emphasis than usual. "You know, some rich sheikh who invests his money abroad, in case the mullahs take over." He ran cold water over his toothbrush, and washed his face.

"Which fits in with Kaji's idea that Mutani is also getting into oil speculation."

"Knowing Mutani, he'll make out fine whether oil is discovered or not."

"If you're finished, it's my turn at the sink."

Striker flipped his face towel behind my neck and gently pulled me to him. "Have I ever told you that you have great lips?"

5

"THIS IS FOR staff only. The public entrance is around the corner." The guard pointed with a big knuckled hand toward the main entrance to Kenya's world-famous natural history and ethnographic museum. When I didn't move, he bent his whole body into the gesture, as if I hadn't noticed it the first time.

I pulled my chin in, but held my ground. "I was just at the main entrance. They sent me here."

I'd been to the National Museum countless times to admire the fabulous collection of tribal artifacts, the world's largest butterfly collection, or—my favorite—to stare in awe at the fossil footprints of three early humans, two adults and a child. Today I wanted one specific piece of information: was the scorpion we found deadly enough to kill a man?

I shifted the straw satchel holding the scorpion. "I want to speak to one of the scientists."

The guard straightened, pulling down the jacket of his military-looking uniform. "The name, please?"

"I don't know the name."

The guard smiled, as if to a retarded child. "I cannot let you in without a name."

"I want to speak to someone in the insect department." I tried to remember my high school biology: was a scorpion an insect, or did arachnids and insects both come under arthropod? Arthropod Department sounded even more unlikely than Arachnid Department.

"You don't have an appointment?"

I probably should have lied, but I'm not quick enough. I admitted I had no appointment.

30

"That is a pity. You see, I am not allowed to let in someone to wander about the halls on their own. There are too many things lying around, you see. If you give me a name, I can call the person to escort you." He gestured toward a battered phone mounted on the wall behind him. "Otherwise . . ." He shrugged his shoulders.

There was no point butting my head against this wall. I went back to the main entrance, paid for a ticket, and entered the museum. I passed the hall of African animals without a glance and headed straight for the gift shop. Yes, as I remembered, there was a door just before the shop labeled STAFF ONLY. If I was unlucky, it would be a ladies' room.

I waited until the clerk in the shop was busy with a customer, walked briskly to the door, looking neither right nor left, and pushed. It was unlocked, and it opened on a dim corridor. I was backstage at the museum. Now I had to find a scorpion expert before someone noticed me and kicked me out.

I looked for signs, but there were none. I was in a warren of hallways lined with dusty cabinets. One direction was as good as another. I turned right. Dim bulbs suspended from the high ceiling marched in a straight line into the distance. The chain of halls telescoped, like Van Gogh's painting of his insane asylum. My heart started to pound.

This must be the Geology Department, for the walls were covered with ceiling-high cabinets holding dust-coated rocks—big, small, smooth, deformed, red, black—each identified, with the name and date of the expedition that collected them. Were these the treasures the guard thought I might steal? A distinguished-looking black man with a bulging briefcase passed me with a curious glance. I nodded and kept going. In the next corridor faded labels identified bone fragments from Olduvai Gorge, where Mary Leakey discovered *Zinjanthropus*; the shelf above was scattered with Stone Age hand axes. Here, I admit, I was tempted—what a thrill to own a tool made by a Stone Age hand—but I hurried on.

I came to a fork and took the wider hall. This too was

lined with dusty cabinets, like a giant attic filled with forgotten junk. I was beginning to lose hope of ever finding the biology section. A person could get lost in here and wander forever, getting dustier and grayer, until she too became one more item in the collection. Every stone and fossil and bone had been brought here at tremendous physical and mental effort, with courage and gritty determination. Now they lay asleep in their blankets of dust like Sleeping Beauty, waiting for the Prince's kiss—or at least the attentions of some poor graduate student seeking a new scrap of information to add to the fund of human knowledge.

Another person was approaching, footsteps ringing on the gray stone floors. This time I had to take the chance of revealing I was an outsider. It was a young man with glasses and a patchy beard. His skin was a warm brown.

I flashed him my friendliest smile. "Excuse me, I'm looking for the Insect Department. I'm afraid I'm lost." If eyelash batting hadn't gone out of fashion, I'd have done that, too.

Even so, it took him a moment to focus on me, as if his thoughts had been far away. "Oh. You mean Invertebrate Biology."

"Yes."

He pushed his glasses back on his nose. "You have to retrace your steps. Return down this hallway about a hundred feet. You will see a big door on your right. Go through there and take the stairway up one flight. Turn left and . . ." He noticed the look on my face. "Maybe I'd better take you." I trotted after him. "Who are you looking for?"

"Someone who specializes in scorpions."

"Hmm." We headed up the stairs. "That's probably Dr. Otieno, and he's away this week. He's the department head. I'll take you to his assistant. If she can't help you, I doubt anyone else can. What's your interest in scorpions?"

"I have a specimen I want to identify."

We trotted down the dim crowded corridors, through a blue door reading INVERTEBRATE BIOLOGY and into a suite of brightly lit offices. We passed several people at a long

32

table crowded with vials and piles of paper and journals, too busy peering into microscopes to notice us. He led me to a cubbyhole separated with a glass wall from a slightly larger office, presumably that of the absent Dr. Otieno. Lopsided stacks of papers reached halfway up the glass.

"Helen? Here's someone who wants you to ID a scorpion specimen for her."

"Jazz Jasper." I shook hands with a medium-height black woman, all plump curves, with a gentle smiling face. Her bright round eyes were framed in horn-rim glasses.

"Helen Wambui Wakaba," she told me. "I have to be at the university in half an hour to teach a biology section." She frowned at her watch, as if disapproving of its message. "But"—relenting, she waved a hand—"show me what you've got, and I'll see what I can do."

The university was a quick walk downhill from the museum. "This shouldn't take too long. I hope."

"It's not that easy with scorpions. There are only three or four people in Africa who can differentiate species; we feel pretty good if we can get to genus."

"They aren't different sizes and shapes and colors?"

"You'll see when we go down to the collection. Show me what you've got."

Was she going to take me into the bowels of the museum? I'd already had enough of those hallways to last me a lifetime.

"The size and color will locate you within the genus," she continued. "But to identify the species, you have to get them under the microscope: count how many spikes they have along their jaw, see if there's a tubercle in front of the stinger or not, count the number of hairs along their legs. It takes a lot of skill."

She held her hand out, and I pulled out the jam jar filled with ethyl alcohol that Kaji had fixed up for the scorpion that bit Nick. It lay on the bottom of the jar, waving back and forth in the liquid like a creature from the bottom of the sea.

Dr. Wakaba smiled. "Ah, you already have it in preservative. I see you know a bit of biology."

"A friend does, actually."

33

She located a tweezers and petri dish among the jars on the counter, carefully extracted my scorpion and set it in the dish. "It's not in the best of condition, but we'll see what we can do. I'll leave the broken legs in the jar, I think. As long as we have two or three still attached, that should be enough."

She sat down in front of a large microscope. Two high-intensity lights on flexible metal necks were focused on a glass slide. She extracted the slide, adjusted the height of the scope, and slipped the dish with the smashed scorpion under the lens. "Have a seat. This will take a moment."

I looked around her cubbyhole, wondering where exactly I was supposed to sit, since every available surface was covered with piles of paper. Finally, I perched at the edge of a chair with half my fanny on what looked like someone's thesis. A huge-bellied spider floated in a bottle of preservative at eye level. I quickly looked away.

It wasn't much better. The shelf opposite contained a small aquarium with screen mesh over the top, a sandy bottom, and a naturalistic tumble of flat rocks. It looked empty except for a large cricket, when suddenly a sand-colored scorpion darted from the rocks and grabbed the cricket with its front pincers. The cricket struggled to free itself, and as fast as sight, the scorpion unfurled its lethal tail and stung the cricket two or three times.

I must have made a funny sound, because Dr. Wakaba glanced toward the cage. The scorpion was tearing the cricket apart with its claws and chewing up the pieces. "Oh, good, she's finally eating." She returned to studying the scorpion.

"It's kind of you to be helping me."

"Please don't mention it. I only wish I knew more, and had more time." She looked up and caught me staring at her. She couldn't have been more than twenty-five. As if reading my thoughts, she explained, "I'm a post-doc; I work directly under Dr. Otieno." This last was said with pride. She looked into the scope and twisted the big black focusing ring on its side. "It's really a shame he is away this week. He knows more about arachnids than anyone here." She got up and waved me into her chair. "Want a look?"

I took her place and bent over the scope. The scorpion had jaws like crab claws, and dot-sized spectral eyes close together on the top of its head. I moved the dish so I could see the stinger. It was a wicked curve, sharp as a cat's claw. The tip was a brilliant red. "Is that blood on the stinger?"

"No, it's the natural color. Pretty, isn't it? Once we identify the genus, we can look it up. I have an excellent reference on the biology of scorpions." She looked at her watch again. "Let's go look at the collection."

She picked up the petri dish and we left the area of brightly lit offices, descending past two levels of dim corridors to a sub-basement. They seemed to be saving electricity by keeping the lights off. Dr. Wakaba left them off. A single window onto a light well shed a gray light over the first row or two. Extending into the darkness beyond were row on row on row of metal shelves crowded with glass bottles. It reminded me of a champagne cellar I'd once visited in Reims, France, but instead of champagne, these bottles held dim horrors floating in alcohol.

Dr. Wakaba went straight to a cabinet opposite the window, and bent over to scan the labels. "All right. Here we are, then." She slid the shelf out and handed me two ball jars, then moved to another shelf and took three herself, pinning them against her chest with her lower arm. Scores of crayfish-size scorpions with sharp claws sloshed against the glass.

We set the jars down on a stone counter next to the light well. A hand-drawn sign announcing NEATNESS TAKES TIME presided over a clutter of jars and stoppers and labels, including a few beasties that hadn't been filed away.

Dr. Wakaba arrayed our collection of jars in a row and turned to me. "We have to be quick now."

One of the jars I held was labeled NATIONAL MUSEUM. KENYA LOBEROT. JUNE 1964. B. PATTERSON. Dr. Wakaba opened it and extracted a wet label from the midst of the scorpions with her tweezers. She held it out for me to read.

35

Odonturous dentatus. Then she reached in and extracted several scorpions and placed them in their own petri dish.

They were sand-colored, and the largest was only half the size of my scorpion. The smaller ones were the size of my pinkie nail.

"Those are tiny."

"I'd guess they are juveniles."

"Do they turn black when they're older?"

"I don't believe so. Some species are tan, some are black. They don't switch about."

She shoveled them back in their jar and pulled another one forward. This jar was full of tiny test tubes stoppered with balls of cotton sopping with preservative. She handed me one tube and held up another.

It read: *Buthidae. Parabuthus* species. Somali Republic. Villagio Squss. Five miles north of Balad. 11 August 1961. C. Gans.

I wondered how far that was from Nick and Wynn's. A single large scorpion was crammed into the vial. Dr. Wakaba pulled it out and measured it against a long metal ruler. She moved quickly but methodically, and seemed to be enjoying herself.

"*Buthidae* is the family, you see, and *Parabuthus* is the genus, but the species is unknown." She prodded the biggest one with the tweezers. It was the same size as my specimen. But again it was the wrong color.

"We need to find a black one."

"Right you are."

We both bent over to scan the labels. "This one's too big." I held up a quart jar with only one scorpion. It was longer than my hand. "*Pandinus.* From South Africa."

Helen picked up another jar. "Ah, here we are, here we are. Look at this fellow. *Androctonus.*" She pulled out a four-inch black scorpion and placed it in the second petri dish.

To the naked eye, it matched the one that bit Nick. A chill went up my spine. Now I knew the name of his killer.

Dr. Wakaba looked at her watch, then handed me the two black scorpions in the petri dishes and scooped up the empty *Androctonus* jar. "I have ten minutes. I'll put those others away later. Let's get these fellows upstairs and compare them under the microscope."

Back in her office, she got busy with the scope.

"I can be looking up toxicity in the book, while you're doing that," I volunteered.

She swiveled over on her chair and plucked a thick volume from the first shelf. "We acquired this recently. It's an excellent book, edited by an American from the University of Arizona."

I opened the tome and scanned the index for *Androctonus*. It directed me to table 10.1. It was in the chapter on toxicity. The chapter was headed with a quote from Kings 12.11: "My father has chastised you with whips, but I shall chastise you with scorpions."

Table 10.1 compared the lethal doses of some of the world's deadliest toxins. The only scorpion listed was the *Androctonus australis*, or Sahara scorpion. Then there were the snakes. I recognized the Latin for rattler, *Crotalus durissus terrificus*, then the cobra and other snakes I'd never heard of, bacterial toxins such as botulism and tetanus, and miscellaneous toxins such as curare, an Amazonian Indian arrow poison, the Japanese fugo fish, and cyanide. *Androctonus australis* kept distinguished company.

Dr. Wakaba swung her chair around. "As I said, this isn't my area, but your specimen certainly appears to be an *Androctonus*. If you want to leave the specimen with me, I can show it to Dr. Otieno when he returns."

"Thank you. I'd appreciate that."

She came to look over my shoulder. "Have you found anything?"

"Yes, look at this chart of lethal doses. It says *Androctonus* is two-and-one-half by ten to the minus nine. Can you translate that?"

"Let me see." Dr. Wakaba bent over the book, her cushiony dark hair brushing my forehead. "You compare these numbers." She ran her finger down the last column. "*Androctonus australis* is less poisonous than a cobra or fugo fish, but a million times more deadly than cyanide."

37

"Someone told me that scorpion bites are only fatal in children."

"I can explain that." She flipped through some pages and came to another chart. "Look, this one compares the toxicity of fourteen scorpion species." She handed me the book.

Androctonus was at the top. Gerry Weller knew less than he thought.

"Let me explain. These charts represent doses used to kill a mouse in the laboratory. Toxicity of a bite in the field depends not just on the species, but also the dosage, which depends in turn on the size of the scorpion, the number of stings, the size of the person." She took off her glasses and rubbed the bridge of her nose. "It is true that most fatalities occur in children. I've never heard of a scorpion bite killing an adult here in Kenya."

"But if it's a million times more poisonous than cyanide, even a minute sting could easily kill a big, healthy man."

"Health has nothing to do with it." She leaned back in her chair and made an arch with her hands, her voice shifting into professorial gear. "Scorpion venom is a neurotoxin. It simultaneously affects both the somatic and the autonomic nervous systems, causing a massive release of neurotransmitters." She paused.

"I'm with you—the chemicals that carry messages from one nerve cell to another."

"Yes. Most importantly, it excites the nerves in your adrenal medulla, sitting on top of the kidney. There's an explosion of adrenaline. We call it an adrenergic storm."

"What does that do to you?"

"All your organs"—she opened her hands wide like a fireworks display—"gone. Hemorrhaged. Your blood pressure—" She pointed to the ceiling with her thumb. "Your heart races, you lose coordination of your muscles, there may be severe emotional agitation, a seizure, frothing at the mouth . . . ending with respiratory failure."

A cold hand went down my back. "I saw somebody die like that, yesterday."

"How awful! Where?" She looked shocked, genuinely distressed.

38

"In the northeast. Samburu Province."

"You mean here in Kenya?"

"Yes."

"And you think that this scorpion stung him?" She picked up the petri dish with the broken black scorpion.

"No question. The man had just come out of the loo, and we found the scorpion crushed on the floor. He must have killed it after it stung him."

"Oh, but that's quite impossible."

"He didn't die instantly. He was able to walk halfway to the house before he collapsed."

"No, I'm telling you, it's impossible. It couldn't have been this scorpion."

I shifted back in the chair, sending the thesis cascading to the floor. "Why not?"

"Because, look here." She tapped the second paragraph with her finger. "*Androctonus australis* doesn't extend south of the Sahara. It's listed for Morocco, Algeria, even Egypt. But in Kenya? No."

I picked up the jar the museum *Androctonus* had come from and extracted the wet label floating in the preservative. IVRAM LEVI, it read. HEBREW UNIVERSITY 1973. ISRAEL. JUDEA. NW OF LAHAV. "This one came from Israel?"

"Yes, across North Africa and the Middle East, right down along the Arabian peninsula. But not south of the Sahara. Kenya has *Odonturus* and *Parabuthus*. Those are the golden ones we looked at."

"But I was there. We found this scorpion in the loo."

An emphatic shake of the head. "If it was in a loo in Kenya, someone put it there."

39

6

I WENT STRAIGHT from the museum to the police station and pulled Omondi out of his office, accepting no excuses about having already eaten lunch at his desk, paperwork for a case of domestic homicide, the latest *panga* gang hacking a homeowner to death, or anything else. The thought that someone had purposely planted the world's deadliest scorpion . . . that Nick's death . . . I couldn't even finish the thought, I was so angry.

By the time we got to Shabaan's it was crowded, not a table free, and we had to settle for two stools at the bar. Raj, the Indian bartender, greeted us without pausing as he halved an orange for the famous Shabaan screwdrivers. I could see the bulk of Shabaan in the shadowy interior, dressed in white Muslim robe and embroidered cap, chatting with a table of businessmen in dark suits.

Omondi pushed back a lock of my hair that had fallen over my cheek. His fingers felt soft on my ear. "You're looking tired and upset," he said.

"Yesterday was hell, and I have a bad feeling about today, too."

"Money problems?" Omondi knew that I was struggling to keep my safari business going. A few well-publicized murders of tourists had dried up business for months, and now we were hit with the recession in the U.S. I was up to my ears in debt, and two months behind on rent. "If there's anything I can do to help. . . ?"

"Thank you, but it's not money, it's much worse. Nick Hunter is dead. He was bitten by a scorpion."

"The journalist?"

I nodded. "And a good friend. I met him through Striker

40

the first year I was here. Nick and his wife, Wynn, own a big stretch of land in Samburu Province. I've been spending a lot of time up there lately helping them with a pair of cheetah cubs they're returning to the wild."

"I'm very sorry to hear of his death. A scorpion? Not a kind way to go."

"A horrible death." My voice got a bit wavery, and I stopped to keep the tears back. "Right in front of Wynn, me, and his sister and her husband."

Omondi put a comforting hand on my shoulder. "I sense that you didn't drag me away from work for sympathy. You suspect his death was not an accident?"

I told him about bumping into Gerry Weller and William Mutani, and what Gerry said about scorpion bites being painful, but not fatal to adults.

"Yet you saw the scorpion bite him?"

"No. That's just it. I was in the barn grooming one of the cubs when the cub heard something and went racing out. I followed her and found Nick collapsed behind the house, near the privy. He was in a very bad way, frothing at the mouth, having trouble breathing. By the time I got there, he couldn't talk." I had to stop again to take a breath, and pressed a finger against my lips to keep them from trembling.

Omondi put a hand on my knee. It felt warm and comforting. "It is okay, take your time."

"His right hand was swollen, big as a grapefruit."

"So you could see he'd been stung."

"Right. Roger Porter—that's Nick's brother-in-law— checked out the privy, since Nick had evidently come from there. He found a smashed scorpion. We figured Nick stomped on it after it bit him."

"Sounds reasonable. This oil man, Gerry Weller, may not know what he's talking about."

"He seemed to me like someone who likes facts. He's a geologist, and spends a lot of time in the desert. I imagine he's seen his share of scorpion bites. Anyway, I took his words seriously."

"So you got curious."

41

"I showed the dead scorpion to a specialist over at the museum, Helen Wakaba. It turned out Gerry was wrong, but only half wrong. She identified it as an extremely dangerous species called the Sahara scorpion. Said it definitely could kill a grown man."

"But."

"Yes. But Dr. Wakaba insists this scorpion is only found north of the Sahara: Morocco, Algeria, Egypt, the whole Middle East right down to Arabia. Not Kenya. She was very insistent on that point. She said there was no way that scorpion got in the loo on its own eight legs."

Omondi beat a rhythm on the bar with his long elegant fingers. Tat, tat, ta tat. "You have the scorpion?"

"No, I left it with her. She's going to show it to the head of the department for verification. He's away till next week."

"Does anyone know you have done this?"

"Kaji—that's Marianne Kanja, who works with the cheetahs—saw me with the scorpion and suggested I keep it in preservative. I told her I was taking it for identification, but she's a biologist, so that seemed natural to her. She didn't ask why."

"Pity. It would be better if no one knew, but you have done well. Very well."

I couldn't help smiling. "You're usually less approving when I get involved in a murder investigation."

"Who—eee." Omondi shook his head as if a fly were annoying him. "Now you are jumping ahead. Remember the methods of science: a theory does not rest on one fact alone. A good investigator is like the scientist: curious and impartial."

Raj came over to take our orders, and we paused while he poured us each a fresh orange juice screwdriver. I took a long gulp. It's the most refreshing drink in the world.

"Ah, most delicious." Omondi traced a line in the condensation on the cool glass. "Do you have any reason to think someone wanted Nick dead?"

"How can I answer that? He was a journalist. I'm sure he pissed off a lot of people."

"Any scandals he'd uncovered recently?"

"He did a story on fifty wild monkeys illegally captured and shipped to the U.S. They all suffocated on the way over. He was personally angry about that one; the wild pet trade is wiping out a lot of species. Other than that, he'd been spending most of his time in the northeast covering the collapse of Somalia. He told me he made himself unpopular by writing a sarcastic piece on Feed the World giving their food to the warlords and calling them 'local distributors.' The Red Cross people were also irked that he was exposing dirty laundry instead of mobilizing world support. But leading to murder? Seems unlikely."

"And before covering Somalia?"

"I don't know. Just the usual." I took another long sip from my orange drink. "I could drop by *The Nairobi Star* this afternoon and get a file of his stories for the last few months."

"Good idea. What about his family? He's married? Any children? Girlfriends? His wife have a lover? Who's going to inherit?"

"Wynn is a good friend, although we don't talk that much about personal stuff. She and Nick were the most compatible married couple I know. I doubt very much if either of them had a lover on the side. No children."

"Did he leave a will?"

"Don't know."

"You say his sister was there."

"Viv Porter."

"How is his relationship with her?"

I shrugged.

"What did you observe?"

"They got along, but with no warmth. They seem like very different people. Viv and Roger were dressed to perfection for a country outing. But then fashion is her business."

"What does she do?"

"She owns a boutique and organizes an annual fashion show from Paris, which takes place soon. I forget—this week or next. Wynn and Nick could care less about anything like that. I don't think Nick invited her up very often. Viv kept exclaiming 'how quaint' over the lack of electricity and plumbing, which didn't endear her to the Hunters, I'm sure. It made me want to kick her in the pants."

"So why now? Was there a reason for this particular visit? She must be very busy with her upcoming show—an odd time to visit her brother."

"Good question."

"What about Roger, the brother-in-law?"

I shrugged. "One of those hearty fellow-well-met types. A lawyer. Other than that, I don't know a thing about him."

"It would be good to talk to those two, find out why they visited, how Viv is taking her brother's death, what their relationship with the Hunters was like. Not a formal interview. We don't want to seem like we're investigating in any way."

"She's having the fashion show opening at her house a few days after the funeral. I'm sure I can get an invitation through Wynn, and bring an escort. You want to go?"

"They're still holding it?"

"Viv said there was no way she could cancel it at the last moment."

Omondi tapped his fingertips together soundlessly. "Yes, going to the fashion party sounds like a good idea. You can pick up a lot of information from someone's social circle, and we will be relatively free to wander about the house, form our own impressions of the Porters. There's a lot of work ahead of us."

"It could be worse. The killer had to be on the spot to plant the scorpion in the privy. It couldn't have been done too far ahead of time, or the scorpion might have stung anyone, or wandered off. That narrows the possible suspects considerably. If you take me off the list, it leaves Wynn, Viv, Roger, and possibly Kaji."

"What do you know about Kaji?"

I told him all I knew about Kaji's background and situation. "She's been working for them for about three years, think, and absolutely loves her job, which is pretty unique. I doubt Nick's death affects her for the better. It unsettles everything. If Wynn decides not to live all alone up there, Kaji would be out of a job."

"We have to add Gerry Weller and William Mutani to your short list. There's no way to know if they were arriving or leaving when you came across them on the Hunters' land."

"I was about to bring them up. There's one more wrinkle. Kaji and I were on a hill, looking around with our binoculars for a lost cub, and we were surprised to see a big camp easy driving distance from the Hunters'. I'd bet anything Weller and Mutani are connected with that camp."

"A safari camp?"

"No, that's just it. They seemed to be surveyors. Kaji wondered if they're prospecting for oil."

"Ah." Omondi slapped the bar. "Now you are talking about high stakes."

"Mutani is not the sort of person to fly up to Samburu to see a reticulated giraffe. Not unless they started shitting money." Omondi winced at my language, and I remembered, too late, that he's a lot more proper than I am. "And why would Weller go to Samburu for a vacation, at a nice hotel, okay, but still stuck in the desert. Wouldn't he come to Nairobi for his R and R? He seemed sex-starved."

Omondi laughed. "A man need not be starving to look at you as a delicious dish. I wouldn't mind a nibble every now and then, myself." He looked at me with mock sorrow. "But you don't believe in snacks."

I smiled ruefully. Turning down Omondi took a lot more discipline than resisting sweets, even though Striker and I were getting along better than ever. Omondi was one of the nicest, sexiest men I'd ever slept with—that one time, before Striker—and he made a love affair between us seem like it could be all fun, all easy and natural, no emotional or cultural complexities, no problems with betraying Striker's trust. I half regretted that I was too old to believe life could be so easy.

45

Shabaan's arrival brought me back to the present. His pockmarked face, dark as espresso, was alight with a smile of greeting. "Inspector Omondi! And my dear friend, Jazz Jasper." He put a meaty hand on each of our shoulders. "Welcome to Shabaan's! It has been far too long since I have seen you two here together. Have you ordered lunch? We have some beautiful rock fish, flown in this morning from Mombasa. I will have them pick out an especially beautiful one for you."

"Thank you, we dropped in for a drink only, this time." Omondi pumped Shabaan's hand. "You are looking very fine. And how is your flourishing family?"

Shabaan beamed. "You know I have a new son? My first wife's seventh son! Allah be praised."

We both congratulated him, and then had to promise we'd return to eat sometime soon. Actually, I had chosen Shabaan's for more than his fresh orange juice and Indian Ocean fish. I'd learned in the past that giving information to Shabaan was a form of currency that he could be trusted to spend wisely and repay in dividends many times over.

"Shabaan." I lowered my voice. "Have you heard that Nick Hunter died yesterday? He was at home. Bitten by a scorpion. Death was instantaneous."

Shabaan's heavy face drooped. "This is bad news, indeed. His poor wife. Will she stay on in Samburu with only Marianne Kanja for company? Two women alone, it is not possible."

"You know Kaji?" It was a silly question. Shabaan knew everyone.

"I know her family. They are devout Christians. The father works in WorldCorp Bank, and the mother is a school administrator. All the other children have done very well. The sons have gone into business or government work, and the daughters are married. Marianne is their one worry. They sent her to university in America to get her away from a suitor here they didn't like, and she came home with many poor ideas. It is so hard to raise respectful children these days. Maybe now she will move home, and gladden her father's heart."

"The father can be proud," Omondi said. "He has done well for his family."

"Oh, yes. His uncle is married to William Mutani's wife's cousin. They had arranged a good job for Marianne as a manager at the Buckingham Court when it first opened, but she quit after two weeks."

I thought of telling Shabaan that Kaji was doing important work, studying cheetah reproduction, but I doubted that would rehabilitate her reputation with him.

Shabaan asked what I knew about the funeral arrangements. I told him Nick's sister was arranging it. "Yes, Viv Porter. She is active in many charities and cultural events. A very capable woman."

Omondi shook his head in admiration. "You are a walking social encyclopedia."

"The Porters are well known." Shabaan waved a hand.

"Nick and Viv are the only brother and sister?"

"Yes." Shabaan was going to say more, but an important customer came in the door, so he repeated his regret over Nick's death and moved off to greet him.

Omondi pushed out his lips thoughtfully. "Before going any further conjuring up Nick's enemies, let us proceed in an orderly fashion and make sure a crime was, indeed, committed."

"I hope it wasn't." The memory of Nick's suffering was seared on my brain. "But if it was, I swear: I won't rest until we find the cold-blooded monster who did it."

"If this was a murder, it is an extremely lucky and clever one." Omondi finished his drink and pushed away the glass. He started ticking things off on his fingers. "So. We shall proceed. First: it looks as if Nick was bitten by this Sahara scorpion, but the evidence is circumstantial. Let us confirm the cause of death. I will make sure there is an autopsy. Discreetly. Then we must check the possibilities of how this foreign scorpion got to Nick's place. Perhaps it can be explained without foul play. Did he and Wynn receive a shipment from the Middle East, for example, in which the scorpion might have stowed away? Might it have been unwittingly carried south by one of these popular camel safaris?"

47

"You really think it could be an accident?"

"You know my methods: assume nothing, examine everything. This is going to be an especially delicate case, and we must test each step before trusting our weight to it."

"Delicate?"

"William Mutani is a very powerful man, and could be dangerous if we get in his way."

"It may not even involve him."

"Mutani operates in the uppermost circles of power. Even if he is not the killer, he may not welcome an investigation that touches on the edges of his activities. I could find myself demoted, even transferred out of homicide. You could find it impossible to renew your work permit."

"And that's if he's not really threatened."

"Exactly. It is fortunate you dragged me out of the office. I'd rather keep this unofficial as long as possible. Once Mutani gets wind of police involvement, he will be receiving the daily reports on his desk, sooner than I write them, even. The law only reaches so high in Africa. If he is the spider in the middle of this web, we must weave a special net to catch him." Omondi threw some bills on the counter. "You are my guest today. No, no arguments. I have paid." He took my elbow and rushed me out of Shabaan's. "I have just enough time in my lunch hour to find out who signed the death certificate."

I freed my arm. "For *us* to find out."

We decided to go to my apartment to arrange the next moves by phone. My answering machine was devoid of messages, reminding me that I had problems of my own. I'd sent out a major publicity mailing to travel agents across America specializing in adventure travel, and so far I'd gotten exactly zip, zero, nada in response. I was running out of ideas of how to keep Jazz Jasper Safaris afloat. Instead of feeling upset, I heard myself thinking: good, if it turns out someone murdered Nick, I'll have time to find the bastard.

Omondi called the funeral home to find out who signed

the death certificate. It was Dr. Alexander, Viv's family physician. As expected, the doctor had put down scorpion sting as cause of death.

Instead of requesting an official postmortem, which would mean a police report, Omondi arranged for the coroner, a personal friend, to do a private autopsy after work hours—as long as Wynn signed a release form.

I groaned when he told me. "You mean I have to tell Wynn of my suspicions now? Can't we wait till we're more certain?"

Omondi patted my arm. "You must tell her. It is not possible to do an autopsy on her husband behind her back. I would tell her myself, but I think it is gentlest coming from you."

I had to agree. I called Wynn and arranged to meet her around five, out at Wilson, where she'd be checking out her plane.

"How did she sound?" asked Omondi.

"Not good. Very tense, almost mechanical. I asked how she was doing, and all she talked about was arranging the funeral and getting her plane fixed."

"You're worried about her?"

"In a way it's good that she has stuff to keep her busy, but what about afterward, when she has to go home alone? It would be better if she would let out some of her feelings now."

The doorbell rang and I went to answer it. It was my landlord, Alvin Matua. He was a homely man at the best of times, with bad teeth and a sour expression on his narrow face, and I never enjoyed my dealings with him. Today he looked positively malicious.

"Mr. Matua!" I backed up and let him into the living room. His eyes darted around, as if itemizing my furniture, and rested on Omondi, who was lounging with his feet up on the cocktail table, dialing, phone to his ear.

"Let's go in the kitchen." I led Mr. Matua into my pocket-sized kitchen and stood with my back against the refrigerator, feeling like a cornered rat. I held up my hand. "I know I'm late on my rent again, and I'm really sorry.

49

I can pay you a quarter today, if you want, and another quarter by the end of the week."

"Too late."

"I'll try to get it by Thursday. Have a heart, Mr. Matua. You know I've always paid you. I'm in a financial squeeze right now, but I'll definitely get the money to you. Please don't worry about that."

"I not worried. I take back the apartment."

I was so nonplussed I was struck dumb.

"You owe big. Two month rent." His eyes flicked around the kitchen.

"Wait just a minute! You can't kick me out for being a bit late with my rent!"

"My daughter has new baby. Needs a bigger apartment."

A bigger apartment than what? This kitchen was so small I could practically touch all four walls while standing in one place, and the one bedroom could fit only a single dresser and a small double bed. "Can't you at least wait till the end of the month?"

"One week." Mr. Matua's crooked teeth gleamed. "You pay your rent, or you be out." He turned and left.

I stomped around the kitchen, seized my dirty breakfast dishes and ran hot water over them, swearing and wondering what the hell I was going to do. Nairobi was growing like a horrible human fungus, but never quite fast enough to house the exploding human population. Finding a cheaper place was impossible. In my whole life, I'd never been late with rent. It was humiliating. If I didn't get the money together by the end of the week, I was well and truly screwed. "Damn, damn, damn."

Omondi noticed my savage attack on the dishes. "Who was that?"

"My landlord. What did the coroner say?"

"He was happy at the thought of some moonlighting. Once we get the release signed, he'll call Dr. Alexander, and make arrangements with the funeral home. We've got to move quickly."

I wiped my hands on my jeans and turned to face him. Omondi looked at me piercingly. "Something is wrong."

50

"Do you have any big pieces of cardboard, or some oil cans lying around, maybe a piece of corrugated iron?"

"What are you talking about?"

"For my shanty."

"You are thinking of moving to Mathare?" Mathare was a notorious valley on the south side of the city that had been swallowed entirely by the pitiful shacks of Kenya's poorest. "I always thought you had a rather nice place here." He gestured to the Vermeer print on the wall above the sink.

It was a relic of my former life, when I was Dr. Jasper, art historian, specializing in the golden age of Dutch painting. I stared at it, unable to think of a bigger contrast between the placid scene of a music lesson, full of calm, beauty, and order, and the current chaos and uncertainty of my life. Although not all was as it seemed in the Vermeer, either: to Dutchmen of the time, a music lesson was a euphemism for a lovers' tryst.

"Jazz, what is it?" Omondi took both my hands in his. "What did your landlord say to you?"

I realized I'd been gaping into space. "He's threatening to evict me if I don't give him two months' rent by Friday."

"No!" He squeezed my hands. "I didn't realize things were that bad. You should have let me know. I can help you out with money." Omondi's kind, intelligent eyes looked straight into mine.

"Thanks, Omondi. You're a good friend to offer, but I don't want to borrow money from you. I'll deal with this somehow. Let me drop you off at headquarters."

I was actually waiting for some big checks, the deposits from a safari scheduled for the winter. The money should come in any day now, and would cover the rent I owed. But it worried me that Matua seemed more interested in getting rid of me than in getting his money.

I hated living hand to mouth like this. I was also missing Striker in a way I didn't used to, actually thinking it might be nice to live together. But I wanted to do it as an independent person, not because I couldn't pay my own

51

rent. I know myself: moving in with Striker with my tail between my legs would not be a good start.

I grabbed my keys, carefully locked the door behind us, wondering how I could stave Matua off. All I needed was time, but time was in short supply.

7

THE NEWSROOM AT *The Nairobi Star* was not a big room, and the staff had no trouble filling it end to end with noise, bustle, paper, desks, clacking printers, humming computers, and plain old-fashioned typing for those lower on the totem pole. The squarely built editor-in-chief had a cubbyhole of his own, demarcated by a chest-high bookcase stuffed with reference books. I explained I was a friend of Nick's and asked if he had a few minutes to spare, that I was writing the eulogy and wanted to talk with some of Nick's co-workers. It seemed like a lame story to me, but the editor bought it, apologizing for being too busy himself. He didn't even bother to ask my name.

"Kamau!" he shouted.

A man in his early thirties, wearing a turtleneck and light leather jacket, poked the upper half of his body around the bookcase. He glanced at me without curiosity from half-closed eyes that looked permanently sleepy. "Hey."

"This lady is a friend of Nick's, doing his eulogy. Talk to her, would you?"

"No problem." He led me over to his scarred metal desk, piled high with papers, pulled over a chair for me and perched on the edge of the desk. "Peter Kamau."

"Jazz Jasper."

"Oh, sure. You're the private investigator who solved the Laird murder, right? And you were involved in those safari murders in the Mara, too."

"I didn't realize I'd developed a reputation."

"Hey, that's our business. What can I do for you? Are you working on Nick's death?"

I had a split second to calculate how to answer. The last thing I wanted was to encourage the paper to trespass on Wynn's privacy. I had the feeling that if I gave Kamau one little opening, he'd extract every lurid detail I knew, and some I didn't.

My confusion must have been written on my face, because he laughed, a sleepy sort of laugh that went with his eyes. "Hey, bull's-eye. Who are you working for?"

"I'm not working for anyone," I said. "I'm one of Wynn's closest friends, and I offered to drop by and talk to a coworker so I could include Nick's work life in his eulogy."

Peter tilted his head and smiled. "You're not too good at lying. That must be a real liability in your work."

"I'm sure I could take lessons from you. Besides, I'm not an investigator, I run a custom safari company." I pulled out a card and gave it to him.

He didn't bother to look at it, just sat there swinging one leg and flicking a fingernail against the little stiff card. "So what information do you want from me? And why should I give it to you with no quid pro quo?"

"To butter me up as a future contact. You never know when I might have an interesting story for the paper."

"Fair enough." He flipped my business card onto the mess of papers behind him. "Anytime you want to chat, off the record, on the record, whatever you want. You'll find I'm very good at my job; I could even be a help to you, too."

I thanked him, pretending I didn't understand the innuendo in his tone, and went on to ask a bunch of eulogy-type questions about Nick's career, his relations with the *Star*'s staff, his reputation in the newspaper world. I asked if there were any important stories that Nick had covered, stories that made a change in the world, resulted in some beneficial actions.

Kamau's eyelids drooped a fraction of an inch more. "You have an exalted idea of the journalist." He gave his lazy smile. "Make a change in the world?"

I refused to be embarrassed. "You know, an exposé of some wrongdoing, things like that."

"Things that may have brought him enemies?" He pursed his lips in a sly smile.

"Do you just want to tease me, or are you going to co-operate? In a quid pro quo, somebody's got to do the *quo* first."

Peter got up and rummaged around in some papers on his desk. "Oh, but teasing is such fun." He came up with a pack of Camels, tapped out a cigarette halfway, extending the pack toward me. I shook my head. "Nick's been covering the situation in Somalia. It's a very hard beat, takes a lot of heart and a lot of courage to cover a story like that." He lit up and squinted through the smoke. "Nick didn't spare himself. He pushed himself to the limit, and beyond."

"Did Nick talk over those stories with you? I'm sure there was a lot of material that didn't get into the paper. I know you have to tread a narrow line between telling the whole story and not treading on any government toes."

"You mean like profiteering from the refugee camps?"

"Is there a lot of that?"

"Is there any government program that doesn't involve cream-skimming? That's not news, is it? And the big guys know that we won't ever print it anyway if we want to stay open. Believe me, they're not quaking in their shoes over what some reporters know about them."

"Were there other angles on the Somali story that you couldn't print?"

"Like what?"

"You're supposed to be doing the *quo*, remember?"

"Sounds like a new dance step. Do you like to dance?"

"For example, was there anything on the oil exploration going on near the border?"

Peter gave another sleepy smile. "How about if I do the *quo* by taking you out to lunch?"

"Thanks, but nothing will satisfy me except information."

"You're a hard woman."

"The oil story? There must be some big money riding on that." I didn't finish my thought out loud: enough to kill for if it was threatened.

Peter's eyelids drooped lower. "You're right. That the story is off limits."

"Why?"

"Nothing scandalous. Kenya has enough trouble with Somalis trying to claim the northern part of our country. The *Star* was not about to yell censorship on that story. We have to pick our battles."

"What about Njck's piece last week on that shipment of fifty monkeys from Kenyatta Airport that were dead on arrival at JFK? Was he doing any follow-up?"

"There was nothing to follow up on. The documentation was to a phony name, and no one stepped forward to claim the shipment. End of story."

Nick once told me he wanted to do an exposé on the wild pet trade as soon as he got a good local angle. Buying a wild animal for a pet is a kind of murder: ten are killed during capture and export for every live animal delivered. I imagined those monkeys crowded into a box, dying one by one. To my embarrassment, my eyes filled with tears. "I know Nick considered it a big story. He was waiting for a good hook."

Kamau's lips turned up in a patronizing smile, and I could feel my face grow flushed. "The wild pet trade is an American story, not a Kenyan one. It's legal in America, not here." He blew a smoke ring and poked his finger through it.

"Yeah, but this time there was a Kenya angle: those fifty monkeys started out either in Kenya or were brought here, probably overland from Tanzania or Uganda."

Peter shrugged. "Nick was already on to other things."

"Stories that haven't been printed yet?"

"Yeah." Peter took a long drag on his cigarette, then stubbed it out in a dirty ashtray. "You may find notes on it at his desk at home; he worked entirely out of his house. All I can tell you is he refused my last assignment, saying he had a lead on a dynamite story."

My antennae went up. "A dynamite story? On what?"

"He didn't say."

"Any guesses?"

Peter said slowly, "If I had to guess, I'd say the lead

56

came from one of his recent stories, but that leaves a wide net. He dropped off a scathing piece about Selfhelp's water projects with the Samburu, which will be coming out in tomorrow's paper. You might do better asking his wife."

"Can I get a copy of it, and his recent stories? Say, the last few months?"

"Sure, if you're up to slogging through a lot of old papers."

"It's not filed in the computer?"

"Computer?" He gave a short sarcastic laugh. "They're not filed at all. Tomorrow's story is down the hall in the production department; you'll find last week's papers hanging on a rack at the back of the office."

Peter led me past the double row of desks. A reporter hunched over his phone followed us with a curious eye. Against the far wall stood a rack like that found in hotel lobbies, with a selection of papers from the *International Herald Trib* to the *Star*'s competitor *Daily Nation*, hanging over wooden batons that looked like pool cues. He hefted the baton holding *The Star*. It dipped downward. A week of newsprint weighs a lot. He let it slip back into its hooks on the rack.

"Then, if you want to look further back, we have these." He thumped his hand on a three-foot stack of maroon-bound volumes.

I opened the back cover, confirming my worst fear: no index. "You mean I have to go through this page by page, looking for Nick's byline?"

"It looks that way." Kamau started out the door. "Come on, I'll take you next door."

Next door was the same size room, but instead of desks, a counter ran along three walls. Two young women were busy in front of large-screen computer work stations. One of them wore her hair in a fountain of skinny long braids. Beads in her hair perfectly matched the yellow and green pattern of her blouse, beautifully set off by her dark skin.

"Hullo, Peter. Deigning to look in on the plebes?" Peter Kamau bent over to breathe something into her ear, and was rewarded by an embarrassed smile. "Get out of here. I'm too busy for your nonsense."

We walked around an angled drafting board as big as a barn door, and found a stocky girl doing the paste-up of tomorrow's newspaper. She was not more than twenty, pretty with the freshness of youth, wearing a tight outfit with an unmistakable style that said Art Student. Peter slipped a hand around her waist and she slapped it away. "You have Nick Hunter's piece on the Samburu water projects?"

"What do you want it for?"

"It's for me. For Nick's eulogy," I said.

"Isn't that terrible? We were all so sad to hear that—the news." She gave me a sympathetic look, pushing away Peter's hand, which was reaching for her waist again. "I'll Xerox it for you." She sorted through some foam-core boards with the finished paste-ups, found the right one and made me a copy.

Peter cleared off a desk for me in the newsroom, and showed me the Xerox machine, crowded between a water cooler and a stack of computer paper. Scanning six months of newspapers at high speed, page after page, quickly becomes tedious, especially with a small voice inside my head whispering that this was a wild-goose chase. I reminded myself of Omondi's admonition to examine everything, assume nothing.

By the time I turned the last page of yesterday's paper, I was more caught up on local events than I'd ever been in my life. I'd seen half a dozen pictures of William Mutani getting out of limousines or shaking hands with cabinet ministers. There was one of him with Viv and Roger, at some charity ball. I copied that, too, not quite knowing why.

I fended off another request for a date and finally got out of the *Star* offices, blinking in the sunlight like a mole. I had a thick manila folder of Nick's stories under my arm, and felt more hopeful than when I began. At least I had some steps I could take. If Nick's investigations had set off his murder—which was pure conjecture—my instincts said it would be about something not yet in print: a story that could be killed only by killing the author.

It might be on a completely new subject, from a lead out

of nowhere. Except most leads don't come out of nowhere. As Kamau said, they were likely to come out of a recent story. I'd probably have to travel north to the Samburu settlement, or manyatta, that Nick had visited for his latest water project story. Tomorrow's article didn't give any indication specific enough to locate it. If Wynn didn't know, I would have to find out through Selfhelp.

Meanwhile, I'd found one name here in Nairobi that seemed worth a follow-through, and that I could do right away. I pulled out last week's story on the dead monkeys at JFK. Midway down the column I'd circled a paragraph, one Nick obviously included to provide local color and a lively quote. "There's nothing Allah breathed life into, that a pet dealer can't get." Next stop was Mr. Amin Ali, Pet Dealer Extraordinaire.

8

THE TINY SCRAP of a monkey raced about the cage in a panic, whimpering and crying. Stacked above it, a serval cat—which feeds on vervet monkeys—had curled itself into a catatonic ball of spotted tawny fur. Farther along, two lion cubs were in adjacent cages. Their faces were cut up, probably by flinging themselves against the wire mesh. A hanging cage next to a shack held a dispirited parrot, who gave a piercing whistle.

A short, slight man stepped out of the shack. He had the light skin and delicate features of a Somali, with a worried, tired look on his face. A small boy, maybe ten years old, in a ragged shirt and sneakers a size too large, sidled out behind him and stared with shy curiosity.

Seeing me, the man gave a broad smile, arms outstretched to the cages ringing the shack. "You are looking for an unusual pet? If you don't see it, tell me, and I will get it for you. I am Mr. Ali, Pet Dealer Extraordinaire. You want a monkey?" He gestured. "A lion cub? If you don't see it here, do not worry. There is nothing Allah created that I can't get. A zebra, perhaps? Tell me. Tell me and it is yours."

He shuffled to the vervet's cage in a pair of down-at-the-heel slippers and scratched a finger against the mesh. The baby monkey fled to the farthest corner and cowered. "Would you like a nice little vervet? They make excellent pets."

They make terrible pets, and owners who are beguiled by a vision of a cute monkey hugging them affectionately are less beguiled by a house in shambles and a high-strung pet that bites. When the monkey gets sick and dies, as ninety percent of them do, they tell themselves it was a chance for the children to learn about death.

On the way over, I'd thought about how to approach Mr. Ali, and hadn't come up with anything brilliant. Asking him to tell me everything he'd told Nick didn't seem destined for success. I wished I knew what questions Nick had asked. And how would I recognize a lead even if I heard it? The obvious cover story was to act like a potential customer, as long as I didn't end up walking away with a pet. I remembered Mutani asking about buying Tonic, and decided to pretend I wanted a cheetah cub.

"Hello, Mr. Ali." I extended my hand. His handshake was firmer than he looked.

"You are American?"

I nodded.

He smiled so that his face lit up. "I like Americans very much. I can ship to any state. If your state has restrictions, we ship to the state next door, and you will pick up from there. America is my biggest customer. You people really love animals."

"I'm actually looking for a very special gift." I scanned the cages. "Some friends of mine have two cheetahs. Do you have any for sale? I'd prefer two that have already been pets, but wild ones will do, if they're young enough."

Mr. Ali folded his hands. "Ah, a cheetah. A very beautiful animal. A cat fit for kings and queens. And not one, but a matched pair." I nodded. "That means two the same age. Now, you are asking me something difficult. Now, that is a harder proposition. An endangered animal, and finding one for sale becomes much more difficult. Finding two for sale, even more difficult." He made a circuit around his cages, as if in hopes of finding a cheetah cub there, then turned to me. "Perhaps they would like a pair of lion cubs, the king of beasts?" He reached into the cage, pulled out a cub, and before I knew what was happening, deposited it in my arms. "That is the boy."

The little cub's fur was dirty and it smelled strongly of cat piss. I got an arm around his bottom to provide good support and he cuddled against my chest. When I gave him my hand to smell, he took a finger in his mouth and began to suck rhythmically.

"Ah, see. He likes you. He is still on the bottle, an excellent age for adoption. See, he is better than a cheetah."

The cub looked up at me wide-eyed. Another minute of this and I'd end up taking him home. To what? Life in an apartment? As if I even had an apartment. Feeling like a traitor, I thrust him back in Mr. Ali's arms and turned away as he stuffed the mewing lion cub back into the cage.

Lions are social animals. Sticking a cub in a cage by itself is like solitary confinement for a toddler. I wanted to take the cub back, but it's next to impossible, I reminded myself, to return a lion to the wild. Hand-reared lions, unafraid of humans, are so dangerous that the national parks won't allow the release of a former pet. George Adamson, with all the financial resources of the Elsa Fund, had only been able to save a few pet lions from zoo or circus life, and only by living, at the age of eighty-three, in the Kora Reserve, out in the middle of howling wilderness. Somali bandits had gunned Adamson down in 1989, and as far as I knew, there was no one to continue his life's work.

"Would you like an easier pet?" Mr. Ali coaxed. "A little monkey." He started toward the cage.

"No, please, I don't want to hold any of the animals."

The boy slipped over to the cage, quietly opened the door and coaxed the little monkey out of the corner. It climbed along his arm, then jumped to his chest and clung there, holding onto his ragged shirt with tiny long-fingered hands. The boy petted the monkey's head, murmuring softly, and came over to stand by Mr. Ali. The vervet looked into the boy's face and chattered back, as if they were having a conversation. The boy gave me a shy sidelong look, and I couldn't tell whether he was relieved I didn't want the monkey or was trying to help make a sale.

"It has to be cheetahs?" The worried tired look came over Ali's face. "I am a simple small businessman," another wave at the cages, "who loves animals. I am not looking for these high-price rarities." He rubbed his head. "But if that is what you want, I know everyone in this business, amateur and professional, I know collectors around the world, I know people no one else knows. I can match you up with a dealer who likes that kind of a challenge. For a price. You are looking at an expensive acquisition."

"How expensive?"

"I cannot tell you exactly, of course, but let us say that it will be somewhere, let me think. No, perhaps I should say nothing, I will let the seller first discuss price." He studied me from under his fine brow. My jeans and khaki shirt were not designed to impress. "As long as you know we are talking now about big money."

"How big?"

"No, how can I say, when I do not even have such an animal?" he showed me his empty palms.

"Price is not a problem, as long as the cheetahs are in good health."

"Excellent." Ali inclined his head. "Excellent."

"And who is this other dealer?"

"Ah, you see, I do not know yet. It will take me some time to find the contact. I must do it discreetly, because the cheetah is a rare animal. There are fewer in the world than people living in one city block. But if, for example, an orphaned animal is found, there is no law that says you must leave it in the bush to starve. No, the law is not so unreasonable. You may not shoot a cheetah mother to take the cubs, no, of course not. But if you find two cubs who have been abandoned—you see? And then all it takes is the right paperwork, which is also a question of . . ." He rubbed his fingers together. "You must have the right contacts in the Customs Service. That is the difficult part. I can do it for you. I don't charge much, only a small commission. And also, I will crate up the animals for you. That is most crucial. The most crucial. You read about that shipment of dead monkeys in the newspaper last week? The reporter came to talk to me, to learn. I told him, that is what happens when they are overcrowded and not crated properly." He put a hand to his throat. "Suffocation. So the crate is most important."

"I remember that article. In fact, that is where I learned of you." The monkey scrambled up to the boy's shoulder,

63

grabbed the top of his ear with one hand, the boy's shaved skull leaving little else to grab, and examined me with huge wise-looking eyes in its small wrinkled face.

Mr. Ali looked pleased. "I was able to give that reporter much information. He knew very little. And then he included only one small sentence. He was here for an hour. One small sentence." He held up an empty palm.

"Do you know who shipped those monkeys to America?"

"No, because it was badly done, you see, it was not done by someone experienced. What I think happened is this: an American dealer tried to bypass reputable businessmen, get a cheap price by buying direct from the trapper. You see where it got him. All dead. A pity. A waste. You must know how to crate. You can't stick too many animals in one box and expect them to survive."

"Were you able to give the reporter any leads on the trapper?"

Mr. Ali shrugged. "I told him they probably came from Tanzania, because they do a big wildlife trade overseas. One of the biggest in the world. Tanzania." He made a face. "They were socialists for twenty years, and what did it get them? They have nothing. No money, no business, no foreign investment. They have great animals, yes, but in that whole country, there is not one good hotel. In their best game park, the hotel may or may not have running water, depending on the day. See, I know all about these things. We in Kenya have more tourists in one week than they get in one year. We know how to make the tourists happy: good hotels, many animals, no hunting, no trapping. In Tanzania, for money you can kill anything."

"So you think the monkeys came from there?"

"Possible. It is possible. Everyone knows they trap monkeys there. You wonder why, then, ship them through Nairobi, where it is illegal, instead of through Dar Es Salaam? Because we have direct flights to the States. So that is why."

"Does that mean someone in Kenya helped arrange it?"

"Yes, certainly. You drive up from Tanzania, you find a good place to cross the border where there is no road, you

64

go to Kenyatta Airport and pay to ship your box, plus a little extra for the Customs. That is where you need a local person who knows how to arrange things."

"Are there trappers working in Kenya?"

"Of course. What do you think? As I said, it is very difficult in Kenya. But I know someone who works near the Somali border, and he has been able to buy some very interesting animals recently."

I knew someone who worked near the Somali border, too: Gerry Weller. "Did you tell the reporter about this dealer, also?"

"Why should I make trouble for someone who has never harmed me? But we discussed Somalia, yes, of course, because the reporter had spent much time there. You know, everything is destroyed in Somalia. There is no sense anymore, no order, nothing. They are living like beasts. A gun in every hand. If a man is treating other men like beasts, then for the wild animals—what do you think?"

"A disaster."

"Slaughtered. Gone. They will never return. It is possible to kill so many in so few minutes with these filthy automatic weapons." Mr. Ali's voice took on force. "Those who make and sell these weapons are truly doing the devil's work. A man must carry a knife, yes, of course, a man needs a weapon. But a gun? Did our fathers carry these guns? Godless Russian guns? When the clans went on camel raids before, they would sneak, take the animals, and run, fast, before a big fight could start. Maybe kill one man for the feud. That family has killed one relative before, so now you kill one also. This is honor. Now, every teenage camel boy is given a gun, to make their clan leader look big. They can do what they like. You are not in my clan? My sub-clan? My family? I will steal every goat, every camel, every scrap of food, and leave a whole village to starve. To starve!"

He gestured for the boy to approach us and rested a hand on his head. The boy stared up at me with luminous brown eyes. The monkey clung to his ear and chattered. "This is my sister's son. I am Kenyan, a Somali Kenyan, but my sister married a Somali from Kismayu, the place

65

they call the City of Death. Inshallah, they are all out safely, seventeen people, living with my family in one apartment. My brother-in-law was a teacher." Mr. Ali showed me his empty palm. "What is he to do here? We have our own unemployed teachers. So now he helps out a cousin who has a good stall in the market, selling carvings, but business is not good."

"The whole tourist industry stinks right now," I agreed with conviction.

"Ah, see? You know, too. I am trying to find a job for my sister at a hotel. She would do anything. Maybe I have a connection, we shall see. They would like their own place, but there is no room anywhere, there are so many refugees. The rents are impossible anyway, and to build a shanty—shantytowns are so dangerous." he shook off the black mood with a dismissive gesture. "Anyway, Somalia is impossible, but near the border, it is a good time to get wild animals, if you do not mind the danger. That has discouraged most people. Except this one person that I know. See how lucky you were to come to me? No one else would know this man, but I, I know everyone."

"I know someone who works in that area. An oil man named Gerry Weller."

A guarded look came over Mr. Ali's face. "I do not know this man."

I wondered what the look meant. Was he lying? "William Mutani is also doing some work up there."

"Ah, Mr. Mutani." Ali beamed. "A big man. He started out as a worker on a tea plantation, and look at what he has become. The Kikuyu are very good businessmen. Look at Kenya and look at Somalia. You know why? I told my brother-in-law. In Somalia, everything is honor, honor, honor. A knife, a gun, honor. The Kikuyu were farmers. They never went around stealing cows to show how brave they were. No, they take care of their family, they work, they think. Look at Nairobi. We have skyscrapers like America, we have beautiful hotels, offices, homes. Inshallah, all the tribes get along. I know a cousin of Mr. Mutani. He has a good job as a driver. He is Kikuyu, I am Somali: I told him about my sister, he said he would put in a word for me, to help my sister. Mr. Mutani has made jobs for many Kenyans."

The monkey had been eyeing me intently all during Mr. Ali's speech. Suddenly she let go of the boy's ear and flung herself straight at me, flying easily through the air onto my head, wrapping her tail around my throat and grabbing onto hanks of my hair with both hands.

Mr. Ali stopped the boy from rushing forward to rescue me. "See, she likes you. We call her Tumbili. That is Swahili for this kind of monkey. I will make a very good price for you."

I tried to loosen her grip on my hair, but she shrieked and held fast. I stopped tugging, and she cuddled into my head. I could feel her little heart beating ta-dum, ta-dum against my ear. "Thank you, Mr. Ali, but I don't want any pets. Except the cheetahs, for a friend," I added quickly.

"This is a very good monkey. Very sweet. See how she hugs you. She is going to be a star next week at a big party."

"A party?" I could picture the shambles as she leapt from hairdo to hairdo.

"Yes. I am renting her for a few hours to a very nice lady from Karen, who is having all the important people to her house. She comes to me and says, 'Mr. Ali, you must rent me a nice gentle cheetah to walk on my terrace among the guests.' I told her a cheetah is impossible, so she decide on serval cat—beautiful spots like a cheetah—and a monkey. She was very happy."

The monkey cautiously lowered herself, clinging to my collar, and made a dive to get inside my blouse. We had a brief tug of war, during which Mr. Ali and his nephew got to see more of my breasts than I'd prefer. I won, and handed her back to the boy. She scampered up to his shoulder again and chattered at me reproachfully. I needed to get out of here soon if I wanted to get out alone.

A feeling of frustration washed over me. All I'd gotten was vague allusions to Kenyan trappers, and that someone was getting animals from near the Somali border. I'm sure Nick would have jumped on that and squeezed out a lot more information than I had. As a last desperate attempt

67

to bring Nick back into the conversation, I said the rich lady's party sounded like a good newspaper story, and had he told the *Star* reporter about it?

"I see you think like a businesswoman. Publicity. Am I right?" I nodded, and he beamed. "As soon as he came in, I thought, I will tell him about the party, they will send someone, they will take a picture of Tumbili on the shoulders of a beautiful woman, it will be good for business."

"Was the reporter interested?"

"He was very interested. Especially after I told him the name of the nice lady." He paused expectantly.

"Oh, is she well known?"

"To him, yes. It is his very own sister!"

9

I STRAPPED MYSELF in, offered a prayer to the gods, and gave Wynn a weak thumbs-up.

"Lion. Hippo. Giraffe. Requesting takeoff clearance." She got the okay and did something complicated with what looked like a multiple gear shift, and her Cessna's twin engine propellers twirled into a blur. She released the brake and we began to move forward. As usual, my heart started pounding in my chest. The little plane taxied down the runway, and suddenly we were aloft. Wilson Airport was a bisected circle below us. As soon as I felt the air under the wings buoying us up, I could breathe and give a genuine smile.

"That time I was hardly scared at all," I told her, raising my voice to be heard above the engine's roar.

"Next time, you'll share the controls. Agreed? Then you'll really lose all fear."

Wynn's small, heart-shaped face was serious as she monitored the bank of dials in front of her. The plane climbed steeply. The shoulder of the Great Rift Valley rises to nine thousand feet ten minutes north of the city. If you fail to gain altitude in time, you slam into its wall. Pilots who do that don't come back.

I pressed my face near the window. In a single glance I could see the glass and steel downtown, the sprawling shanties of Mathare, and the plains of Nairobi National Park. It looked gloomy under the ceiling of clouds typical for August in Nairobi. "I'm not sure I want to lose all fear. Fear is a survival instinct."

"Fear is a ball and chain. You must grab life like an orange and savor its sweetness."

"I agree with you there," I said. "Losing Nick makes me feel it all the more: savor every moment. But flying is not my idea of an orange."

"Well, I won't press you."

"Very punny." I'd made several attempts to help Wynn talk about Nick, and each time she'd deflected me. She obviously wasn't ready. I didn't know whether to be worried about her or not. Being strong is great, except for the times when you need to be weak. If she wouldn't unbend, she might break.

"I can see they've fixed the altimeter." Wynn tapped one of the dials. "That was the important thing. One of my wing lights is still broken, but the mechanic promised he would poach one from a plane that's out of commission. I can put it in myself. The fuel gauge will have to wait until next time. I can get home and back easily on one tank, so that's no problem."

"So you're heading north tonight, and then back down for the funeral?"

"Yeah." Wynn gave a big sigh. "I can't wait to get home, see Gin and Tonic, take some of the load off Kaji. Besides a burning desire to get out of Karen. A little of Viv and Roger goes a long way." As we lifted above the Rift, wind gusts from the valley below buffeted the plane. Her hands shifted on the levers in front of her.

I gripped the armrest and tried to ignore the fact that the angled window next to me was showing only sky. Then I saw a black shape, a nine foot wingspan, another and another. "Wynn! Vultures!"

At one hundred and fifty miles per hour, colliding with a vulture is not a joke. They've been known to smash through the windscreen and kill the pilot and copilot instantly. One vulture whooshed over the right wing. I could see its yellow eye and the slashing hook-tipped beak. The naked skin on its head and neck flushed red with fear, like a splash of blood, and it was gone.

"Hold on!" Wynn radioed the problem to the control tower as she quickly worked the controls and put the plane into a tight descent. Next to us the shoulder of the Rift was a terrifying blur. It looked as if the vultures were yanked upward with a sky hook, but it was us falling. I tried not to picture us splattering against the ground. My stomach tried to climb into my throat, and this time I gripped the armrests with no shame. We leveled off above a small farm, so low that I could count the goats behind a shack.

"Well, that added a touch of excitement," Wynn said dryly. "You can let go of the armrests now."

I practically had to peel my fingers off one by one. "How much longer are we staying up here?"

Wynn pushed the throttle forward and we mounted at a more gradual angle to a vulture-free sector of the sky. "Ten minutes? Can you take it?"

"Sure." I kept rehearsing how I would tell Wynn about the scorpion, wishing I could chicken out. Finally I forced myself to speak. "Wynn, there's something serious I want to talk to you about. Will you have some time when we land?"

"Not much. Tell me now. I can fly and chew gum at the same time."

"It's about the scorpion that bit Nick." Wynn stiffened. "Wouldn't it be better if we wait?"

"Why? I'm not going to lose control of the plane. I do my best thinking when I'm flying."

Yeah, but what about feeling? I thought to myself.

Wynn gave me a quick glance. "What is it?"

I hesitated. This wasn't what I'd had in mind.

"C'mon, spit it out!"

I steeled myself. Here goes. "It's about the scorpion that bit him. You know that Gerry Weller character Kaji and I bumped into? He said scorpion bites aren't fatal to adults."

"That's not true."

"I wasn't sure, so I found the dead scorpion and took it to the National Museum. They ID'd it as a Sahara scorpion."

"Yeah?"

"They're one of the most poisonous animals on earth. It's just that we don't have them here in Kenya."

There was a long silence. The earth below us was a patchwork of small green fields. To the northwest, the Abedare Mountains were shrouded in clouds.

71

"Wynn?"

She turned the plane in a wide arc, and we headed back to Wilson. "I don't understand what you're saying. We obviously do have them here in Kenya, since one stung Nick."

"There's a big difference between *them* and *one*."

"The scientist you spoke to is wrong."

"She'll corroborate it when her boss gets back, but she was very certain."

"So it's a crazy fluke."

"Maybe. Did you get any packages from the Middle East or North Africa lately? Perhaps a scorpion snuck into the packing material as an unintended stowaway."

"No, nothing like that."

"There are only two choices: it got to your house by accident—or on purpose."

Wynn took a big breath and let it out slowly. "I don't know if I can take this, Jazz. You know how much I loved Nick. He was the world to me."

"I know." There was a lump in my throat.

"Losing him is hard enough." She fought to gain control of her voice. "At least I can tell myself it was part of the natural world. We knew it was dangerous to live out in the desert. We've had scorpions in the house before. The place is crawling with them, and they like hiding in little dark places, like among your clothes, under things left on the floor, a hundred places. They're horrible, but they're not evil." Her voice became adamant. "I don't want Nick to be touched by evil."

"But if it has? Touched him, I mean. If the scorpion was put there on purpose?"

"That can't be so. I won't believe it."

"Why, Wynn?" It felt cruel to be hitting Wynn with this, but the autopsy couldn't wait. I knew she was still in the first stage of shock. Nick's death didn't seem real yet, let alone that he might have been murdered. Still, Wynn wasn't a person to close her eyes to unwanted realities.

She was silent for so long I thought she wasn't going to answer. Nairobi was below us. The clouds had thickened,

72

and the city was dreary, spreading across the landscape like a skin rash.

"If you don't want to talk about it, that's okay."

"I'd like to talk about it. It's been so long since I've told anyone. No one here in Kenya knows now."

Now that Nick was dead.

Still, she said nothing. I decided not to push it. Bringing this up while flying was not the greatest idea. We finished the flight in silence. Wynn made a somewhat bumpy landing, but I was too preoccupied to feel scared. We taxied to a halt and then slowly rolled down the asphalt toward a hangar.

Wynn turned off the engine and peeled off the radio headset. She ran her hands through her short hair, and then swiveled to face me. "I don't think I ever told you why I came to Kenya, why I gave up nursing." I shook my head. Her dark blue eyes looked past me into the distance, as if the corrugated steel hangar wasn't next to us. "I don't think I told you I was married before Nick."

"No." I was realizing there was a lot that Wynn hadn't told me. We'd picked up our friendship from where we were in our lives, and hadn't touched on our past. I didn't like talking about my former life too much. The memory of my ex-husband telling me he'd gotten a grad student pregnant and wanted to marry her was still like a knife going into my stomach. And to remember my identity as Dr. Jazz Jasper, art historian and curator, was bizarrely irrelevant to my life in Kenya. So I'd never noticed that Wynn was equally quiet about her past, too.

"We were both twenty-one, married two years. One night he got this headache." Her voice caught. "He was screaming from the pain. It was an embolism. Tom died before the ambulance could get there. And I stood there, completely helpless."

I put my hand on hers. "Oh, Wynn. I'm so sorry."

Wynn pulled back her hand and shrugged. "I survived, but part of me was dead, too. I went to nursing school— you can imagine why. I worked like a maniac, worked until I was numb. After a couple of years, my mother was crazy for me to remarry, to start a family, but I couldn't. Having him snatched away from me like that . . ."

"How awful . . ."

"Still, I had friends, eventually I had lovers, I had a life. I took a year off and traveled around the world with a backpack. The grief was still there, but it had its own room with a door, if you know what I mean." She shot a glance at me. "If I didn't open the door, it didn't rush out."

My heart went out to her. "I know exactly what you mean. As long as you avoid that wing of the house, you can even forget the room is there."

Wynn fell silent, her eyes staring at memories deep within her.

"There's more, isn't there?" I asked.

"Yes. I hate to think about it."

"You don't have to—"

"No. I want to tell you. If you can take it." She gave me a searching glance. "It's been on my mind."

The unspoken name of Nick hung between us. "I'm your friend. You can tell me anything you want."

"I was beginning to think about marriage again, about loving someone that much, when my younger sister disappeared while on vacation in California. We were frantic. For a month we heard nothing. We didn't know if we were sleeping or waking, eating or not eating, on earth or in Hell. And then finally, word. She must have been hitchhiking, picked up by some—" Her voice choked to a whisper. "He tortured her before strangling her." She had to stop, press her lips together to stop their trembling. Her hands were clenched so hard her nails bit into her palms, drawing blood. She opened her hand and looked at the bright red drops without reacting.

I dabbed at the blood with a crumpled tissue, then put my hand on top of Wynn's small one. There was nothing I could say. I felt so fortunate to have been spared such tragedies.

"The police had no leads." Her eyes stared into nowhere. "It was hard to think of anything else but my sister, the hell she suffered. It got so bad, I was angry at all men, scared to go out by myself."

I squeezed her hand gently.

"Okay," she continued in the same bleak voice, "that was a phase, too. I began to study self-defense, got good enough to teach it. That helped me more than anything." She glanced at me sideways to see how I was taking it.

"It must feel good to know you can protect yourself."

"I sure can. I learned from all of them: how to fall from judo, how to block punches from karate, how to immobilize someone from aikido. And not just the martial arts. I learned street fighting. No one is ever going to pull a knife or a gun on me and get away with it."

"Did it help?"

"Yes and no. I stopped being scared. And then, out of the blue, they caught the guy. He'd murdered another girl, got careless, and they traced him. He confessed to seven murders, including my sister's."

"God, that makes me mad."

"Listen to this." Her voice went rough with anger. "He didn't go on trial, because he was declared legally insane. They kept him in a hospital three years, and released him."

"To kill again."

"It ate away at me, little by little. Maybe it was job burnout, like my supervisor said. I could do my work, but I couldn't care anymore. I was getting twisted tighter and tighter inside."

"I know what you mean. After my divorce I was so full of anger, not just anger, *bitter* anger. It was so horrible. Especially the self-pity." A shiver went down my spine. I hated to remember myself like that. "That's why I came to Kenya, to get away from that person I was becoming."

"Yes, exactly. I didn't want to be a dark, bitter, paranoid person. If I did, it was as if my sister's killer had destroyed me, too, had won, you understand?"

"So you decided to leave the States and start a new life?"

"I never decided." Wynn gave a sad smile. "I met Nick when I was on a tour in Israel. He was Jerusalem correspondent for the *Trib*, but he missed Kenya so much, he decided to come back here and free-lance. He convinced me to come with him for an extended vacation. I never left. I took an extra two weeks, then a month's leave of absence, then an indefinite leave. It was such a relief to be away from nursing, from my mother, from the pressure cooker. And then we found Gin and Tonic. Those two cheetahs saved my life. I mean it. They brought me back to myself, to the loving person I knew I really was. I still think about my sister, more than you can imagine. But I keep that in its own room. Every now and then I go there, and I fall apart inside. But then I leave and close the door, and return to Kenya."

"Wynn, I don't know what to say." I felt so sad for her. "I wish I could hug you and make everything better."

"So do I!"

"Let's forget what I said about the scorpion. Enough is enough. It's already too much. I told Inspector Omondi what I told you, and he said there wasn't enough evidence to make an official inquiry. We could stop everything right here."

Wynn ran a weary hand through her hair. "The truth is also the truth. If somebody planted that scorpion in our house, they have to be caught. They could be a danger to others. I don't see you and Omondi ignoring a possible murder because it upsets me to think about it. That's ridiculous."

"I wish I'd never picked up the damn scorpion."

She shook her head sadly. "I'm so tired of evil. The world is hard enough as it is."

"Wynn, would you like me to come stay with you in Samburu for a while? Would company be nice or a burden?"

"Oh, you're never a burden." She thought a moment. "Thank you. It would be good to have you there, maybe for a few days or a week. I'm going to be all right. Really. I'm a survivor."

"I know you are. I've never met a stronger person."

"Even after Gin and Tonic are on their own, back in the wild, I don't think I'll lose my connection to life again, no matter what happens."

"I know what you mean. Here in Kenya, the wilderness—it gets inside you, heals you."

Wynn nodded. "So, I can face the scorpion. What's the next step?"

"Omondi is arranging a quiet autopsy to confirm cause of death. He'd like you to write a note authorizing it."

"No problem. Will he want to talk to me?"

"At some point."

"Any time. You can give him my number. What about Viv and Roger?"

"We thought we'd go to Viv's opening party and nose around. Without an official investigation, we can't very well conduct a formal interview. Can you get me an invitation?"

"To Viv's gala? Of course. It's on Saturday. I hope you know what you're letting yourself in for. And after that?"

"Nick told Peter Kamau at *The Star* that he had a hot lead on a new story. Did he tell you about it?"

Wynn looked thoughtful. She shook her head slowly. "Nothing I can think of. It was probably on his latest trip, to that Samburu manyatta where Selfhelp installed a pump. He was there at the end of last week. We hadn't played catch-up yet on all our news, because of getting ready for our weekend guests." The lines in her face grew deeper.

We got out of the plane and headed toward the hangar and Wynn's mechanic.

"There was one thing he mentioned," Wynn said slowly. "He saw signs of poaching on a big scale. He was really bummed out, but he said something interesting might come of it."

"Hmm. Do you know the exact location of this manyatta?"

"Yeah, we always left the coordinates of a destination if we were flying solo."

"What do you say I come up to your place after the funeral and Viv's party, and we head north, see if we can find what his hot lead was?"

"And if it threatened someone enough for them to kill him."

10

OMONDI CALLED ME as soon as he got the results of the autopsy to say he'd drop by after work. His line at police headquarters was not private, so he wouldn't say a word on the phone. I put a bottle of wine in the fridge to chill, and paced around my apartment. I was really eager to get the cause of death confirmed. Then at least we could be sure what had happened. The who, why, and how a Sahara scorpion was used as a murder weapon were going to be a lot harder to discover, as I was already finding out.

I'd spent the last couple of days looking into the wild pet trade, talking to knowledgeable people in the Wildlife Department and animal protection groups, asking if Nick had contacted them lately. The answer kept coming back no, and I was getting pretty frustrated. It looked like Nick hadn't been pursuing a follow-up to the story of dead monkeys shipped to JFK. That in itself seemed odd to me, but this early in an investigation everything can look suspicious. Still, as I'd told Peter Kamau, Nick had been *waiting* for a local hook so he could do an article on the mass killing behind collecting parrots and monkeys as pets. This story was exactly what he'd been waiting for. Why hadn't he pursued it? Was it because he'd found a more urgent "dynamite" story?

Omondi arrived at last. I hustled him to my couch, gave him a glass of wine, but before I could start pumping him about the autopsy, he popped up to look at my bookshelves—full of mysteries and books on Africa. He admired a Rembrandt print of a quiet Dutch house and pond, then sniffed around the kitchen to see what I was up to on the stove, which was nothing.

"You've created an oasis of peace, with your prints and books."

"A necessary illusion."

"No, the peace is real. It is realer than your money worries. I can feel it. You have made a true home for yourself in Kenya."

"That's true. I wouldn't be anywhere else in the world."

"How are things with you and Striker these days?" Omondi asked. "You haven't mentioned him much lately."

"Probably because things are going so well. I'm afraid to put a jinx on it by saying it out loud."

"That good?" Omondi raised his brows.

"Are you proud of your handiwork, Mr. Cupid?" I always teased Omondi about getting Striker and me together, by breaking me out of my self-enforced isolation from men.

"You were already half in love with him."

"That's why I was running away so hard."

"All I did was point it out. You only needed a friend's encouragement to give you courage."

"Encouragement? Is that what you call it?"

Omondi laughed. "Anytime you need more, let me know."

"Maybe I need some friendly advice." I looked into my wine, then up at Omondi. "I'm sort of thinking of . . . maybe . . . I've thought of suggesting . . ."

We both burst out laughing.

"I'd like to move in with him, but the timing is so bad with all my money problems," I blurted out.

"The timing seems good, given your money problems."

"No. Because then I'm in a dependent position. It would feel crummy to both of us. But it's been months that I've been waiting for the economic recovery they keep promising us, and business is still getting slower."

"Are you thinking of marriage?"

"Marriage!"

"Pardon me!" Omondi put up his hands, laughing.

"Marriage is the furthest thing from my mind. I don't

79

want it. Not now. Not with Striker, and not with anyone. A nice, loving, sexy friendship is great. It's wonderful. I have no desire to force it into something bigger than it is. Striker feels the same."

"So, you know what you want and what's right for you." Omondi came and sat down next to me. "If you love each other and want to be together, who cares if you can pay half the expenses? That's bookkeeping, not independence. Follow your heart. The rest is fear."

"Not having any money makes it harder."

"You are independent. That's not going to go away. It comes naturally to you."

I made a doubtful face.

"Are you afraid Striker will have all the power if you're living in his house, on his income?"

"Wait. I still have some tours coming through. It's not like I can't feed myself, or chip in. . . ." I heard the defensive tone in my voice. "Yes, you're right. Power gets in there, too. Striker assumes he'll get everything his way as it is. It's one of his least lovable traits."

"And what happens when he acts that way?"

I shrugged. "Either I go along, we talk it out, or we fight."

"So, you'll do the same when you're living there."

I smiled. "You always make things sound so easy."

"You always make things sound so complicated." Omondi smiled.

"So what did the coroner say?" I got up hurriedly, walked to the window and back.

Omondi leaned back on the cushions and twirled his wineglass. "Dr. Singh. Have you heard about him?"

"I've heard the name."

He emptied his glass and put it on the table. "One of the best forensic doctors in all of Africa. A middle-aged man, very experienced. A true man of knowledge. By good fortune, he has a keen interest in snakes and scorpions, poisonous sea creatures and so forth. He's treated or consulted on dozens of incidents, so he can speak with some authority."

"And?" I sat on the edge of the couch and searched Omondi's face.

"He said there is absolutely no doubt Mr. Hunter died of a scorpion sting."

"Can he tell which scorpion?"

"No, that he could not say. Some are more poisonous than others, but they all kill the same way."

I suppressed a shudder.

"Apparently scorpion venom is a highly complex chemical solution." Omondi put his fingertips together, in what I thought of as his lecturing mode. "It consists of five classes of chemicals: enzymes, amino acids, neurotransmitters, and so forth. They assault the body simultaneously, causing convulsions, massive internal bleeding—the complete collapse of the internal organs."

I tried not to picture what the words meant. I'd seen the toxin in action all too well. "And the only thing that does that is the sting of a scorpion?"

"Some snakes are similar, but if it was a snake, there would have been fang marks. He found nothing."

"No sting mark, either?"

"Singh said with scorpions there is often no punctate. Sometimes the site swells and is painful, other times there's no sign at all."

"Nick's hand did swell."

"Singh left no room for doubt. Mr. Hunter died of scorpion venom."

"So it was definitely the sting, and not the snake antivenin that killed him. I told you Viv said he was allergic to the antivenin as a kid."

"An allergic reaction kills through shock and respiratory failure," Omondi said. "The scorpion kills by—"

"Please, I saw it."

Omondi touched my arm. "My dear Jazz, I am sorry."

"No, don't apologize. We need to know all these facts. What did he think of a scorpion killing him?"

"Yes. That is the one point that Dr. Singh admitted was odd. He recently treated a Samburu teenager who sat on a scorpion and got stung in the rump. His leg was stiff for

81

twenty-four hours. He recovered completely. Here in Kenya, it is only small children who die of scorpion bites."

"So the question remains: how did a deadly Middle Eastern scorpion find its way to Kenya and into Nick's outhouse?"

Omondi tapped his fingers together thoughtfully. "We have only a single drop of suspicion, but this is actually good. Without other evidence, the identification of a Sahara scorpion by Dr. Wakaba is too flimsy to convene a grand jury, even if we wanted to."

"So you and I are free to investigate this privately."

"Yes." Omondi tapped a jauntier rhythm. "Without bringing in the police."

Saturday afternoon, a few days after the funeral, I picked up Omondi, who looked resplendent in a tropical suit, and headed for the Porters'. He nodded at me approvingly. "It is a rare treat to see you in a dress."

"It's camouflage. I hope to blend in and pick up a lot of information." I was wearing a turquoise and mauve tunic I used to wear to exhibit openings, and my one piece of good jewelry, a heavy Navajo necklace. "I wonder what Nick said to his sister about using wild animals in her show? According to Mr. Ali, she's still going through with it."

"They sound very dissimilar, this brother and sister."

I turned left at Karen Road and passed the members-only country club, set well back from the road. The Porters lived not five minutes from the home of Karen Blixen, who wrote *Out of Africa* under the pen name Isak Dinesen. Blixen's stone house, surrounded by an English garden with a broad green lawn, was a staple of my Nairobi tour, and I found it with no trouble. "I had a farm in Africa, at the foot of the Ngong Hills," I recited. The hills were still there, purple-blue against the darkening sky, but the Blixen house was now a museum, and her immense coffee plantation sprouted the mansions of Nairobi's old settler elite. The suburban town was named Karen, in her memory.

I guided my old Rover smoothly down a long allée of jacaranda trees. The Porter house was half timbered, a

Kentish cottage grown to monstrous proportions. A male peacock strutted on the lawn, vibrating his fanned tail, as if to rival the ladies arriving in their latest fashion statements. We waited while a chauffeured Jaguar disgorged its passengers.

A handsome young man in uniform opened the front door and directed us straight through a central hallway to an open terrace in the back, where a lavish buffet had been laid out. Africans in white chef hats were lined up behind bright copper warming dishes, while black-coated waiters walked through the crowd. I accepted a wild mushroom pastry and popped it in my mouth. It was going to be a challenge not to get distracted by the food.

I looked around the terrace. The crowd was mixed racially, but almost all women. One or two faces looked vaguely familiar, probably from the newspapers.

"Hullo, Jazz. I'm glad you could come." Roger Porter was beaming at us with a hearty host's welcome and a bottle of champagne. "Ah, no glasses. Well, let's correct that." He plucked two tulip-shaped glasses from a passing tray and filled them for me and Omondi. "Viv is sick at having to go through with this function so soon after the funeral, but she had no choice," he told us in a low voice. "She's brought all these models from Paris ... can't let them down, it would be the end of her business for keeps."

"How is she doing?"

"She's upstairs now. I told her not to feel she has to make an appearance, but she insists she'll come down later. She's a trooper, I tell you."

I introduced Omondi as a friend, and asked Roger about the other guests. "Ah, let's see." His pale blue eyes roamed the crowd. "You see the whey-faced woman in the red Chanel suit? Regina Thorpe. Her husband is a financial advisor with Stone, Wellby, and Lamont." He raised one brow. "She is well known in her own right as an unending fountain of scurrilous gossip. Now who else?" He turned slightly. "You see that absolutely smashing woman in green?" A tall woman with café au lait skin and regal bearing, wearing a flowing emerald robe and head scarf, was smiling and nodding, as a stockier, medium-brown

83

woman chatted happily away. "A Somali. From one of the wealthiest families in Mogadishu. They've sublet a house in Karen. The woman talking with her is Joyce Mutani, wife of the Casino King. Notice the number of diamonds on her fingers if you get a chance. The fat woman in blue who just joined them is married to the Minister of Culture." He went on this way, pointing out the wives of Nairobi's richest and most powerful. He turned his gimlet eye to Mr. Omondi. "Now, Mr. Omondi, tell me, who you are connected with?"

"Nothing so high and mighty," Omondi answered. "I am a mere mid-level government employee. My only claim to be part of this august company is as Jazz's escort." Roger didn't press him further. "And yourself? Do you work in the public or private sector?"

Roger rolled on the balls of his feet and sipped the champagne. "I am that lucky man who works for himself and has no master." He smiled smugly. "You might also say I have no trade."

"No master and no trade. A riddle." Omondi smiled. "Does that mean you have a mistress and no gainful means of employment?"

Roger threw his head back in a loud laugh. "I'll have to tell Viv that one." He shook his head with mirth. "She keeps me on a short leash, I'm afraid. As for my employment being gainful, sometimes I wonder myself."

"So what is the answer to the riddle, Mr. Porter?" Omondi asked.

"You might call me a matchmaker. I put together people who have money and people who want to spend it. A consortium of Korean businessmen want a lucrative investment. A Kenyan developer wants to build an office tower. I put them together, act as facilitator in the negotiations, explain the ways of Kenya to foreign investors, and so forth. If you've ever tried to get anything done, dealing with government bureaucracy and all that, you can appreciate the service I provide. Sometimes the deal falls through and I get nothing for my pains. If it works, I can make out very well, indeed." He finished his champagne and refilled our glasses. "Have some more bubbly, and enjoy. I believe I see the first model parading through."

A long, angular woman walked down the center of the terrace, transforming it into a walkway and all of us into an audience by the sheer projection of her presence. She wore billowing harem pants, a scanty gold halter made of metal, and a leopard cape draped over one shoulder. The cape, obviously fake fur, was dyed bright pink. A vervet monkey balanced on her shoulder. It was dressed in matching gold collar and chain and pink leopard cape. I couldn't tell if it was Tumbili, the monkey I'd held at Mr. Ali's pet shop; it was about the right size. The monkey's bright eyes darted around in a mixture of curiosity and fear. Its little hand clutched the model's hair.

"What a darling outfit," someone behind me said. "Does the monkey come with it?"

It was Regina Thorpe, the woman in the Chanel suit. Omondi pulled back, leaving the two of us to chat. Regina led me through a brief genealogy, quickly sized me up as nobody, and gave me her shoulder. I got her attention back by saying I was a friend of Nick's and had been with him and Viv when he died. Like any semipro gossip monger, she cross-examined me with all the thoroughness of a trial lawyer. From there I was able to segue into Nick's relationship with his sister and brother-in-law, and the family's place in Nairobi's power elite.

"It was Viv and Nick's uncle George who came out to Kenya first, and got a very nice farm indeed, in Thika, raising tea." Regina fondled the gold chains around her neck with a beautifully manicured hand. "Their father came later, after most of the good land was already divvied up. He was never really keen on farming, anyway. Much more interested in horse racing." She smiled thinly. "And then, so sad, George's only son was killed fighting the Germans, and so Nick and Viv ended up inheriting the lot."

Nick never talked about coming from a moneyed background. I wondered how much of his inheritance was left. Enough to kill for? A lot of white farmers lost everything after independence, when—righting colonial wrongs—they

85

were pressured to sell their land to blacks for a token sum. "Did they sell before Uhuru?"

A white-coated waiter carrying a silver tray offered us a selection of exquisite miniature sandwiches. Regina paused for a delicate bite of smoked salmon and cucumber. A crumb of white bread clung to the down around her lips, trembling as she spoke. Regina was not the sort of person you told that she had food on her face.

"No, they lost the farm. But there was also some rather valuable property in Nairobi, as well as that worthless piece of land in Samburu Province. So eccentric of Nick to live there like a hermit, but then he also married that dreadful American woman, so make of it what you will. Viv was wonderful about that, she never so much as uttered one word of reproach, although you know she must feel terrible about it."

"Have you met his wife, Wynn?"

"I?" Regina looked startled. "No. I believe Nick brought her to the Muthaiga Club, but just one time, and I wasn't there."

"Would they stay at Viv and Roger's when he was in town?"

"Oh, no. Absolutely not." Regina looked over the crowd and lowered her voice. "Viv and he never had much use for one another. I mean, look at this," she gestured at the lively terrace, "going on with the fashion show, and Nick barely in the ground. How broken up can Viv be?"

Maybe, but running a one-woman business myself, I understood the pressure on Viv to hold this show, even if she was collapsing with grief. "Does Nick's half of the inheritance revert to her?"

"What's left might, but I doubt it amounts to much. Nick liked expensive toys. How many journalists have their own Cessna?" Regina continued without pausing for breath. "It's funny, but even though Viv is older, Nick was the one lost in the past, living up in the wilds and all that, while Viv has adjusted to the new Kenya as well as anybody." Regina took another bite of the salmon sandwich and the crumb was knocked off. "Half the ministers wouldn't take one step without Roger—you know, all these skyscrapers and new hotels." She waved her hand vaguely in the direction of Nairobi. "Viv has to do an awful lot of entertaining," her voice dropped again, "of all sorts of people, but she is an angel about it, really, an angel."

I looked at the crowded terrace. The noise of animated conversation rose like the sounds of birds in a rookery. "She certainly does a beautiful job."

"Oh, Viv is a marvel, an absolute marvel. Deals beautifully with a crisis. Last year the entire consignment of dresses was stolen at the airport. Imagine! And this year, I happen to know Roger's latest project, that new casino on Limuru Road, is dreadfully behind schedule, and so far it's cost three times more to build. But development projects are always like that here, aren't they? You know that half that money is going straight into someone's pocket and from there to Switzerland. They complained that the British were taking all the money out of the country, but really, is it any different now? I'm sure it's worse. At least we created wealth, built roads, developed agriculture. Now it's all back to subsistence farming—soon they won't be raising enough corn to feed the country anymore. In *Kenya*. But don't get me started on that."

She pasted a bright smile on her face as a dowdy woman with sweet English features joined us. "Caroline! Isn't this fun? Don't you just love Viv's fashion shows? Such a clever idea. But then she's so good at this sort of thing, isn't she?"

"Why does she bother?" Caroline asked. "Horrible clothes. Who wears that rubbish?"

Another model came stalking through the crowd. She had heavy blond hair in a bizarre cut, a small, perfect nose, and a big red mouth, this season's measure of female beauty. She swirled, showing the lines of a full-length fur, this one in fake giraffe, dyed fuchsia. She slipped it off mid-twirl and draped it over her shoulder, to reveal a very little, very tight, very revealing black dress.

"I know what you're saying, dear. It's a tremendous amount of work, and the money involved—bringing models direct from Paris."

"The dresses are on commission, aren't they? It's not like she gets stuck with them." Caroline nabbed a seafood puff pastry from a passing tray and popped it in her mouth.

"Yes, but all that airfare, whether people buy or not. And no one has the same kind of money to throw around today as they did even a few years ago. I'm sure that's why she's having the preview here this year, instead of at the Buckingham." Regina's eyes fixed on someone across the terrace, and I followed her gaze: two women, one old and plump, one young and svelte, talking vivaciously with Viv. Their gold jewelry was visible even at this distance. "Except the Saudis, of course. Have you met those two? The thinner one's a princess. Married to Sheikh Farid."

"I bet they go to Paris every year," the dowdy lady, Caroline, said. "They don't need Viv."

"I feel rather sorry for her, don't you? Fawning over those two," Regina stated with satisfaction. "Of course, all the government muckedy-mucks' wives love this fashion show; it probably is very good public relations for Roger. You see, that's why I say Viv's adjusted better to the new Kenya than a lot of people. There's Mrs. Mutani, joining them. Viv will be happy about that. She always buys a lot."

A woman smooth as agate joined us and accepted Regina's gushing welcome. No one bothered to introduce me. I took the hint and wandered on, picking up a few tidbits here and there. I found Omondi at the other end of the terrace talking with Mrs. Mutani and two other black Kenyans, waggled my fingers at him and moved on.

A model finished her saunter through the crowd and disappeared inside the house. I followed and found myself in a morning room, prettily decorated in white wicker and yellow floral couches. A fabulous aquamarine parrot sat in a ceiling-high wicker cage. It examined me with one bright yellow eye, turned its head and studied me with the other. I could imagine Nick's opinion of Viv and Roger owning a wild-caught parrot. The model was already out of sight. "Where did she go, beautiful?" I asked the bird, but he wasn't talking.

I heard the sound of excited female voices cut off by the

sound of a shutting door. I walked down a wide hallway. The voices were from a door on the left. I knocked softly, immediately opened the door and stepped into a spacious room. All the furniture was pushed against the walls to create a large open space that was filled with racks of clothing. Five models were in various states of undress, surrounded by several assistants hanging up and taking down dresses, lending a hand with zippers and the proper drape of a coat. There was a sweet smell of powder mingled with a hint of female bodies that went with the air of tension as each woman moved swiftly, almost in a panic of haste.

"Hello, ladies," I said. "Is there anything you need? Sandwiches? More champagne? Another lamp? A helping hand?"

"Oof. I cannot eat a thing when I am working." The blond model I'd noticed outside pouted her thick sensual lips in a dismissive Gallic gesture. She studied her image in a large gilt mirror that leaned on a tabletop, evidently dragooned from another room. A short, sturdy woman dressed in a simple black dress stretched on her toes to place a toque decorated with a fluffy ostrich feather on the model's thick hair. The model shifted the hat slightly and pouted into the mirror.

"*Non.* You will leave it just as I placed it, mademoiselle," said the woman in black, reaching up and readjusting the hat. "So." She looked at me over her shoulder. "It is perfect, no?"

"Beautiful," I admired. "Do you need more light in here?"

A pale Oriental woman with exquisite bone structure called out that another lamp would be fabulous. I dashed out of the room and into the room next door, which turned out to be a formal dining room. There was a floor lamp with an alabaster shade against the wall. I unplugged it and carried it to the dressing room, where its soft light was greeted with cries of appreciation. Having thus provided myself with credentials, I sat down in a straight-backed chair, kicked off one slipper and rubbed my foot. It would have taken an ogre to ask me to leave. "Are you going to model all those clothes?"

The stocky woman was sewing an emaciated girl with haunting eyes into a skintight dress. "No, no. *Mon Dieu.* Tonight is just a little hors d'oeuvre. The tasting menu, perhaps. Tomorrow we do a few private showings, and then the big show at the hotel. I have not seen you before. You are an assistant to Madame Viv?"

"No, a friend. She's tied up outside, so I thought I'd check in on you for her."

She had sewn her way up to the nape of the girl's neck, looped her needle swiftly to form a knot and cut it off with a little silver scissors. I wondered how the poor occupant could breathe. "Hold still a moment, Martine." She grasped the fabric at the girl's hips and lightly tugged. *"Parfait."* She turned back to survey the progress of the other models.

"Wasn't that terrible last year when all the dresses were stolen!" I said.

Her face darkened. "A disaster. They threw a poor idiot from the airport into jail, but nothing was ever recovered. You know that to do such a job, there were higher-up people involved." She gave an exaggerated shrug, getting both her shoulders and lips into it. "It was a tremendous blow to your friend."

"But the dresses were insured, weren't they?"

Another model entered the room and immediately presented her back to the woman I was talking with, who started pulling out straight pins and slipping them into the shoulder of her own dress. "Oh, insurance. It is so expensive these days it can eat up all of your profits, and then they refuse to pay. Imagine."

"They paid Viv, didn't they?"

"There was a technicality. There was going to be a lawsuit, and then I think they settled out of court. Madame Viv received only a fraction of what they were worth."

"You're talking about thousands of dollars! She never told me."

"Thousands?" The woman in black smiled at my naiveté. "I am not surprised she cannot bring herself to mention it. That stolen shipment was probably worth as much as this grand house we are sitting in, mademoiselle."

11

OMONDI CAUGHT ME as soon as I stepped through the French doors back onto the terrace. "I was wondering where you'd wandered off to." He looked relaxed and elegant, as if he attended functions like this every day of his life. "You look pleased."

"I was talking to the models."

"And?"

"After last year's fashion show, the entire shipment of dresses was stolen. Viv was only partly covered."

"How much did she lose?"

"A small fortune. Literally. Plus"—I waited for a woman in a paisley dress to get past us—"Viv and Nick shared a sizable inheritance from an uncle. We'll have to find out if some of Nick's share reverts to her, instead of Wynn."

"So Viv might be desperate for money—"

"—and Nick's death might bring her some."

"This is the first hint of a motive we've found. Good work. Meanwhile, you have missed the big excitement."

"What is it?" I could see a clump of women down near the end of the buffet. "Dessert?"

"No, a cheetah cub."

"What!" If Nick had learned Viv was using a cheetah to sell dresses, he'd have killed *her*. "One of the models has it?"

"Not at all. The older Saudi woman suddenly appeared carrying it."

"Suddenly appeared? You mean they didn't bring it with them?"

"It was already here and she went to fetch it. I asked the

doorman and he told me Mrs. Mutani brought it. Tiny little thing. I didn't know they were gray."

"Gray!" I wanted to scream. "That's a special coat they're born with for camouflage in the lair; you're lucky to ever see a baby that young. How the hell did Mutani get it?" I stared at the clump of women. "He was asking about buying Tonic the day Nick was killed. Did I tell you that?"

"Yes, you did. Calm yourself." Omondi patted my arm. "Let's try to find out what we can. Perhaps it is better if I approach them alone. I can see your diplomacy has deserted you."

"I'm coming, too. I'll be good."

I clenched my jaw into a pretend smile and followed Omondi as he wove a way through the crowd to the knot of women surrounding the cheetah. Little oohs and cries of "Isn't he darling" rose from the center of the circle. I couldn't see a damn thing except a lot of hair-sprayed heads.

By standing our ground as people left, we eventually ended up face-to-face with a beaming Mrs. Mutani, Viv, and the two Saudi women. The thin one held a cheetah cub who didn't want to be held. Sure enough, it still had its fluffy baby coat of long gray-blue hairs. It squirmed and spat, showing sharp little teeth that scared no one. Its round brown eyes met mine for a split second, and I could feel its panic. It could have been a home-raised cub taken too early from its mother, but my intuition told me otherwise. This was a wild cub that was not acclimated to people.

"Princess Rana, this is Jazz Jasper, and her escort. . . ."

"Mr. Omondi. Enchanted." Omondi gave a formal bow.

The princess was much younger than I thought, not older than eighteen. She had the adolescent's heavy hand with makeup, thick pancake a shade too dark for her coloring, turquoise eye shadow and enough mascara to coat a giraffe's eyelashes. She was painfully thin. The heavy gold jewelry festooned around her neck, wrists, and fingers, and dangling from her ears looked more like a burden than an embellishment. Not that she needed embellishing. She had enormous black eyes and a wide, bright smile.

Viv introduced us to Mrs. Mutani next. She was medium height, with a dumpy full-breasted figure and a motherly face, dignified by an aura of power and wealth. She was full of smiles, evidently delighted with the sensation her gift had made, and barely acknowledged the introduction.

"Isn't this the most marvelous gift that Mrs. Mutani has found for me?" The princess's jeweled fingers tightened on the cheetah's neck as she giggled at the cub's efforts to free himself. "I have wanted one for ever so long." Her accent was cultured Brit—the result of a British tutor perhaps, or of schooling in England. She tried to kiss the top of the cub's head, but he was squirming too much, and she dissolved in laughter.

The older Saudi woman next to her smiled indulgently. She wore a satin dress with a full skirt covered with sequins and metallic thread that did nothing for her stout figure. She, too, was festooned with gold. Her bad taste made the princess's spare black dress all the more elegant. No one bothered to introduce her. Was she a chaperone?

"Isn't he amazing!" I cried. "Where in the world did you find such a sweet darling?"

Mrs. Mutani smiled. "They're hard to get. Almost impossible."

"Was it through Mr. Ali?" I asked.

"Mr. Ali?"

Viv gave me a sharp glance, but Mrs. Mutani was not self-conscious.

"A local pet dealer."

"Oh, no. You cannot find a cheetah in a pet shop." Mrs. Mutani laughed condescendingly. "My husband knew the princess had her heart set on one, so he looked and looked, and found him through someone he knows."

"Do you think he has others?" I asked.

"I doubt it very much." Her tone said I was becoming a nuisance.

Rana held the cub up over her head and waggled him with a chortle of pleasure, as if he were a human baby. "I must think of the perfect name for him."

"Do you know that Viv's sister-in-law has two cheetahs she's returning to the wild?" I asked.

She had a firm grip around the cub's throat and he had temporarily subsided. "Yes, Viv told me of this. I wanted to buy one of those cheetahs. Now I am glad they wouldn't sell. This one is so much nicer, a little itty-bitty fluff ball, aren't you?"

"My brother and his wife named theirs Gin and Tonic," Viv said.

The woman with the princess had been staring at the food table. Now she darted a suspicious look at Viv from under her heavy brows.

"That wouldn't do in Arabia," Omondi said.

The cub squirmed and chirped in the princess's arms. "Quite right," she said. "Drinking is strictly forbidden." She looked mischievous. "So is listening to music."

"Music?" My voice sounded like a squawk. Ms. Diplomacy in action.

"You can be arrested for whistling in the street." Luckily, the princess seemed to enjoy my horrified reaction. "The religious police carry whips. Yes, it's true. They used to just patrol the streets and shopping malls, but now they raid private parties. If they catch you with music, liquor, forbidden videos: wshht! Off to jail." She wrinkled her nose with a sidelong glance at the woman with her. "For a while we had satellite dishes to get uncensored western TV, but now they have started to climb on people's houses and smash them."

"Even if you're a member of the royal family?" I asked.

"Being a princess is not such a special thing as in England, you know. My great-grandfather conquered all the other tribes in the twenties and named the country after our family, Saud. He was very clever, and very virile. He united all the important tribes by marrying one wife from each of them."

"You mean hundreds of wives?"

"No, no. Twenty-two only. Four at a time as allowed by the Koran, and divorcing them as they conceived." She smiled at my shock. "We like to do things our own way. He had forty-five sons. His eldest son, King Saud, who came to the throne in the fifties, had fifty-two sons and fifty-five daughters."

95

"You must have a thousand cousins."

The princess had a broad, infectious smile. "More than five thousand princes and princesses. What really counts is what branch of the family you come from."

"Are you from a good branch?" Omondi asked.

"Medium." The little cub suddenly lunged, trying to escape, and scratched the princess's wrist with his back foot. She cuffed him sharply in the face. He spat, and she hit him again.

I stiffened, and Omondi squeezed my wrist for a brief instant. "If you hit them, it makes them more aggressive," I said.

"I didn't hurt him. I wouldn't hit him hard, would I, my little prince?" She crooned into the cub's ear, giving him an affectionate shake.

"It has been enchanting talking with you, Princess Rana." Omondi gave a small bow. "We don't want to monopolize your time. May I wish you a pleasant stay in our country. Will you be going on safari?"

"Yes, a camp has been prepared for us. We are heading to Samburu tomorrow at dawn."

"Have a pleasant journey," I forced out, and Omondi hurried me away. "Why would Mrs. Mutani bring the cub here to give to the princess?" I whispered to him.

"She got a lot of social mileage out of it."

"Yes, but she could have done that at a party of her own."

"What are you getting at?"

"Is there some link between Viv and Mutani? I know Nairobi's elite is a small world, but he pops up at Nick and Wynn's the weekend Viv and Roger are visiting; now he chooses to give this big deal gift to the princess at their house."

"Let's see if we can find out," said Omondi. "Time to visit the other half of this household."

"The other half?"

"The servants' house."

I followed Omondi down to the lawn. By watching the waiters, we figured out which end of the house held the kitchen, and from there picked up a brick path that led to

96

the back of the lot. Behind a thick screen of bougainvillea pruned into a twenty-foot hedge were three metal-roofed cottages. Pots and pans lay on the ground near a dripping outdoor spigot. Next to it was an outdoor toilet that smelled like it hadn't been cleaned since it was built. A row of faded dresses and ragged shorts hung from a wash line made of old electric wire.

Omondi called out "Jambo!" and a young woman appeared with a baby on her hip. We introduced ourselves. She was the cook's wife; her name was Valerie. She stared at us, tongue-tied, rubbing one foot against the other. Hearing voices, a heavyset woman came out of the next house. She was dressed in a white maid's uniform, and greeted us with more confidence, and some suspicion. She was Catherine Wainaina.

Omondi bowed. "This is a friend from America, Jazz Jasper. She has been living in Nairobi a few years. She was a good friend of Mrs. Porter's brother's wife, and was also visiting them last weekend." Both women looked at me with curiosity.

Omondi then introduced himself, shook hands with Catherine and kept her hand in his. "Miss Wainaina, it is a pleasure to meet you. How is your family? I hope they are all in good health?"

Catherine smiled, showing dimples, and directed Valerie to get some chairs. Within minutes Catherine, Omondi, and I were sitting on some beat-up old chairs in front of the houses. Valerie sat on the stoop and dandled her baby on her knees. The child looked skinny, with a round swollen belly that signaled protein deficiency.

Catherine and Omondi chatted in Kikuyu, which I don't know, then Omondi switched to English. Omondi asked about the various guests at the party. Catherine knew all their names and positions, how often they visited and how important they were.

"And Mr. and Mrs. Mutani? Do they visit often?" Omondi asked.

"Sometimes, yes, for a dinner party. Mr. Porter works with Mr. Mutani many years. He helps Mr. Mutani on his projects." Catherine nodded emphatically. "He is always helping him."

"And Mrs. Porter works for Mr. Mutani, also?"

"No, no. Mrs. Porter has her own shop. A dress shop. Very expensive and beautiful. All the rich ladies shop there." Catherine smoothed the white fabric of her uniform's skirt.

"I thought this was owned by Mr. Mutani," Omondi said.

"It is in Mr. Mutani's hotel, the Royal Lancaster, but Mrs. Porter has a lease and owns the business herself. It is hers, not Mr. Porter's. She used money from her uncle to start it."

"A rich uncle! That is convenient!" Omondi joked.

"This uncle is dead long ago. He gave money to Mrs. Porter and her brother. The brother spent his on an airplane and a sailing boat on the coast to go fishing once a year and on cars." Her mouth drew down in disapproval. "It was Mrs. Porter who had the business sense in the family. She works very hard."

"Last year her dresses from Paris were stolen?" I said. "Wasn't that terrible!"

Catherine shook her head in sympathy. "Very terrible. Very, very terrible. 'What am I going to do?' she kept saying. Round and round the house. 'What am I going to do?' So I told her, go to Mrs. Mutani." Catherine's eyes lit up with pride. "I said, 'Go to Mrs. Mutani.' "

"She followed your advice?" Omondi asked.

"She got all dressed up, she went in the afternoon, and the next day, she is smiling, she says to me, 'Catherine, it is all fixed. Mrs. Mutani is going to be my partner in the next fashion show.' I said, 'Congratulations. She will be a good partner.' She tells me, 'I will still organize the show, but she will put up the money. And she has agreed to pay for the stolen dresses.' She took my hands and said, 'Isn't that wonderful? I owe it all to you.' "

"She must have given you a big gift," Omondi teased.

"Oh, yes. She asked me what I want, and I said for my oldest son to live with me, here, so he can go to school in Nairobi. That way he has a much better chance of passing his exams and going on to high school. He is a fine boy. Very studious. A serious boy."

"You must be proud of such a son," Omondi said.

We chatted on awhile longer about her family, then Omondi rose and thanked her, and we followed the path back to the house.

"That was worthwhile," I said. "Maybe Mrs. Mutani gave the cub to Princess Rana here to butter her up so she'll buy a lot of clothes."

"You don't sound completely satisfied."

"It's not that. I'm thinking about the money. It doesn't match up. The seamstress said the stolen dresses were worth as much as this house. Even if that's a gross exaggeration, I don't see Mrs. Mutani covering the loss simply to be a partner in one fashion show."

We paused on the lawn, looking up at the colorful crowd on the terrace and the half-timbered walls rising behind them. The women's high voices sounded like a rookery.

"Yes," Omondi said. "I would say Viv Porter owes the Mutanis a great deal."

"You wonder what she promised in return."

"She might have discovered that she made a bargain with the devil."

12

THE NEXT DAY found me driving up to Samburu, fulfilling my promise to keep Wynn company for a few days. She was still acting like a woman of steel, but I figured she needed me, even if she couldn't show it. We planned to visit the manyatta that Nick visited the week of his death, and check out any leads from that end. Still, I was frustrated: I'd much rather have stayed in town and followed the Mutani-Porter connection, instead of leaving that to Omondi. I felt like a dog on a scent, whistled away just when it turned hot. I was also nervous about telling Striker I wanted to move in with him, but I knew Omondi's advice was right: follow your heart.

So as usual I stopped at Mount Kenya on the way. Striker met me at the car with a kiss and hug that swooped me up into his arms and circled me round and round until we were dizzy and laughing with kisses.

"Have you eaten?"

"Yes."

"Want some coffee?"

"Later." I moved in for another kiss. Striker picked me up effortlessly, carried me into the bedroom, still kissing, and deposited me on the bed. We separated only for as long as it took to peel off our clothes. Striker has a broad chest, round ass, and thighs like lithe columns; the Greeks were on to something when they worshiped the male form.

Sex this time started with hot romantic kisses, moving from my lips to neck and breasts. I was in a ball gown, sweeping down a curved stair into the arms of my Italian lover, straight out of a perfume ad. The electricity between us began to build, and I got lost in a world of sensation nd pleasure, touching here and there, now slow, now urgent, now smooth, now sharp, now soft, now hard. I had several climaxes along the way, then Striker's rhythm became steady and urgent, a huge wave building momentum. He stroked me to bring me along with him, and we rode the wave together, slow and sweet. I caught hold of the cresting edge of Striker's climax and joined with him. What a great feeling!

I stroked the soft hair on his chest.

"I love you so much." He kissed my eyebrow. "Aren't we lucky?"

"Mmm. Lucky." My eyes were closing. "Sleepy." I drifted off.

When I woke up, the sun flooded the room, falling in a warm band across my face, turning my closed eyelids gold. I opened my eyes a crack, and through iridescent eyelashes watched Striker gather his scattered clothes and get dressed.

"Hey, sleepy. Aren't you going to wake up? Let's walk over to the blind before it's too late."

Striker had built a wonderful blind a few months ago overlooking a pocket marsh that attracted all sorts of animals. The trick was to get there during the midday heat, to be in place before the animals left their shady noontime resting places and came in search of green vegetation, water, or prey.

As we approached, a shy bushbuck with spiral horns froze for an instant, then burst into the undergrowth and was gone. I climbed the wooden footholds hammered into the fever tree's trunk and crawled onto the viewing platform. Striker had built a banister around the platform and hung it with camouflage netting, which meant we could move around invisibly up there and not frighten the animals. We'd brought a blanket with us, and a basket of refreshments. We sat and munched mango, pawpaw, and grapes, drank white wine, and made love again, long and luxurious, building up to a delicious sparkling finish, like a superb champagne. We lay in each other's arms, silently listening. A tropical boubou gave his bell-like call, and a little bee eater paused for an instant on the banister, an emerald and topaz jewel. It studied us for a moment with shiny brown eyes, piped *teeep, teeep* and flew off.

I took Striker's hand. "There's something I want to talk about."

He brought our linked hands to his lips and softly kissed the back of my hand. "Anything you want."

"No, this is serious." I looked up at the tree surrounding us.

Striker lifted himself on an elbow so we could face each other. "Okay. I'm ready."

I looked into his hazel eyes, reflecting green now from the tree canopy. "I've been missing you a lot, wishing we could be together more."

"Me, too." He bent over me and we kissed. "Being together a day here and there isn't enough anymore. Not nearly enough."

I knew Striker was feeling it, too, so why was I so scared? "I've been waiting for my business to be more settled before suggesting this, but the recession is going on forever, and we can't put our lives on hold." I took a big breath. "Maybe it's time for us to think about living together." I searched his eyes. "What do you think? How about it?"

"Fantastic!"

We grinned at each other.

"I was going to ask you the same thing!" Striker said.

"You mean today?"

"Yes, today."

"It must be the right time." I could feel happiness and excitement expanding inside me.

"Now comes the hard part," he said. "Where?"

"That's not hard anymore. I know you won't live in Nairobi." I sat up and crossed my legs. "I'll have to do the best I can running Jazz Jasper Safaris from here; I'm hoping Alicia might rent me a room for one or two nights a week, if I have to be in town. I have so little business, I might as well be semi-employed on Mount Kenya as in Nairobi."

"You're doing almost as much private investigator work as running safaris, anyway."

"I know."

"Can you see yourself quitting the safari business?"

"No, I love it too much. And I'm not a quitter." I paused. "It's funny to say it, but I also like murder investigations. There aren't many things in life where right and wrong are so clear." I studied my palm for a moment. "I'm good at it, and fighting for justice—well, it sounds hokey, but it's very satisfying." I laughed. "Also, there's no competition in Kenya."

"Which brings me back to the question of where."

I sat up. "Here." I gestured around us. "Your place is big enough for two, and I can't think of a more wonderful spot in the whole country."

Striker looked serious. "Jazz, I can't stand it here anymore."

I looked at him, dumbfounded.

"I also got some bad news. They're improving the road. The convention center wants to straighten out that bad curve just before my driveway."

"Isn't that good?"

"It will bring the road right past my front door."

"My God, this is unbelievable! Can't you fight it?"

"Mutani—"

"—has very good connections," we said in unison.

"Besides, he's right," Striker continued. "It was folly to build a huge convention center up a narrow dirt road full of blind corners. There've been two accidents already."

"There's got to be some way to modify the plans. You're the only person living within miles on either side of the road, and they have to reroute it through your yard?"

"Believe me, I've spent the last three days talking to the road engineer, and the surveyors, and everyone I know, in government and out, who might have some power. Mutani made a big concession. Originally they planned to move the road right through my living room."

"What do you mean concession? He doesn't have the right to take your land!"

Even as I said the words, I knew it was futile. In Kenya, the laws bend for powerful people like Mutani.

103

An elephant mother and baby emerged from the foliage on the edge of the swamp. Mom lifted her trunk to sniff the air carefully, recognized our familiar scent, and began to tear off branches and stuff them into her mouth. She carefully chewed off the leaves and bark, and spat out the peeled branch.

"The baby's about two weeks old," Striker whispered. "Male."

That part was obvious. He was small enough to fit comfortably under his mother's huge, round belly. He tottered out from under, approached his mother's two human-shaped breasts between her front legs, and searched for her nipple with his funny little trunk. It took him a moment to find it, then he curled his trunk out of the way and suckled with his mouth. We could see his head move rhythmically as he gulped the warm milk.

Mom finished eating the bush, having reduced it to a stump of shredded branches, gently pushed her baby off her teat with her left leg, and moved on to the next. He followed her on his rubbery legs, almost made it over a small fallen log, but made the mistake of placing a hind foot on the log. It slipped off with a jolt and he teetered, saved from a fall by his mother's trunk. A second matron emerged from the forest and positioned herself on the other side of the baby, to give him extra protection. All we could see were the three rear ends, two huge and one tiny, and three tails whisking away flies.

What was going to happen to this marsh when they moved the road? Would it still be here? Would the animals feel safe enough to use it? Would they be safe? The answers I could imagine were not good.

I sighed. "It sounds like we're both house hunting. At least we're together. That makes it a bit easier, doesn't it?"

"It certainly does." Striker gave me a sweet kiss.

"Maybe we can find something near here."

"I want to go someplace really wild, where there'll never be encroaching development."

"I don't know." I watched the elephants selecting branches with their clever trunks. "The only places like

104

that are in the desert. Too far and too hot and too danger-ous. I need to be within a few hours drive of Nairobi."

"No place that close is going to stay wilderness." Strik-er's face was long and serious. "I don't want to go through this again. And again. I want to find a place I can guaran-tee won't be destroyed."

"On planet Earth?"

"Yes, there still are a few remaining places."

"Like where? Siberia?"

"If need be."

"It's a hell of a long way to go to find an apartment."

"Jazz, I'm serious."

I stared at him with a horrible feeling growing inside me. He really wasn't kidding. "You're thinking of leaving Kenya?"

"I've made the decision."

"But Striker! What about us? Weren't we just talking about living together?"

"That's part of my plan. I want you to marry me."

13

WE'D BEEN FLYING for an hour through a vast landscape. I glanced at Wynn's profile against the bright sky. Her face looked drawn and preoccupied; not too preoccupied, I hoped, to concentrate on flying. We were already farther out over the desert than I'd ever been, and it gave me an uneasy feeling.

Wynn and I were on our way to the Samburu manyatta that Nick had visited last week. *The Star* printed his story on their water project the day after his funeral. I tried to get hold of the water expert Nick interviewed, but he was in the field, so I hadn't been able to question him yet. Wynn had found notes in Nick's desk at home: he'd underlined *heavy poaching*. We were hoping it was the "dynamite lead" he mentioned to Peter Kamau. Had Nick picked up a thread here that had unraveled to his death? Or was the answer down in Nairobi with his sister and Mutani?

The Selfhelp people had cleared and marked an airstrip at the manyatta, and Nick had noted the coordinates, so we didn't expect any trouble finding it. Below us rolled a plain of hard-packed sand covered with thorn trees, leafless in the August dry season. The ground was pale tan or ochre, the thorn branches were silver. Grandeur came from the distant volcanic hills, flattened by distance, blue-purple against the heat-whitened horizon. Their varied shapes—cones, mesas, ranges—changed with the miles, overlapping in different ways, a never-ending sequence of form and color.

The only sounds were the drone of the engine and wind roaring around us as we sliced through the air.

Wynn checked the mileage and the compass heading. A

stiff crosswind had been threatening to shove us off course. "We should be seeing the manyatta soon. Keep your eyes peeled."

A manyatta consists of a wall of thornbushes surrounding a half-dozen or dozen igloo-shaped homes made of dung and wattle. Most of the families are related, although some may be friends from the same clan. The colors of the huts are the same as the landscape around them. Still, the circular thorn wall stands out for miles from the air as a man-made shape; they aren't that hard to spot. We hadn't seen any sign of human life for a long time. Thanks to the brutality of Somali bandits, the *shifta*, many of the local people had abandoned their homes and moved farther west, away from the border. The world seemed empty and our plane suspended in time.

"I smell av-gas," Wynn said sharply.

"Me, too." A thick, oily smell seeped into the cabin. I looked out. "There's something greenish running over the wing."

"Shit." Wynn looked out my window. "That's where the fuel tank is."

The smell was sickening. So was the image of us bursting into flames and rolling over and over into the desert below. "It's starting to spatter the rear window."

"We must have a leak in the fuel tank." Wynn scanned the instrument panel. "The gauge is still broken," she reported. "No telling how much we have left. This is serious."

I didn't need her to tell me. The leak seemed to be growing, spreading across the wing and spraying against the side of the plane. One spark of electricity and we'd be a barbecue.

Wynn opened the window on her side so we could breathe. "We're going to have to land immediately."

"Won't the friction . . ." My mouth was too dry to talk properly. "A spark . . ."

"We have no choice." She flipped a switch. "I don't know how much gas we have in the intact tank. They haven't been drawing evenly. We could be running on empty any second." She banked the plane steeply and we

107

started to descend. "Once we're down, and this leaking tank empties out, I can check the other tank. I hope there's enough to get home on." Her worries about getting back sounded overly optimistic.

The ground below us was covered with thorn trees. There wasn't a clear patch to land a plane anywhere. I had a pounding headache from the sickening fumes. Wasn't it bad enough to face death, without feeling nauseous at the same time?

Wynn broadcast an emergency call. The response was static. We were long out of range. The ground zoomed toward us. Now I could make out large rocks scattered among the thorns.

Wynn banked the plane sharply the other way, scanning the ground. "There's a fairly clear bit." I could hear the relief in her voice. "A trifle short, but it's the best we have. Hold on."

At that instant the leaking tank ruptured. Fuel gushed across the wing and spattered the outer cabin wall. We were rushing above the blurred tops of the thornbushes at a terrifying speed. Wynn yanked back on the throttle and the control yoke, bringing up the nose. The bare patch flashed under us. I felt the wheels touch and bounce. The plane bucked, the wheels touched earth again, we were down. We'd made it! Wynn stood on the brakes, the plane roared and slowed. It wasn't slow enough. My foot stomped an imaginary brake on the floor. Slow down, damn it! An acacia tree stood smack in front of us. The distance shrank.

Then the wheels hit a soft patch of sand and the plane flipped to the left, slewed around and dug its nose into the ground. "Quick! *Out!*" Wynn yelled.

I was already fumbling with my safety belt. My weight hung against the straps, and the damned catch wouldn't release. The av-gas flowed through the port window, now above me, spattering me with the green high-octane fuel. My T-shirt soaked it up like a rag. Great. I was going to be first flambéed, then roasted like a trussed turkey.

Wynn tried to release the damn thing. "It's jammed." She jiggled and tugged. It wouldn't give.

"Where's your day pack? That giant knife of yours—"

Our loose stuff had settled against Wynn's seat back and door. She searched rapidly, flinging things about. "I don't see it. Shit."

Sweat was pouring down my face; I could feel it running between my breasts. I was going to be nicely basted, too. "In front of your seat?"

Wynn looked. "No."

I felt around the space between me and the door. There was a backpack strap. "I've got it." I yanked. The damn thing wedged more tightly. I gave the pull of my life and it broke free. I fumbled with the zipper, got it open, and my hands closed on Wynn's knife. "Thank God!"

I pulled the knife out of its scabbard and sawed at my safety belt. Wynn must have kept the thing razor sharp, because it slashed through the reinforced fabric like it was muslin. I fell against her, luckily missing her with the knife. She got her door open and we both half jumped, half tumbled to earth. I got to my feet and ran the hell away from the plane as fast as I could.

Wynn wasn't next to me. I looked back and saw her tugging at the luggage hold. "Wynn, are you crazy? Get away from there!"

"Without water we're dead," she yelled over her shoulder. I ran back and helped her toss out our bags. Behind them was the case of bottled water she always traveled with. I grabbed the bags, she got the water, and we raced away from the plane.

The rest was an anticlimax. We sat at a safe distance, watching the last drops of gas run into the sand and evaporate off the shining aluminum plane. There was no explosion, not that it mattered at this point. The left wing was crushed, the propeller bent like a hairpin. We wouldn't be flying out of here.

I got out of my gas-soaked T-shirt, cleaning myself off as best I could, and changed into a long-sleeved shirt I'd brought for the cool of evening. I'd need the protection from the sun anyway. We figured we were within a few hours' walk of the manyatta we were heading for, less if

109

we were lucky. The trick would be finding it. We filled our day pack with as many water bottles as it could hold. That left no room for food or a sweater. It was well over a hundred now, but if we didn't find the manyatta by nightfall, we'd find ourselves out in a desert night, which meant freezing temperatures. Still, there was no choice. In the desert, if you're cold you can keep moving, or bury yourself in sand. If you run out of water, you die.

Wynn stuck her long knife in her belt, took a compass bearing, and we set off side by side. Before our unscheduled landing, I had noticed the line of a watercourse snaking its way to the north, and we headed for it. At best it might be a permanent spring, where we'd be likely to meet a herding boy watering his flocks. At worst it would be a seasonal river with high enough banks to afford us some shade.

Slowly the landscape became more brutal. Black lava boulders were strewn more and more thickly upon the ground. They held and magnified the heat, bouncing it up at our faces, so even our broad hats gave us no relief from the sun. The phrase "Out of the frying pan and into the fire" took on a personal meaning. My legs grew heavier and heavier, until walking felt more like weight lifting than locomotion. The land began to slope upward, calling on ever greater expenditures of energy. I stumbled and cut my shoe on the sharp-edged lava. After that I walked more carefully. I didn't want to take a tumble onto those rocks.

The only signs of animal life were flies, which appeared from out of nowhere to bombard our faces, crawling into our noses and eyes in search of moisture. Keeping the flies off my face meant brushing them away second by second. Keep that up for an hour and you've waved your arm 3,600 times. Now I understood why the desert nomads ignore the flies crawling on them. Or why, in some tribes, one of the attributes of chieftainship is a fly whisk. My arms started to feel as heavy as my legs. The only thing that kept me going was the range of hills rising ahead of us, at the bottom of which I hoped to see that stream.

"Look." Wynn pointed to the ground. A patch of clear dirt showed the footprint of a large antelope.

"Kudu?"

"I think so."

"You think it was heading for water?"

"Kud-be."

We quickened our pace. A spine of bare lava rose to our west, but where we were, the rocks petered out, and once again we were surrounded by the twisty branches of thorns and acacias. Ahead there was a telltale tearing and crunching. We swung around in a large circle and climbed a rocky outcrop to look for the source of the noise.

We could make out a lone elephant, undoubtedly a bull since the females are always in family groups, decimating a thornbush. He tore off five-foot branches and stuffed them into his mouth, ignoring the thorns, chewed off the bark and spit out the pale, splintered remnants. When he got to the thicker branches, he lifted his front foot and smashed them to pieces, until the thorn was collapsed around his feet. In the raking light I could trace every wrinkle in his gray hide, see the pink inside of his mouth. He chewed methodically, with a peaceful look of satisfaction.

We made a wide detour to avoid him, but after that, walking seemed easier. The elephant was a good indication of water ahead. Then it was only a matter of time to find people, and then we'd be safe. I took a big swig of water, finishing off a bottle, and started to hum under my breath. Even the flies didn't bother me so much.

The sun passed the zenith, and flimsy shadows began to develop under the thorns. We gave ourselves a short rest, but there was little relief from the heat and the glare. We forced ourselves back onto our feet and kept going.

I kept my eyes soft-focused on my entire field of vision, ready to spot any peripheral movement. We didn't want to stumble on a dangerous animal as we grew closer to the water. I peered into the shadowy tunnels under denser bushes, a favored lie-down spot for leopard or lion. Even though I was looking, when my eye first fell on the lion, I didn't notice him immediately, his tawny coat blended so well into the desert soil.

I grabbed Wynn's arm and pointed, mouthing the word

111

lion. My pulse started pounding in my ears. He lay with eyes closed, flat on his side, stomach bulging obscenely and blood matting the fur around his mouth. He was an older fellow, with a big scar across his nose and hunks missing from his mane, signs of past battles. He'd obviously passed out after gorging. His feet jerked, as if he was running in a dream. This guy wasn't going to wake up for us.

My pulse started to quiet down and I stepped back quietly. Wynn stopped me and pointed ahead at a lioness, her head on her paws, eyes closed, ears twitching at flies.

We quickly scanned the bushes around us. There were two more lionesses to the left. They were also sleeping. Their stomachs were so distended, they looked as if they'd been eating basketballs.

One of the lionesses whooshed her tail back and forth, obviously plagued by flies attracted by the blood on her face. She opened one eye with a bad-tempered look and snapped at one, then caught sight of us. The hairs rose on the back of my neck. I stared into her cold yellow eyes, trying to project fearsomeness. I didn't dare move, fearing that would trigger her charge. She gave a low growl of alarm and ran. Her pride mates started up, saw us, and scattered into the bush. Five seconds later we were alone.

Wynn and I looked at each other, our faces slack with shock.

"That was odd," I said.

"It sure was. Something has spooked those lions."

"Lucky for us."

"Well, let's be careful. One of them might decide to ambush us."

A mile farther on we heard the quarreling of vultures, the thorns thinned, and we came to the edge of a long, clear slope.

Wynn gave a gasp of horror. There'd been a massacre of animals. I quickly counted the mounds of red flesh, some covered with a writhing mass of vultures, jackals on several of them, others barely touched. The jackals lifted their heads and studied us for a moment, then went back to feeding. I counted ten bodies. The one closest to us had been a Grevy's zebra, to judge from the horse size and shape. Animals had eaten into its belly and left the rest. But no animal had skinned it. There was not a trace of hide.

Farther downhill the remains of what I guessed to be three oryx lay in a group, skinned of their shiny taupe and black-striped coats, two missing the tops of their skulls and their straight, deeply ridged three-foot horns. The third was a youngster, and its horns were apparently too small to bother with.

Wynn and I couldn't speak except for incoherent sounds of protest and disbelief. Next to the body of an oryx were three other skinned corpses, with short, thick legs that I couldn't decipher at first.

"They killed three lions!" Wynn said. The jackals' heads shot up at the sound of her voice. The vultures ignored us.

"Bastards! They waited for lions to come at the smell of blood and shot them, too."

"You figure it was Somalis?" Wynn studied the ground, looking for tracks.

"Probably. I wonder if this is the same group responsible for the poaching Nick saw." I had to turn away. The stench of meat and the shrill cries of the vultures were horrific.

Wynn kept looking for tracks. "They have a car, same size as my Land Cruiser."

"There are so many prints here." I noted some small ones. "Including children. I bet the folks at the manyatta have been by to check out what happened."

Wynn gestured at the vultures. "This is recent. It wouldn't be the same slaughter that Nick saw last week."

"No way. The scavengers have hardly gotten started here." I looked around again. "There's something funny about this." Wynn looked around, too. "Wouldn't a band of Somalis have taken all or at least most of the meat?"

"Maybe they were interrupted."

"Interrupted by Samburu? Spears against guns—they'd have shot anyone who tried to interfere." I looked at the poor, naked carcasses, not feeling entirely satisfied.

113

Wynn touched my arm. "Let's get out of here."

"Keep your eyes open. The last thing we want is to bump into whoever did this."

14

We ENTERED A zone of riverine forest. Once under the shelter of the trees, the tension that had been gripping my chest for hours loosened, and I took a big breath of the green-scented air. It's not what you'd call a forest in America, except perhaps on Cape Cod. The trees were widely spaced, some bare in the dry season, others with small drought-resistant leaves that cast only dappled shade. Any shade at all was preferable to that malevolent sun. Although much of the ground was bare, sandy soil, it was obviously a haven for wildlife. The ground was covered with prints and animal droppings, from the elephant's heap to the dik-dik's tiny dark pellets.

We startled a dik-dik family—antelopes only knee high—sheltering under a silver thorn. They froze and stared with huge dark eyes, then leapt away on matchstick legs. We worked our way to the bank, which fell away steeply at this point. Below us a few waterbucks lay with their legs folded under them on a broad mud bar. In the middle ran a trickle of water. It was the most beautiful stream I'd ever seen. We were going to be okay. As long as we had water, we could survive for a few days, and eventually a herdsman would come to water his flocks and lead us out of this wilderness.

As it was, we didn't have long to wait for rescue. We walked along the bank, looking for a way down to the water; we were dying to splash ourselves. We flushed a large flock of vulturine guinea fowl, exquisite birds in black and white and cobalt blue. The waterbucks heard the commotion and reluctantly got up and trotted off. We found a good spot and clambered down the bank. The water was warm from the sun, but it still felt like heaven on my superheated skin. We rested in the shade for a while, and then followed the stream north, still heading in the general direction of what I thought of as Nick's manyatta. The lovely call of a drongo echoed through the woods.

Wynn was ahead of me when I noticed a set of bare human footprints, almost adult size, with no animal prints on top of them. They must be recent. "Hey, human prints!"

Wynn rushed back and I pointed them out to her. "And goats!"

"Hooray!"

Wynn threw her arms around me and we hugged, jumping up and down and laughing.

"Hooray!" We yelled and grinned at each other like idiots.

A half an hour's walk following the tracks and we came to a Samburu boy watering his motley herd at a pool. His head was close-shaved, he wore a knee-length faded red and white cloth tied around his middle, and no shirt. He had a high, round forehead; smooth, even features; and slightly buck teeth.

After an initial bout of shyness and staring, he warmed up, proudly showing us his goats, joking back at Wynn's friendly teasing. Luckily he'd picked up a few words of Swahili, Kenya's lingua franca along with English, so we were able to communicate the essentials. After the goats finished drinking—staying cautiously as far from the pool's edge as possible, and stretching their necks full length to reach the water, on the alert for crocs—he started them toward home, reassuring us in words and gestures that the manyatta wasn't far.

We left the forest and had another long hike, slogging across heat-blasted terrain. We passed two ragged boys with a herd of goats, who stared and shouted a question at our companion. The smaller of the two ran ahead. Our arrival would be announced.

We crossed the brow of a low, sloping hill.

"There it is!" Wynn shouted.

A crude airstrip had been cleared along the flat area at

the bottom of the slope. It even had a wind sock. It was Nick's manyatta. Opposite us was the thorn wall of a manyatta. Several young men lounged around the opening in the wall, which would be closed up at night against predators.

We'd made it. How we'd get from here back home was the next hurdle. It might be a very long visit.

We sat in the shade of a hut, our backs against the dried manure wall, drinking home-brewed beer with several elders in their blankets and old hats. A crowd of teenagers and children, dressed in bright red and white cloths tied at the waist, watched from a short distance, nudging each other, giggling and whispering. Near them, a woman with her small children gathered around her—the entire family shaved bald—sat on the ground in the sparse shade of a thornbush and simply stared.

One of the junior elders or maybe an older *moran*, or warrior, a man in his late thirties, introduced himself as Lembirdan, and did the translating in broken but adequate Swahili. My Swahili is good enough to catch the gist of things, and Wynn's is very good. He had a warm, open face that made a great impression on me.

We must have looked quite outlandish to him, with our unshaven heads and sober attire. He was dressed in a red-checked cloth reaching to his knees. His hair was shaved high on his forehead, creating a noble brow. He'd colored both his hair and forehead orange with ochre clay, then added a string of beads across his forehead with a big opalescent button in the middle of his brow. Not content with that, he'd put on bead armlets and bracelets, hung two long strings of beads in an X across his bare chest, and added a broad choker that emphasized his graceful neck. He slouched against the dried manure wall in a pose of complete ease, and studied us with friendly curiosity.

The elders asked after our journey. When we told them about wrecking the plane, there was a moment of awed silence. I imagined they thought we had very strong magic to have walked away unharmed, and they probably thought

117

we were the targets of a witch, but such things are not talked about.

Wynn explained she was Nick's wife, and everyone brightened. Sure, he had been here last week. They had showed him their well and pump. Unfortunately, it was broken right now. Yes, he'd also been very interested in signs of poaching near the river. No, he hadn't been able to track the poachers; no one knew who they were; they were undoubtedly back in Somalia by now.

I didn't know whether to believe them or not. I had the feeling they knew more than they were saying. If someone from the manyatta was involved in poaching, they certainly wouldn't tell us. Why wouldn't they be able to track the poachers? Nick might not have the skill, but the *moran* certainly did. If Nick had received the same evasive answers, I'm sure it would have piqued his curiosity.

When I asked how Nick had gotten along with the well man, there was a decided pause, and the group of children had a fit of the giggles. Lembirdan shrugged and said, "Between two stools, you fall to the ground."

Obviously something had happened between Nick and Claude Lavalle, the French Selfhelp engineer Nick had mentioned in his article. It was a follow-up to a long feature Nick had done last year about the Sahara expanding southward, turning semidesert to desert and arable land to scrub. His first article was titled, "A Well-Meaning Disaster," and made him extremely unpopular among the aid workers.

According to Nick, man tampers with a fragile ecosystem at his peril. Livestock concentrated around the permanent wells meant the surrounding land was stripped of every scrap of vegetation by the animals and people. No new shoots were able to replace the vegetation that was eaten or taken for firewood. The land degraded. The drought grew worse. The desert grew. The people concentrated even more around the wells. The herds starved. The people starved. Charity killed the people it was trying to help.

Had charity killed Nick as the trumpeter of bad news?

Claude Lavalle must have contacts with aid workers farther north, in the region where the Sahara scorpion lived. Had he found a scorpion hitchhiker among his things, say, and transferred it to Nick's car? It might even have been done as a nasty joke, not realizing how deadly that particular scorpion was. The scenario wasn't impossible, but neither did it seem likely.

Lembirdan asked why Nick wasn't with us, and Wynn told them rather stiffly that Nick had died, bitten by a scorpion. Blankness came over their faces, and Lembirdan switched the subject to the drought. Wynn and I tried to bring it back to Nick's visit, but we were stonewalled.

Too late, I realized we should never have told them Nick was dead. To traditional Africans, there is no such thing as a natural or an accidental death. In Nick's case, I suspected they were right, but they saw every death as murder. To them, misfortune is guided by the malevolent will of a personal enemy working through black magic. Black magic may be a curse, it may be a spell—or it may be a potion that consists of very real poison. The sorcerers who sell it are hated and feared, and no one wants to trespass on their business. People wouldn't tell us a thing now.

I was filled with a sense of futility and wasted time. I wished we'd never come on this damned expedition. There was nothing for us here. We'd questioned them like clumsy amateurs, learned nothing, wrecked Wynn's plane, and wasted more time than I wanted to think about. I could have screamed with frustration.

Lembirdan must have noticed something, because he inquired solicitously if we needed anything. To eat, to rest?

Wynn assured him the honey beer was all she needed at the moment.

"We appreciate your hospitality very much, but what we really need," I said, "is a way to get home. Is there any way to send word that we are here?"

"We will ask the well man when he comes."

My heart sank. That had been the answer I was dreading. It could be weeks. God, it could be months before the guy returned.

The Samburus' ears were better than mine. One of the children must have heard it first, for he said something in Samburu to the elders, for which he was firmly hushed. Children are meant to be seen and not heard when around grown men.

Lembirdan listened a moment and then held up his hand. "Do you hear?"

"No." Wynn and I shook our heads.

"Car. Car of water man. He be here soon. He be to manyatta, not too far."

Wynn and I smiled at each other with relief.

In a few minutes we saw a cloud of dust, and then Claude Lavalle's dusty truck came lumbering over the next ridge. There was a round Selfhelp insignia on the side. He pulled up to the manyatta's open fence and hopped out. Claude was a chunky man, with big homely features and a sun-roughened skin. He greeted the elders in rapid Samburu, which impressed the hell out of me, before acknowledging our presence. We introduced ourselves. He didn't seem that excited to see us, and when he heard Wynn's last name, he looked even less enthusiastic.

"We're in kind of a jam," I told him. "We flew up, had some engine trouble a ways from here, had to make an emergency landing. The plane is totaled. We were hoping you could give us a lift back to civilization."

"You mean away from civilization and back to the modern world," he said.

I half smiled and waited for the rest of his answer.

"I wish I could help you, but I'm heading north from here, on to the Sudan." He paused, waiting for us to be impressed. The Sudan has been ravaged by war for years: the Arab government in the north has wiped out a million or more southerners, because they are black Christians and animists. Recently, as the government pushed south, four million blacks had been herded into camps in the desert and told to convert to Islam if they wanted food and water. International relief agencies were trying their best to get access to those camps. It was one of the most

120

dangerous relief assignments in the world. So I was impressed.

Claude ruined it by saying. "You don't want to go there, do you?"

"Perhaps you can drop us off—"

He didn't even let me finish my sentence. "My truck is completely filled with well parts and spare fuel, and I've offered a ride to two *moran* in the next manyatta. I'm afraid there's nowhere you could fit, even if you wanted to go with me, which I assure you, you don't." He gave a Gallic shrug. "I am so sorry."

The bastard looked so unsorry I wanted to smack him. I'd met these I-love-Africans-more-than-thou types before, and they gave me a shooting pain. "You must have a radio."

"We are out of range here." He curled his lip. "Let me think. Yes, next week, or maybe ten days, depending how things go, I will be in range to radio one of the camps. They can pass on a message for you, if you wish."

"Yes, we wish."

Wynn could see I was losing it, and stepped in. Claude grudgingly wrote down how to contact Kaji and Striker, and Wynn dictated a short message. And with that he turned his back on us and started talking to the elders in Samburu again.

I was so angry, I walked away, out of the manyatta. I'd wanted to ask him about Nick, but there really seemed no point. He wouldn't tell me anything, and the idea that Nick had quarreled with him seemed self-explanatory. I kicked a small rock that lay in my path. Several of the children followed me, staring. An older boy with wide-set eyes shyly introduced himself—his name was Kariankei—and asked me in halting Swahili if we were going to the camp.

"No, the well man won't take us," I said.

"I can show you where it is," he offered with a broad smile.

"It is very far. Many days' walk?" I asked.

"No." Kariankei grinned. "It is right over there." He pointed to the next hill. "Right there. A few minutes." He laughed at the disbelief on my face. "Right there."

"A camp for the Somalis?" I asked. I didn't know the word for refugees.

"No Somalis! Tourists!"

15

THE CAMP WAS like nothing I'd ever seen. A row of two ton trucks were parked at the outskirts, next to huge water and fuel tankers and a number of Land Cruisers. Enough tents were set up to house a small town. They must have had an incredible staff-client ratio. How could this be profitable? It looked awfully strange. The tents were not the usual green canvas. They were black, and were suspended by interior poles and guy wires that created swooping curves as graceful as a hawk's wing. On the highest ground there were several the size of small ballrooms, and next to them, a satellite dish.

"Those are Saudi tents," Wynn said. "I wonder what we've walked into."

A man with a semiautomatic slung over his shoulder seemed to be asking himself a similar question. His yell in Arabic didn't sound very polite as he barred our path. We introduced ourselves in English with no appreciable results. Another man with a gun joined him. They didn't exactly point them at us, but looked as if they wouldn't pass up a chance to use them. When I looked for the Samburu boy who had led us over, he was gone. We were on our own.

Curious servants poked their heads out of tents to stare. They seemed to be various Asian nationalities, Pakistani, Filipino, maybe Bangladeshi. Modern-day indentured servants, Nick once told me, preferred by the Saudis because their abject poverty made them powerless. I didn't see one Kenyan; it looked like they'd brought their entire staff from home. The guards issued guttural orders, and the Asians melted away.

123

I tried to ignore the semiautomatic, but it was somewhat distracting. I turned to Wynn. "This must be the safari the princess was telling me about at Viv's. Why did they choose this spot—I mean, it's quite a coincidence. Nick had no contact with them, did he?"

"Not that I know of. I suppose Viv might have asked his advice about a place to recommend for a private safari, far off the beaten track. They do have that airstrip."

Aside from the airstrip, the area didn't impress me as a great place for a safari. Too bleak. If you wanted semidesert, you could have plenty of privacy in Shaba, near Samburu Game Park. The volcanic scenery there was spectacular. Setting up a camp here spelled an extreme desire for privacy. Why? Did it come with being royalty, or was something else going on?

An old woman, to judge by her forehead—the rest of her was swathed in black from head to foot, with a black scarf over her nose and mouth for good measure—walked up, eyed us suspiciously, exchanged some words with our guard, and hurriedly threaded her way to one of the big tents. She returned at a faster pace, gestured for us to follow her, still unsmiling, and led us up the slope without turning to see if we were following.

The large black tent soared just as beautifully close up. A pudgy woman standing by the entrance pulled open the heavy flap, which I could see was a dense handwoven wool, probably goat's hair. I brushed my hand against it as we entered. It was slightly prickly to the touch.

Inside, I blinked in the sudden dimness as my feet sank into a lush Oriental carpet. It was much, much cooler inside the tent, far too cool to be the result of simply being under shelter. There was also a telltale humming, like a small lawn mower.

The pudgy woman saw the look of confusion on my face and giggled. "It's air-conditioned," she explained, in slightly accented English. "We carry our own generator."

We were in a medium-size space created by interior walls of hanging damask. Louis XIV sofas lined three of the walls. The remaining side of the room was furnished with multicolored pillows on the floor, some woven, some

124

in silk, others in painted leather. The older woman who'd led us here disappeared behind the damask wall.

An Asian servant helped the pudgy woman take off the heavy black robe that encased her. I couldn't imagine anything more hot and uncomfortable for these temperatures. I wouldn't even wear a black T-shirt in the desert sun. Underneath she wore a rather fancy orange dress, and gold jewelry. She turned to a second servant, a slim girl who looked about sixteen, and gave a long order.

"Princess Rana will be with you in a moment. My name is Halimah. Please, be seated." She gestured at the red silk sofas. "Make yourself as comfortable as if this was your own home. I have ordered some iced tea, or perhaps you would prefer a Coke? Or lemonade?"

"We're so filthy," I began.

"Oh, no, you mustn't mind that. This is your home." She gestured again at the couches.

I gingerly perched on the edge of the red silk seat. Wynn hesitated, then joined me. "This is so very kind of you," she said.

"It is the hospitality of the desert." The cultured voice spoke from behind us. Princess Rana had entered from behind one of the damask interior walls, followed by her older companion. The princess wore a bright green dress with a tight bodice that showed off her figure. She was as heavily made-up as at the party, and emeralds dangled from her ears.

The fuzzy baby cheetah was struggling in her arms. There was a long, angry-looking scratch on her forearm. The cub's little round eyes stared at us with fear, and he chirped piteously. There was a wide diamond-studded bracelet fit tightly around his neck as a collar.

"Why, it is Jazz Jasper!" Rana turned to her pudgy companion. "We met at Viv Porter's delightful fashion show."

I exclaimed, "Princess Rana," and introduced Wynn as Viv's sister-in-law. The princess welcomed her cordially, with no sign she knew of Nick's existence, let alone death.

"Let me introduce my little darling," Rana smiled at me archly. "I have picked a name for him. Saladin. In honor of the great warrior." She grasped one of his paws and waved at us with it, as if he were a stuffed toy. "Say hello, Saladin," she lisped in baby talk.

I looked at Wynn. She had plastered a slight smile on her face, but her jaw was clamped shut. I could see the muscles in her cheek bunching.

The tent flap opened again, letting in a gush of hot air and sunshine, and three servants entered with our drinks: one to hold the silver tray, one to pour iced tea from a crystal pitcher, and the third to hand about the cut-crystal glasses. They were prechilled. A wafer-thin lemon slice floated on top.

I drank mine in about three gulps. I know it was crude, but it was the most welcome cold drink I'd ever had. It was sweeter than I like it, but who was quibbling? I could get into being princess for a day. I leaned back on the couch and admired the swooping black ceiling created by mahogany posts of different heights. "This is the most beautiful tent I've ever seen."

Rana smiled with pleasure. "It is a classic Saudi tent, except of course, a bit larger. My husband loves the desert." The cub squirmed ferociously, and she flipped him onto his back in the crook of her arm, like a human baby, where she could keep a good grip on him. "Every year we go camping in Pakistan for several months, far from the capital, and hunt for houbara." She giggled over the last word.

"Houbara?" I asked. I glanced at Wynn. She was staring at the cub with a big frown on her face.

"They are like the bustard you have here—like a wild chicken. Delicious." The princess's dark eyes glinted with mischief. "They are good for helping men to—you know—to father a lot of babies. The princes like to eat one every day." She giggled. "They are extinct in most places now, so you must be quite lucky to get enough to last the whole year. He hunts them with falcons. It is a very ancient and beautiful art."

"Do you hunt, too?" I asked.

Rana laughed. "Women don't hunt." She lowered her voice. "To tell you the truth, I get bored in the desert. If I didn't have videos with me, I'd go mad. Stark raving mad." She roughed up the cub's fur and laughed at his protests. "Of course, I never tell him so. Let him think I love the Romance of the Desert."

"It's a funny coincidence," I said. "Wynn's husband Nick was visiting that manyatta near here just last week."

"Last week? That is funny. I arrived only yesterday. My husband wanted to have everything set up for me beforehand. My son is two," she said proudly. "I miss him very much. I have never left him before. The first few days in Nairobi I was crying all the time, I missed him so much. I was calling home every hour to see how he is. My husband was becoming quite irritated with me." She gave an embarrassed smile. "I have been trying to get pregnant again." The smile turned wistful. "Perhaps on this trip I will be lucky."

She kissed Saladin's fuzzy gray head. "Saladin, will you bring me luck? Another son? Make Wafiyyah jealous?" She switched to us. "That's the sheikh's youngest wife. She just had a baby girl, and does she hate me for having a son! Men are so much nicer than women, don't you think?"

The tent flap was thrown back, saving us from having to answer. Yet another Filipino servant entered with a large brass platter of fruits, nuts, and dates, and pulled out one of the Louis XIV end tables to place it on. The princess picked out a date with her long red-enameled fingernails and popped it into her mouth. "Please, eat."

I was famished and didn't need a further invitation. Wynn wasn't shy, either.

"Do I remember correctly that you have your own safari company?" Rana asked. I nodded, my mouth too full to answer. "What a lucky chance that you are camping nearby."

"Actually," I stammered, "we're here due to a mishap."

"I'm a pilot," Wynn explained. "We were out for a test flight in my plane after some repairs, and developed engine trouble."

"A pilot?" Rana looked at Wynn with curiosity and respect. "Saudi women are not even allowed to drive. My husband gave me a beautiful red Mercedes sports car for the birth of my son, but I have to leave it in London. Can you believe, the religious police arrested an American friend of mine in Riyadh who they caught driving her sick child to the hospital. The child almost died." She seemed to enjoy our expressions of shock. "Yes, it's true. The king does not dare go against the *ulemas*. The fundamentalists are always waiting to jump on us and say the ruling family is corrupt and western. And it is not just the old men, either, the young fanatics are even worse." She made a face. "But it is boring to talk about politics. When my husband gets back from his morning game run, he will send our mechanic to take care of your poor stranded plane. Meanwhile, you must tell me all about yourselves."

Wynn gave a wry smile. "We're the worst kind of guests, I'm afraid. We're really throwing ourselves on your mercy. The plane's totaled. One wing smashed, the propeller gone."

Rana's mouth and eyes opened in amazement. "How calm you both are! I would be shaking with terror. How lucky you were to walk away without a scratch! How lucky we were here to help you! This is absolutely terrible. A plane crash! Well! Of course, you must be our guest on safari for a few days, and fly back with us. We have another guest arriving tonight. I think the sheikh plans a nice, cool night drive in the desert."

The older woman said something sharply to Rana. Suddenly I recognized her as the chaperone with Rana at Viv's party. The princess looked sullen, and didn't answer. She turned to us and excused herself, saying she'd see us after we rested, and disappeared behind the curtain, whispering in the cub's ear.

Halimah, who'd been sitting quietly in the corner all this time, got up. "Perhaps you would like to wash up now?" She led us out into the pounding sun again. We walked a short way and she ushered us into the bathing tent. Plumbing had been rigged up, with hot and tepid water. It wouldn't be cold unless they chilled it. Slipping in their standards. We both stripped and a servant took away our clothes, leaving only the day pack, which still held Wynn's knife and a couple of bottles of water that we'd rescued from the plane.

I let Wynn take the first shower. Water flowed from a saucer-sized shower head, while a latticed wooden mat kept the bather's feet from the floor. She lifted her face to the water. "Ah, this is great."

I sat on a stool. "We're being treated like royalty."

"Yes, but don't take it personally." Wynn found a shampoo bottle conveniently placed on a shelf and sudsed her hair. She had a nice, compact body, with round breasts and pretty dark-rose nipples, which were now standing erect as the water coursed over them. "Tradition prescribes elaborate hospitality to guests. As long as we stay in that category, we're fine." She massaged her scalp, and ran her head under the water to wash the soap out. She began to soap herself all over.

"Why wouldn't we stay in that category?"

"Because I plan to take that cub back with us."

I stared.

"I know I'm crazy. But the world doesn't have any extra cheetahs to waste."

"He didn't look in very good shape."

"She's not feeding him properly. If we leave him, he's not going to survive long enough to be smuggled out of the country. He has a right to be free, and I plan to free him." Her voice was determined. "I can't walk away and let him die."

I flashed on the memory of Nick dying in her arms, and couldn't bring myself to argue with her. "You are crazy. Unfortunately, I'm crazy in the same way. But how can we get away with it?"

"I don't know, but we have to try." Wynn looked grim. "Your turn." She stepped off the wooden pallet, and I handed her a thick towel from a pile on a bench. She wrapped it around her wet hair, turban style, and I handed her a second. "I have a very bad feeling about this whole setup," she continued. "No one would camp this far north for game viewing."

"I've been thinking the same thing. If you want beauti-

129

ful scenery all to yourself, there are a lot nicer places than this, which are private but not totally isolated."

"Exactly."

"Do you think these guys are hunting?" I took Wynn's place under the shower, and for a moment I could think of nothing but the pleasure of being wet and clean.

"Remember that big scandal with two Saudi princes several years ago?"

"That was before I got to Kenya."

"The then-Minister of Tourism gave them phony hunting licenses and personally escorted them, right in Maasai Mara."

"Inside the park? You're kidding." Maasai Mara was Kenya's part of the Serengeti Plains, the most spectacular concentration of wildlife on earth, and Kenya's biggest, most popular national park.

"They were shooting lion, buffalo, zebra, giraffe. God, was that an international stink. The minister had to resign."

"And what happened to the Saudis?" I soaped up and let the water run over me. Pure bliss.

"They had to go home without their trophies."

"Oh, poor things."

"People as rich and powerful as a Saudi prince don't get in trouble for breaking laws, at least not the laws of another country. They could probably kill with impunity."

I thought of Nick. He might very well have caught the Saudis hunting, or stumbled on a scene of slaughter and checked out their camp. A scandal in the papers couldn't damage them, but it would cut their party short. The same scenario I'd thought up for Claude Lavalle could apply here. Someone who wants to shut Nick up, one of the Saudis, finds a Sahara scorpion among their things, in a packing crate or something like that, and decides to plant it in Nick's car, give him a scare or a nasty bite. Maybe they'd threatened him and meant it as a warning to cease and desist. I finished washing and turned off the water. Or maybe they'd found out where he lived and sent someone to kill him in a way that wouldn't show.

"Hand me a towel, would you?" I reached out a dripping arm. Wynn handed me a towel and I dried off. "During the siesta let's poke around camp a bit, see what we can see. I'm wondering if Nick might have come across the Saudis last week, gotten suspicious, or even caught them hunting."

As if waiting for the sound of running water to cease, a servant entered with two luxurious terry robes over one arm and two black head-to-toe jobs in the other. We emerged from the bath tent dressed as shapeless black bags, and were led to another tent with two single beds along one wall, a plush Oriental carpet and low brass table in the center. We were invited to take a nap. Our clean clothes would be ready for us when we awoke.

We waited half an hour, lying naked on the beds and sweating—our tent was not air-conditioned—before putting on the black robes and going for a walk. We figured almost no one would be about in the sweltering heat of afternoon; if we were caught, we'd simply say we'd gone for a stroll.

A young Asian woman was doubled over, sweeping with a primitive broom of bound reeds. She seemed to be smoothing the sand between tents. I guess you don't want messy sand in camp.

"Do you speak English?" I asked.

"A little," she said with a grin. "American?" She pointed at us.

"Yes. American. You?"

She touched her chest and laughed. "Pakistan." She nodded. "Well-come."

"Thank you. Can you show us the lion skin? From the hunt." I mimicked a lion's roar and shooting a gun.

"Yes." She lay down her broom and guided us through the cluster of tents. "Good hunt. Many animals. Beautiful."

Inside a thorn enclosure were the zebra and oryx skins missing from the scene of carnage we'd passed on our trek to the manyatta. The zebra was an especially beautiful species, large as a horse and with fine stripes. They were found only in this area, and were endangered. Their skins were stretched on frames. So were those of several lions,

131

two leopards, and a cheetah. Wynn reached forward and touched the cheetah skin with a trembling finger.

"This is awful," I whispered. Wynn nodded without speaking. Her eyes were full of tears.

The smell of death festered under the hot sun. Pale oryx skulls with their magnificent horns lay in a pile. The bits of flesh still attached to them had attracted flies. There was another pile of curved impala horns, next to the entire head of a little dik-dik. Except for the buzzing of the flies, the scene was utterly silent.

"Beautiful," said the Pakistani girl.

My throat was closed up with rage and grief, and I couldn't answer her.

"I wish we had a camera, to document this." I wanted to see the photo splattered across the front page. They weren't going to get away with this, even if they were the richest people on earth.

Wynn gestured, Let's get out of here. Somehow we thanked the girl, and walked away as quickly as possible. The vision of death wasn't as easy to leave behind.

"If Nick saw this . . ." Wynn's face was white and drained.

"Are you all right?"

"Yes," she snapped. "I'm fine."

"You look terrible."

"I'm just mad as hell. If they killed Nick to keep this quiet . . ." She hurried her pace, not paying attention to where we were going.

"Slow down." I caught up with her. Sweat was pouring down my body under the black robe, plastering it to my back and chest. "Let's pass by the princess's tent. If she's asleep—"

"You mean, steal the cub now?" Wynn interrupted, mind reading. "Shouldn't we wait till just before we leave?"

"After what we just saw, I'm thinking we should leave on our own, and the sooner the better." The sun beat down on us like a fist, making each step an effort. We passed no one in the sand alleys between tents.

"And forget getting a ride back on the sheikh's plane?"

"I wouldn't count on him for help. In fact, I don't even

want to wait for nightfall—let's get out while we can."
The princess struck me as pretty naive about having
strangers show up at an illegal hunting camp. She might
not even know it's illegal, or care about such plebeian mat-
ters. I didn't imagine the sheikh felt much danger in coming here, either, until a newspaperman showed up. And
now the two of us.

Wynn nodded. "You're right. Let's get the pack first.
Then we go to the princess's tent, and see where she keeps
the cub."

We hurried back to our tent, getting lost only once,
quickly scooped up the day pack, and refilled the water
bottles from a carafe thoughtfully placed on the brass table. Our clothes were neatly folded on the beds, dried and
pressed. We got dressed in about two seconds. Wynn took
her big knife out of the pack and stuck it through her belt,
and we put the robes back on.

Wynn stopped me from rushing right out and looked directly into my eyes. Her eyes were a pretty blue, with a
star pattern around her iris in lighter blue. She looked
scared but determined. "Jazz, you realize we're risking our
lives to save this cheetah. I'm willing to take on that risk.
If you're not, I understand completely. You don't have to
do this, you know. You can head back to the manyatta, and
I'll get the cub and meet you there."

I returned her steady look. "We got in this together, and
we'll get out together."

We gripped each other's hands in a big handshake, then
headed for the princess's tent. We walked swiftly and silently through the sleeping camp. It was so quiet I could
hear the sand squeak under our feet.

Ahead of me Wynn stopped and whispered, "There it
is."

The big black tent hunched at the top of the slope like
a giant beast.

"I'll go in," I told Wynn in a whisper. "If I'm caught,
I'll try to bluff my way out of it. You stay here. If someone approaches, talk loudly enough for me to hear you."

She argued she should be the one to go in. I won.

I took a deep breath, drew my shoulders back and

133

walked up to the tent as normally as possible. I paused in the shadow of the wall and looked around as if admiring the camp. No one was around to see me. I walked quickly to the flap and slipped in.

The old lady, still wrapped in her black robe, was lying on one of the red sofas. I froze. My heart pounded in my ears. Had she heard me come in? Her chest rose and fell as she breathed lightly and evenly. Fast asleep. I looked quickly around the room. No cub. The sheikh must be back, though. A dusty hat and safari jacket had been thrown down on one of the pillows. As I passed it I noticed a camera poking out from under the jacket. Just what I'd been wanting, but first things first.

There was a moan of lovemaking from behind the damask partition. I snuck across the room and put my eye to a crack between the damask and the outer wall. My hands were slippery with sweat. I could see the end of a bed, and tethered to the bedpost with a belt, the cheetah cub. He looked at me and chirped piteously.

I cursed silently to myself. The damn princess wasn't letting the cub out of her sight. It was going to be impossible to steal it. The movement and sounds from the bed stopped, and I could hear covers being thrown back. I retreated in a panic, quickly, under the sofa, not the one the old lady was sleeping on. I scrambled under it and flattened myself against the back wall. My black robe would be invisible against the black goat hair.

Bare feet and a man's hairy legs crossed in front of my eyes. The sheikh moved out of my vision, fumbled in his jacket and pulled out something that crackled like cellophane. I heard the snick of a match being struck and smelled the acrid smoke of a cigarette. My heart was pounding like a crazy drum: dan-ger, dan-ger, dan-ger.

He crossed back to the bedroom. I heard the bedsprings squeak. The princess said something in a sleepy-sounding voice, and he hushed her gently. I waited five minutes, and then I heard a sound from the bed that was music to my ears: the sound of light snoring. Please, God, let them both be asleep.

I crawled out from under the sofa as silently as I could

and put my eye back to the curtain. The crack was wider now—the sheikh hadn't pulled the damask back completely. I could see two shapes cuddled in the bed under a satin sheet. Nothing but a gentle snore disturbed the peace.

Behind me the old lady on the couch stirred and her breathing changed pitch. My heart jumped. I didn't think we were going to get a better shot at the cub. I tiptoed across the room, picked up a pillow, and tiptoed back. Put my eye to the crack. Still asleep. Shaking with a rush of adrenaline, I slipped into the bedroom, dropped the pillow over the cub to muffle his chirps, hoped I wasn't smothering him, pulled the loop of the belt securing him off the bed, and raced out of the tent.

Wynn was right there. I thrust the wriggling cub mashed into the pillow at her and darted back inside. There was one other thing I wanted.

I slipped the camera out from under the sheikh's jacket and ran.

Wynn grabbed my arm and pulled me around the corner. She had her arms wrapped around a struggling bulge under the front of her robe; I could guess what she'd done with the cub. "Let's get out of here."

"Listen, I took a camera," I whispered. "I want pictures of their hunting trophies. You start for the manyatta, and I'll catch up with you."

"No, Jazz. It's too dangerous. We've got the cub. Let's go now."

Wynn seemed more focused on saving the cub than the possibility we'd found Nick's killer. Maybe that was healthier. This was one life she could save. I wanted to do both. "We need evidence if we're going to go up against these guys. I want to make sure we can nail them to the wall for what they've done."

"Okay. But I'm not leaving without you."

"This will just take a minute. Everyone's sleeping like a baby in there."

We threaded our way between the tents and found the enclosure with the animal skins after only a few nerve-wracking minutes of searching the wrong alley. Wynn took up a position as lookout, and I finished off the sheikh's roll of pictures. I took a few shots of the enclosure with the unmistakable Saudi tents all around it, and the piles of animal parts visible through the doorway. I took several of the lion, leopard, and cheetah skins, did a close-up of the dik-dik's little head, the pile of oryx and gazelle horns.

"Hurry," Wynn said.

I quickly rewound the film, opened the camera and pulled out the exposed roll. I'd hide the camera somewhere on our way out.

"Jazz! Run!" Wynn's whisper tore through me like a buzz saw. I pushed the roll of film into my sock, the only hiding place I could think of in one second, and swiveled, poised to run. My heart stopped.

"Not so fast." The sheikh stood in the opening of the enclosure. A guard with a semiautomatic in his hands stood behind him.

The sheikh said something in Arabic. The guard stepped forward and seized the camera. The sheikh spoke again. The guard raised his gun and struck me along the side of my head. It sent me reeling, and I could feel blood pouring down my cheek.

"Just exactly what do you think you were doing?" asked the sheikh in a clipped British accent. He was at least thirty years older than his wife, and shorter than my image of a prince, but the dark expression on his face was certainly imperious.

"The skins are so beautiful. . . ." I stammered. "I was just taking a few photos with my camera."

"Don't toy with me!" His eyes flashed. He spat out some Arabic to the guard, turned on his heel and left.

The guard seized me by the arm. His fingers dug painfully into my biceps. I tried to break his grip, and he hit me again with the gun, threw me to the ground and gave me a kick in the ribs. Before I could recover my breath, he yanked me up and frog-stepped me to a wooden hut with a padlock on the door, threw me inside and snapped the padlock shut.

I burst out crying. I sat in a miserable heap on the floor and sobbed for a long time. My ribs hurt like hell, and I was scared. Somehow I didn't think the sheikh was going to hand me over to the Kenyan police for stealing his camera. I didn't like to think what his plans might be. Something discreet, like a quiet drive into the desert after dark, and a quick shot to the head.

Eventually I got done crying and looked around me. I was in a storage hut piled high with cases of mineral water, wine, soda. At least I wouldn't die of thirst in here. They didn't seem to worry that I'd use the heavy glass bottles to break my way out. I put an ear to the wall. I couldn't hear anyone, but there was probably a guard.

I sat down again. I got up. Examined the walls and ceiling, looking for I don't know what, but didn't prisoners always do that? My only hope was Wynn. I prayed they hadn't caught her, although that seemed overly optimistic. If she saw them in time to warn me, they'd probably seen her. At least she was in a black robe. It made it harder to run, but easier to hide. But then I thought: even if she escaped, where can she go for help?

We were in the middle of nowhere, with no radio, no car, no weapons. The manyatta was the only place Wynn could go for help, and somehow I didn't see the *morans* coming to rescue me, their spears pitted against automatic weapons. I remembered Claude Lavalle and felt a brief flare of hope. He had a radio! He could radio Omondi, and the police would fly in and— My heart sank again. The police would fly in, and at the first sight of their plane, I would be quickly disposed of. I had an image of being efficiently strangled and buried under the sand floor where I was sitting at the moment. Cheerful thought. I tried to think of a better scenario, and remembered that Claude said we weren't in range to use the radio, anyway.

My future didn't look very promising.

16

WAITING FOR THE sheikh's next move did not seem like a good idea. They wouldn't have more than one man to guard this shack. Since I couldn't open the door myself, I'd have to get him to open it for me. I doubted he would simply stand there and listen to me destroying his boss's wine cellar.

I opened up a case, pulled out a bottle of champagne—a vintage Dom Pérignon, to be more precise—and smashed it against the side of the crate. It made a hell of a noise but didn't break. I pulled it back across my shoulder and belted it against the edge of the crate. Smasheroo. A yell in Arabic and pounding on the door. I smiled and pulled out another bottle. By the third bottle, I could hear the guard fumbling at the lock.

The door swung open. I raised an unbroken Dom Pérignon like a club, and the guard hesitated in the opening. There was a flash of movement behind him, like a big, dark shadow. He started to turn, and I stepped forward and belted him across the jaw with my bottle. He hit the doorjamb and crumpled, revealing Wynn standing behind him with her knife. I was glad she hadn't had to use it.

We pulled the guard into the shack by his armpits, shut the door and snapped the padlock closed. Then we ran like hell.

More people were awake now, but wearing black robes seemed to confer some status on us, since the Asian servants we passed lowered their eyes and asked no questions. With the cub under her robe, Wynn looked pregnant. We reached the edge of camp and paused. No guard in sight. No shouts. No one running after us. We walked calmly but quickly over the hill and out of sight of the camp. At that point we ran until we were winded. We paused to catch our breath, and silently but triumphantly intertwined our hands and raised them in a victory salute. Wynn's face was a big happy grin of relief. I felt the same.

"I've got to get out of this sweat lodge," I said.

We took off our black robes and stuck them into the crevice of some rocks, where they wouldn't be seen. I also took the film canister out of my sock, where it had been biting into my ankle, kissed it and put it in my pocket. It brought the sweet promise of future justice.

When I turned, the teenage boy with the wide-set eyes who had first led us to the Saudi camp was standing there, watching us intently. "Wynn. Look who's here. Kari-ankei."

Wynn held the bulging backpack against her stomach and looked at him thoughtfully for a moment. "How about if we ask this guy to hide us, instead of going directly to the manyatta? The less people who know about us, the better."

"And ask Claude Lavalle to come to us? Judging from his first reaction, he's more likely to refuse."

"If so, one of us can sneak into the manyatta and contact him. The more discreet we are, the better."

"Fine with me."

Wynn told the boy in Swahili, "Bad man." She pointed at the camp. "We run away. Hide. You." She pointed. "Hide us. No tell bad man."

It was a simple story, but it worked. The kid grinned, pulled our black robes out of the crevice, and tucked them under his arm. He motioned for us to follow him. He continued in the direction we'd been following, led us over one hill, turned left and down a gully where we were hidden from any observers, walked for half a mile, then scrambled up a rocky tumble. We rounded a sun-warmed boulder and there was a low cave, looking like an open mouth. We spread out the black robes and lay on them, looking out on the desert vista. We could see but not be seen. It was a perfect place to plan our next move.

Below us was the manyatta and its airstrip. The Saudis'

plane was still away, presumably picking up supplies. The empty space in front of the manyatta took a moment to register.

"Oh, shit. Claude Lavalle's truck is gone!" I exclaimed.

Kariankei confirmed that Lavalle had left hours ago and wasn't planning on coming back. I groaned aloud. "How the hell are we going to get away now! Why, oh why, did I assume he would still be here?"

"I did, too," Wynn comforted me. "Who sets off at midday in the desert?"

We looked at each other with disbelief and growing panic. "We are well and totally screwed."

"Let me take care of the cub, and then we can work on what to do," Wynn said. She zipped open the day pack that she'd been wearing on her belly, and pulled out the orphan cub. He was shaking. There was dried mucous in the corners of his eyes, and his fur was dull.

I felt awful for him. It made me forget our predicament for a moment. "Is he sick?" I asked.

"Badly dehydrated, I think."

"Should we try to get him milk?"

"No, it's worse than nothing. Cow or goat's milk will make him sick, and he'd lose even more body fluids. That may be his trouble. I wish I had an electrolyte solution, but water will have to do till we get him home." She pulled a water bottle out of her pack, soaked a corner of her shirt, twisted it into a nipple shape and offered it to him. He didn't react. She wrung a few drops onto his tongue. He squirmed. "Suck, wild one," she crooned to him, but he didn't get the idea. She ended up squeezing it into his mouth drop by drop.

We decided to call the cub Comet, in promise of the space and speed that were his birthright. At the moment, speed was our biggest problem. With water and a guide, we could hike from manyatta to manyatta and eventually reach a place with contact to the outside world, but it would be all too easy for the sheikh to catch up with us before we got to the first one.

"That's enough for now." Wynn put the cub on the floor of the cave, and he took a few shaky steps.

"Let's get that collar off him," I suggested.

Wynn undid the safety clasp and slipped off the jeweled bracelet the princess had fastened around his neck. She handed it to me. I weighed it in my hand. Diamonds and emeralds, obviously worth a small fortune.

"Pretty," said Kariankei.

I handed it to him, and he dangled it over his wrist, next to the two bead bracelets he already wore.

"I wonder when their plane is coming back."

Wynn gave me a disbelieving look. "Are you thinking of stealing it?"

Kariankei handed the bracelet back to me, and I held it up so that it dangled and sparkled in a shaft of sunlight. "Maybe we could bribe the pilot to let us borrow it."

"Maybe." She sounded dubious.

"What are our options? Even if we walk all night, they'll catch up to us. Once we have the plane, we're home free."

The cub began to call piteously, little chirps of distress like a baby bird.

"I bet he'd feel safer inside the open pack, where he's enclosed and out of sight," I suggested. "More like a den."

"Good idea." Wynn put him into the day pack, and he immediately snuggled deep into it. He stopped chirping, his little golden eyes grew to sleepy slits, and he fell into a slumber. I swore to myself we'd get him out of this mess.

From our bird's eye perch, we watched the activities of the Samburu manyatta. In the center of the manure-dotted enclosure, a group of women sat in their red robes, feet straight out in front of them on the ground, stringing beads. Their shaved heads gleamed in the sunlight. A gaggle of small children played noisily nearby, exciting two dogs who raced around, barking.

Several women, bowed under a towering load of wood on their shoulders, trudged toward the manyatta from the direction of the stream. An eight-year-old girl came after them, carrying an infant tied to her back, undoubtedly her latest brother or sister.

About a dozen adult men sat in the shade of a big tree

141

outside the thorn wall, passing a gourd of beer. They called out something to the approaching women that cracked everyone up, and there was a lot of laughter and shouting back and forth. A gray-haired elder rhythmically slapped a fly whisk against one shoulder and then the other.

The boys were presumably still out with their herds, younger boys with goats, older adolescents with the prized cattle. The *moran*—the most privileged male age set, circumcised but not yet able to marry, aged fifteen to thirty years old—were nowhere in sight.

"Where are the *moran*?" I asked Kariankei.

"Visiting," he said, with a lewd-sounding laugh. "The lion doesn't avoid the place where he has fed."

They must be off visiting their lovers. They're only supposed to have sex with prepubescent girls who can't get pregnant, but few obey the rules. Since girls are married at puberty and men don't marry until after *moran*hood, and then keep taking more wives as they amass cattle over the years, Samburu marriages often have a thirty- or forty-year age difference between husband and wife. The result is an age-old tradition of married girls and *morans* being illicit lovers, which in turn leads to jealousy and wife-beating. At the same time, elders share their wives with each other as a mark of hospitality—at the wife's consent, of course. Since a girl's clitoris is cut off at puberty to prevent her from enjoying sex, I didn't understand what women got out of all this lovemaking. Or maybe I did: wooing and attention. I thought of me and Striker, and how much he expected me to give up for love.

I pulled my mind back to our situation. I had more pressing problems to think about. As the afternoon wore on, Wynn and I played out alternate strategies of how to approach the pilot. Best scenario: he might be a Kenyan charter pilot and Wynn would know him. Worst scenario: he'd be a Saudi, have heard of our escape from camp by radio, and try to grab us. Wynn gave me a lesson on how to break a hold, how to immobilize someone who's coming at you, and other highlights from her street fighting course.

Kariankei watched with great interest, until he was so intrigued he asked to join us. Wynn had Kariankei get me in a choke lock, with his elbow around my throat. He was all sinew and muscle, incredibly strong from the physical demands of herding, plus teenage competitions of spear-throwing, fighting, and dancing. If I could break his choke hold, I could get free from anyone.

"Okay, tuck your chin into his elbow to get the pressure off your throat. Left hand grabs attacker's wrist, right hand goes for his nerve center." Wynn directed my hand to a spot about three inches above Kariankei's elbow on the inside of his arm. "Can you feel it? You should be between the biceps and triceps." She repeated it in Swahili for Kariankei's benefit.

"Yeah, I've got it," I said dubiously.

"Okay. Apply strong, direct inward pressure."

I squeezed. Kariankei made a surprised noise and involuntarily lost his grip.

Wynn circled us. "Keep the pressure up. Both hands. Okay! Now bend and draw his arm over your head. Yes! Keep twisting." She directed me with her hands. "That's it. See? Now twist his arm behind his back. Direct his momentum into your chosen line of force. You're not using muscle power, you're using anatomy. Good!"

I let go of Kariankei and we grinned at each other. Then it was his turn. At the end of a couple of hours I was dripping with sweat, dirty from landing on the floor, far from proficient, but I knew how to break an arm lock, and I could use my opponent's weight to avoid a blow and maybe even trip him up.

It was a welcome distraction when Comet woke up and wriggled out of the day pack. He gave a forlorn chirp like a little bird. Wynn twisted her shirttail into a nipple, soaked with water, and offered it to him. This time he cuddled against her leg and started to suck, while rhythmically pushing his paws into her thigh. "That's much better."

Outside a francolin gave its far-carrying call. *Tee-dee-jee, tee-dee-jee.*

"*Duma* needs meat," Kariankei said, using the Swahili word for cheetah.

"Yes," Wynn agreed.

"*Kwale* good?" he asked. *Kwale*, or the francolin, a quaillike bird, is part of a cub's natural diet.

"*Kwale* very good."

Kariankei selected a few well-shaped rocks from the cave entrance and silently disappeared. Within twenty minutes he was back with a francolin dangling in his hand. He lay it on the ground and Wynn slit it open with her knife. Comet, who'd been exploring the cave, trotted over as fast as his little legs could carry him. He sniffed the bird, patted it with a paw as if to see if it would move, and settled in to feed. It took him a long time with his tiny baby teeth, but he managed to eat until his tummy was round and swaying under him.

While Comet was eating, we asked Kariankei about Nick's visit last week. All he could say was that Nick walked around, looked at the well, at the herds, talked to people.

"Did he visit the camp, the strangers' camp?" Wynn asked, pointing toward the Saudis.

"Yes. Visit everywhere."

It sounded to me like a typical African yes, said in order to please and encourage, regardless of the facts. When we tried getting some details of Nick visiting the Saudis, Kariankei came up blank.

At last we heard the sounds of the returning herds, signaling the approach of evening. Clouds of dust were converging on the manyatta from different directions, as the cows were brought home to the safety of the thorn fence for the night.

The plane flew in before dusk, as we knew it would. Landing on a bush airstrip at night is only for the foolhardy or an emergency. The Samburu ran out to watch it land. As the plane's engine died, we saw a Land Cruiser drive up from the Saudi camp. I wondered what supplies the plane was bringing in. Fresh caviar? An air-conditioner part? Fresh papaya for tomorrow's breakfast?

Everyone was outside the thorn enclosure, swarming around the plane and the single Land Cruiser. We could hear their excited chatter, especially the children running

144

around giggling and shouting. The cattle were lowing, the sun was balanced above the horizon, and the Samburus' shadows were long and emaciated. A fat man in a suit got out of the plane and clambered into the Land Cruiser. I saw a flash of gold from a ring and a clear view of double chins and a vigorous profile. It was William Mutani!

I noticed something else with a sinking sensation. The pilot climbed down from the plane and joined Mutani in the car. Meanwhile three Saudi guards, each with automatic weapons, hopped out of the Land Cruiser. The car was loaded with supplies from the plane and headed back for camp. As this was going on, some girls were sent off and returned with firewood. A small fire was built next to the plane, a straw mat was rolled out, and the guards sat.

"So much for our beautiful bribery idea," Wynn said. "It's not going to work with three of them, even if we could speak Arabic."

"And they all know about us."

Fighting off a feeling of gloom, Wynn and I tried to think up some scheme to distract the guards, or to fool them into letting us visit the plane, but each of the scenarios ended up with a beautiful reason and opportunity for them to shoot us.

Wynn ran a hand through her short hair. "We've got to think of a new way out of here."

"Leave tonight on foot. Ask the Samburu to help us."

"We'd be caught too easily."

"Steal a car?" I joked.

"Yeah." Wynn gave a dry laugh. "How? The camp is crawling with people, and the guards there will also have automatic weapons."

"It's either that or decide to trust the sheikh and ask him for a lift home."

By now it had grown dark in the cave and I could barely make out where Wynn was sitting, although we were in touching distance. I stepped outside and looked up at the stars flung across the unfamiliar sky. There had to be some way we could sneak out of here. "Hey, listen to this crazy idea. Remember the princess saying the sheikh is taking his guest on a night drive tonight?"

145

"I bet it's a hunt," Wynn said grimly.

"You're probably right. So here's the plan: we go now and hide outside camp, wait till they leave, sneak into one of the cars left behind and drive after them. Anyone who sees us from camp will think we're part of the hunt. Then, when we're far enough away from here, we turn south."

"Hey." Wynn got up and joined me at the cave mouth. "It's crazy, but I like it. Our tracks will be all mixed in with theirs, we'll have a good long head start." She folded her arms across her chest. "I'd bet anything they're going after leopard."

Leopards are the only nocturnal animal that would interest hunters, so I thought Wynn was right. "The only place for leopard around here is the riverine forest."

"That would suit us fine. We follow them as far as the stream, and then head south through the woods. We'll drive without lights. We'll be invisible."

"It's our best shot."

"We'll do it." We shook hands.

"Who's crazier, you or me?" Wynn asked.

"Me," we both answered, and laughed.

Wynn explained our plan to Kariankei. He was all for helping us, and it took some convincing for him to agree that the only help we needed was as a guide back to the Saudi camp. Wynn zipped the sleeping Comet in her pack, and I put it on. The cub stirred but settled back into sleep. Wynn adjusted the long knife in her belt, and we stepped out of the cave. The manyatta was filled with humpbacked cattle, lowing and milling around. Once more Kariankei led us to the Saudi camp.

Wynn and I lay flat on our stomachs, outside the reach of the camp lights. We had put on our black robes and were perfectly invisible. Kariankei, next to us, was naturally invisible at night. Comet was a warm, soft pressure against my shoulder blades. I felt as protective as a mother cheetah.

The parking area below was like an empty stage before the curtain goes up and the principal actors appear. Half a dozen Land Cruisers and a customized Mercedes were lined up next to the two-ton trucks, polished sides gleaming in the hissing light of high-intensity gas lamps. There was only a single armed guard with the vehicles, smoking a cigarette as he leaned against the hood of the first car.

The lamps illuminated only the first few vehicles, leaving the rest in deeper darkness to anyone near the lights. A swirl of moths and other insects swarmed around the lamps. The night was so still, we could hear the sizzle as some of them collided with the hot glass shade. Several small bats were taking advantage of the baited prey, zooming in and out of the night.

Voices and the clatter of dishes sounded from the other end of camp, and we could see servants going in and out of a big black tent on the slope. Presumably the sheikh and his illustrious guest were dining before the hunt. My own stomach was tied in a knot.

"If we only knew which cars were going, we could slip into an unused one right now," Wynn whispered.

"How about slipping into one of the trucks? Then, at the right moment, we pick our car."

"Right. That one with the high wooden sides."

"Let's go."

We whispered our farewells to Kariankei, pulled back and angled our way to the far side of the trucks. They lay in deep shadow. We moved like shadows ourselves, quick and quiet, and put our backs against the first truck. We listened. Above the hissing lights was the distant cackle of hyenas, and farther off, a lion grunting. The sheikh and William Mutani weren't the only hunters out tonight.

Wynn hooked her thumb toward the next truck and was gone. I imitated her, dashing around the corner and flattening myself against the side. We waited, listened, dashed to the next truck. This was child's play. We came to the last truck. This was the one tricky part, because we'd be within the guard's field of sight when we climbed in—if he turned around.

A moth sizzled loudly against the camp light and I jumped. I put a hand over my pounding heart until it settled down. I stuck my head around the back of the truck.

147

The guard was facing away from us. His head was back as if he were studying the stars.

I signaled all clear to Wynn and we clambered over the tailgate, Wynn first. As I swung my leg over the side, Comet's weight shifted, pulling against the robe, and my foot caught in the hem. In one of those horrible slow-motion moments, I fought to keep my balance and lost. I fell heavily, thudding on the floor, letting out an *oof* as the breath was knocked out of me.

I froze. Wynn was watching the guard through the space between the wooden boards. She dropped next to me, a finger over her lips. There was a big canvas tarp folded in the corner, but no time to unfold it and crawl under. We flattened ourselves against the floor and pulled our black robes over our faces. I strained my ears. Yes, I could hear the sound of footsteps scrunching on sand. Comet, don't pick this time to chirp, I prayed. The guard was approaching. The sound grew louder and louder. I imagined myself part of the truck floor, flat, dark, part of the truck, invisible, not here, don't see. The footsteps came up to the tailgate. They paused. I imagined the guard glancing in and held my breath, waiting for the sound of a bullet falling into its chamber. But his gun remained silently on his shoulder. The footsteps scrunched on.

He walked to the end of the line and back down the other side. After a long interval, Wynn and I moved to the back corner and sat down. If I hunched down a bit, I could see between two boards and scan the entire area. We had ringside seats.

Then came a long period of waiting, getting colder and stiffer and hungrier. We didn't dare talk, so I was left to my own thoughts. William Mutani was here. That could only mean one thing: the sheikh was mixing business with pleasure. I wondered if it was Mutani who had arranged this illegal hunting safari as a bonus for bringing money to Kenya. What was the sheikh's business here? The obvious answer was oil. Did Gerry Weller fit into this picture also? Were those surveyors near Nick and Wynn's working for Kenarabia? Or for Mutani?

But what would Mutani have to do with oil? It was

more likely the sheikh was looking for places to invest his money, and Mutani was cultivating him as a backer for his next hotel. What had Striker told me? That he'd asked Nick to find out Mutani's foreign investors for the Mount Kenya Center. Had that led Nick to Sheikh Farid? Most of all, I wondered how much Nick had found out about the sheikh's activities—both hunting and oil—and how dangerous it was to know.

The sound of people approaching brought my attention back to the row of cars. Two more men with guns appeared and stood talking with the guard. Then a slender man without a gun walked over, got into the customized Mercedes and started it up. Once the engine was running smoothly, he got out and began polishing the already shiny exterior with a cloth. A stocky man with a mustache arrived and started up the Land Cruiser next in the row.

This was a make it or break it moment. My hands tightened into fists. How many guards would be left behind? If all three men with guns stayed with the remaining cars, we'd be in big trouble. I was pretty sure, though, that some of them at least would go with the sheikh. He probably didn't go to pee without his personal bodyguard.

Nothing more happened for about ten minutes. I couldn't see the big tent on the slope anymore, but it must have opened and disgorged the party members, because there was an abrupt din of voices spilling toward us. I pulled my black robe tighter around me. Comet was a warm, gentle weight on my back, a sleeping angel. The phrase "This is it," kept repeating inanely in my mind.

Then they were in view. Despite his lack of stature, the sheikh strode with the self-assurance that power bestows. Instead of white robes, he was dressed head to toe in an impeccable safari outfit. Mutani was also in khaki. He had the same bulky outline as the sheikh, but he was almost a foot taller. I hadn't realized what a big man he was when I saw him sitting in his car, with Gerry. I hadn't expected to see William Mutani in safari clothes, either. I wondered if this was the first business dinner of his life when he hadn't worn a suit. Where could he put his diamond tie clip if he had no tie?

The two men were surrounded by attendants holding lamps, holding hunting rifles, holding warm jackets, holding a blanket, holding food baskets, holding a cooler, holding a spotlight. The princess had not come down to see her husband off. I wondered if she was allowed to eat with them, or if she had to eat alone in her woman's quarters. I hoped she hadn't gotten into trouble because of us.

Mutani and the sheikh got into one car, with their gun bearers. The two men with automatic weapons got into the other, followed by two servants. The food and drink were stored in the second car. It looked like enough provisions to last several days. How many leopards were they planning on killing? More to the point, it reminded me that Wynn and I were setting off with only one bottle of water left. Food we could do without, but water was vital.

With luck there'd be bottled water in the car we were going to steal. When I run a safari, each tourist has a canvas pouch by his seat with his own bottle of spring water. I could only hope this safari was run the same way. If not, we'd deal with that problem when we came to it. First we had to get the car.

And there—the most important—luck was with us. They were only taking two cars. That left the rest for us to choose from. And the extra gunmen were going with the sheikh, as I had guessed, leaving only the one guard for us to deal with. For Wynn to deal with, really. All I had to do was slow him down for a second. Wynn was confident she could knock him out before he could make a sound. Did she still have the skills to do it? When it came to doing it for real, would she have the guts to do it? Would I?

The cars holding the sheikh, Mutani, and their retinue turned on their lights and set off into the night. A few remaining servants watched for a moment, then, feet dragging with fatigue, headed for their tents. The scene returned to an empty stage, but for the one guard. He lit a cigarette and watched the taillights zig and zag between thornbushes.

This is it, this is it, this is it. My pulse beat faster. I climbed out of the truck and quickly walked to the nearest Land Cruiser. The guard saw me and started over. I pulled open the door and peered inside. The key was in the ignition. Thank God, one less hair-raising thing we'd have to do. There was a mess of music tapes in a box that I pulled closer and pretended to be fiddling with, bent over and with my head down. I could hear the guard approaching. He called out something in Arabic. I acted as if I hadn't heard. Now he was next to the car. He spoke again in an impatient voice. He was so close I could smell him.

I straightened and turned, lifting my robe—that got his attention—and kicked him in the balls. As he grunted and doubled over, Wynn appeared behind him. He began to straighten and opened his mouth to shout. She reached forward, grabbed his chin in one hand and his hair in the other, and pulled his chin in sharply, twisting at the same time, as if she were turning a steering wheel hard over. Whatever he was about to say turned into a burble of pain, and he slipped to the ground. His gun was pinned under him.

He was down for only a second. He started to push himself up. Wynn swiftly crouched and snaked her arm around his neck in a choke hold, with his chin in the crook of her elbow and her knee pressing into his back. He clawed at her arm, twisted and bucked. Unfazed, Wynn raised her crooked elbow in a maneuver she'd shown me earlier, which locked her arms in an isometric grip that was impossible to break. She squeezed his neck between the hard edge of her forearm and her biceps, pressing with full force against the carotid arteries on each side of his neck. He tried to scream, but all that came out was a gasp as he struggled for breath. His legs kicked out in a disorganized way, almost like a seizure. I jumped back to avoid his flailing feet. They went still. He was out. Wynn kept her hold on his neck a few seconds longer, then straightened.

"We have twenty seconds before he regains consciousness," she said.

We worked like a drill team. I pulled the gun off his shoulder and trained it on him, while Wynn removed his head scarf and ripped it in pieces. His eyelids flickered, then flew open, but one sight of the firing end of the gun and he didn't put up any further struggle. Wynn flipped

151

him over onto his stomach, bound and gagged him. She hitched her hands under his armpits and dragged him to the back of the truck. One big heave and we lay him on the dirty metal floor. I got the folded tarp we'd hidden in, and we rolled him up in it like a cigar. He wouldn't be able to bend his legs to kick against the floor or walls and attract attention. Any sound he might succeed in making would be too muffled to hear from any distance. No one would think of looking in here for a long time, surely not before morning. They might even think the guard had taken off with the missing car.

We kept the semiautomatic. A minute later we were in our very own Land Cruiser, heading out of camp.

17

Far ahead, the beams of the Saudis' vehicles cut a cone shape out of the darkness. They were heading toward the stream and its band of forest, as we'd known they would, since it was the only good habitat for leopards. I kept my headlights off and followed. They weren't driving for speed, and we were. Little by little the gap between us shrank, until I got close enough for comfort. At that point I let up on the gas and we followed their twisting path through the scrub.

Driving through the bush at night at any speed is not for the fainthearted. All our primate instincts call out: the night is dangerous, go curl up in a cozy nest high in a tree, stay out of harm's way until dawn returns the world to us. A half-moon was rising. It shed a spectral glow over the wild scene. Bushes loomed in front of the car suddenly, while others crowded around, their hulking shadows pressing in on our sides.

The two cars ahead plunged into the denser underbrush that skirted the riverbed. They flushed a herd of zebra that came crashing toward us. I hit the brakes, and the herd split and flowed around us, close enough to touch. Their white stripes gleamed in the moonlight, and the black ones disappeared, making their stocky shape invisible. At night their stripes hide zebra from predators. By the time the last zebra had passed, the vehicles in front of us were gone. I sped forward, closer and closer to the forest, until we came upon the double ruts of a track that ran more or less parallel to the edge of the forest.

I paused. There were fresh tire prints heading to the right. Our way was south, to the left.

"I think we'd better turn right ourselves, for a few hundred feet or so," I told Wynn, "and then circle 'round and hit this trail farther down, so they won't see our fresh tracks branching off. This spot is so obvious."

"Good idea."

It might have been a good idea, except the Saudi vehicles had stopped a hundred feet ahead. I almost drove right up to them. There was a clearing on the bank, where the stream had carved a U-shaped bend. I came around the bend, and there they were, on the far side of the U, facing away from us, their headlights off. I quickly pulled back into the shadows.

The light of a high-powered spotlight, the kind that runs off a car's battery, was trained on a horizontal tree limb some forty feet off the ground. Dangling over the tree limb was not an impala, not a gazelle, the leopard's usual prey, but a large white goat with its throat slit. They were baiting a leopard. Some of the hotels did the same thing, to give their guests a chance to see this most elusive of the big cats, but the sheikh and William Mutani weren't here for a photo opportunity.

"Bastards," Wynn whispered.

The two men, one tall, one short, were standing with their upper torsos poking out of the roof hatch, rifles at the ready. The sheikh braced his elbows on the roof and trained his rifle on the goat. Then their spotlight went out.

I blinked, blinded by the increased darkness, as if someone had dropped a velvet bag over my face. I was flooded with rage and helplessness, my two least favorite emotions, especially in combination. How dare they! I had to stop the leopard from walking into their trap.

A scream of fear came from the other car; no, it was beyond them. The screams grew louder, multivoiced, anger and fear combined. Baboons. They must have a sleeping tree on the riverbank close by. They'd smelled a leopard. Nothing else would rouse them from sleep to scream like that. The leopard was nearby.

What could I do? Turn on my lights and rush the baited tree, after we'd gone to all this trouble to sneak off undetected? I didn't fancy getting my head shot off at close

154

ange. Was there a way to scare the leopard off without the hunters knowing?

"Wynn," I whispered. "We've got to stop them."

"You *are* crazier than me."

"I think I have a safe way to do it." I paused. "Comparatively safe. An acceptable risk."

"Just don't blow our chance of getting out of here."

I took that as acceptance.

Among the tapes I'd looked at when acting decoy for the armed guard, I thought I'd seen one I could use. I fumbled through the tangle of tapes in the box. Damn, where was the one I needed? It wasn't there! I forced myself to slow down and go through them one by one. I was wasting precious minutes.

"What are you looking for?" Wynn whispered.

"This." I held up the tape; animal sounds of Africa. It wasn't a good tape, but it was sold in most lodge tourist shops, and I owned the exact same recording. "A lion's roar."

"To scare the leopard."

"Yes. Are you willing to take the risk?"

"Yes. There's only one problem. We have no tape deck." She gestured at the dashboard.

"Oh, shit. Why the hell do they have this box of tapes, then?"

Wynn scanned the seats behind us, the space under her seat. I checked under mine. Nothing, and time was running out on us. Then I thought of the canvas pouches that hung over the back of the front seats, where tourists could store their binoculars, a bird guide, a water bottle. I scrabbled around in the pouch behind me. Bull's-eye. I pulled out a portable tape deck and slipped in the animal sound track.

The tape began with lions roaring. The only problem was that the announcer interrupted every ten or fifteen seconds to explain what you were listening to. I rewound to the beginning, turned the volume as low as possible and held it to my ear. A fruity English voice announced, "From the vast plains of East Africa come these wild animal voices, telling their own African tales." He had a few seconds of a lion's territorial roar, then of lionesses greeting pride members. There was a specific section I needed. "This is the sound the antelopes of the plains recognize as the pride moves in for the kill." I stopped the tape and turned the volume knob up full blast.

A tree hyrax near us emitted its insane asylum shriek, and I jumped. First, I had no idea how far full volume would carry, if it would sound close enough to scare away the leopard. Second, I'd have to cut off the tape with split-second timing. If I cut it off in the middle of a roar, and the men with guns in the other car were sharp, they might realize it was a tape—although that possibility would be so far from their minds, they probably wouldn't dream of it. But if I waited too long, I'd be projecting Mr. Tooty Fruity explaining the next sound, and that would certainly bring the high-intensity light—and the guns—trained on us.

Lastly, the tape only had thirty seconds of roaring. If I played it too soon, the leopard might not hear it. If I waited too long, the leopard might climb to the goat and the hunters would still have time to get off a shot.

I strained my eyes, trying to see the tree trunk. Was that a hint of movement? The leopard wouldn't make a sound. Its tawny body might be visible in the moonlight, but I needed to see it before the sheikh and Mutani, and they had the better vantage point. I kept my finger on the play button. Wynn put Comet in his pack onto the seat behind us, rolled down her window, and held the gun we'd taken from the guard at ready.

A francolin's call split the darkness, carrying like a siren. *Tee-dee-jee. Tee-dee-jee.* It exploded upward like a small bomb. For one brief second I saw it between the branches of the baited tree, silhouetted against the night sky. Francolins sleep on the ground. The leopard was approaching.

My finger punched the button. At the same moment, the leopard appeared. It leapt up the trunk effortlessly. The lion's roar began as a low rumble. The leopard was already halfway to the horizontal branch. I could imagine the Saudi framing the cat in his cross hairs. The lion broke into a series of wheezes. It sounded deafening to me, but was it loud enough? I could make out the leopard's head

156

in the big notch where the trunk met the baited branch. The tape wasn't working. The smell of goat was more convincing than my lion.

"Keep me covered." I slipped out of the car, walking with the tape held high, speaker toward the tree. The lion's roar changed to basso profundo grunts, getting shorter and faster. It was the sound of lions spurring themselves on to hunt. I trotted closer. The leopard gave a low growl of protest. Its head disappeared. There was a flash of movement near the base of the trunk. I imagined the heavy body hitting the ground and disappearing into the undergrowth. I wanted to cheer.

Without a break, the tape cut from the lion to the alarm call of crowned cranes. I immediately hit the stop button, but it was too late. There are no crowned cranes in this semidesert. If anyone in the other car knew their birds, they'd know something odd had just happened. I raced for the car.

Wynn had her gun out the window, ready to return fire. The only sound was of the sheikh yelling at his gun bearer. I slipped into reverse and backed away from the clearing, then turned around and circled south.

18

IT WAS SLOW going through the forest without lights or a road. The moon was well up and lay in motley patches on the ground, or it would have been impossible.

Wynn craned around for the third time to look through the rear windshield. "I don't think they're following us." She sat back in her seat. "I love you. I can't believe you got away with that crazy stunt."

"I can't believe you let me do it." We laughed, slaphappy.

"Watch out. Nothing can stop me now." I felt like singing. It was a crazy stunt, but it was a victory. A big victory for that leopard. Life against death. Life against extinction.

Echoing my thoughts, Wynn said, "At some point, you have to put yourself on the line and stop the slaughter." She gestured emphatically. "*No* more."

I drove past the point where I figured we'd entered the forest, went a bit farther, found the dirt track that paralleled the stream, and was finally able to get into third gear. I checked the rearview mirror. No lights, no sound of an engine. Obviously no one in the hunting party recognized a crested crane when they heard one, or knew enough about birds to realize something was off kilter.

I turned my thoughts to the journey ahead. "Just remembered. Check and see if there's water in the car. We have only one bottle left."

Wynn checked the back, checked the seat pouches. "Nothing."

"Shit." Once the sun was up, even a few hours in the desert would be dangerous without lots of water. I was especially worried about Comet. Sharing one bottle three ways was not going to be enough.

Wynn said, "There are more water bottles near the plane, plus some oranges, and our camping gear."

"All we have to do is find it again."

"I think we can do it."

"I guess we have to." Even if we had extra containers, which we didn't, stopping to get water from the stream would make us too vulnerable—to both animal and human predators. "Plane ho!"

"I know what compass line to follow," Wynn said. "All we have to do is find the right starting point, and we have some landmarks to approximate the spot."

"We do?"

"I pay attention to stuff like that."

Comet stirred and began to chirp. Wynn put him on her lap, wet the edge of her shirt and let him suck it. He kept at it a long time, and she had to replenish the water several times. She stroked his fluffy coat. "That's the fella. Drink up." She offered him the remainder of the francolin Kariankei had caught for him, but the cub wasn't interested. Like all the great cats, he was a binge eater, and he'd stuffed himself the first time around.

The narrow road lay in front of us like a ribbon of moonlight. A nocturnal aard-wolf, its mane erect, trotted down the path, forcing me into first gear until it decided it didn't like the smelly thing following it and angled into the scrub.

The track was all over the place, now nearer the stream, now farther. We came to a spot where the banks disappeared and we could see the dark stream rushing past.

"Great. This is where we met up with the boy," Wynn said.

"I think you're right." I flicked on the lights. Sure enough, the ground was peppered with signs of his goats.

We discussed it and decided we'd covered enough ground, with no hint of pursuit, to risk driving with the lights on. Not only could we pick up speed, but it would improve the chances of finding our route back to the plane. I continued on the dirt road another few thousand yards.

We came to a messy area where a big tree had fallen years ago. Its great silvery trunk lay in the dust like the column of an ancient temple.

"This is it." Wynn sat upright and peered intently through the windshield. "This is where we came in from the desert. Let's see if we can find our tracks."

I swung the car in small arcs, raking the ground with our headlights. Nothing. Wynn jumped out and walked along in front of the car. We moved to the right and to the left in ever widening circles. Nothing. I was about to suggest we give up, when she clapped her hands and gave a whoop of triumph. "I've found it! Here we are." She indicated the line of our footprints in the sand. I jumped out to look, too. There were a few nice crisp imprints, then nothing over a pebble-strewn patch, another few prints, then a mess of antelope and zebra hoofprints lay over ours.

"We're never going to be able to follow this from the car," I said.

"We don't have to. Now I can take a compass heading, and we'll be pointed at the plane. If we veer too much to the right, we'll hit that long spine of rock."

The worst part was crossing the lava field. The Land Cruiser can do it, but only at a crawl, and with a maddening amount of backtracking when you work yourself into an impassable spot. But eventually, well past midnight, we made it, nerves jangled and exhausted. The wrecked plane was a shadowy blob against the sand. Our things were strewn about, just as we'd left them.

With the feeling of relief came the realization that I was completely used up. We decided to set up Wynn's pup tent and catch a couple hours of sleep before moving on.

I don't know how long I slept. I woke up suddenly, not knowing where I was or what I was doing there. Comet was chirping, but there was another sound, loud and close. A sound that didn't belong. I lifted the window flap and peered into the desert. The moon had set, and the stars were a magnificent blaze, bright enough to reflect off the sand and keep the night from being pitch-dark. I didn't need the starlight to see what was making the noise. It was coming straight at the front of the tent.

The hairs stood on the back of my neck.

"Wynn." I scrambled out of my sleeping bag and started putting on my shoes. "Wynn, wake up." She turned heavily inside her sleeping bag. "Wynn!"

She bolted upright.

"There's a car coming."

"Shit." Wynn jumped out of her bag and hurriedly tied on her shoes. "Oh, shit." She scooped Comet up, zipped him into the day pack and got it on her back.

Adrenaline roared through my body, setting my heart to thumping, my palms to sweating. The sound of the engine was terrifyingly close. Suddenly it cut off.

"They've stopped at the plane," I whispered. "Let's get out the back of the tent."

Wynn stabbed her knife through the canvas and pulled downward. The sound of tearing canvas was excruciatingly loud. I wiggled through, and Wynn followed. We ran, crouching, straight back from the tent, using it for cover, heading for the thorn scrub and darkness. I heard a shout behind us, sounds of feet pounding on sand. I burst forward with a surge of strength and speed. The man behind us was falling back. I couldn't hear him anymore. Once among the thorn bushes, we had a good chance of escape.

A car engine gunned. Shit. Oh, shit. Headlights raked over me. Wynn was slightly ahead and to my left. The thorn trees danced crazily in the headlights. The car roared closer. It pulled ahead of Wynn, swung around so we were caught in the lights. The driver, a large Saudi in white robes, jumped out and grabbed Wynn.

Or rather, he *tried*. I raced toward them. The man rushed her, Wynn's leg jabbed forward, and he sprawled on the ground. He rolled and was up again. He crouched like a wrestler, eluded her feint, and then darted in and got hold of Wynn's arm, twisting it behind her back. She doubled over, and he went flying over her head, landing heavily. By then I reached the car. Its engine was running and the

161

door hung open. I jumped into the driver's seat. "Wynn, come on!"

"Watch out!"

The second man was behind me. I pressed down the clutch, but he already had the car door open, grabbed me around the neck and pulled me out of the car like a cork from a bottle. He was choking me. I clawed at his arm, trying to find the pressure point that Wynn had taught me, but I couldn't. I kicked backward, hitting air. He raised his other hand high. A curved sword glinted against the sky. The bastard was going to kill me. I squirmed desperately, but he was too strong. The sword flashed down, but at the same moment, he was hit in the back by a tremendous force. He fell against me, a horrible scream sounded next to my ear, and we crashed to the ground. The sword stabbed into sand. His scream turned into a grunt as all the air rushed out of his lungs. He didn't breathe in. He was crushing my face into the ground. I couldn't breathe, either.

I pushed up with all my strength and warm liquid gushed over me. I could smell blood, a hot, sweet smell that said I was alive. Thank God I was alive. Wynn helped tug him off my back as I squirmed free from his dead weight.

The other man rushed us. I scrambled to my feet. He must have scooped up the sword, because there it was in his fist, looking as big as a goddamn chain saw. He approached with loose knees, weight low, grinning confidently, as if he fought with swords every day of his life. Maybe he did. Wynn's knife against his sword. His was bigger than ours, and his arms longer. I clawed a handful of sand and threw it straight at his eyes. He saw it coming and quickly turned his head. Most of the sand fell short, and he kept right at us with a guttural laugh. Wynn and I moved away from each other.

"Come and get me, bitch," he taunted Wynn.

He went for her. I jumped forward.

Wynn screamed, "Duck!"

Something in her tone sent the order straight to my legs, bypassing my brain. I changed directions in mid-leap and hugged the sand. He lunged forward. Something bright whirled through the air, and he sank without a cry. Wynn's knife stuck straight out of his throat.

I got up, coated with blood and sand, noticing for the first time that my throat was burning where the other guy had choked me. I stared at the knife hilt in the big one's throat. Maybe I should have felt horrified at killing, but all I felt was a huge bubble of joy that I was alive. Alive.

That lasted less than a millisecond. The rattle of automatic fire came bursting at us from the direction of the plane, slamming into the Land Cruiser behind us. Wynn and I hit the ground. In my short visit to the driver's seat, I'd seen an automatic weapon leaning against the seat. I raised myself into a crouch and sprinted to get it. Bullets hit the windshield, and the ground in front of me was sprayed with glass. Staying as low as possible, I grabbed the gun.

"Wynn!" I tossed her the gun.

We ran behind the car as cover, and she began to return fire. A line of bullets slammed into the engine, and the air was filled with the stink of oil and burning metal. The engine had caught on fire. We moved to the back of the car. The tire I was hiding behind erupted like an exploded balloon.

Next to the wrecked plane, the headlights of our car blazed to life. Wynn stepped out from cover, stood, took careful aim and fired. The car turned tightly with a roar of the engine and angled toward us.

"Get out of the light," Wynn yelled. We both ran like hell away from the car, seeking cover among the thorn scrub in the dark. The headlights of our car raked over us, and I flattened myself into the sand. As soon as the funnel of light passed, Wynn braced herself on one knee, aimed and fired. There was the sound of shattering glass, and the car zagged wildly and stopped. I stayed put, while Wynn ran from cover to cover, approaching the car with full caution. When she got close, she stood and yelled. "All clear. This guy's dead, too."

I'd been sweating and my back was covered with blood. The desert night is cold. Even the stars looked frigid. I shivered and hugged myself, feeling numb and keyed up at the same time. Wynn dumped the slumped body at the steering wheel onto the sand and took his place. We drove the short distance back to camp. Part of me wanted to collapse, shut my eyes, block everything out, and the other part was hyper-alert, like I'd never sleep again. I looked around, knowing I'd be back to this spot in nightmares.

"Well, this answers the question about the sheikh killing to hide his illegal hunting," Wynn said.

"How the hell did they know where we were?"

"They probably fly over here on the way to the manyatta airstrip. Their pilot must have seen our downed plane and noted the coordinates."

"So they took a lucky guess and figured we'd return here."

"When these guys don't show up, they'll be back with reinforcements. We've got to get as far away as possible and find a good place to hide."

19

WE COULD TELL Comet had survived the fight, because he was chirping like crazy and clawing Wynn's back from inside the pack. As soon as we got back to the tent, she sat down in the sand and zipped the pack open. Comet's cries turned from scared to reproachful as he crawled out and cuddled into her lap. He put his head down, accepting her gentle stroking for the first time. It felt odd to care so much about Comet's survival when we'd just killed three men. Of course, Comet wasn't trying to kill us, and they were.

I cleaned myself off as well as I could, discovering that I'd picked up some glass when the other car's windshield was shot out; pulling out the splinters would have to wait until daybreak. It was hard to tell my blood from the Saudi's, but I concluded my cuts weren't bleeding much; I'd survive.

Wynn and I struck the tent and threw everything into the back of the car in one big mess.

"Hey, this isn't the Land Cruiser we came in," Wynn said.

We both turned and watched the burning hulk of the other car. Our car. The car into which we'd packed all the food and water we'd salvaged from the plane, like good little campers. We were left with one water bottle we'd had in the tent with us, and that was half empty.

I groaned. "We're back to square one!"

We should have kept going instead of returning to the goddamn plane wreck. We should never have stopped to catch some sleep. Neither one of us said it out loud. It was too depressing.

Wynn kept Comet on her lap. I took the wheel. "It sounds hokey, but thank you for saving my life."

Wynn waved an arm. "Anytime, sweetie."

"I can't believe I dragged you up here into this disaster."

"Hey, you didn't drag me into anything. We have an idea why Nick was killed and we're going to get out okay. By the time they send more people, we'll be far, far away."

I had to keep my eyes straight ahead, focused on weaving in and around bushes without losing our south-by-southwest heading. Wynn checked periodically with the compass. Now and then our headlights were reflected in the eyes of animals, predators and prey. The lowest were spring hares, bat-eared foxes, jackals, and dik-dik antelope, also gazelle resting on the ground, and the big round eyes of hyena. Higher up were the eyes of oryx and zebra—a whole bunch of little fluorescent circles as the entire herd swung their heads around to face us—higher still, like low-lying stars, were giraffe eyes. Disembodied eyes of the night.

Normally I would have considered it a great nocturnal game run, but somehow being targeted as prey myself took a lot of the pleasure out of it. My mind kept replaying the fight, especially the moment when that sword shone in the moonlight above me and I'd believed in my own death. A spring hare darted in front of the lights and froze. I swerved to avoid him, and crashed through thorn branches that noisily raked the side of the car.

"They thought we'd be as easy to kill as a rabbit," Wynn said.

"We are really going to nail him. Between the pictures I got and this attack on us—I can see the headlines now."

"I wonder how deep Mutani is into this whole thing."

"He might not know about it. He probably wasn't up here when Nick came."

"Or he might be the mastermind, not the sheikh."

I darted a glance at Wynn. "Hold on a sec." I downshifted and edged the Land Cruiser slowly into a gully that ran across our path. The car tipped at a forty-five-degree angle. My heart was in my throat, waiting for the car to tip over on its side, but the low center of gravity saved us. I inched forward and up the other side of the gully. The Land Cruiser groaned and lurched over the rough ground, but kept going.

Wynn picked up where she'd left off. "Think about who has the most to lose when we expose this hunting party."

"I see what you mean. The poor sheikh will go home without his trophies. Big deal. Mutani, on the other hand, could be ruined."

"His hotel empire is a house of cards."

"If his backers pull out, if he loses his credit, if someone decides to call in an overdue loan, the whole thing could collapse."

Wynn was silent for a moment. "But Mutani couldn't have sent out these three thugs without the sheikh's permission. They wouldn't have gone."

"For a big enough bribe?"

"No, I don't see it. They'd be too scared of the sheikh. They don't belch without his permission."

"Too bad they weren't more scared of us." I gave a dry laugh, and we lapsed into a long, exhausted silence. I had another worry, which I didn't mention to Wynn. We still had the princess's diamond bracelet. It was proof that we'd been in their camp, as if the photos wouldn't be enough. But they could use it to undermine our story, claim that we were thieves, that their men had been sent merely to recover the jewels, and that we'd murdered them in cold blood. In the hands of a top-notch lawyer, it would be a strong argument. It was a chilling thought. All we had to link the sheikh to Nick's murder was conjecture. I could see us ending up in jail and the sheikh going scot-free. I told myself I was tired and shaken up, and not to entertain morbid fantasies.

After a couple of hours we got out of the car to stretch our legs and take turns driving. The stars seemed immensely far away, cold, impersonal, and beautiful. Being reminded of infinity was oddly comforting: our lives and deaths counted for little in the cosmic order. Even the life and death of our planet was merely a speck in time.

A movement in the headlights caught my attention as I

167

went to get in the passenger side. Something tiny was scurrying across the sand. Something the size of my finger and shaped like a crayfish, with a pointed tail curled above its back. A cold finger of fear went up my back. The scorpion scuttled out of the light.

The farther we got from the plane wreck, the more our spirits revived. Wynn started singing a folk song about captivity and freedom, which I half remembered from a Joan Baez album I loved, back in the late sixties. I taught her "Hallelujah, I'm a Bum." From there it was straight downhill to summer camp songs, but at least it kept us awake. When we got tired of singing, we talked about family outings growing up, then about family relationships. Comet was a warm furry circle on my lap, his sides heaving up and down rhythmically with each breath.

Wynn started to talk about Nick. I said "umhum" every now and then to let her know I was listening, and let her talk herself out. She told me the story of finding Gin and Tonic as tiny cubs, next to the dead body of their mother. It was Nick who had the idea of raising and returning them to the wild. It was the most wonderful experience either of them had ever had, and sharing it brought them such joy. She reached over to stroke Comet, and I realized why it had been so important to save him. The older cubs would be off on their own in another six months. Raising Comet would be a way to hold onto Nick, still carrying out their joint dream of saving cheetah.

Wynn asked what my plans were.

"Striker is leaving Kenya."

"Oh, no! You're kidding. Why didn't you tell me?"

"He's asked me to marry him."

"Jazz! Does that mean you're leaving, too?"

"No, it means everything's a mess."

"Oh, God," Wynn groaned sympathetically.

I sighed. "I'd just screwed up my courage to suggest we should try living together. It was a big step for me. After my divorce, I swore I'd never depend on a man again, not ever."

"It was a bad one, huh?"

"We'd been married ten years. Happily, I thought. My

168

husband thought it would be fun to screw one of his pretty grad students. She got pregnant. He walked out on me."

"Ouch."

"Yeah. It really makes you question your judgment. I didn't know a thing was going on."

"What a shit," Wynn said with feeling. "Why are men such bastards?"

"Yeah." I felt a twinge of the old familiar pain. "But good things come out of bad things. I would still be living the staid life of an art historian. God, that seems like another universe."

"You came out here after you split up?"

"I *ran*. I ran for my life. If I'd stayed in the States, I'd have ended up one of those lonely, bitter women who despise all men and can't tell a good one from a bad one." I paused. "Maybe I still can't."

"You mean Striker?"

"We still have a lot of walls between us. It's easy to love someone as a boyfriend—sex is great, we're best friends, we have wonderful times on safari. But we also fight a lot. I have trouble asking for anything, and he has trouble giving. It's not a good recipe for a marriage. We have a lot to work out first, and he knows it, as well as I do."

"Then why . . . ?"

"He's furious about Mutani building that casino near his house, and he's decided in a huff that all of Kenya is ruined and that he's leaving. Asking me to marry him is a bribe to get me to go with him. He's lived here his whole adult life, and he's scared to set off alone."

"That's lousy. It's an ultimatum, not a proposal."

"Exactly."

"So who needs him?"

I felt so sad. "But I'm not ready to say goodbye to him, either."

"You're sure he'll go without you?"

"Yes." My voice sounded bleak.

"Have you tried to convince him to stay?"

I stroked Comet's soft fur with one finger. "You know what, Wynn? The thought didn't even cross my mind.

That's what I mean when I say I'm not good at asking for things."

"Don't give up without trying your best, or you'll end up blaming yourself, or always wondering. What have you got to lose?"

"Nothing. It's not pride that stops me—I don't think of asking."

"Do you want to marry again?"

"Sure. Someday. Marriage is the greatest thing going, when it's good. But I'm in no hurry to make another mistake."

"It's not your fault when someone changes and stabs you in the back." Wynn was quiet for a while. "Nick was the last man for me. I thought we were going to spend our whole lives together, working with cheetah. And look what happened." Her voice sounded as bleak as the desert around us.

"He was a wonderful person." I reached out and squeezed her hand.

The sky was still black and star-spangled an hour before dawn, when the car died. Not stalled, died. No response, nada, nothing, dead. I craned over to look at the green glow of the instrument panel, and stared at the gas gauge needle in disbelief. "We're out of gas."

We sat there cursing and saying we couldn't believe it for as long as possible, and then we had to face the facts. We were stranded, with no food, too little water, no hope of being rescued, and some danger of being killed if we stayed with the car. We were in big trouble.

I put Comet into his pack, along with the half-full water bottle, and hopped out of the car. "Let's go."

Wynn checked that she had the compass, and put her knife in her belt. I rummaged among the stuff we'd thrown in the back, looking for anything useful but light. "Hey, I've found half a roll of Life Savers. You think they'll do the trick?"

"Don't mock. We're going to be very happy to have those by midday."

I stuck a towel in the pack; we could tie it onto a thorn-bush for a patch of shade at midday. A refuge from the

170

sun, however small, might spell the difference between life and death.

Wynn pulled out a folding shovel. "We can dig for roots to get moisture," she explained.

"And hope they're not poisonous."

"Nick made a hobby of Samburu plant lore. I wish I'd paid more attention, now. I think I can recognize one or two that are edible, if we come across them." She picked up the automatic rifle.

I shouldered the pack. "Ready? Let's see how much ground we can cover before daybreak."

Wynn gave me a quick hug around the shoulders. "This will be a good story to tell our grandchildren."

We set off into the dark without a backward glance.

"I figure we'll be able to walk till ten before it gets too hot, then we'll lie up till around four, and walk through the night," Wynn said. "That should bring us pretty close to home."

As long as a lion or hyena didn't find us first. Dark was the time of the hunters, not for a couple of hairless apes to be wandering around far from home. It was hard to keep on a straight course, especially as we were constantly deflected by thornbushes, blobs of darker blackness that would jab you in the face if you weren't alert. A stiff three-inch thorn stabbed me in the cheek, drawing blood.

We set a fast pace for ourselves. Once it got hot, how long could a person survive without water or shelter in the desert? Wynn probably knew, but I decided not to ask her. I wasn't sure I wanted to know the answer. We went through all our marching songs several times, then started a Beatles retrospective. It *was* a hard day's night.

My legs grew heavier by the second, then my head started to get heavier, too. I sang louder. My back was the next to go. My eyes felt like sand was inside them, and my mouth tasted like a locker room armpit. We marched on. My feet started in. I stopped to empty sand out of my socks, but ten steps later they were full again. Our singing became forced, then petered out.

The sky grew pearly gray in the east, then a wash of flamingo-pink slowly spread from the horizon to the ze-

nith. My heart sank. The familiar silhouette of Mount Ol
Kanjo was an ethereal blue shape far to the south. We had
to go right past it before we'd start to see the hills of
home. We had a long, long walk ahead of us.

The sun crept above the horizon. It threw skinny shadows to our right. Wynn put away the compass.

By ten the heat had the force of gravity, pressing down
on my back and shoulders until I bent from the weight. I
stumbled over a pebble on unwieldy legs too heavy to
move. My mouth was so dry my tongue stuck to my gums,
and talk became impossible. I thought of the Somali refugee women, east of here, trekking like this day after day
with their children, watching them grow thinner and thinner, until they were too weak to walk.

When it got so hot I felt my brain shriveling up inside
my skull, we draped the towel over a thorn branch and lay
down next to each other in the tiny patch of shade. We
took Comet out of his pack. I would have cried, except my
eyes were too dry for tears. He was so limp I thought for
a moment he was dead, but then his eyes fluttered partway
open. He looked at us helplessly, and opened his little
mouth in a mute appeal. Please don't let him die, I prayed.

"We have to bring his body temperature down," Wynn
said.

"Any ideas?"

"If we were home, I'd wrap him in wet towels and pack
him in ice."

I blinked at the sun-blinding sand around us. "Not too
much ice here."

Wynn picked up the water bottle and looked at me ques-
tioningly.

"Don't we need that to drink?"

"He's not going to make it."

My entire body was thirsty. For Comet it might be the
difference between life and death. For us, the few mouth-
fuls wouldn't save us, if it got to that point. "Let's leave
ourselves a couple of swallows and give him the rest."

There was too little water left to waste any by soaking
a cloth for him to suck. I held his mouth open while Wynn
dripped the precious liquid in. Then she soaked down his

head. A quarter bottle was left. Not grabbing the bottle and glugging it all down myself took more willpower than anything I'd ever done in my life.

Wynn picked up her shovel and wandered off. She returned with a root that looked like a turnip. We cut it in half and chewed it raw. It was hot from the warm sand, but we didn't complain. It was as welcome as a watermelon. She found a second one and we saved it for later.

Mercifully, even my thirst couldn't keep me awake, and I passed into a stuporous sleep. When I awoke, the sun had moved, but if anything it was hotter. My hair felt as if it would burst into flames at any moment.

We dragged our protesting bodies south, ever south. My mind held only one thought: step, step, step. Raising each leg took an act of will. Step, step, step.

Then it changed to Who, who, who? The sheikh or William Mutani or both? When Kaji and I bumped into Mutani with Gerry Weller, was he dropping by to find out if the murder was successful? Or was his desire to meet Nick and Wynn genuine, connected to the oil survey near their property? Did he want to buy their land? If so, did his presence nearby actually indicate ignorance of the murder?

I worked my tongue against my mouth, trying to get enough saliva to talk. I wanted to ask Wynn if they'd gotten any offers on their land recently. All I could get out was an incoherent sound like rubbing sandpaper together. I filed the question away to ask her later; it wasn't as though I could do anything with the information right now.

We sat down in the almost nonexistent shade of a leafless thorn tree, draped the towel over the branch above us to create an awning, and gave Comet some more water. He was still breathing, but didn't have the strength to open his eyes anymore. The remains of the francolin had started to stink, and Wynn threw it away. There was no chance Comet would be eating it now. My heart shriveled with grief and regret. We sat in silence, gnawing on our second turnip, when we heard the sound of a plane. It was coming from the south.

Wynn and I looked at each other.

"It could be them," I said. My lips were so dry, they cracked as I spoke. Them, the men who would kill us if they could. "They could have circled 'round searching for us."

Wynn reached up and pulled the white towel down; it would stand out clearly against the uniform tawny sand. "Or it could be someone out looking for us. Kaji might have raised the alarm when we didn't come home."

"To hide or not to hide." I stared at the dirty white towel as if it held the answer.

"As long as we find some more roots, I think we'll be okay."

"Maybe, and maybe not. If this isn't the sheikh's plane, we'd be jerks to hide." The plane was now visible, heading from southeast to northwest. I imagined raising a water bottle to my lips, sweet liquid pouring into my mouth, life-giving water. "Let's try it both ways. I'll signal them with the towel. If they land, you keep out of sight and cover me with the gun until we see who they are."

Wynn agreed, and I leaped up, flapping the towel at the sky. I ran to the top of a rocky outcrop. Wynn slashed some thorn branches, leaned them against the rocks and crawled into the tunnel she'd formed. In her dust-covered khaki clothes, she was completely invisible.

I stood tall and held the towel up to the wind, which supported it like a flying carpet. Would the plane see it? Would it veer this way? Would it be a benign person, able to radio our position to rescuers, or even able to land themselves? The sun hit the sand and the towel and reflected into my face. I squinted my eyes and followed the plane. Was it changing course, heading this way?

The sound grew louder, but the plane held a steady course a half mile to the east of us. Then the engine's roar grew fainter. It had passed. They hadn't seen us. My eyes were too gritty for tears. My skin felt incandescent.

We trudged on. I no longer had the energy for singing, talking, or even thinking. Consciousness was reduced to each second, surviving moment by moment. I was an ant, and each grain of sand a mountain to cross.

I didn't even notice the sound of the returning plane. Wynn stopped and pointed. "Let's try again," she urged.

I pulled out the towel and went through the rigmarole of flapping it in the breeze, but my hope had dried up. I was going through the motions like an automaton, without even bothering to look up. Wynn distanced herself from me, and hid at the base of a shrubby thorn, slashing and piling branches around herself, her gun at her side.

The drone grew louder. The plane was close enough to see. I'm stupid about planes, but this one looked very familiar. Was I hallucinating?

The plane dived toward us, raising its nose at the last moment and flying past me only a few dozen feet off the ground. Striker grinned at me from the pilot's window.

"Striker!" My yell came out as a croak. Wynn came running. We jumped up and down, waving like madwomen.

The plane banked and turned. Someone was sitting next to him. It was Kaji! She must have called him when we didn't show up. Striker waggled his wings and climbed higher, described a greater circle around us, clearly looking for a place to land. Relief washed over me like a waterfall.

He had some trouble finding a clear enough spot, and finally came down a mile away, easily visible across the vast expanse of scrub and sand. Wynn and I broke into a shambling trot. We were as good as home. We'd made it. We'd stared death in the face, and death had blinked.

20

AS SOON AS we landed, we headed for the kitchen. I followed Wynn's example, sticking my head under the pump to quickly bring down my overheated body temperature, then downing salt pills. We'd already drunk in the plane, of course, tepid water, and only allowing ourselves to sip slowly. Now I savored a glass of cool spring water, ambrosia of the gods. Striker made us some broth and we ate a little piece of bread. I could feel my energy reviving almost cell by cell.

Kaji had immediately set to work reviving Comet. She'd wet him down also, and with wet fur he looked pitifully shrunk to half size. She wrapped ice cubes in a towel and lay him on the icy bed. He still didn't stir. She wet a cloth and gently washed off the gummy mucus on his eyelids.

Meanwhile, Wynn mixed a simple home formula of water, salt, and sugar that they'd used for Gin and Tonic when they were found semistarved and dehydrated, not much older than Comet, and dripped it onto his tongue with an eye dropper.

I leaned against Striker's chest and he put his arms around me. None of us could talk until we knew if Comet would revive. We watched Wynn patiently drip the liquid onto his rough tongue. The color improved, from a frightening dry white to a shell pink. Eyes still closed, his paws began to rhythmically stretch and contract, as if kneading his mother's belly.

His eyes fluttered open and he struggled to free his mouth from Wynn's big index finger. She pulled back and let him look around. He chirped, and we let out a cheer. We'd all gotten through alive.

Wynn and I took turns at the shower. My face stared back at me in the mirror, dark tan, weather-beaten, and kind of wild about the eyes. Also filthy. I stood for ages under the running water, as if I could absorb it through my pores. My cuts stung, but I found only one splinter of glass embedded in my chest, and I was able to tease it out.

Striker was in the guest room, waiting for me. We lay down on the bed in each other's arms and I talked myself out, telling him all that had happened from the moment of smelling av-gas in the plane. It felt like a lifetime ago. I don't even know if I finished the story before falling asleep on his shoulder. When I awoke, Striker was sitting in an oat-colored easy chair watching me. He immediately returned to my side.

We made love slowly, floating on a sea of mixed languor and excitement, ripples of love and tenderness moving through our bodies until everything was all mixed up and exploded like waves crashing high into the air.

Instead of peace, the release brought a flood of anguish. We had such deep feelings for each other. Okay, I'd call it by its name. Love. We loved each other. Maybe not true love, maybe not lifelong love—I didn't know yet—but still, a lot of love. The thought of Striker walking out of my life wounded my heart. The thought of leaving Kenya was like leaving my soul behind. Why was he forcing me to choose? I thought of Omondi's and Wynn's advice. Was I going to let this happen? I spoke quickly before I lost my courage.

"Striker, don't go."

"I'm not going anywhere." He stroked the curve of my back.

"Don't leave Kenya."

"I want you to come with me." He gave me a sweet kiss. "Be my bride."

I nestled into his neck, breathing in his spicy masculine smell.

He leaned over and kissed my hair. "So?"

I felt his chest rising and falling under my cheek. "We're not ready to get married."

177

"Why not? We love each other, we love the same things. We'd have a great life together."

I sighed. "Love comes in different shapes and sizes. Maybe ours will grow to marriage size, but it's not there yet."

"You make it sound like a pig you're fattening for market."

I suppressed a retort about his sarcasm and took his hand. "You of all people should understand about not being ready to make a lifelong commitment to someone. What kept you a bachelor all these years? It wasn't that you never fell in love."

"Not like with you."

I kissed the warm, sculpted back of his hand, his tiny hairs silky against my lips. "Thank you, sweetheart. That's why I want to live together. Let's give it a try before you make a decision about leaving."

Striker shook his head. "At our age, we don't need to give it a try. I'm ready to get married. And I have to leave. Why keep things tentative when they're not?"

I could feel his muscles tensing, and I pulled back. "Because I'm in a different place in my life than you are. I've just gotten over one marriage, and I'm focused on making a life for myself, building a business—"

"A pretend business that isn't even paying your rent."

"It's not a pretend business! It's a new one, and it takes time and effort to build up. I've wanted to run a safari company my whole life. I'm making a dream come true. Okay, it's not in the black yet, but—"

"You'd choose that over us?"

"Striker, we have a great side and a not so great side. We fight an awful lot. There's so much we haven't worked out yet. Like how to make important decisions, for example."

"We make each other happy." He tried to put his arm around me, but I pulled back.

"Leaving Kenya doesn't make me happy."

"Don't get that mixed up with whether we get married."

I sat up. "Wait a second. It's *you* who's getting the two mixed up."

178

"I am not."

"Would you be asking me to marry you if you weren't leaving?" He didn't answer. "Honest: If for some reason you decided to stay, would you still want to get married?"

He said, "No-o," reluctantly, and hurried on, "but that doesn't mean anything."

"It means you want a traveling companion, and you know I wouldn't go with you otherwise."

"That's a rotten thing to say."

"Well, I think it's a rotten reason to propose marriage."

"Listen, you little shithead." Striker made a visible effort to regain his cool. "You're right, that's why I thought of marriage. But you're twisting it to make it all negative. It's not like that. It was the thought of leaving you that made me realize how much I love you. And feel loved. We belong together. Where doesn't matter."

"So let's stay here. And put off marrying until—"

"Dammit, that's not what I mean. Stop trying to create an argument. I want you to marry me because I want to spend my life with you. I think we can make each other happy."

"Then don't leave me."

"I'm not leaving you, I'm leaving Kenya! Can't you get that through your head? Kenya is over for me. Dead. It would be like living with a corpse."

"Well, that pretty much closes the discussion, doesn't it?"

"This isn't a fucking debate, it's a marriage proposal! Come on, Jazz, stop being so obstinate. Can't you give a little?"

"A little? If you love me so much, don't you care that leaving Kenya now is wrong for me? You want me to give up my business, my dreams, my life here—which isn't dead, but growing and thriving—"

"We'll make new dreams together."

"On your terms."

"On *our* terms."

"You're not listening. Leaving Kenya is your terms. You can't hide that with word games."

179

"They're not word games."

"Striker, this is stupid. We're not listening to each other, we're going around in circles, convincing ourselves how right we are."

"Because you keep harping on Kenya."

"Harping?" I lost it. I could feel my temper rising like a ball of magma surging from the depths. My face grew hot. "If that's how you regard what's important to me, why the hell would I want to marry you?"

Striker's face closed. "Sorry. I guess I was under the mistaken impression that you loved me, too."

I made a herculean effort and pushed my anger down. "Yes, I do. But what's the big rush? We've been together less than a year."

We lapsed into a miserable silence. Striker leaned against the headboard with his arms folded across his chest. His face was in a deep frown. "Jazz, please understand," he pleaded. "I'm not being selfish and wanting everything my way. Don't turn this into a power struggle."

"I'm not. I'm asking you not to leave me."

"I don't want to! That's why I'm asking you to come with me."

"And if I don't, you'll leave without me."

"You think I'm proposing marriage out of convenience, don't you? So I'll have someone to help me pack and unpack? 'Cause I'm scared to go off and try something new on my own? What kind of a shit do you think I am?"

"You said yourself you wouldn't want to get married if we stay here."

"But I'm not staying, so what does that matter?"

"It would matter if you cared about my life—our life together—as much as your own! Couldn't you put off the decision to leave for a while? Give us more of a chance!"

"You turn everything into a battle of wills. And you've always got to win."

"That's unfair!" I wanted to hurl the accusation back at him, but I restrained myself. "That's completely untrue!"

"We have the whole fucking world to choose from, and the only place you want is the one place I can't stay."

Striker got out of bed and started angrily putting on his clothes.

I watched him, propped up on one elbow, my heart sinking. "Where are you going?"

"You know how crazy I am about you. I've never asked anyone to marry me before, and there were a lot of women who wanted to, believe me." Striker's hazel eyes blazed and his mouth was an angry line. "What is there to say? You've made up your mind. You have these rigid ideas of how things are supposed to be. Life isn't that neat. People get married all the time because one of them has to move." He buckled his pants. "It's you who's walking out on us because you'd rather daydream about your damned safari company that only exists in your mind. Grow up!"

I jumped out of bed. "Walk out? Who's doing the walking out? You've made up your mind you're going, and then as an afterthought you try to bribe me to come with you with a marriage proposal. That's bullshit! I'm going to marry someone who knows how to treat me as an equal, not like a portable convenience!"

"A portable convenience!" Striker pushed his face in front of mine. "You are an unbelievable idiot. Fuck you." He slammed on his hat, yanked open the door, and was gone. I threw the pillow across the room, fell on the bed and cried.

When I emerged a short while later, Wynn's bedroom door was still closed. I hoped she hadn't heard us. I drank about a quart of water and ate another hunk of bread, then looked all over for Striker, hoping we could put the fight behind us and really talk. He wasn't in the house, or out on the porch, or at the cheetah barn.

I walked over to check out the airstrip: his plane was gone. I remembered an engine's roar that I'd half heard when I was crying, but it hadn't registered as a takeoff. I couldn't believe he'd leave like that. I picked up a rock and hurled it as far as I could.

I went back in the house, struggled to put Striker out of my mind, and radioed Omondi at police headquarters. The film I'd taken in the camp was a burning coal in my

181

pocket that I wanted to get to him right away. I explained the events of our trip north as tersely as I could.

"My dear Jazz! You are perfectly all right?"

"Yes."

"And Wynn?"

"We're fine."

"Do you have a gun in the house?"

"We do now, an M-16 we got from the Saudis. Do you think they'd come after us here?"

"I don't make guesses about things like that, I make sure you're safe. If this was official, I could send Sergeant Kakombe to guard you."

"Won't it become official now? There are three dead men in the desert."

"Yes, but it will not be under my jurisdiction, not unless the local authorities ask Nairobi for assistance. I do not think they will. No, it is highly unlikely. There are many bodies in the desert these days. At most, they will take a glance, assume the work of Somali bandits, and close the case."

"But when they see they're Saudis? There aren't many dead Saudis showing up in Kenya."

"Even if they make the connection, they won't want to bother Sheikh Farid with questions. If anything, there will be a formal apology for the loss of his men."

"After we tell them we were attacked? I was thinking this would open up the whole can of worms in a way that can't be contained."

"No, it won't happen like that, I assure you."

"You mean the police will ignore the attack on us, and that we killed three men?"

"Jazz, calm yourself. You know as well as I do how the system works. There's no protection here if you go against the people with power. We need to do a lot of work first: the evidence must be overwhelming or it will be quietly squelched."

"Aren't dead bodies evidence?"

"Of course. You and I must return north. We will stop at the scene of the attack, take photos, and gather evidence.

182

Then you can show me the slaughtered animals you found and we will find out from the Samburu exactly what hunting was going on when Nick was there, and what he saw. I'm sure they know. And that is only the beginning."

The thought of going back into the desert was as attractive as shaking hands with a scorpion, but Omondi was right. "I have pictures," I told him, "a roll of film of the hunting trophies in the sheikh's camp."

"Excellent. I will have that developed at the police lab."

"I also have a diamond bracelet that the princess put around the cub's neck as a collar. I want to hand that over to you so we can't be accused of theft."

"There aren't going to be official accusations, but I'll put it in safekeeping. By the way, has Wynn hired you?"

"No, I'm doing this for myself, and for Nick."

"Still, since I am unofficial, and you are going to be the chief investigator, I think it is better if you have a professional role. Have Wynn pay you ten shillings. Now, as to my coming north. If I get a flight to Isiolo this afternoon, can Striker fly over to pick me up?"

"Striker's not here."

"I thought you said he rescued you and Wynn by plane."

"Yes, but"—I gave an embarrassed laugh—"we had a fight. He left in a huff."

"He flew off and left?"

"Yes. He may be back; I don't know."

Omondi fell uncharacteristically silent. When he spoke, his voice was icy with anger. "I will get up there as fast as I can. Please, be cautious."

"Hey, we don't need Striker to be safe."

"Act as if you might be attacked again at any minute. I'm serious. Don't think the sheikh will be frightened off because you defended yourselves the first time."

I was about to argue that he didn't need to come until the next day, realized I would feel safer with him here, and instead simply thanked him. I signed off in a whirl of confusion. What would I do if Striker and Omondi were both here? Striker didn't know I'd ever slept with Omondi, and Omondi insisted it wasn't in his nature to be jealous—after

183

all, it was he who encouraged me to get involved with Striker—but I'd feel awkward. I found myself wanting Omondi to think well of Striker; I wasn't sure he would.

Kaji was outside kicking a soccer ball around with Gin and Tonic. She was dressed in her usual modest outfit of slouchy olive sweater and chinos. When the cheetahs saw me, they abandoned the game and came racing over to rub against my legs. Gin jumped up with her paws on my shoulders and peered into my face with her mysterious yellow eyes. Could she tell what I'd been through? I wondered. Was there a lingering smell of my face-off with death? Or had she heard my fight with Striker? I rubbed my face against hers and she dropped to all fours.

Kaji watched, unsmiling. I'd never seen her look so somber.

"Is there something wrong?"

"I called Margot Willard at the Nairobi Zoo, to get some advice on building back Comet's health. She said our formula was pretty good, but to add extra thiamine and copper, and to keep up the antibiotics. Bad news about Gin and Tonic, though."

"Oh, no. What?" Had we screwed up their health in some way? Horrid possibilities flickered through my mind. Cheetahs raised in captivity often develop bone problems due to mineral deficiencies. People think raising wild animals is like feeding your pet dog. It's not. We know so little about how to approximate their requirements.

"She'd been talking with the new cheetah expert at the National Zoo in Washington, D.C. You know, the guy who's gotten two pairs to breed?"

"Yeah."

"He says handling them after weaning is a no-no."

"Handling them?" The words made no sense.

Gin ran up to Kaji, batting the ball back and forth between her two front paws, inviting Kaji to play. Kaji sent it sailing into the air in a long arc. Gin took off after it, all four legs extended as she flew over the ground, a long line of liquid grace and speed.

"We're not supposed to touch them."

Not to be able to pet and cuddle Gin and Tonic? Not to *touch* them?

Kaji continued, "We're not supposed to get closer than fifteen feet." Her usual smile lines were deep furrows around her mouth.

"We knew we'd have to let them go sometime—but never pet them again! Why?"

"He says the males have to develop aggressive territorial behaviors to trigger courtship and mating. He thinks male competition may even be necessary to stimulate the female to go into estrus. Keep them cuddly, it's like keeping your son a mama's boy: he won't have a normal adolescence and learn to chase girls. Or a daddy's girl: Gin will be more interested in humans than a cheetah mate. Margot, from the zoo, said she'd discussed this with Nick a couple of months ago. She sounded annoyed he never mentioned it to us."

"He didn't say anything about it?"

"No. He probably knew Wynn would hate it, and he didn't like to upset her."

"Have you told her yet?"

"No, I called while you were all sleeping."

"It's going to be even harder on her now."

"I know." Kaji looked glum. "After losing Nick, to not be able to hug or pet Gin and Tonic, and the new cub . . ." Her voice trailed off. "We're supposed to get a long staff, and push them away when they try to approach us."

"Push them away?" I groaned.

Kaji nodded. "Fifteen feet."

"I can't stand it."

The cheetahs lost interest in the ball and ambled over to plop down near us. Tonic lay down first, and then Gin lay half on top of him, starting a biting and swatting match. She slipped off, lay with her belly against the length of his back, the way I like to lie with Striker, and switched to licking the back of his ears. He accepted happily, panting slightly with his mouth half open and his eyes half closed.

"Do you have the willpower to stop touching them?" I asked Kaji.

"To enable these guys to live a normal life? To set them free? To keep cheetahs from extinction?" Kaji gazed at the two cheetahs. Gin had rolled over on her back, all four feet dangling in the air, twisting and knocking against her brother. "There isn't anything I wouldn't do."

"Has Wynn talked to you about her plans?"

"No, but I don't see her leaving until these guys are free. And now we have Comet, too."

Tonic jumped up, pounced on Gin and bit her in the neck, then sped off, his sister in hot pursuit. They raced in parallel, their legs crisscrossing under them and then extended full out in a beautiful geometry of motion.

Kaji looked toward the house. "Listen, don't tell Wynn about not touching Gin and Tonic, at least for a couple of weeks. A few weeks won't make a difference."

Gin jumped half onto her brother's back, holding him around the ribs as he tried to keep running. They both landed in a flailing heap of long legs and switching tails, biting and kicking, until they struggled to their feet and the race continued, this time with Gin out in front.

I agreed it would be cruel to tell Wynn now, when she needed their love and comfort, and went back to the house. Wynn was awake, sorting through a mail bag of condolence letters that Kaji had picked up in our absence. I told her Omondi was coming and about my fight with Striker. She listened sympathetically, reminding me that if this relationship was right, we'd work this problem out, as we had others. It was the same kind of woman talk I'd given Kaji last week, but it actually did make me feel better.

I volunteered to help her with the letters, which she accepted gratefully. She wanted to read them, but not yet. Receiving sympathy was too painful at the moment. I set up a writing table under a tree, from where I could look north to the purple cone of a not-so-ancient volcano jutting up on the horizon. About a quarter of a mile away the black and white feathers of a male ostrich stood out clearly against the drab sand. Off to his right there was a small herd of the endangered Grevy's zebra, though what food they were finding was a mystery to me.

I piled the stack of Wynn's mail on one side of the table, wastebasket at my elbow, and proceeded to rip through the pile of condolence letters in record time. I copied the return address onto a fresh envelope, signed Wynn's name to a thank-you card, and piled those on my left, ready to be stamped. I threw the condolence cards into a flat basket. Nick had a lot of friends and well-wishers who would miss him.

I copied the address of the Office of Conservation and Rural Development onto an envelope and opened the official letter, assuming it was a condolence note from Wynn's boss, Matthew Njagi, the man in charge of reforestry in the Kenyan government. It started out offering condolences on Nick's untimely death, went on to detail how much Wynn had contributed to Kenyan prosperity. Had contributed? It was starting to sound as if Wynn was dead, too.

The last paragraph explained: a sudden financial crisis in the Ministry of Development necessitated a severe cutback in all but essential programs. Since Wynn's reforestry work was considered experimental, it was axed. Her job no longer existed.

Wynn was in the kitchen, stuffing a roast chicken for dinner. The kitchen smelled of browned mushrooms, onions and celery, butter and chestnuts.

I waited until she had finished spooning the mixture into the bird and washed her hands. "There's a letter I think you should see."

"Uh-oh. I can tell by your tone of voice it's not good." She dried her hands on the back of her jeans, and I handed over Mr. Njagi's missive. As Wynn read it, her body stiffened and she set her jaw. "Something smells in this letter. And not like roast chicken."

She sank down at the kitchen table next to me, and I flung an arm around her shoulders. She leaned into me briefly, and sat upright. "What am I going to tell all the people expecting trees? The elders who signed on to the project are going to look like idiots. They're never going to trust a development agent again. After all the time and work, just when the seedlings were about to be delivered. Idiots!"

187

"I don't get it, anyway. You're paid through U.S. foreign aid, aren't you?"

"Yes, but the Office of Development is my official employer. They provide office support—meaning I get to share a secretary with a dozen other people. It's ridiculous."

"Besides, what's this sudden financial crisis? They're continually in a financial crisis. I haven't heard of any new scandal, have you?"

"You never can tell. They may have discovered someone diverted the rest of this year's funds to build a reservoir in his third cousin's village. Someone with high enough connections to keep it out of the papers." She read the letter again, crumpled it, and flung it across the room. "To hell with them. I'm going to finish the project anyway."

I wondered if they would have dared fire Wynn like this if Nick were still alive. They no longer had to worry about him digging up a scandal and writing an unflattering article. "What do you think of passing this information along to Peter Kamau at *The Star*? Maybe he'd want to look into it."

Wynn got up and started working on the chicken again. She sliced a fresh lemon and squeezed half over the chicken. The kitchen filled with the bright scent. "Better not. Whoever masterminded this might take it out on me."

"What more can they do to you?"

"Revoke my permanent resident status."

"They can do that? Even though you're the widow of a citizen?"

Wynn picked up one herb jar after another and vigorously sprinkled a medley of spices over the bird. My mouth started watering with the memory of her chicken: tarragon, thyme, basil, ginger. She looked up at me with a measuring look.

"Swear you can keep a secret?"

I held my right hand up in a pledge.

"Nick and I weren't legally married."

"What!" I jumped out of my chair. "And here I always thought you were the happiest married couple I knew!"

"Sorry. It was a little fiction. You know how concerned Viv and Roger are with appearances. Nick and I couldn't care less, but since it meant so much to them." She shrugged. "So as far as anyone knows, we're married. Except my boss knows we're not, 'cause my work permit and alien resident visa are part of my job file."

"Wynn, does this mean the house isn't yours?" I gestured at the roof over our heads. "And the land?"

"Oh, no, that's all right. When Nick started covering Somalia, he got worried about what would happen to me if," her voice wavered, "if he didn't come back. He went to a lawyer, made out a will, all signed, sealed, and official. The lawyer kept one copy, and Nick has the other in a locked box in his desk. I get everything." She peeled a potato with a few deft gestures and reached for another one.

"Otherwise, Viv would get it?"

"She's third in line. After Kaji."

"Wow. Does Kaji know?"

"Neither of them knows. Nick was afraid Kaji would refuse, and he didn't want to get into a snit with Viv about it. Nick loathed confrontations; he'd do anything to avoid a fight. Not that Viv would want the land herself." Whack, whack, whack. Each potato was sliced in half.

"She could sell it."

"And pile up more money in the bank." Wynn poured a drop of olive oil on her palms, smoothed her hands over each potato, and arranged them in the roasting pan below the chicken. "Not that you could get much for this land."

I remembered the surveyors. "Unless they found oil on it, or nearby."

"Dream on. Even I would sell it then."

"What would you do with the money?"

"Buy a bigger piece of land, even farther away. Share it with Samburu and cheetah." She slid the heavy bird into the preheated oven and turned down the temperature. "Help fund Kaji's research. Pay ranchers and farmers not to kill cheetah on their land. There's tons that could be done, if we only had the money."

She swept up her mixing bowl and spoon, the frying pan

where she'd browned the vegetables and piled them all in the sink. She filled a kettle from the pump and put it on to heat for washing.

It wasn't until later, when I went back to my work table under the tree, that some other questions struck me. Mutani could easily arrange for Wynn's job to disappear, on his own initiative or as a favor to the sheikh. But why? I stared at the horizon, thinking. Nick was gone, and without a job, Wynn had even less reason to stay. In only a few months Gin and Tonic would be out on their own, and the house would seem empty. She now had Comet to take their place, but no one could have predicted that.

Still, once Nick was out of the picture, why would Mutani or Sheikh Farid also want to get rid of Wynn? After all, she knew nothing about their hunting, and Nick's murder had successfully come off as an unfortunate accident. Maybe Mutani and company felt more secure that it would stay that way by getting Wynn out of here. The explanation didn't completely satisfy me, but I couldn't take it any further.

A lilac-breasted roller flashed by on cobalt wings and perched on a twig two bushes over from where I was sitting. He folded his wings, which were cinnamon-brown on the back, then flashed them half open, showing the iridescent-blue again as he fought the wind to keep his balance. It ruffled the lilac feathers on his breast and the long blue tail streamers. He eyed the ground and swooped down to grab a small lizard, and returned triumphantly to his post. He was making out better than I was.

I was still moving the puzzle pieces around in my mind when Striker came back. I decided not to be childish, put stones on the letters to keep them from blowing away, and went to the airstrip to meet him. He got out of the plane, grabbed me and gave me a big kiss, half remorse, half passion.

"I'm sorry for losing my temper." He leaned back and looked into my eyes. His green-brown eyes were full of sadness and worry. "The thought of losing you tears me apart."

190

"Me, too." His eyes were so beautiful. What would it be like to never see them again? "I love you. I want you in my life."

We kissed again, a gentle, almost trembling kiss. I was waiting for him to say, "Let's make us a priority and put the decision on where to live on hold." He didn't.

Instead he gave a big sigh and said, "If we can't work this out somehow, I guess we'll have to accept it. I can't stay and you can't leave."

"Is that how you want to leave it?"

"*No.* Of course not. I want you to come with me."

For the second time I screwed up my courage. "Striker. Don't do this. Please don't be in such a rush. Can't you stay until we know about us?"

His jaw tightened. "I already know about us. And I know you, too. It could take you years to make up your mind. You're not in any hurry, but I am. My life is over in Kenya. And yours is, too, Jazz. Face it: Jazz Jasper Safaris is defunct. You haven't had a tour group in months. There's nothing keeping you here."

"Two months."

"Your safari business is dead, Jazz. I'm sorry, I know how much it meant to you. It's the economy—it's not your fault. Can't you admit that and come with me?"

My hands bunched into fists. If he told me one more time my business was dead, I was going to hit him. "It's not over until I give up, and I'm not giving up. Don't you tell me there's nothing for me in Kenya just because you want to leave. I happen to love this place. There's no place like it on earth."

"More than you love me!"

"Yes, more than I love you!"

"That's what I thought," he said quietly.

Before I could add anything, he said he needed a cold drink, and headed toward the house.

At least his return made things much simpler. I radioed Omondi that we'd be coming down to Nairobi. Wynn needed to lease a plane, and then she could fly us all up north tomorrow. For safety, Kaji agreed to take the cheetahs in the Land Cruiser and spend the night at some friends' who had a place outside Isiolo.

Miracle of miracles, Striker, hater of cities, agreed to spend the night with me in Nairobi.

21

THE FIRST THING I did was drop by police headquarters and quietly pass Omondi the exposed film and diamond bracelet. Then I headed straight home. My neighbor, Helen Kimani, must have been listening for me, because as I was unlocking my apartment's dead bolt, she poked her head into the hall and told me our landlord, Alvin Matua, had been showing my apartment to a bunch of Somali refugees. "Are you moving?" she asked, crinkling her nose in dismay.

"Not if I can help it," I said. "I owe two months' rent. He said I have a week to get the money. Can he evict me anyway?"

Helen shook her head. "It all depends how much they're bribing him for the apartment."

"Thanks for the tip, Helen." I went in, seriously contemplating throwing myself on the floor and kicking and screaming like a toddler. I regretfully accepted that I was a grown-up and would have to deal with Alvin. Should I ask Ibrahim, my friend and safari cook, whom to bribe to tell Alvin to lay off me? And where was I going to get the money to pay bribes and my back rent? I wasn't about to ask Striker for it. Ibrahim wouldn't have it. Omondi? I hated to impose on his friendship. Wynn would give it to me, but I didn't know if she could afford it. Shit.

I pushed my own problems aside. I needed to make some calls before offices closed for the night. I was looking for the connection between the sheikh and Mutani. First off I called River Lodge, but was told that regretfully, Mr. Gerry Weller was no longer a guest. He'd checked out two days ago.

193

Next, I called Kenarabia Oil's Nairobi office. I knew the chances of their telling me the location of the oil camp were precisely zero, so I pretended to be a nurse calling for Gerry Weller's doctor, who needed to reach him immediately regarding some test results. I tried to sound as if there would be a medical emergency unless I could reach Mr. Weller personally. A receptionist with a snippy manner put me on hold for ages, and then the line disconnected and it took me a while to realize the static had changed and that I was hanging onto a dead phone.

The second time, I managed to talk to a person, but all he could tell me is that the man I needed to speak to had stepped out of the office for a moment. Then I had to twist his arm to name someone else who could tell me Mr. Gerry Weller's whereabouts. When I got hold of that person, he kept repeating that he'd pass the doctor's message to Mr. Weller as soon as he returned to work. When would that be? He still had one week to go on a temporary leave without pay. He wouldn't tell me if Weller had left the country, or where he was likely to go within Kenya.

As soon as I hung up, I thought of a question that would tell me if the sheikh was involved with Kenarabia. I called the receptionist back and this time asked if the sheikh was at this afternoon's meeting. She said Sheikh Farid wouldn't be back in the office until next week. I hung up with a satisfied smile. So, the sheikh was expected at Kenarabia: his trip *was* combined business and pleasure.

I picked up the phone again. Now to establish the third leg in the triangle. I dialed Mutani's office and said I had a message for Sheikh Farid, when would he be coming in to see Mr. Mutani? A sweet-voiced woman told me that Mr. Mutani was currently the guest of the sheikh on safari. As far as she knew, there was nothing on the schedule about the sheikh coming into the office, but Mr. Mutani didn't always formally schedule appointments.

Next, to find out when the sheikh arrived in Kenya. I was pretty sure he'd use a private plane. I called the airport, to ask the straightforward question of when he'd flown into Nairobi. It took a half hour of being passed

194

from the operator to various offices, none of whom would tell me a damn thing. Why the secrecy?

Finally I remembered that Ibrahim, my safari cook, had a nephew or cousin or some relative that worked in the control tower. I dropped by his house, chaotic as always. He wasn't there, but his younger wife told me the air traffic controller was a cousin named Simon Gathu. Simon was on a break when I called, so I left my number, identifying myself as Ibrahim's employer.

He called me back ten minutes later. I chatted about Ibrahim and how much I valued him as a friend and employee, before asking about the sheikh's arrival.

"Why do you want to know? Are you a reporter?"

"No. It's for a private matter."

"I think perhaps it is better to discuss this after work."

We arranged for me to pick him up a few blocks from the airport at the end of his shift. Despite his sober brown suit and black-framed glasses, Simon looked young and nervous. He rejected all my suggestions for a bar or café as too public.

"How about if we go to your uncle's and talk there?" I finally asked. I had the feeling I might need Ibrahim's help to get anything out of Simon, but I was wrong. As soon as we spotted Ibrahim's portly frame lying on a lounge chair inside the courtyard of his sprawling house, Simon relaxed and even became expansive. Ibrahim led us onto the blue stucco porch in front of his first wife's apartment, and pulled forward three mismatched chairs from among the clutter of wooden stools and wobbly chairs, pots and pans, a charcoal brazier, and mounds of assorted household items that had landed here long ago. He offered us Tuskers, called to one of his school-age sons, or perhaps it was a nephew or cousin, and gave him money to go and fetch the beers at the corner store.

I felt funny not knowing all of the children living at Ibrahim's. He shared the compound with two wives, his own eleven children, several brothers and their many wives and children, plus a constantly changing number of visiting relatives, and on top of that called all the boys *son*, and all the girls *daughter*, and they all called him *Father*.

I'd long ago given up my attempts to keep track as hopeless.

Ibrahim knew that I'd dropped by earlier and gotten Simon's name from his younger wife, so he wasn't surprised to see us. I explained that a Saudi sheikh was hunting up north, that I wanted to stop him and hoped Simon could tell me exactly when the sheikh had arrived in Nairobi.

Simon tilted back on his rickety chair. "You might as well give up. You will never touch even the hem of his robe."

"Still, I would greatly appreciate any information you can give me."

Ibrahim put a hand on my knee. "You can trust her with your greatest secrets, my son. She will tell no one where she found out. She has caught rich and powerful killers before." He gave me an inquiring look. "Killers of men."

Simon's voice became grave and important. "The sheikh arrived on August fifteenth, at midnight. I, myself, was on duty, and Stephan—that's a nephew," he added, nodding at Ibrahim, "was on ground crew."

That erased the smile from my face. Nick went to the manyatta on the sixteenth. The sheikh arrived in the country only eight hours before Nick went north. Being in the safari business myself, I knew his camp would be set up either in advance, or while his party waited comfortably at a Nairobi hotel. Even if it was set up in advance, that cut things pretty close. It seemed unlikely Nick caught the sheikh hunting his very first day in the country. Shit. Either Nick saw something that made it obvious it was a hunting camp, or the sheikh rushed right up and started popping his gun off at animals. I hoped the Samburu knew what Nick saw, and that they would tell us.

Ibrahim and Simon were staring at me, waiting for me to return to the present. "Sorry, I was trying to figure something out." I looked at Simon. "Is midnight a normal time for a private arrival?"

Simon laughed. "For a sheikh, nothing is normal. They are as rich as gods, and even more conceited." He described how they'd come in a Learjet and a customized Boeing, landed in a remote corner of the airstrip—met by

196

a government minister, no less—and had been whisked away in limos without customs clearance or passport control.

Not only that, but they also had a reconfigured C-130, whatever that was. From Simon's vivid description, it was obviously big. The C-130 brought in a two-thousand-gallon water tanker and eight-thousand-gallon fuel tanker, plus a dozen safari vehicles, mostly customized Land Cruisers, and even a customized Mercedes with a gold-plated royal crest on the hood. The sheikh also brought his own generator and a satellite dish, not to mention small items like thirty air conditioners, VCRs, large screen TVs, and enough fixtures and plumbing to outfit a mansion's worth of marble bathrooms.

"This is unbelievable!" I said. "And no reporter got a whiff of it? There was nothing in the papers."

"The sheikh wanted his privacy. Many gifts were passed around the airport, and also a few threats."

The children came back with our beers, and conversation turned into more social channels. Simon decided to stay at Ibrahim's for dinner and I went home. Striker wasn't back from his errands yet. I poured myself a second beer and sat down to think. When Omondi gave me the go-ahead for publicizing the sheikh's hunting, it was going to make an incredible story. I could picture Peter Kamau at *The Star* having a field day with it. Tomorrow we'd document the Saudis' attack on Wynn and me, and try to find out from the Samburu exactly where Nick had gone while he was up there, and what he had seen. Even with Omondi, I didn't feel safe returning to the Saudi camp.

Striker came back, we made dinner together, both talking as if life was normal and we weren't breaking up. After dinner we sat at opposite ends of the couch and listened to a blues tape he'd bought. It was Willie Dixon singing his own songs, many familiar to me from the borrowing of sixties rock groups, but it was the first time I'd heard "Abyssinia, My Home." Go far enough back, and we're all from Africa. All our roots are here, in this wonderful land. It was the greatest privilege of my life to come to Kenya, to spend some years here. I knew I wouldn't stay forever, but I wasn't ready yet for exile. Not from Africa, not from my freedom.

I thought of Striker leaving, and I started to cry. He slid over to my side of the couch and held me. I sobbed, deep wracking sobs of woe. And then Striker was crying, too, a wrenching sound, as if he hadn't cried in decades. We held each other for a long time.

"Darling, I wish I could stay here and be with you." Striker's voice was low and soft, a warm breath on my brow. He squeezed me close. "But I feel like I have to leave Kenya or die."

I knew I was hearing the truth. There'd be no more arguing now.

"I've been here twenty years." Striker rested his cheek against my hair. He spoke gently. "You can't know what it was like then."

"I know."

"You think it's Eden now, but this is just a shadow, a pathetic remnant—the wildness, animals everywhere you went, elephant herds in the hundreds, the plenitude, people in balance with the rest of creation, room for everyone."

"Mmmm." I took his hand in mine. His long, wonderful hand. Soon I wouldn't be seeing it anymore.

His sad, thoughtful voice went on. "It may be worse other places, but at least there I won't know how much has been lost." He paused a moment. "Nick and I were talking about this the last time I saw him. He felt the same way. You can take it for so long, and suddenly you snap. He thought I should get a big boat and sail around the world."

"A boat? You'd hate being confined like that, with no plants and no animals around you."

"That was the idea—get away from wildlife, from people, from everything. The ocean isn't for me, but I've got to find something." He fell silent, but I could tell there was more, so I held his hand, felt his chest warm against my side, and waited. He began to speak again, almost whispering. "I don't want to see the last remnants being torn away and destroyed, shrunk and shrunk until the parks are just big outdoor zoos where you see as many people as animals, and Nairobi as big and as horrible as Calcutta, and poor, suffering people everywhere you look. This place used to be about Nature's greatest glory, and people living age-old, traditional lives. I won't deny them progress, but where is it? Now Kenya is about AIDS and families with twelve children on a farm big enough to feed two. I love this place too much. I can't stay and watch it all change into something so far below—" His voice cracked, and he stopped talking, squeezed me tight again.

"I understand. But I can't go with you. My course runs in a different direction."

"I know."

We sat, and the music washed over us. There was nothing more to say.

Later, in bed, Striker and I made love with aching tenderness. He fell into sleep like a rock tossed into a pond, then whimpered and moved restlessly with bad dreams. I lay at his side, staring into the dark. Salty tears ran down my cheeks and onto my pillow. It was over.

Flying into the desert the next day with Wynn and Omondi was not a relaxing experience. Every time the wind bucked the plane, my heart started racing. Omondi must have noticed my white knuckles because he picked up my hand, laid it on his thigh and covered it with his own, like a warm tent. He loved the plane ride, as usual, peering out the window and exclaiming with excitement over the red and ochre colors of the earth, the zigzag of dried watercourses, and of course, the animals, like miniature toys, far below. By the time we landed, I'd started to forget for moments at a time that planes can and do fall out of the sky, and started watching and enjoying along with him. That's one of the things I love about Omondi.

First we flew to the site of the wrecked plane, expecting to take pictures of the burned-out car and the remains of the men who'd attacked us. The plane with its crumpled wing was there. So were our possessions, scattered around over a wide area, as if animals had been at them. There were no corpses, which wasn't too surprising. The Saudis undoubtedly came back for them. There was also no burned-out car. We circled low. There were no signs in the sand of the life-and-death struggle that had taken place. All had been swept clean. Even the marks of our tent, even the tracks of our Land Cruiser—gone. We headed south to where we'd run out of gas. The car was gone; so were its tracks.

"Very interesting," said Omondi. "It looks like the sheikh has preferred to clean up the site himself. As I said, I doubt he will be making a charge against you."

We continued on to the manyatta, and in seconds flew across the couple of ridges that separated it from the Saudi camp. The camp had disappeared. There was nothing there but blowing sand and the wind. A chill went down my back. I'd known it wouldn't be easy to bring the sheikh and Mutani to justice; now I wondered if it would be possible. Omondi's refrain about getting the proof first took on new meaning.

Wynn made a perfect landing at the manyatta airstrip, with only one little bump, for which I was grateful. Arriving in a plane was different from straggling in half-dead from the desert. Instead of offering us home-brewed beer, the Samburu immediately started digging out beaded calabashes and necklaces to sell. We asked for Lembirdan, the junior elder we'd talked with, and Kariankei, the kid who'd hid us in the cave, but neither of them were around. We'd have to start from scratch.

Since we were going to be pumping them for information, it seemed wise to cooperate, so I bought a calabash with a lovely mahogany sheen and long, beaded strap; since I wasn't going to use it to hold milk, I didn't mind that the gourd was old and had a tiny hole. The seller got a small fortune in hard currency for a useless old thing, and I'd bought a beautiful and authentic piece of craft for a few hundred shillings, so we were both quite happy.

Then a tall young woman draped in beads came out of her hut with a zebra skin. She wanted a thousand shillings for it, about ten dollars. I bought it and asked if there were more. She shook her head and rattled something off in Samburu. A young man dressed in ragged pants and shirt instead of a Samburu toga was in the crowd hovering around us. "That is all she have," he said in English.

"Hi." I extended my hand. "My name is Jazz, what is yours?"

He smiled and shook hands energetically. "Bernard. Welcome."

"Thank you. Can you tell us where she got the skin? Can she get more?"

Bernard explained in quite adequate broken English that it was not permitted to hunt, that no one there hunted, and that the woman had not gotten the skin from any man in the manyatta.

"Not from a man here," I repeated. "From another Samburu, not here?"

"No. No Samburu. From Dorobo." The Dorobo are a hunting and gathering people who live in the mountains, where many Samburu herd their flocks in dry season. A Dorobo was courting this young woman, Bernard explained, and had given her a skin as a present.

We asked if there were also some tourists hunting in the area, from the nearby camp. Bernard shrugged and said they knew nothing about that. Ha. Either they'd been paid off, or they didn't want to have anything to do with the illegal doings of the Saudis. I asked when the tourists arrived, were Claude Lavalle and Nick Hunter also here? There was a discussion: it was around the same time, but they couldn't be more precise. No one had actually taken either of the men to the tourist camp. It was beginning to look less and less likely that Nick had uncovered the sheikh's hunting, but there was no proof either way. I groaned inwardly. We were going to have to rethink everything.

Omondi broke in, talking Swahili. "These tourists would like to see the scene where this Dorobo hunted recently." He pulled out a few hundred shilling notes. Bernard took the money, explaining to his companions what the deal was, and without more ado, started out of the manyatta. We followed, along with half a dozen curious young men wearing red and white togas and carrying the graceful Samburu spears. I dropped off my gourd at the plane, we picked up water bottles and headed west.

We marched along in silence through the dry landscape.

201

A dun-colored bustard exploded from under Bernard's feet, startling him and giving a reason for teasing and laughter. Farther along, a solitary male impala guarded his territory, waiting patiently for a group of females to wander through. His strategy was to corral them for as long as possible, while he mated with those in estrus. But even that wasn't easy. When the females came, they'd be followed by a gang of young bachelors who had no territory of their own, looking for a chance to sneak in and grab some nooky. The territorial male would be kept so busy herding and guarding his temporary harem that he wouldn't have time to eat. Eventually he'd be too tired and weak to hold off his well-fed competitors. He snorted and stamped his delicate hoof as we passed, holding his head and lyre-shaped horns high. He looked lonely and hot, but that might have been projection. Why had I agreed to this reprise? As far as I was concerned, I'd done enough desert walking to last me for years.

I caught up to Omondi and whispered to him, "Why did you ask to see the Dorobo hunting site?"

"They are going to take us to the nearest scene of hunting. It might be the work of this Dorobo, if he exists, or more likely, of the Saudis. Once we are there, it will be easier to find out more about Nick's visit and what he saw."

When it came to worming information out of people, Omondi was a master. I just hoped this long walk was worth it. We crossed the crown of a low hill and ahead lay the riverine forest, its band of startling green slashing across the tan and silver landscape of earth and thornbush. Several herds of goats and cattle attended by adolescent and younger Samburu boys dotted the scrub between us and the forest. The closest ones waved and shouted, but instead of going toward them, we turned left and walked across two more low hills.

Another hot mile or so later we came upon something, but it was hard to tell what had happened there. Unlike the fresh site that Wynn and I crossed after the plane crash, there were no vultures or jackals, and almost no bones. That didn't mean anything, except that the killing here was at least a few days old. Hyenas can crunch up and digest even large thigh bones and the toughest hide. We walked slowly around the site. There were so many animal prints it was hard to find the signs of man, but toward the periphery we spotted tire treads and the mark of running shoes.

"This doesn't look like a Dorobo." I pointed out the shoe print to Bernard.

He and his friends discussed the print. He turned to me and said, "This is a car that came after. Maybe some tourists who wanted a horn or wanted to look, like you." He gestured for us to follow him and pointed out some scruffed-up earth and bone chips, then another area and another.

"Poacher," contributed one of his friends, a handsome young man with a round, open face, strong straight features, and warrior locks down to the small of his naked back.

"Yes," Bernard nodded. "No tourist. Poacher."

The fellow with the warrior locks stepped forward and said in a loud clear voice. "We know this man. Lodogia." He pointed at the scruffed earth with its bits of bone. "Lodogia. Dorobo."

"Is that his name?" Wynn asked. "Lodogia?"

The young men nodded.

"Do you know Nick Hunter?" she asked. They nodded. "Did Nick see this?"

Bernard said, "No," but the guy with the long hair shook his head yes.

"Who brought Nick here, to this spot?" Omondi asked in Swahili.

There was some discussion in Samburu, and then Bernard reluctantly pointed to the fellow with the waist-long locks and friendly face who'd told us the Dorobo's name. His name was Alawan.

He looked to be in his early twenties. He wore a red cloth tied toga-fashion over one shoulder and falling halfway to his calves. On his feet were crude sandals with broad straps. He wore a band of tiny colorful beads across his high brow, a thinner one stretched from ear to ear across the top of his head, an elaborate bead choker around his neck, large white plugs in his earlobes, assorted bead bracelets, two narrow strings of beads crisscrossing his chest, and two more earrings dangling from the tops of his ears. The bright colors gleamed against his dark skin. You could never accuse a Samburu warrior of being uninterested in personal appearance.

Instead of asking him questions, Omondi asked him to recall the day, to describe meeting Nick: who was there, what each person said, how it came to be that he, Alawan, had accompanied Nick to this site, who went with them, what did they see that day, what had everybody said. Like many nonliterate people, Alawan had a phenomenal memory, especially for social situations. He brought the day to life for us, and made Nick so vivid it brought a lump to my throat.

He described Lodogia, the Dorobo hunter, creeping up on a herd of zebra, shooting swiftly and accurately with his rifle, quickly skinning them and taking some of the meat, and carrying it away on his back. How had a Dorobo, who lived pretty much outside a money economy and are famous for their poisoned arrows and clever snares, managed to buy a rifle?

I asked this and Alawan laughed. "Lodogia has shillings."

Bernard cut in. "Lodogia sells skins to a white man. Has many shillings."

Goose pimples rose on my arm. Was this the lead Nick had stumbled on? A white man in partnership with a Dorobo poacher must be someone who knew the area well, who passed through regularly. Claude Lavalle, the aid worker? Would he endanger his work by engaging in smuggling? The only other people who came through here regularly were the oil prospectors. I flashed on Gerry Weller's tanned face. If it was an oil man, there could be a connection to the Saudis' hunting in this same area. All very interesting.

Omondi prompted Alawan to play Lodogia creeping away with his skins. Then he took the role of Lodogia and assigned Alawan the name of Nick, with a tap of his chest and a hand held five inches above his head to indicate

Nick's six-foot-four frame. Alawan/Nick began to creep after Lodogia. He pretended to catch and shake him. Then he showed them becoming friendly and going off together. Everyone laughed with appreciation of his performance.

Bernard, feeling slighted perhaps that Alawan had taken over the starring role, put a restraining hand on Alawan. "Nick here," he gestured around us, "Lodogia no here. No here." He gestured to the west. "Lodogia live inside mountain. Far. Come here, see woman he wants marry. You be my wife. She say no, he go away same day. Lodogia and Nick, no meet."

A discussion in Samburu ensued. Omondi asked some questions in Swahili, while the Samburu switched languages back and forth. From the scraps I understood, some of the men maintained that Alawan's skit was true, while others backed Lodogia's version.

Omondi switched to English. "It seems Lodogia comes to the manyatta now and then to do some trading, and to visit this woman, who is Bernard's sister. Perhaps that is why he insists that the Dorobo and Nick never met. All the men have seen Lodogia's gun, and know he is trading in skins and live animals, too. No one has actually seen this white man, but they say Lodogia has been trading with him from before the last circumcision, which would make it a year ago."

The Samburu have mass circumcisions every fifteen years, in which males aged fourteen to twenty-four undergo the ordeal and move from the status of boys, who do all the herding, to that of warriors. In the old days the warriors' job was to prey on other clans and tribes, but now, with tribal peace, they mostly hang out, visit their lovers, have competitive dancing and spear throwing, and secret ceremonies in the bush in which they consume a lot of wine, drugs, and meat. Needless to say, male circumcision was eagerly awaited by boys, the biggest event in the life of each generation, and a reliable way to mark the calendar. There is no female equivalent. Girls have their clitoris cut out whenever they hit puberty, without much fanfare, and are immediately married to an elder.

"Do they know where Lodogia lives?"

Alawan, who had been listening to our conversation with a frown of concentration, said, "In mountain. Two days." He pointed west.

Kenya is divided by a line running straight down the middle from north to south. To the east of the line, where Nick and Wynn lived, is lowland. It is semidesert, inhospitable, thinly populated by nomadic herders such as the Samburu. To the west are the highlands, lush, fertile, temperate, blessed in every way, crowded home to many agricultural tribes. The dividing line is a broken wall of mountains. Mount Kenya's snow-covered volcanic peak, smack in the center of the country, tops 17,000 feet.

The Dorobo were the original inhabitants of Kenya, smaller and less warlike than the waves of Maasai, Samburu, Kikuyu, and others that colonized the country centuries ago. Little by little the Dorobo were dispossessed and retreated into the safety of the mountain forests. They were joined by Maasai and Samburu who lost their herds in tribal warfare, so many of them that some people claimed the original Dorobo never existed. Like the elusive mountain antelope, few people had seen them. Dorobo were skilled in the arts of the hunt: spotting game, tracking, setting snares and traps, killing with poisoned arrows. Their healers were feared sorcerers who knew every plant, every herb, and their uses—beneficial or deadly. And they alone could gather the wild bees' honey, from which the other peoples made their beloved wine.

I had heard of the Dorobo ever since I came to Kenya, but had never met one. The northern mountains are inaccessible, and I hadn't visited them. It sounded like I was about to have the pleasure.

Alawan claimed to know the exact location of Lodogia's personal honey territory. Wynn was confident she could fly us to within reasonable hiking distance, and we had canteens and a packed lunch.

Omondi turned to Wynn and me. "I think it is wise to hire Alawan to lead us to this Lodogia. He has less English and Swahili than Bernard, but he has been more honest with us."

"Hold on," I said. "Should we be doing this? We were

looking for evidence Nick knew about Farid's hunting. This is taking us off in a different direction."

"You know my method. Examine everything, assume nothing." Omondi patted my arm. "Reality is not cooperating and following our theories, so it is better that we follow reality. We must use the information we have. You don't know where this road will lead us. It may be forward, back, or sideways. But it is a road Nick walked on, at least for a while, so we must explore it."

I had to agree with him, and Wynn did, too. My guts told me this would lead us back to oil, one way or another.

Alawan was jumping with excitement about going up in an airplane, until the moment of climbing on the wing and through the door, when he went quiet and still. Omondi helped him with the seat belt. As we taxied down the runway, I heard him ask Omondi above the roar of the engine, "Will we be able to touch the stars?"

22

THE ELEPHANT TRAIL climbed up the valley and disappeared among the trees. We'd landed the plane at the edge of the desert at least an hour ago and had been hiking uphill ever since. The sun was near the zenith and weighed on our backs with a heavy hand. The beginning of trees was a welcome sight.

Alawan turned with a triumphant smile that lit up his face. He pointed up the mountain. "Lodogia. Cave."

We started the climb. The signs of elephant were plentiful: piles of turds the size of melons, still fresh enough to sting our noses, and every now and then a smashed shrub where an elephant had stopped for a snack. The shape of a bare human foot was superimposed on the elephant's dinner-plate-sized prints. Omondi tapped it with his toe. "Lodogia?"

Alawan nodded.

Wynn put her foot alongside the human print. They were almost the same size.

The brush grew darker and denser around us, absorbing light and sound. The dainty hoofprints of a bushbuck crossed the path, and farther on, the pug marks of a big lion. The trail became steeper and the day hotter. I leaned into the hill, head up, alert for danger. This kind of trail was especially dangerous because we could come around a corner right on top of a lion or elephant. We wouldn't live long enough to regret the mistake.

We climbed into a true forest zone, where the air was cooler, a pungent mix of fresh-growing green and the danker smells of rot, mushrooms, and decay. We heard elephants, and pushed our way off the path, creeping up on a pool of water gleaming in the green darkness. An elephant family of a dozen or more crowded into the water, happily scooping mud with their trunks and slapping it onto their bulging sides.

The matriarch was over ten feet at the shoulder, with magnificent tusks. Few mature elephants have escaped poachers' bullets; I'd never seen full-grown tusks before. I stared in awe. We were close enough to see her long, sparse eyelashes, and every wrinkle on her imposing trunk.

A hefty youngster was more interested in milk than mud. He folded his trunk over his forehead and reached with open mouth for the matriarch's breast. Like all female elephants, she had two breasts between her front legs the same shape as a well-endowed woman's. Mom was not cooperating, however; she blocked each attempt with an adroit shift of her leg. She was weaning him. The youngster tried from the other side, and when he was thwarted once more, tooted with annoyance. This attracted another youngster; the two entwined trunks and began a game of shove.

One of the adults caught a whiff of us. She stretched out her long trunk for a better sniff. I could see the coarse hairs on the triangular tip, its two fingers opened wide. She stared right at us, but luckily we were well-hidden among the leaves. Still, the smell made her uneasy, and she brought her ears forward and raised her trunk. Her mother and sisters immediately came toward us, massive heads up and ears out. As an intimidating sight, it was very effective. My mouth went dry. If they saw us and charged, we had nowhere to run. But elephants are pacific animals, as long as they've never lost a family member to a hunter. This group decided they were no longer in the mood to dawdle in the bath, and disappeared soundlessly into the forest.

We picked up Lodogia's footprints on the trail and pressed on. The game path grew narrower and less distinct, with a muddled mix of prints: baboon, jackal, fox, mongoose, hyena, various antelopes, the skunklike zorilla. Several times we saw the large, pointed hooves of greater kudu, and once, peering into the shadows, I caught a glimpse of white stripes on a dark face topped by magnificent spiral horns, so brief it was like a dream.

Alawan stooped to examine another of Lodogia's footprints, and I passed him, attracted by some curious fruits a few feet farther on.

"This one looks very recent," Omondi was saying.

Almost at the same time, Alawan yelled a warning, as I tripped over a raffia cord tied across the trail and sprawled to the ground. Alawan urgently shouted a word I didn't understand.

I rolled to the side as I sensed a commotion of movement in the tree above me. Something dark and heavy whistled past me and pounded into the earth. It hit my leg, a glancing blow that felt hard enough to break it. A startled bird flew off, complaining noisily. Clenching my jaw against the pain, I stared in disbelief at the black object. It was a three-foot length of log, obviously cut by a person. If I hadn't rolled in time, it would have broken my back.

Wynn and Omondi rushed to my side. "Did it hit you?" "Are you all right?"

I sat up and gingerly moved my leg. "It hurts like hell." I straightened and bent it. "If I can move it, does that mean it's not broken?"

"Probably. See if you can stand on it," Wynn said. She and Omondi helped me to my feet.

I hobbled a few steps. "Ouch. Ow. I can walk. What in hell fell on me?"

"I think it's called a drop trap," Wynn said.

Alawan's beautifully muscled arms bulged as he strained to move the log. He turned it over to reveal a short spear embedded in a socket in its side. It had fallen with enough force to jam the spear deep into the earth.

"Ah, yes. The Dorobo are famous for their traps," added Omondi, the city slicker. "I've wanted to see one ever since I was a boy."

I stared at the ten-inch shaft tipped with an iron barb. The space between my shoulder blades went cold.

Alawan pulled out the shaft and pointed to the iron barb. I noticed he didn't touch it. "Poison."

"Most fascinating," said Omondi.

I looked closely at the spear's tip. Damp earth clung to it in patches; the poison was nothing I could see. I shivered. Alawan laid it down carefully next to the log. I supposed the iron made it a valuable possession, one the Dorobo could not make for himself.

We paused where we were to give my leg a rest and bolt down a late lunch, hunched over, quick to startle at a rustling bird, feeling an ominous presence. Anything or anyone could be hidden in the undergrowth around us, and we wouldn't know until it wanted to be known.

Alawan broke off a stout, straight branch as a walking stick for me. I tried it out. My leg had stopped throbbing, but it had stiffened during lunch, and if I stepped on it wrong, a jarring pain made me grit my teeth. The staff helped. I walked back and forth a few times. If I relaxed and kept an even rhythm, it wasn't too bad.

"Decision time. Keep going or head back?" Wynn asked me.

"Keep going," I said. "The more I walk, the better it feels."

We continued on, now looking up as well as front and side, which was a good thing, because we found, and avoided, another five drop-spear traps. Then we came upon a broken trip wire. Fifty feet farther on, there was the sweet heavy smell of blood. We paused, listening for sounds of tearing and rending. All we heard was the plaintive call of a forest bird.

Around the next curve was a carcass of a greater kudu. The beautiful white-striped roan pelt had been stripped off, leaving a mass of red flesh crowned with those beautiful spiral antlers. The choicest meat had been cut off in hunks. The blood was still scarlet. Lodogia must have butchered it recently.

We'd barely walked out of sight of the kudu when Alawan stopped abruptly and hissed, "Simba."

We froze. Through a tangle of branches twenty feet or so down the path, I could make out a patch of tawny pelt. I put one foot behind me, then another, slowly backing up, controlling the urge to run. Running would trigger the lion's instinct to pounce. A lion can sprint at thirty-five miles an hour over short distances. I stepped unevenly on a root and almost lost my balance. A jolt of pain flashed like fire through my ankle. My throat felt as dry as swallowing a mouthful of sand.

The patch moved and a lion in the prime of his youth pushed his enormous head through the foliage to get a good look at us. Cool yellow eyes assessed me. He had a big nose and even bigger mouth, surrounded by a foot-thick black and tan mane. He stepped out on the path, all nine feet of him. He was twitching his muscular tail in an edgy way I didn't like.

I heard a soft moan of fear, and realized it came from me. My pulse was beating loudly in my ears, sending up such a clamor I couldn't think or breathe or move. Somehow I kept my legs going, one foot behind the other. The phrase "Fight or flight, flight or fight" ran over and over through my mind, as if putting one more foot between us could save me. But I knew with a dreadful certainty in the pit of my stomach that we were already too close, that it was too late, that the next move was up to the lion.

A burst of hope! The lion lay down, paws in front like a stone lion in front of the public library, studying us with what I hoped was simple curiosity. He was still twitching his tail like a heavy rope whip, but at least he was stationary. And then he visibly made up his mind. His look sharpened. There could be no misunderstanding. I read his intentions as clearly as my own. His eyes became more focused, more aggressive. He didn't like the look of us. He gathered his legs under him. He was going to spring.

I turned and ran. My leg was on fire. Behind me the lion growled, low and ominous. Ahead of me Wynn leaped sideways, smashing her way through the undergrowth toward a large tree. It looked like a great idea, except there were no trees near me. I jumped into the middle of a thorn bush, which tore at my skin like a hundred claws. But at least there was no mouth attached. I scratched and clawed right back, working my way deep among the thorns. To my right, Omondi balanced precariously in the notch of a tree so thin it was bending over with his weight. This all happened in an instant, one of those nightmare split seconds that from the inside feel like slow motion, giving you time to fully realize that you are in big trouble.

Where was Alawan? At the price of a thorn raking down my neck, I craned my head to look for him.

Alawan was motionless, at the very spot where we'd first seen the lion. The lion approached in a hunting crouch, tail whipping, teeth showing in a snarl. Alawan had spread out his arms and legs like Leonardo Da Vinci's drawing of a man inscribed in a circle, the perfect embodiment of human proportions. One upraised arm held his spear. He stared straight at the lion and a growl ripped from his belly, the roar of a giant primate, a scream of power and defiance.

The lion paused. But he was too close, he wouldn't stop. His crouch gained speed. He was leaping. Alawan thrust his spear down, into the lion's mouth. The lion twisted his head, bit the spear savagely and tore it out of Alawan's grasp. Alawan flung his right arm across his throat. Lion's rip out the throat of small victims and suffocate large ones. It's the spot they go for first. The lion reared up, raked Alawan's arm with immense claws and hurled him to the ground.

I roared and tore off a huge branch of the thorn tree as I jumped to the ground. I was running. Wynn and Omondi were there, too. We charged, mouths open in primate screams, arms whipping our branches through the air. I wasn't scared. I was twelve feet tall. I was an enraged beast. I could best any lion.

The lion looked up with his cold yellow eyes, decided we were more trouble than we were worth, and sped away. Our shouts turned to peals of triumph. Alawan struggled to his feet, grinning, while he stabilized his torn arm against his chest. Blood, bright and warm, was pouring from the scratches. Omondi tore off his shirt and pressed it against the open wounds.

"Let's get this bleeding to stop," he said gently.

I looked around nervously. "There're sure to be more lions attracted to that kudu, unless he's a bachelor without a pride of his own yet."

"Even if he's a bachelor, he may have a brother he's

roaming around with. The faster we can get out of here, the better," Wynn said.

I took my canteen from its holster on my hip and passed it to Alawan. He drank some down. Omondi was using both hands to exert enough pressure to stop the bleeding. The shirt was soggy with blood.

"We also need antibiotics, and fast," Wynn added. "Lion maulings are very dangerous."

Alawan looked at his torn arm without expression. A small thing like a lion attack obviously wasn't enough to disrupt a warrior's sangfroid. It must have hurt like hell.

Omondi asked Wynn why the wound was dangerous.

"Lions scavenge rotten meat, and when their teeth or claws go in, they carry filth deep inside your muscle. If you can't clean the wound properly, it turns septic. Gangrene. Blood poisoning. Very dangerous. You can lose the limb, or more likely, your life."

"Just as well it is bleeding so freely, then," Omondi said.

"There's, a first aid kit in the plane with antibiotics," I said.

"Find Lodogia now," Alawan said. His voice was weak. I looked up sharply. His gleaming dark skin had a greenish pale cast to it.

"I think he's in shock." I tried not to let my fear show in my voice. I took a step forward to see if the bleeding was slowing down. A stab of hot flame ran through my ankle and calf. My leg buckled under me and I fell.

I hit the ground hard. "Oh, hell." I rolled over and flexed my foot. My ankle was swelling visibly. It hurt so much I wanted to cry, but I wasn't going to, not with Alawan standing there smiling heroically with his arm torn open. If I couldn't walk . . . and you weren't supposed to move people in shock, either. How the hell were we going to get down the mountain?

Omondi and Wynn helped me stand, but at my first attempt to put weight on the leg, it buckled. "Can we improvise some crutches for me?"

"Let's see if Omondi and I can carry you," Wynn suggested.

"And what about Alawan? If he's in shock, he might keel over at any second."

"We'll worry about that when we get there," Omondi said. He and Wynn made a seat with their linked hands.

I sat gingerly, letting down my weight, and put my arms around each of their shoulders. They felt strong and warm, and I felt a rush of gratitude. As soon as they tried walking, their hands slipped, tumbling me back onto my good leg.

"Let's try that again," Omondi said lightly. This time they gripped each other's wrists and the seat held, but for how long? I doubted they had the strength to do this for several miles. How the hell were we going to get off this goddamned mountain before nightfall? Before the microbes bred and infected Alawan's wound? Before another lion was attracted by the smell of blood?

Stop, I warned myself. Panic was a luxury none of us could afford. Wynn and Omondi walked carefully, trying not to jounce me, with frequent stops to rest their arms. Alawan walked ahead. He looked unsteady, his stride ragged. Progress was practically nil, but we kept on. There were no other options.

"Jambo."

The four of us whipped our heads around. Another option had appeared on the path. It was Lodogia. He had big soft eyes in a dark, wrinkled face, hugely callused bare feet, and a white loincloth that set off his ebony skin.

"Jambo," we chorused.

Wynn and Omondi lowered me to the ground. Lodogia came and crouched next to me. His deep eyes looked into mine, and he put a warm, horny hand over my ankle and moved it slowly. Then he rose and went to Alawan, gently pulled back the bloody shirt to examine his mauled arm. He signaled for us to wait, turned, and disappeared silently up the path.

Fifteen minutes passed. At Wynn's insistence, Alawan lay down. His eyelids fluttered closed, as if against his will, and he was breathing unevenly.

I had a horrible feeling that Alawan was not going to

215

walk off this mountain. "What do you think Lodogia's doing?"

"I don't know." Wynn's face looked tense and serious. "The Dorobo know a lot about plants. Maybe he's looking for medicine. Let's wait a bit longer."

I sat next to Wynn and took Alawan's hand, willing the Dorobo to come back swiftly with some herbal magic that would make everything all right, wondering if we were doing the right thing by waiting. "His hand is freezing. This is dangerous." Every first aid book I'd ever read told you to wrap a shock victim in a warm blanket. Very helpful advice for the middle of nowhere. I lay down next to Alawan and put my warm body against his. He barely reacted. He wasn't unconscious, but he was out of it.

"Jambo." Lodogia reappeared, carrying a zebra skin bound to two stout poles. A stretcher! We put Alawan on it, Lodogia picked up the front and Omondi the back. Instead of facing downhill, Lodogia started up.

"Hey, wait a second!" I gestured down the mountain. Lodogia gave a long explanation in a language I couldn't understand, with many gestures, insistently pointing up.

"Listen," Wynn said. "I don't see you hopping down the whole way to the plane. It's just not on. We can rest at his hut and send for enough men to carry both you and Alawan down."

It was the voice of reason. I limped heavily behind Omondi, leaning on Wynn and using Alawan's spear as a crutch. Sweat poured down my face from the exertion and the pain. We climbed steadily, higher and higher into the forest. Several times the Dorobo uttered a warning as he stepped over the trip wire of a drop-spear trap, and once we had to squeeze into the bushes to avoid a pit trap.

He turned right and we pushed into a narrower trail that snaked around among the trees. I could see a pool of light ahead. It was a long narrow clearing of tumbled stones at the base of a hundred-foot cliff. Lodogia flung his hand upward, smiling to encourage us, and trotted up a narrow ledge.

"I hope you're not scared of heights," I told Wynn.

There wasn't enough room for the two of us to walk

abreast. I hopped, limped, and finally crawled, not looking down, gripping the sheer rock face with the pads of my fingers for an illusion of security. The ledge grew narrower. I counted my forward movement, one, two, three, four, anything to keep from thinking about the drop-off on my right. I was up to sixty when Omondi's back disappeared, the ledge grew wider again, the cliff face fell back on my left. We'd arrived at the Dorobo's cave.

23

LODOGIA KNELT AT the mouth of the cave, whirling a fire stick between his palms. The point of the stick fit against a bit of flat wood, on which Lodogia had put a strawlike wisp of dried elephant dung. The friction he was creating threw out a spark, a tendril of smoke rose, then a flame. He fed the flame with more dung, lifted the burning straw onto the ashes of his previous fires, added twigs, blowing gently, coaxing it to fiery life.

Above him a rock overhang merged into the roof of the cave, which extended back into dimness. Alawan lay near the fire on a pile of skins, his eyes half open and unfocused. He was shivering. I crawled to the wall near him and leaned against it, panting and sweating.

I pulled out my canteen and took a few gulps. Now that I was a safe distance from the edge, I allowed myself to look out at Lodogia's million-dollar view. The treetops rolled away a few feet below us, as if we were floating on their waves. Forested mountains dipped and crested to my right. Ahead, all along the mountain face the earth fell away in a three-thousand-foot waterfall of trees and rock. At the bottom lay a long narrow plain, lavender-blue at this distance, featureless except for the cone of a solitary volcano. The plain ran north and south forever, but directly opposite it ended abruptly at a towering wall, tall as the perch where I sat.

We were looking into the Great Rift Valley, the largest feature on earth, two thousand miles long and at places a mile deep, a giant crack in the earth's surface where two tectonic plates are pulling apart. A long-crested eagle floated by, coasting down from a thermal, whistling a shrill *kee-eee-eee*.

Lodogia pushed the ends of five arm-length sticks into the center of the fire, like spokes from a wheel, balanced a small blackened earthenware pot on stones sticking out from the coals, and half filled it with water from a wood-stoppered gourd. Omondi emerged from the darkness of the back with a lion skin and arranged it over Alawan. The mane alone covered him from chin to thigh. Lodogia nodded his approval.

Turning away from the bright cave mouth, I let my eyes adjust to the dimness within. The cave was deeper than I expected, the size of a rich man's living room. The roof started out at a comfortable eight to ten feet, but sloped downward so that by the end it was only half as high. Wynn was stooped over near the back, examining several large wooden drums capped with buffalo hide, the hair still on them. She struck one. It emitted a surprisingly dull thump. Lodogia laughed and went back to pry open the hide lid.

"They're honey barrels," exclaimed Wynn. She dipped in a finger and sucked off the sweet golden honey. "Ummm."

Lodogia went to a smaller drum and used a small gourd to spoon out a bowlful. He handed the gourd to Omondi, gesturing that he should help Alawan drink. Omondi supported Alawan's back and held the gourd to his lips, while Alawan sipped obediently. I could smell the fermented honey wine from where I was sitting.

Alawan emptied the gourd and Wynn refilled it. We passed it around. It was as sweet as Passover wine. Lodogia was the only one who drank more than a sip; he finished it in a few gulps and had a second gourd. He returned to the fire with several thick slices he'd cut from a hunk of meat, skewered them and lay them across the fire. *"Tandala,"* he said. Kudu.

Next, Lodogia fetched an antelope horn stoppered with grass, took out a handful of colorful pebbles and cast them on the ground. He studied the resultant pattern with quiet

219

concentration, then scooped the divining stones back into the horn.

A bundle of leafy twigs lay near the zebra-skin stretcher. They were a fresh green, as if newly picked. Lodogia must have gathered them while we were below, waiting for his return. He stripped off several handfuls of the leaves and added them to the pot on the fire. A lovely herbal smell rose in a cloud, overlaying the fermented wine and the greasy smells of wood smoke, meat, and hides that filled the cave.

I might be in the cave of a dangerous sorcerer, but a great feeling of peace descended upon me. It was wonderful not to be hopping around on my bum ankle, to be safe from lions, to smell dinner roasting on the fire, but it was more than that. I looked around the cave. A bow and cluster of poison arrows hung from one peg. A bulging leather bag hung next to them. Bundles of herbs tied with raffia hung from a third peg. Scattered near the fire were two crude iron knives with wooden grips, a second earthenware cooking pot, several gourd bowls, a little vase-shaped basket with a top. In the back were drop traps in varied stages of manufacture, and a small blackened pot that I suspected was used for making poison.

A bee flew into the cave and buzzed around the honey barrel. The fire crackled. In the trees below two drongos sang a duet. Everything here Lodogia had made himself, with the exception of the iron points for his arrows and traps. We had stepped not hundreds, but thousands of years back in time.

Wynn came over and plunked down next to me. "How's the leg?"

"It's not great," I said. "I'm glad I'm not walking anymore."

"It looks like we'll be here for tonight. Quite a place, isn't it?"

"Like a visit to the old ancestral home."

"Yeah. Except for his pelt business."

"What's he got in that pile back there?"

"Don't ask, you'll get apoplectic."

"More lions?"

"Cats big and small. And under the whole pile, he's got a new rifle."

"Wonderful. Progress touches every corner of the globe."

Omondi joined us. "I wonder why Nick didn't tell you about meeting Lodogia. He's such an extraordinary man."

Wynn smiled sadly. "Nick and I liked to keep the interesting bits from our work trips to share when we could really listen to each other. He had a lot of other stuff to tell me about his week away, but we were busy getting the house in order for our weekend guests." She gave a big sigh.

All this while, Lodogia stirred the pot on the fire. Next he scooped out the wilted leaves with his gourd spoon and set them aside. He gently pulled Omondi's bloodied shirt from Alawan's arm.

"How does the wound look?" I asked.

Omondi craned over Lodogia's shoulder. "A mess, but it's stopped bleeding."

Lodogia spread the herbal poultice liberally over the wound, then wrapped it with some large leaves. Alawan didn't flinch.

Lodogia transferred a browned hunk of meat from the roasting stick into the pot, to which he added more water. He got some bundles of dried herbs from the back of the cave and added two sorts to the pot.

Now it was my turn. Lodogia crouched by my ankle, turned my leg until I winced, pressed gently on the puffiness. Again he cast the divining stones. When the broth had simmered to his satisfaction, he handed Omondi a calabash to feed to Alawan, and brought over one for me.

I sipped, and discovering it tasted like a delicious herbed beef broth, gulped it down. A feeling of warmth and energy flowed through my body. "I'm suddenly ravenous!" I remarked. Lodogia was already returning with a large portion of roast kudu.

Omondi asked Lodogia something in Samburu, and translated for me. "He has put a special plant in the broth that the *moran*, the warriors, use in their retreats, to make themselves strong. The way he describes it, I believe it is

221

a sort of amphetamine." I was already wolfing down the buffalo steak, tearing off hunks with my teeth. "The *moran* drink this brew, and then they stay up singing and dancing all night, and they can eat meat like a lion does, twenty or forty pounds for each man."

I paused in mid-bite. "How much did he give me? Am I about to turn into a werewolf?"

Omondi passed on the question; Lodogia laughed. "He says not to worry. He has made it very weak, because he wants Alawan to sleep. It will help your ankle to heal faster. Eat as much as you want. There is plenty."

Lodogia served the rest of the meat, and we all concentrated on eating. The broth seemed to have a good effect on Alawan. His skin was back to its normal, warm color. He ate some meat, too, looked around the cave with a strange look. It was not so much curiosity as suspicion. He asked Lodogia some questions, and launched into a long recital.

"He is describing the lion attack," Omondi told us. "He had thought it was Lodogia himself, transformed into a lion; now he asks if it was a rival sorcerer. They are striking a deal. When we leave, Lodogia will give us some protective magic, plus several kilos of honey, and Alawan will send him a cow. Alawan's younger brother has the family herd in the mountains several hours to the north. Lodogia says there are so many cows in the mountains, there's hardly any forest left."

"I'm surprised this mountain is so untouched," Wynn said. "None of the Samburu graze here?"

Omondi asked Lodogia. "He says that he is a powerful sorcerer, and that nobody enters his honey territory without his permission."

"Ask him about meeting Nick. And where he meets this white man the Samburu says he sells pelts to," I asked Omondi. "How did he meet him? Is it someone from the water project? Or the Somali refugee camps? Or an oil worker?"

"And how much did he tell Nick?" Wynn added.

Omondi thought for a moment. "I must build up to these questions. Be patient." He started by walking over to

222

Lodogia's bow and arrows and admiring them. Without being asked, Lodogia took the bow down and demonstrated, then invited Omondi to test his strength by pulling back the bowstring. Wynn tried her hand at it, too.

"It feels great to hold," she told me. "Beautiful balance."

Next Omondi examined the arrowheads, and Lodogia showed where he dipped them in the pot of poison and lay them down to dry. Omondi moved over to some clusters of dried herbs. I heard Lodogia say Nick, and gesture as if wrapping up his hand in the leaves.

"What's he saying about Nick?" I asked.

Omondi listened as Lodogia explained further, and translated. "Lodogia had brought this herb to the manyatta to treat a child with an infected foot that he'd sliced on a sharp rock. It is a secret cure he learned from his father. Nick was interested, and he gave him some."

Next came the honey kegs. Lodogia explained how he carved out five-foot segments of logs to create an artificial hive. He would place them high up in trees and regularly visit them to harvest the honey. At this time of year it was only at these higher elevations that bees found flowering trees; after the rains began, he would rejoin his family in the more open forest in the foothills.

At last Omondi came to the pile of animal skins. Lodogia offered to sell them to us. It was heartbreaking. He asked a few dollars for the life of a lion, a leopard, even less for a lynxlike caracal or a spotted serval. What the hell did he need the money for, anyway? To buy bullets so he could wipe out more animals? And so it went, all the way up the line, human greed and selfishness, right up to the one who drove the whole engine of destruction, the woman who thought it was romantic to wear wild fur.

"Who is his buyer?" I tried to control my voice, but it came out rough with anger. "Who?"

Omondi patted my arm. He and Lodogia continued their cordial conversation. I had to walk away. Alawan was sleeping, his chest rising and falling in a slow, regular rhythm. The sun was lower in the west, like a giant cat's eye staring into the cave. Below it, the Rift Valley was a trough of purple haze, its far wall lost to view. My shadow reached across the stone floor to the others, still standing by the pelts. Lodogia was talking. He tapped the pelts with his toe, talking in Samburu. Suddenly, two words stood out with all the clarity of the sunlight.

"Gerry Weller."

Our enemy had a face.

24

SPENDING THE NIGHT in Lodogia's cave was uncomfortable but wonderful at the same time. It got pretty cold, and the skins I slept on seemed to have retained their fleas after death, so I slept fitfully. The tearing and chewing sound of feeding elephants arose from the woods below us, making the stillness that followed even more complete.

Sometime in the small hours of the morning a bone-chilling cold crept into the cave. I huddled into my little pocket of body warmth, reluctant to burrow under more skins and gratify a fresh batch of fleas. My mind began speeding with thoughts about the case, no matter how hard I tried to put it out of my mind and fall asleep.

I heard a faint whisper of movement in the dark, and sensed a dark shape crouching over me. As I began to sit up, the person put a reassuring hand on my shoulder.

"Don't worry," a voice breathed in a whisper. It was Omondi. "Are you cold?"

"Yes."

He slipped under the lion skin with me.

"Omondi!" I whispered vehemently.

He put a soft finger on my lips. "Don't worry," he said again. "We shall keep each other warm." He lay with his belly pressed against my back, thigh to thigh, our feet nested together, his arm around my waist. I snuggled against him. His breath was warm on my neck; his breathing grew deep and regular as a lullaby. The next moment I was asleep.

I awoke to a cheery breakfast fire and a sky of high mackerel clouds that briefly glowed pink in the rising sun.

Alawan was not only awake before me, he was standing at the very edge of the ledge, looking out at the mountains' plunge to the Great Rift Valley. I joined him, Omondi came to my other side, and then Wynn. The four of us stood in silence and looked out over the immensity and grandeur of the earth.

We breakfasted on cornmeal mush. To my relief, Alawan ate and talked with energy. The only sign of his mauling was the poultice on his arm; looking at him, you'd never know anything bigger than a flea had bitten him the day before. My leg was stiff, but I didn't need a stretcher service, either. We took the trip back down the mountain slow and easy. Lodogia came with us, carrying the honey he was bartering to Alawan, and we had no encounters with either traps or animals on our way back to the plane.

By the time we dropped Alawan and his honey off at the manyatta, Omondi and I didn't get back to Nairobi until the tail end of the afternoon. The first thing I did was call Kenarabia again. The secretary admitted Weller was back in town but wouldn't tell me where I could reach him.

I left a number for him to call me, then paced around my apartment like a caged animal, trying to plan my meeting with him. Confronting Weller on buying pelts was easy; the hard part was finding out if Nick's discovery of it threatened Weller enough to commit murder. Would Weller kill to protect his job? Perhaps, if he had a stake in the new oil exploration near Nick's land. He'd be the first to know how much that land was worth. Oil was the explosive ingredient. Or was this a sideshow that led Nick to the sheikh, still our main suspect?

I couldn't think of any brilliant ideas of how to get Weller to talk: "Hi, Gerry, according to an anonymous source, you are involved in the wild skin trade. Nick Hunter found out about it a week before his death and was going to expose you. We also believe you may have links to a Saudi hunting party in the same vicinity. Explain yourself." It wasn't going to fly.

Mercifully, the phone rang in under an hour. I pounced on the second ring.

"Jazz? Gerry Weller here. I was pleased to hear from you. How're you doin'?"

Even the man's voice was sexy. It made me more nervous. I stammered something about wanting to get together to talk over some things.

"Great. I'd love to see you. I've been thinking about you." His voice held the slightest trace of a purr. "How about this: I'm staying at a friend's house downtown, a very interesting person I'm sure you'd like, named Gabriella Casale. Why don't you drop by here for drinks, say around seven, and then you and I can take off for a nice supper somewhere."

I agreed, feeling horribly duplicitous, and he explained how to find his friend's house. Gerry was acting as if I'd called to ask him out on a date. I couldn't very well declare that I wanted to grill him about a possible link to Nick's murder. Actually, he was making things easy for me. I'd have to play along.

"See you at seven. Looking forward to it," he signed off.

Gabriella's house was on a once-residential side street downtown that was now engulfed by larger-scale apartment and commercial buildings. The stucco house was set back and hidden by trees, so you'd never know that between a ten-story apartment complex and a furniture showroom lay a private home. The front door was protected by a wrought-iron antiburglar grill, but bougainvillea climbed up the bars, creating a lush and welcoming effect.

Gabriella, a distinguished-looking woman in her fifties, with dark hair pulled straight back from her face, stood on the steps. She was dressed elaborately, wearing a curiously designed silver necklace that contrasted with the simplicity of an Italian knit dress and three-quarter-length jacket.

She flung her arms out. "Welcome, welcome." She gave me an energetic handshake. "I am so happy to meet you." She led me into the house, still holding my arm. "Gerry has been saying nice things about you."

"Oh, really?" I laughed. "We only met once."

227

Gabriella studied me for an instant with piercing dark eyes. "No, that doesn't matter. I can see immediately why he is attracted to you—you have a special spirit." She squeezed my hand. "I hope we will become good friends, too."

Although I don't usually warm to people who judge me by first impressions and talk about people's spirits, I couldn't help liking Gabriella's warmth.

I looked around the entry. Gerry was standing to one side, with his big white-toothed smile, ready to enjoy my reaction. The house was stucco within as without, but while the outside was ordinary, the inside was intensely personal. It was as if a sculptor had carved out each room by hand, with great spontaneity and a hatred of rulers. There was not a straight line in the place.

Opposite the door was an asymmetrical niche with a West African fertility sculpture—a female figure with protruding cone-shaped breasts and an infant on her knee—and a cymbidium orchid in bloom. The speckled pink flowers filled the entry with a scent of cloves and cinnamon. On the wall next to them, an abstract painting of the Madonna and Child glowed in jewel tones.

"Nice to see you," Gerry drawled, and gave my hand a squeeze with his callused palm.

There were doors off to the left and right, but Gabriella led me up the curving stairway. "Let me take you to my favorite room," she said, throwing open the door. "This is where I live. For my soul to breathe, I need plants around me."

It was a conservatory. Huge jungle plants reached to the glass ceiling, philodendrons with table-size leaves, smooth-trunked palms, a banana tree with its hanging flower looking like a giant male organ. Somewhere a jasmine was casting its scent onto the lightly humid air, and I heard the sound of tinkling water. I rounded an orange tree and there was a low marble table set up for drinks, surrounded by wicker chairs with puffy cushions. Behind them, water percolated down a slab of black volcanic stone and disappeared among the leaves.

The chair was even more comfortable than it looked. "This is an extraordinary place, Gabriella."

"Thank you. I live in Rome half the year, but this is where my heart stays, always."

"Gabriella's a painter," Gerry explained.

I asked if the Madonna and Child was her work (it was), and exclaimed over the beauty of the painting, and the entire house, while Gerry took our drink requests and Gabriella grew excited as a child telling me about her recent safari to Maasai Mara. She'd timed it to see the peak of the wildebeest migration: tens of thousands of animals crossing croc-infested rivers to get to green grass.

"It is like watching an opera," Gabriella exclaimed. "Pathos, tragedy, comedy—it is all there."

Gerry handed Gabriella a campari and soda, then a gin and tonic for me and himself. I asked Gabriella a hundred questions about her life and work, and we discovered a shared passion for wildlife and Renaissance art, when she looked at her watch and jumped up, saying she was meeting friends for dinner. Gabriella was the first person I'd met in Africa who could relate to the first half of my life, as Dr. Jasper, art historian, as well as Jazz the lover of wildlife, owner of Jazz Jasper Safaris. I hadn't realized there'd been a cost in suppressing that other part of myself, but being with Gabriella, I felt more whole than I had in a long time.

"I hope we see each other again," I told her.

She threw her arms around my shoulders. "Of course we will. We are going to become friends, I hope. Don't you feel it?"

"Yes. I do. Till next time, then."

If Gerry had attempted to disorient me on purpose, he couldn't have done a more effective job. I assume most oil people are conservative and conventional, untouched by the far-off places where they work. Gerry was obviously different. He wasn't going to be an easy person to read.

Gabriella's departure left an awkward hole. Gerry didn't seem to notice. He told me how he'd met her, managing to fit into the conversation that they were mere friends, that he'd been divorced for several years, that he much preferred working in Africa to the Middle East, because of the interesting people, Africans and expatriates, that you could meet here, as opposed to the walled-in country club life of expats in Saudi Arabia. We talked about the Samburu; Gerry loved visiting the manyattas near the oil camps, and had begun to make one or two Samburu friends in the year he'd been there.

The more I enjoyed myself, the more I felt myself in an untenable role, acting like a potential friend. Better get to what I'd come for, then depart. I approached the topic by telling about my visit to the manyatta, seeing signs of hunting and going to find Lodogia. Gerry acted fascinated and slightly envious. I couldn't detect the slightest sign of unease. Was I all wrong? Or was Gerry incredibly slick?

There was only one way to find out. I approached the end of my tale. "Lodogia showed us this pile of cat pelts he had in the back of the cave—leopard, lion, serval, caracal. He wanted less than ten dollars a piece."

Gerry looked disgusted. "Somebody's making a bundle. It would be great to find the middleman, the guy who's smuggling the stuff into the international market. Those are the real lowlifes."

"We asked him about that. He told us the guy's name."

"Fantastic. Have you turned it over to the Wildlife Department? They'll have to find the goods on him, or catch him in the act of buying from Lodogia."

"You want to know the name he gave us?"

"Some government minister?"

"No. He told us he sells to: Gerry Weller."

The look of interest on Gerry's face was replaced by surprise. "That's why you called me," he said quietly. Was it my imagination, or did he look hurt?

I nodded.

"Why in heck would he give my name? How does he even know it?"

"You deny knowing him?"

"Sure, I deny it." He leaned forward and looked into my eyes. His were a piercing blue. "Listen, Jazz, you don't know me very well yet, or you wouldn't have believed him for a second. I love the wilds, and I despise people who kill animals for money."

"You sounded pretty cavalier about keeping cheetah as house pets, the other day."

"I'm not a fighter, like you. I'm a cynic: I think you're fighting the force of history. The pressure of human population will swallow everything on this continent, like a huge tidal wave that leaves only bare soil and destruction when it recedes—except this wave is never going to recede." He picked up his drink and sloshed the ice around. "We're going to lose most of these animals, and there's not a damn thing anyone can do about it. But I admire you for trying," he lifted his glass in a mock toast, "and I would never do anything—"

"How do you explain Lodogia telling us your name?"

"I'm asking myself that same question." Gerry thought for a moment. "He could have heard about me from the Samburu I know."

"But why would he make up a thing like that? Give the name of someone he's never met?"

"I'd have remembered meeting a Dorobo, I'm sure." Gerry seemed puzzled, not perturbed. He took a sip from his drink and leaned back in the wicker chair, crossing his long legs. He was wearing tooled leather cowboy boots. "You know, I'm wondering if my driver knows something about this. We had a camp not too far from the mountains, oh, maybe six or eight months ago. Louis doesn't usually mix much with the locals, and I remember being surprised to see him hanging out with an old geezer in a red toga, who I assumed was a Samburu elder."

"You think that might have been Lodogia?"

"I'm wondering. It would be easy for Louis to stow a pile of pelts among our other equipment. He travels with an enormous duffel bag, now that I think of it, big enough to smuggle a small horse."

"Wouldn't Lodogia have given Louis's name?"

"Heck, Louis may have pretended he was buying as my agent. He's in the kitchen. Come on, let's go talk to him."

231

Gerry sprang up and swung out of the room. I hurried after him, down the sculpted staircase to the first floor, down a short hall to a dining room filled with more orchids and paintings, and through a swinging door to the kitchen.

Two black women in servants' uniforms were eating at a beat-up table, while a third one carried a set of dishes to the sink.

"Is Louis here?" Gerry asked.

"No, sir. He left this minute to deliver your package. Said he'd be back later."

Gerry looked at me. "I didn't give him anything to deliver."

"Let's try to catch him."

As we ran to the front door, I could hear a car's engine shift from first to second gear. We burst onto the front steps in time to see the taillights of Gerry's Land Cruiser go through the gates.

"Come on." I pulled out my keys, we jumped into my old Rover and followed. Louis rounded the corner as we pulled through the gate. I cut off a guy on a motor scooter and drove after Louis. He was heading toward Uhuru Highway, where the traffic would be heavier, and I didn't want to fall behind. At the roundabout where Kenyatta and Uhuru meet, a lorry lumbered in front of us, cutting off the view. By the time I got into the roundabout, Louis was gone.

"Can you spot him?" I asked Gerry. I had to keep my eyes on the high-speed chaos that passes for a traffic pattern at the roundabouts.

"No. Stay on Uhuru. Maybe we'll catch up to him at the roundabout on Haile Selassie."

I drove the length of the big grassy expanse of Uhuru Park, dark and uninviting at this time of night. On our left we passed the Parliament Building. The road was crowded with buses, vans, lorries, and a lot of Japanese cars. Every now and then we were passed by a Wabenzi, member of the rich black elite, in his chauffeur-driven Mercedes or Jaguar, and once by a dusty Land Rover that had come into Nairobi from safari. Gerry's Land Cruiser was nowhere to be seen.

"We've lost him," I said.

"Let's go on to dinner," Gerry suggested. "We can catch him when he comes back. Louis is going to have some questions to answer."

"Does he have permission to use your car when you're not using it?"

"Only if he asks. I told him I wouldn't need him tonight. I thought I'd drive us to dinner myself. He must have assumed I didn't need the car. But he shouldn't have taken it without telling me."

"I wonder what he was in such a hurry to deliver."

We ate at a seafood restaurant with double-height walls painted tropical blue. It was like eating in a giant aquarium. Gerry announced it was his treat, and urged me to join him in ordering spiny lobster, which is usually too steep for my budget. I told a story that involved me and Striker while we were still ordering, with the covert message that I was in a serious relationship and unavailable. Saying Striker's name made me feel alone and scared. Would I soon be going out on real dates with other men? Or only with potential murderers?

Gerry finished a funny story about getting lost only a few thousand feet from his own camp. I managed to work the conversation around to his employer.

"What's the connection between Sheikh Farid and Kenarabia?" I asked.

"Sheikh Farid ibn-Dawud's family owns controlling shares in the business. He's nominally a vice-president in their central office. I don't think he does much but sign off reports from his foreign underlings. This is his first visit to Kenya in a few years."

"What's the occasion?"

Our food arrived. Gerry speared a succulent piece of lobster on his fork and popped it in his mouth. "Isn't this sweet?"

"Mm. Delicious. I hear they're opening up a new oil field."

"Never believe rumors about oil. Those who know, don't talk. Those who talk, don't know."

233

"Isn't the sheikh's visit a tip-off that something big is happening?"

"No, he's a lightweight. His older brothers are the ones who count."

"I met Princess Rana at a fashion show, and was her guest on safari."

"In Samburu?"

"Yes. You know about it?"

"I suggested the site."

"You know he's hunting there?"

Gerry snorted. "No, but I can't say I'm surprised. The bastards."

"It could get him in real trouble."

"You are naive." Gerry put down his knife and fork. "The sheikh could kill with impunity."

"Only if he manages to keep it secret."

"That's what he pays for."

"If his hunting becomes public . . ."

"Nothing can get someone that rich in real trouble. A nuisance, yes, a little mess for the lawyers to clean up. It's nothing to them."

"What about world opinion?"

"Listen, when you own forty percent of the world's oil, you don't care a hoot what people think of you. The Saudis despise infidels anyway, so why should they care what you think?"

"What about Farid's big brothers? Would they welcome him back with open arms for creating a major international stink? A lot more people are concerned about preserving wildlife than there used to be."

"Not enough. But you have a point about his brothers. Farid would certainly care about their reaction. And they want to keep a low profile. You know, the more I think about it, maybe a scandal—even about hunting—would hurt Farid at home, because of the playboy angle. The young generation of fundamentalists have the whip hand over the royal family. They're sure the only reason the princes go abroad is to drink and whore, so any publicity about their vacations makes the royal family nervous."

234

"Well, Farid's safe now that Nick Hunter's dead."

"Hunter's not the only journalist in Kenya."

"He's the only one who was visiting that manyatta on August fifteenth, the day Farid arrived at his hunting camp."

"Farid didn't go on safari till the seventeenth."

"How do you know?"

"Because he flew to my oil camp on the sixteenth and I gave him a nice little tour and briefing."

Gerry seemed unaware that he'd just ruled out the sheikh as Nick's killer and left himself as the prime suspect. In fact, nothing in his demeanor showed a hint of fear or subterfuge. If Weller had something to hide, he was doing it awfully well.

"I meant to ask you," Gerry said, "was it really the scorpion sting that killed Hunter?"

"As far as I know."

"Did they give him scorpion antivenin?"

"No, snake antivenin. That's all we had, so Wynn tried it. It didn't have any effect. Why?"

"Some countries won't sell scorpion antivenin anymore, because there've been fatalities associated with it. I guess it's trickier than with snakes to get the dose right, or make sure the venin has been rendered harmless or something."

"Well, there was an autopsy. The doctor said for sure it was the scorpion and not the shot."

"Unlucky bastard. You never know when death is going to come knocking on your door." He signaled the waiter for the check. "That's why it's so important to do what you love, eat plenty of lobster, spend time with friends: make every minute count."

"Nick had plenty of gusto. I'm sad for him not getting to enjoy the rest of his life."

"I'm sorry about you losing your friend," Gerry said sympathetically.

"You said you met him once?" I remembered quite well that Gerry had denied ever meeting Nick, but I was testing.

"No, I never had the pleasure. How's his wife doing?"

235

"Wynn? She's taking it hard. Very hard, but she doesn't show it much. She has a tough side to her."

"That's good. Life can be a bitch, especially in Africa."

I'd heard enough to feel sure Gerry was not our killer. I believed him when he said he'd never met Nick. Questioning me tonight about the real cause of death was the clincher. The killer wouldn't do that. Yes, Gerry might have had a reason to wish Nick out of the way, he might have had the access to Sahara scorpions from his experience in the Middle East, he might have been near the scene of death, but that didn't add up to murder. Hell, without Gerry's questions, there never would have been a murder investigation.

I was eager to speak to his chauffeur, Louis, and find out about this package he'd delivered, purportedly for Gerry. I found myself hoping that it was the chauffeur and not Gerry who was buying animal skins.

By the time we returned to Gabriella's, Gerry's Land Cruiser was parked neatly in the graveled area in front of her house. A maid answered our ring and told us Gabriella wasn't back yet. We followed her to the kitchen, where we found Louis entertaining the cook and her assistant with funny stories and beer, to judge from the bottles on the table and the general mood of conviviality. Before Gerry could ask him, Louis jumped out of his seat, all apologies for taking the car, explaining at tortuous length that he'd thought Gerry wasn't going to need it.

"Where did you take it?"

"To the garage, sir. There was a sound I didn't like and I wanted them to check the engine. It was a loose fan belt, and they put in a new one."

"Your cousin's garage?"

Louis nodded.

"That's okay, then. We took Jazz's car, so it wasn't a disaster. Next time, tell me if you are taking the car out."

"Sure thing. I am very sorry." He launched into the whole explanation from the beginning, but Gerry cut him off.

We left the kitchen, and I declined the offer of a nightcap in the conservatory. Gerry walked me to my car.

"Where is this cousin's garage?" I asked.

"Off Muranga Road," Gerry said with a crooked smile. "The opposite direction from the one he took."

"Yes."

"Why didn't you say anything?"

"I'm going to find out what this is all about. But the direct approach is useless. I'd prefer he thinks I suspect nothing. That way I'll be able to catch him in the act."

The direct approach was the one I'd used on Gerry. Had I messed things up? Tipped my hand and been easily deflected by a smooth line and a lopsided smile?

As I was entertaining these doubts, Gerry popped the hood on his Land Cruiser and bent over the engine. I joined him. He pointed to the fan belt. It was newish, but not what anyone would call brand new.

"As I thought. We replaced the fan belt a few months ago." He let the hood down softly and pressed down till it clicked. "Louis Mutani is going to have some explaining to do."

"What did you say?"

"I said Louis is—"

"No, his last name."

"Mutani?"

"Any relation to William Mutani, the casino king?"

"Yeah, William sent him to me. There's some kin connection, not close. You know."

"How long has he been working for you?"

"A little over a year. Why?"

"What were you doing with Mutani that day I met you?"

"Just driving around."

"Come on."

"I bumped into Mutani at the lodge where I was staying, and he told me he was going to look at some land and drop in on an interesting couple that were raising cheetahs. I'm always up for meeting interesting people; especially a pair of desert lovers like myself, practically living in my neck of the country. I'd still love to see the cheetahs someday, when Wynn's feeling up to visitors."

237

"What was the story with the land Mutani wanted to look at?"

"I really can't tell you that."

I leaned back against the Cruiser to take the weight off my bad leg. My ankle had begun to throb. "Why not?"

"Because it's Mutani's business, not mine. I didn't ask him what in hell he wanted that worthless scrap of land for, and he didn't tell me. That way if word leaks out and speculators start swarming like sharks, he knows it wasn't from me."

"Did he ask your opinion of it as oil-bearing land?"

"Hey, if I thought there was oil to be found down there, believe me, I'd move my outfit, rent one of the cottages at the lodge and commute to the worksite. Wouldn't that be comfy?" He smiled, watching my lips for an answering smile.

I crossed my arms. "Not that you'd tell me if there was oil."

"No, I certainly would not, even if I knew you a whole lot better than I do now."

"What about Mutani and Sheikh Farid? What's their connection?"

"Why the third degree about Mutani?"

"Just curious."

Gerry leaned one hand against the car. "I'm curious about something, too." He leaned forward and pressed his lips against mine.

My first impulse was to escape the kiss, but the car was behind me, and it would have taken a real shove to move him back. It's hard to shove somebody you've just spent a pleasant evening with, even if it felt wrong to kiss someone other than Striker, someone who I hardly knew and didn't trust. But the kiss had its own imperative. Gerry poured a beam of sexual energy into that kiss, and my whole body lit up. He pressed his lower body against mine, his hand in my hair, his lips soft and insistent on mine. I closed my eyes and kissed back.

After a moment I pulled back a few inches, and Gerry's blue eyes stared into my brown ones. "I really like you, Jazz."

I stammered something, I don't know what, flew into my Rover, and was out of there. I imagined Gerry standing there and laughing as I fled. Whether it was friendly or triumphant laughter, I wasn't sure.

25

IT WAS TIME to visit Mutani in his lair. I'd tried to think of some clever, indirect method of finding out about Mutani's connections to the sheikh and what he was up to near Wynn's property, but I came up blank. I didn't even know whether to believe Gerry Weller that the land was being surveyed by Mutani and not by Kenarabia Oil: when I saw them, they were driving around in Gerry's Land Cruiser, with Mutani as the guest in the backseat.

William Mutani's office was downtown, near the Standard Bank Building on Kenyatta Avenue. I pushed open the heavy glass door to his suite and felt my feet sink into the plush carpet. The receptionist was enthroned behind a gleaming mahogany desk. She was the color of mahogany herself, and shining with bright jewelry and a red silk blouse, matched by her red-manicured nails. She wore her hair in the latest style, a fountain of thin two-foot braids cascading from a knot at the top of her head. The fact that the hair was fake took nothing away from the smashing effect.

"How may I help you?"

I didn't merit a smile. And I'd put on a dress and makeup, too. "Jazz Jasper. I have an appointment with Mr. Mutani at ten." It was a lie, but I figured the truth would get me nowhere.

She didn't even look at the fancy appointment book at the corner of the desk. "Did you make the appointment with me?"

"No, I saw Mr. Mutani last week, when he was up north."

"I'm afraid he didn't mention it to me. Perhaps it

slipped his mind." Her tone and look implied that I appeared quite forgettable. "He's in conference now, and then he has a meeting elsewhere. If you leave your name and number . . ." She didn't bother to end the sentence.

"I'm in town only for one day. Mr. Mutani will be disappointed if he misses me." I paused. She didn't look impressed. "Perhaps he has a few minutes between his other engagements."

"I doubt he'll be able to see you, but if you want to wait, you're most welcome. Please take a seat." She gestured toward a set of low stuffed chairs that looked like carnivorous muffins.

There were magazines on a glass side table: old copies of *Financial Times*, a magazine called *Business in Africa Today*, and the latest edition of a fancy European travel magazine featuring Mutani's new casino on Mount Kenya. That brought on glum thoughts about Striker. Why did things have to change when we were getting along so well? Why did Mutani have to build his stupid road through Striker's front yard? Why couldn't Striker find another wild place to live in Kenya?

A buzz from the intercom interrupted my unhappy thoughts. Mutani's secretary arose and swayed into his office. She returned only to go into a utility closet filled with a table and coffee machine, and start setting up a tray with several cups.

I walked over to her. "Did you let Mr. Mutani know I'm here?"

"No. This was not the proper time." She didn't bother to look up.

I had an impulse to upend the coffee tray all over her bright red dress, but controlled the urge.

"He's going straight from this meeting to the next. After lunch, I will have time to tell him you are here." She picked up the tray and looked at me, but I don't think she saw me. I don't know if she saw anything except herself playing a starring role as the king's secretary, wielding the keys to the realm. "Do you still want to wait?"

Without giving me time to answer, she pushed through the heavy door into the conference room. There was a babble of male voices and a waft of sour smoke before the doors closed. I left without leaving my number, but I didn't go far.

I got my car, tipped the man with the *rungu*, a Maasai club, who had offered to guard the car from vandals, and positioned myself across the street from Mutani's office. His destination might tell me something interesting, and if not, at least I'd collar him and set up a time to talk.

Following Mutani's chauffeur-driven Mercedes was a breeze. He took the Limuru Road, passed the Aga Khan Hospital, and a mile farther, on the right, turned into the stone gates of one of his own latest creations, the Royal Parklands Hotel and Casino. The drive wound among lush tropical plantings, past thatched guest cottages, to a large semicircle in front of the lobby. I pulled to the side until Mutani disembarked, then surrendered my keys to a valet, with a tip to park the car close to the entry.

I hurried into the lobby—a giant thatched hut a hundred feet across and sixty feet high—and paused a moment to let my eyes adjust to the dim interior. These new hotels made me feel like I'd wandered into a movie set. In the center of the lobby was a life-size plastic model of a charging bull elephant. Under its upraised trunk, I caught sight of Mutani's back disappearing out the opposite side of the lobby.

Following him, I exited onto a high terrace which overlooked a multilevel garden. A complex of paths and bridges led over a pool graced with live flamingos, leading to a stream complete with water-smoothed boulders, which ended in a waterfall pouring into the swimming pool. The pool was divided into several areas by two tree-clad islands. Purple bougainvillea dripped from the bridge crossing the pool, where Mutani was shaking hands with two familiar figures.

They were none other than Viv and Roger Porter. Roger looked distinguished in a well-cut silver-gray suit, while Viv was the picture of femininity in a softly falling dress with English wildflowers scattered on a lavender background. She even had on a cream-colored sun hat with a floppy lavender rose on the brim. After exclaiming over the pool and garden, they crossed the bridge to the restaurant on the other side, where the maitre d' awaited them at the door, all bows and smiles.

Funny that neither Viv nor Roger said a word about knowing Mutani when I reported bumping into him the day of Nick's death. Although, given how stunned everyone was, I couldn't make too much of it. It would be interesting to know what brought the three of them together today. I'd wait for them to get settled, and then wander in and discover them.

I watched the flamingos for a while, some preening, others napping with their long necks improbably twisted backward. They reminded me of camping out with Omondi at Lake Nakuru during a murder investigation earlier in the year. We'd arrived in darkness, and at dawn the sun rose on a million flamingos floating and flying and massed along the shore. I wondered if the Royal Parklands flamingos missed their compatriots on the soda lake.

Descending, I crossed above the waterfall and found myself at a fork in the path. I heard sounds of heavy machinery to the left. It sounded like earth-moving equipment. I headed toward it, thinking I might pick up some useful information. The path took me past a charming outdoor restaurant under the broad limbs of a tree with huge, glossy leaves. It wound about some more, past a dress boutique and other lobby shops, a third restaurant decorated like an Indian palace with walls of carved sandalwood. To the right the path was blocked off with a rope and a sign begging forgiveness for the inconvenience posed to the guests by the construction site of a new conference facility.

I squeezed past the rope and headed for the construction site. A black man in a tropical suit and a hard hat was conferring over some plans with what looked like the work foreman. I waited until they were finished, then walked up and asked the man in the suit what they were building.

He looked surprised to see me, but perhaps not wanting to be rude to a hotel guest, explained this was a site for a conference center. He seemed like a nice person, with an open, friendly face, as he waved at the big messy hole in the ground and chaos of workmen with a self-confident gesture, helping me picture what would someday soon adorn the spot. I chatted with him about his design and what other buildings in Nairobi he'd worked on.

"Are you interested in architecture?" he asked. "Or in development, perhaps?"

"Both," I answered. "Are you working on Mutani's new one up in Samburu Province?"

"As a matter of fact, I am."

"What are you building there?"

His face lit up. "Oh, a very exciting design. We want the hotel to fit perfectly into the landscape, like a manyatta, and yet be airy and open to the magnificent views of the hills, yet also a shelter from the heat and the sun. It poses some interesting design challenges."

"It's an unusual place for a hotel, isn't it? Rather far from the park."

"Not really. It has to be outside the park because we are to have a casino. The site has a magnificent view, and there is abundant water."

"It's not on the Oaso Nyiro, is it?" The Oaso Nyiro was a shallow muddy river that flowed year-round, providing a haven for wildlife in the National Park, and elsewhere a watering place for Samburu stock.

"No, but there is a very good spring on the adjoining parcel, which Mutani is acquiring. He plans to put in a golf course. Did you ever visit Palm Springs?" He grinned. "I went to school at UCLA. Palm Springs is amazing. Dozens of golf courses in the desert. I never thought Kenya would have anything like it."

I wondered if they'd import live flamingos to the desert, too, like hotels did in Palm Springs. "Where is he getting the money?"

He shook his head, smiling. "Ah, that is something Mr. Mutani is very good at. The Koreans are investing in this project." He indicated the red clay hole and cement machinery in front of us. "And I think there is some money from Oman, or one of those rich oil kingdoms. There's a lot of money in the world. The trick is knowing how to tap into it." A piece of heavy machinery started up and he had to shout to be heard. "Mr. Mutani is a one-man multinational institution. He has brought much money into Kenya. We have the best tourist industry in Africa."

There was no point trying to talk over the racket, and besides, I'd found out what I needed. I wished him good luck and headed back to the restaurant. I was happy that Gerry Weller hadn't lied to me. It sounded like Mutani was building his biggest project ever, and meant to include the Hunters' land. Why hadn't he approached them already? Or had he approached Nick—and been turned down? Turned down because Nick had started to uncover Mutani's web of illegal activities, from smuggling pelts to arranging a hunting safari for a favored client?

"One for lunch?" The unctuous maitre d' gave a little bow.

I was in another gargantuan thatched hut. This one seemed to have been crossed with a Tudor cottage and a Stately Home, producing half-timbered walls and dark rafters worthy of any Great Hall in Britain. In place of the lobby's life-size elephant there was a circular buffet on a raised dais, splendid with an ice sculpture of an elephant, brass serving globes with flames underneath to keep the hot food hot, mounds of ice displaying masses of sliced pineapple, papayas, melons, and passion fruit, salads of every description, Indian curries, and on and on. It effectively blocked off sight of the other side of the room.

"I think I have some friends here," I murmured, and kept walking. I circled the buffet, glancing at the double outer circle of tables: businessmen in suits, hotel guests in pool attire, a busload of Germans in bright resort wear. There was a babble of voices in English, Italian, Swahili, French, German, Swedish. Where were Mutani and the Porters? In the round room, there were no dim corners for them to be hiding in. They couldn't have gobbled down lunch and left this fast. I circled a second time. The smells of the curries and fruits were making me ravenous.

The maitre d' was seating a French couple with a small sunburned child. When he returned, I asked him if William Mutani was lunching there today.

"Ah, yes. He is with a party in a private room. Are you expected?"

This was starting to sound familiar. "No, but if you would please give them my name—Jazz Jasper—and apologies for disrupting their lunch."

"Of course." He bowed, called over a lackey and gave him instructions. I loitered by the entrance, looking out at the islands in the pool. In a few minutes the lackey returned and escorted me to a curved door in the curved wall that led to a small hall with a gilt mirror and a carpeted stair. We climbed the stair, he knocked on the first door, opened it and ushered me inside.

William Mutani and his guests were at a white damask-covered table overlooking the pool and garden. The three faces turned to me with inquiring expressions.

"I'm terribly sorry to interrupt," I stammered, "I happened to see you coming in, and I thought, perhaps, you hadn't heard Wynn's bad news."

"Not more bad news?" Viv asked in a strained voice. She put a hand to her flowery, lavender bosom. Now that I saw her closer, her careful dressing couldn't hide the fact that she had lines of strain from nose to chin, and a pinched, unhappy look. What did I expect? The woman had just lost her brother in a most horrible way.

Roger seemed his usual tanned, hail-fellow-well-met self, although he did shoot Viv a glance filled with concern. "What appears to be the matter?"

"I didn't mean to scare you," I said. "It's not life-threatening. She's had her work permit revoked."

"Please, have a seat." William Mutani's tenor voice always surprised me, contrasted with his bulk. He waited until a chair was brought for me, and a table setting, and dismissed the waiter. "May I pour you some wine?"

"Yes, thank you."

"What is this about?" he asked. A diamond twinkled on his tie clip, and another on a heavy gold ring. He'd have appeared more impressive if the puffiness of his face didn't look so dissipated.

I explained to him and the others in a few words about Wynn's work situation and the letter she'd received.

"Oh, this is terrible," Viv said. "She must be so upset. Just when she needs her work to steady herself. If I didn't have tomorrow's fashion show to think about, I'd be a complete wreck. Wynn must be frantic." She put a hand on her husband's arm. "Roger, can't you do something? Do you know someone in that department? You must."

William Mutani bent toward Viv. "Please, do not concern yourself about this. I know the minister like my own brother, and I even know the head of the forestry department himself. He is a fine fellow. I will make a phone call for you, and clear this misunderstanding up." He turned to me. "Tell Wynn it is taken care of. If her job has been dropped, we will find her another. I will let Roger know what we work out."

"William, you are marvelous," Viv gushed.

So that's how it's done, as easy as that. I wondered if it was Mutani who'd also had her fired. Just as easily—with only one phone call—at the sheikh's bidding, or on his own.

"Will we see you at the fashion show tomorrow?" Roger leaned back in his seat and gave me an appraising look, at odds with the jovial tone of his words.

"Is it tomorrow? I'm afraid I don't have an invitation." This was my punishment for barging in on them. I didn't see how I'd learn anything new by going to another of Viv's events, but I was trapped.

Viv said, "Do come, Jazz. Three o'clock, in the Raj ballroom, to the left of the lobby as you come in, past the boutiques." She lowered her voice, and the lines in her face deepened. "There's been gossip about my holding the show so soon after Nick's death. But what could I do? I'm a businesswoman. Everything's paid for—if I canceled, I'd have to default on my backers. I'd never get credit again. You have your own business. You understand."

"People are like that, you mustn't let it get to you," said Roger. "No one who actually knows you would dream for an instant of criticizing you."

"You can tell them I forced you to go ahead." Mutani gave a deep laugh. Roger shot him an intense look that I couldn't decipher. It looked like fear.

"I understand completely," I told Viv, wishing it were true. "Although I must say, in my business, the problem of backers hasn't come up yet. My only backing at this point is an overdrawn checking account."

Mutani laughed again. "You are very frank. I like that. Maybe I can help you. After all, we are both in the tourist industry. I have a talent for finding money. Call my secretary and make an appointment."

I left wondering if I would make the appointment or not. It would be worth it for the satisfaction of getting past that harpy secretary. On the other hand, Striker would kill me if I accepted money from Mutani. I didn't condemn Mutani that harshly myself. We were both in the tourist industry, as he said, although I was a flea and he was an elephant. The Kenyan economy certainly got more from Mutani's efforts than mine. Was his offer serious? And why? To show off his largesse in front of Roger and Viv? Did knowing them give me an entry into the old boy's network? As I drove out of the hotel grounds I had another thought: was Mutani trying to buy me off?

26

VIV STOOD NEAR the entrance to the ballroom, looking nervous and proud. She extended a hand to me as thin and cold as a lizard's claw.

"So glad," she murmured, already smiling past my shoulder.

The ballroom was filling quickly, and most of the seats near the model's runway were already occupied. Karen's female population was there, and a healthy cross-section of the African elite, wives of government officials and their business cronies. I spotted Mrs. Mutani in a beautifully cut afternoon dress that conferred dignity on her dumpy figure. She had a front-row chair, surrounded by a small circle of women who seemed to be hanging on her every word, twittering and laughing at all the right cues. There were several empty seats next to her.

A commotion at the door caught my attention. William Mutani was ushering in a dark-haired woman in a peacock-colored dress contoured to her pudgy but voluptuous figure. It was Halimah, the princess's companion. Released from the head-to-toe black sack, she looked like a different person. A woman behind me said, "Look who just walked in."

Half hidden by Mutani's bulk was Princess Rana in a stunning raw silk dress. The older woman with the sour expression was behind them. Her eyes scanned the room and passed over me without pause. She obviously didn't recognize me, dressed up, as the same disheveled person who'd dropped in on them in the desert. Perhaps she was looking for young men to guard her princess from; if so, she'd find no threat in this room.

"Excuse me." I sidestepped past a bunch of silken knees, got to the aisle and hurried toward the group at the entrance. When the princess saw me, her face lit up.

"So! You got out safe and sound." Her smile was guileless. "It must have been a tiring trip by car. How long did it take?"

"We camped overnight." Still nothing in her face but friendliness. I was sure she didn't know about the attack on us. Obviously the sheikh had fed her some story to account for our disappearance. "Sorry that we scurried away without a chance to say good-bye."

A look of sorrow came over her face. "My little Saladin was not so lucky. He ran away and was lost in the desert."

"Are you heading back north after the fashion show?"

A smile lit up her eyes. "No, the safari has been cut short. I am returning to my son tonight."

"Why so soon?"

She raised her eyebrows and shrugged. Hers not to wonder why.

I was spared elaborating my lies by the sudden appearance of Viv with the last member of their party.

It was Sheikh Farid himself, looking taller and thinner than I remembered him, in an elegantly cut suit. Did the man inside change as easily as he changed his clothes? He gave me a penetrating look.

I returned his icy stare. The bastard had sent men to kill me. Again I saw the curved sword above me, felt the big Saudi's weight crushing my face into the ground. If the sheikh thought closing his camp was going to save him from scandal, he was in for a nasty surprise.

If any of this showed on my face, Viv was oblivious. She didn't bother to introduce me, indeed pretended not to register my presence. I could read the thought in her mind easily enough: I was an unwelcome addition to the royal party, out of my league and rude to be pushing myself forward. I wished the princess a safe return home and returned to my seat.

The lights dimmed and the fashion show began. It was hard for me to pay attention to the clothes, however outrageous they were, because the young women wearing them were even more fantastic. They had long, sloping bodies, thin and sleek as a cheetah's. Their eyes had the indifferent, mysterious expression of the great cats. No human quality of the irregular or imperfect remained. Everything about them was artifice, under tight control: their terrible thinness, the cosmetic masks, the stylized hair, the walk. The clothes were no more artificial than any other aspect, indeed fitted them so naturally they might have grown in place.

The emaciated model who was being sewn into a little black dress when I went backstage at Viv's was still in black, this time tight-fitting pants and a leather brassiere adorned with metal studs and chains. It was hard to imagine the ladies in the room going for that sort of outfit, but perhaps the designer knew something I didn't.

The next model was in a totally different mood. A big fluffy wrap of bright purple fake fur was matched by a purple wig of exploding curls. On her heels came a strikingly tall model in what looked like hot-pink mink, followed by a black model in a turquoise fur bomber jacket over black leggings.

"Now those are fun," murmured the woman next to me.

"Lucille says they're as expensive as real fur," her companion whispered.

"Maybe they're fake fakes," I quipped.

"That's one way to avoid someone throwing blood on you for wearing furry animals."

It could also be a clever way for someone to smuggle fur pelts out of the country. I remembered Mutani's joke that he'd forced Viv to go on with her show. I wanted to see those furs more closely.

Again I stumbled past the row of silken knees, slipped out the double doors at the back of the room and turned right. I followed a corridor leading to the stage-end of the ballroom. Near the end, on the right, was an unmarked door. I poked my head in. As I'd hoped, it was the dressing room. It was a scene of frenetic activity. Women in all states of dress and undress were aided by a crew of seamstresses, cosmetic specialists, coiffeurs. I could faintly hear

251

a French-accented voice from the ballroom describing th
next set of clothes.

The seamstress I'd talked to at Viv's was a spot of caln
amidst the chaos as she ripped out threads to release th
model from the metal studded pants. Instead of the charm
ing welcome I got at Viv's, she gave me a harsh look
"This is not the time for visitors, mademoiselle. I an
sorry."

I raised my palms in what I hoped was a placating gesture. "I'm leaving right now. I just wanted to check tha
you have everything you need. Do you need a setup of
drinks? Some cold bottles of Evian? Or perhaps champagne?"

"Yes, that would be good. Some of the girls get nervous,
and it makes the mouth very dry. That is kind of you."

I headed toward the door via the rack of fake furs. I ran
my hand along the candy-colored row of sleeves. Some
were solid colors, some had leopard or cheetah spots, several had zebra stripes; others sported fanciful patterns that
nature had never invented. They were as soft as they
looked; except for the ones with phony patterns, it wasn't
screamingly obvious if they were real or a petroleum prod-
uct.

A six-foot Valkyrie blonde stripped off a violet fur wrap
and flung it in my general direction. Perhaps she mistook
me for a dresser, or rather, an undresser. I stumbled forward and caught it; she was already turning away, unbut-
toning her blouse. I didn't see any free hangers, which
gave me a good excuse to go more slowly through the
rack.

Stuffed among the other coats was a chartreuse stole
with cheetah spots. The pattern was authentic, with an un-
predictable scattering of large and small spots. I ran a finger along the sleeve. The spots were slightly raised and
had a coarser texture than the surrounding fur. The hair
rose along my arms. This was the skin of a young cheetah.
There was no question. No one producing fake fur would
know or care that in some young cheetahs the spots stood
out from the surrounding tawny fur.

If I tried walking out with it, I'd certainly be seen and

stopped, maybe even accused of stealing. Better to leave it and return with the police—if they would come. Was this being done under the direction of Viv, or behind her back? As her own sideline, or for Mutani? I didn't want to ask questions that would draw attention to the stole and cause it to disappear. Maybe I could get some answers without asking questions.

I slipped it off the hanger and brought it over to the seamstress. "Would you describe this as a light green cheetah stole?"

She talked without removing some pins from her mouth. "Of course."

"Could you please send it out during the intermission for Princess Rana? She wants to feel the fabric."

She pulled the pins from between her lips. "But this one was not even in the show."

"Really? I wonder how she knows about it."

"Perhaps Madame was saving it for her." Her face showed no guilt, fear, or avarice, only annoyance. She fingered the jacket. "It's rougher than some of the others, but the pattern is excellent. Tell her that a model will wear it out to show her during the intermission." She looked at her watch and checked around the room. She went back to her work.

I left the jacket with her, trotted outside, waylaid a waiter with a tray of champagne and directed him to the dressing room, and returned to the ballroom, where the fake fur segment had given way to ball gowns with tube miniskirts and bodices encrusted with sequins in flashy designs. Tacky is not limited to low budget wardrobes.

The last model stalked down the runway, swirled and stalked back, and the lights came on with a babble of excited voices. Ladies began to stream through the double doors to the tables of food and champagne. I worked my way over toward the princess and her entourage, staying out of their direct line of sight, but within hearing.

The wardrobe mistress knew her job. Exactly enough time passed for the princess to finish off a small plate of exquisite salmon and watercress sandwiches fetched by her companion, and down half a glass of champagne, when the Valkyrie model approached in the chartreuse stole.

"Oh, look, they are bringing me a cheetah stole!" The princess broke into a radiant smile. "Let me try it on. It will look smashing with the dress I have on now."

Now for Viv to notice. Or would it be Mutani?

The princess handed her champagne to her companion and reached for the stole. The model gracefully whirled it off and laid it gently across the princess's shoulders. The princess caressed it as she pulled it around her bosom, and looked adoringly at her husband, whose face softened in response. He dismissed the model with a flick of his hands.

The royal party stayed in place while the room circulated around them, each eddy throwing up wealthy women in pairs who chatted for just the proper length of time before drifting off and leaving room for the next.

Viv was at the other end of the room, also receiving homage. She must have brushed off her well-wishers, for suddenly she was at the princess's side. She held a demitasse of coffee perched on a little plate of petits fours. Unfortunately, she was pressed forward by the crowd, the stole brushed against the plate and the coffee tipped over, dousing the chartreuse fur.

"Oh, no!" The princess jumped back. The cup bounced harmlessly on the thick carpet, but the damage was already done.

"Did I burn you?" Viv asked, dabbing at the soggy fur. "I'm so sorry. How terribly clumsy of me. I feel an utter fool!"

"No, no, it is nothing. I am perfectly all right."

"Coffee stains so terribly!" She dabbed some more. "Let me return it to the wardrobe mistress and have her wash this out before it sets." She reached out an arm, the princess relinquished the stole, and Viv bore it out of the room. Very deftly done. So Viv knew about the fake fake.

The princess's companion patted her arm. "If you like that one, they'll deliver it to our hotel later. It will be perfect again. Do not worry."

I headed for a phone and called Omondi.

"Most interesting. If Nick found out that his sister has a scam for smuggling furs out of the country—"

"—and especially a cheetah skin!"

"—he certainly would have stopped it. Add this up with her financial crisis, and it must have been quite a family fight. If Mutani was behind it, she would have had to warn him that Nick knew."

"Can you get a search warrant and confiscate it? It will probably be either with the designer clothes or else in the Saudis' suite."

"I cannot ask for a warrant without a case; besides, animal products aren't in my jurisdiction."

"You must know who would handle it."

"Yes I do: nobody. No underling would dare to ask a judge for such a warrant without his superior's backing. Such things not only take time, they take political courage. Who wants to go into William Mutani's newest hotel, upset wealthy people, insult a foreign power, and turn the wonderful publicity of the fashion show into a scandal? It will not further anyone's career to stir up such a hornet's nest."

"You must get tired explaining the facts of life to me over and over. So what can we do?"

"See if you can find out more information about this stole from the models. You have already done good work."

"I'm afraid I tipped my hand to Viv, if she asks the wardrobe mistress why she sent it out."

"Maybe not. She will say the princess asked for it, and Viv isn't likely to give the princess the third degree. Be equally skillful in finding out when this stole joined the rest. Who made it? Who brought it? Was the princess promised a cheetah stole?"

"Well, I know where to find the models: suntanning around the swimming pool."

"And Jazz? Be careful. I don't think the sheikh will dare go after you at the hotel, but stay alert."

"Aren't I always?"

"And you're not staying at your apartment tonight?"

"Right. I'm staying at a friend's. Wish me luck with the models."

"I know you can do it."

I wished I felt the same confidence.

I was pretty sure I knew where to find them after the show. I lingered to congratulate Mrs. Mutani on her husband's latest success. She was having a great time holding court, laughing about the models' skinny rear ends, and discussing the pros and cons of the different outfits. It sounded like the fake furs were a big hit.

I headed for the lobby shops, where I bought an unbelievably expensive swimsuit, with a designer label, of course. It had a single broad strap that crossed one shoulder and draped across the torso like a toga fit for Diana, goddess of the hunt. It was the most smashing suit I've ever worn—but would it get a model to talk?

I checked my watch. I'd given the models plenty of time to begin sun-worshiping. A flowering jacaranda tree littered the walkway with purple blossoms. I passed under its cool shade, crossed the bridge over the garden pool, and was rewarded with the sight I expected: a row of thin, tanned bodies on lounge chairs oriented to face directly into the sun.

With a smile at the pool attendant, I walked into the cabana as if I were a guest, changed into my new swimsuit, picked up a pool towel, and chose a lounge chair next to a lithe brunette. She had sleek hair, the big pouty lips that were fashionable this year, and exquisite breasts with rosy nipples, gleaming with suntan oil. I could tell her nipples were rosy because, like the other models, she was wearing only the bottom half of her bikini. I'd heard that was how they did it on the Riviera; I wondered what the Africans thought of it, after generations of missionaries had convinced them that nakedness was shameful.

The beauty beside me stirred, opened an eye and pressed a finger against her oiled flesh to check her tan.

"You're the perfect color," I told her. "Like toast."

"You are *gentille*. Is it your first day here?" She glanced pityingly at my pale body. "You must be ver-ry careful or you will be burned." Her lips pouted even more as she rolled her *r*'s in a French accent.

"I live in Nairobi, but it's the usual story. I rarely get the

256

chance to lie by a pool. I'm only here today because of the fashion show."

"It is a good collection this year, is it not?"

"The clothes were amusing."

"Yes. Especially these furs in candy colors. It is a good idea, no? It is *depassé* to wear real fur in Paris. And to wear a fake masquerading as real, it is not charming. To wear a fake proud to be fake—that is genius."

"I noticed the Saudi princess was already wearing one. A green cheetah stole."

"A green stole?" A crease appeared between her carefully shaped brows. "There was an orange one that Krista showed."

"This one was brilliant green, like a parrot."

"It is not part of our collection," she stated with certainty.

"Perhaps it was made especially for the princess, and not included in the show."

She shrugged, curling her upper lip the way the French do. The woman on her other side had been lying still as a mummy. She flipped over on her belly, face toward us, and opened her green eyes into slits to keep out the sun. "That little stole was delivered yesterday evening. I saw Marie-Odile sign for it."

"Oh, by one of those international delivery services," I said.

"I don't think so. Those services use a uniform. This fellow was in a navy sport coat and mud-brown pants. Terrible. And a red baseball cap."

"Yes, I saw him, too," interrupted the other model. "He was hanging around afterward, clinking his car keys as if that would attract a date, and trying to talk to the girls. Marie-Odile came out and told him to leave, and he was rude to her."

Thanks to American movies, there were a lot of men in Nairobi wearing baseball caps these days. You saw them everywhere you went. It didn't prove anything that Louis Mutani, Gerry Weller's chauffeur, was wearing a Cincinnati Reds cap the day that Nick was killed.

257

27

OMONDI HAD TOLD me that there was no legal way for us to seize the cheetah pelt. That left illegal ways.

Things were beginning to fit together. We knew that Mutani's cousin, Louis, working for Gerry Weller as a driver in the northeast, bought pelts from Lodogia. It was also Louis who delivered the green cheetah stole to Viv's fashion show. If someone was to deliver it now to the Saudis, who were staying at the Buckingham, it wasn't hard to figure out that it would probably be Louis again.

I hurriedly got back into my clothes, cashed a check at the front desk, and returned to the corridor outside the models' changing room. I could hear Viv's voice, and that of the French seamstress, supervising the packing up of clothes. I retreated around the corner and waited until I spotted Louis in his Cincinnati Reds cap coming up the stairs. I darted into the ballroom before he saw me. If I kept the door open a crack, I had a clear view of the top landing.

Ten minutes later he reemerged from the corridor carrying a large glossy shopping bag with the logo of Viv's store: her name in splashy red letters and a line drawing of a woman in an elegant hat. I let him start down the stairs and followed. He wasn't being secretive. He led me across the bridge over the swimming pool, past the cascade, up through the garden and into the lobby with the life-size charging elephant. He crossed the lobby and went out the main door, where he tipped the doorman and headed for his car, conveniently parked at the curbside.

I hurried my steps to catch up to him, and got to the

passenger side as he was climbing behind the wheel. I hopped into the seat next to him, moving his shopping bag from the seat to the floor to give me room to sit.

"Louis! Hi! This is a stroke of luck. May I ask you to drop me off at my car? I'm way at the end of the parking lot." I put the shopping bag holding my bathing suit at my feet, next to his bag.

Louis scowled, but what could he do? "No problem. Did you enjoy the fashion show?"

My car was actually within sight, but I thought my plan would have a better chance of success if Louis felt we were unobserved. I chatted about the show as I directed him through the maze of tree-lined parking areas to the very end.

Before getting out, I fumbled in my wallet and pulled out five twenty-dollar bills. American money is considered hard currency here, and has a black market price way above the official exchange rate. Louis's eyes grew alert.

"Thanks so much for the ride." I handed him the hundred, picked up his shopping bag, leaving mine in his car, and hopped out. He took in what I was doing, grinned, pocketed the hundred and drove off.

I smiled triumphantly and headed home. Confronted with the stole, in the right way, Viv Porter was going to do some talking. If I showed up with it at her house, though, she could accuse me of stealing it, and try to bully her way past my questions. If Omondi came with me, she would assume it was the police who had confiscated the stole, and feel herself in a position of weakness. As a lawyer's wife, there was always the chance she would simply clam up and refuse to say a word, which would be her safest route. That's why I wanted to go in hard, with Omondi carrying the stole, and rattle her.

I called Omondi and he agreed with my plan. Next call was Viv's house, to learn what time she was expected home. I left a message that I would be dropping by soon afterward. I counted on her curiosity to make her keep the appointment. Sure enough, when we rang the bell an hour later, we were ushered directly to the terrace, where Viv was ensconced on a white wrought-iron couch with floral cushions, sipping a glass of white wine. She greeted us graciously, offered us drinks, and gestured us to our seats. We both said we'd join her in what turned out to be a glass of South African chardonnay. Omondi was carrying the glossy shopping bag with her logo, and placed it at his feet.

"Inspector, have you been buying presents at my shop?" Viv pretended to be pleased, but I thought she eyed the bag suspiciously. She would have known by now that the package Louis had deliver to the Saudis contained a bathing suit instead of the immensely valuable stole.

We didn't keep her in suspense. Omondi pushed aside the cloud if tissue paper and pulled out the chartreuse cheetah fur. "Do you recognize this?"

"Of course. It wasn't part of my show, but through some mistake," she darted a poisonous glance in my direction, "it was placed among my fake furs and shown to Princess Rana. She asked for it, and I sent it over with a messenger this afternoon. It never arrived. That's all I know about it."

She sounded smooth. If she kept that line up, we'd get nowhere. I tried to look confident and all knowing. "Good try, Viv. But we know all about where the fur was procured, and your part in laundering this stole."

"Smuggling a cheetah pelt out of this country is a serious charge, Mrs. Porter." Omondi's voice was gentle. "The reason I came to your home instead of calling you in to police headquarters was the hope that we might persuade you to talk freely. If we can get enough information on"—he hesitated, as if about to state a name and changing his mind—"on the person in charge of this smuggling operation, it may not be necessary to level official charges against you at all."

"Inspector Omondi." Viv inclined her head in what was supposed to be a gracious gesture, but looked painfully stiff. The tendons of her neck were standing out like tightened cords. She was more scared than she was letting on. "I appreciate your thoughtfulness." She reached under the side table and must have pressed a button, because within moments Catherine appeared in a gray and white uniform. She didn't show she knew us.

"Catherine, would you please bring me my checkbook?"

Omondi and I exchanged glances.

"I realize that I forgot to donate to the police benevolent association this year," Viv said with a pinched smile. She finished what remained of her wine in one swallow. The maid returned and handed her a checkbook with a monogrammed lavender cover. Viv dismissed her and hurriedly scribbled out a check. "I always like to be as generous as I can."

She handed Omondi a check.

"Thank you, indeed, Mrs. Porter, but you have made this out incorrectly. It should be made out directly to the policeman's benevolent fund." He held up the check. "As written, this could be misconstrued as an attempted bribe. The laws governing bribery of a police official are severe, indeed."

Viv's fixed smile cracked. "Oh, what a silly error." She reached out for the check. "Let me tear that one up, and I'll write out another."

Omondi placed it on the side table next to him, out of her reach. "Let me keep it for now. It depends how our conversation goes. It may constitute evidence, if—as I hope we can avoid—we have to make this inquiry over your role in the pelt-smuggling business official."

"Oh, Inspector," Viv gave him a coy look. "I'm sure it won't come to that. After all, I know nothing about this fake fur that you say is a cheetah skin. I haven't the slightest notion how it came to be among my things."

"That's a pity." Omondi looked right at her. "We were so hoping you had some information to trade for immunity." He shrugged. "But if you don't, you don't. It leaves you in a vulnerable position, should one of our other informants make accusations against you."

He handed the check to me. It was made out to Omondi for one thousand dollars. "Jazz, I'm going to ask you to write on the back, 'Witnessed Vivian Porter handing this check to Inspector Omondi.' Date and sign it. Then would you please draw a cross through the front and initial the cross, so no one will think that I accepted this as a bribe."

Viv stood and grabbed at the check. "*No*. Wait!"

I held the check out of her reach.

She sat again, wringing her hands and looking miserable. She pressed the button for the maid again.

"Catherine, refresh our drinks please. And call Mr. Porter at the office and tell him—"

Omondi shook his head no, once to the right, once to the left. Viv broke off. "No, I've changed my mind. Don't call him." Catherine left to get the drinks, and Viv gave a brittle smile. "Well, now that we've cleared all that up, how can I be of help?"

"Who arranged for the cheetah stole to be delivered to your show?"

"William Mutani." Viv's mouth must have gone dry, because her lips were sticking to her teeth. Catherine returned, and Viv remained silent while the maid refilled our glasses from a newly opened bottle of wine. "Thank you, Catherine. Please leave the bottle here."

"Details, if you please."

Viv gulped her wine and spoke quickly. "Last year the shipment of dresses was stolen at the airport, and I had to make good the loss. It was a sizable amount of money, and I would have had to sell my shop to cover it had not Mr. Mutani—who's a client of my husband's—stepped into the breach. He gave me a low-interest loan in exchange for a half share in this year's show. Mr. Mutani was also kind enough to invite Sheikh Farid and his wife to the show."

"What is Mr. Mutani's connection to Sheikh Farid?" I asked.

Viv clutched her wineglass like a child clutching its favorite stuffed animal. "They have some common business, I don't know what."

"What business is that, Mrs. Porter?" asked Omondi, ignoring her disclaimer.

"Oh, I believe the sheikh has invested in some of Mr. Mutani's projects. I really will have to direct those questions to Roger."

"Which projects do you know about?"

"What does this have to do with me?" Viv asked.

"Their names?"

Viv look flustered. "The Mount Kenya Conference Center, I believe."

"Did Nick tell you that?"

"Nick? We might have discussed it, I—I don't really remember."

"But you did discuss Mutani's investments with Nick."

Viv finished her wine and refilled it. "Yes, Nick did call to talk with Roger about it. Not on newspaper business, though. He was asking for a friend."

That was probably Striker, I thought.

"What other Mutani projects has the sheikh invested in through your husband?" I'd never seen Omondi so severe. Usually he used charm to worm information out of people.

"The casino that's going up as part of the Royal Parklands."

So Roger was a middleman between Mutani and the sheikh. I tried to keep my face neutral as I assessed this new piece of the puzzle.

"The one that's behind schedule and costing far more than the estimate," said Omondi.

"Yes."

"And the one planned for Samburu?"

"I don't know." Viv twisted the wineglass in her fingers. Omondi stared at her without speaking. "Yes, that one, too. I don't understand why you're asking me these things."

"Both you and your husband are deeply involved in Mr. Mutani's projects. Including his pelt-smuggling project."

"No!"

"Your fashion shows are the perfect vehicle for smuggling millions of dollars worth of furs out of this country."

"No! It was just this one time." Viv didn't watch what she was doing, and tilted her wineglass so that it sloshed onto her skirt. She dabbed at the wet spot distractedly. "I don't know anything about Mutani's pelt business. All I know is that he told me to make this gift to Princess Rana. I didn't know the fur was going to be a real one."

She was lying.

Omondi picked up the bribe check and flicked it against his fingers. "Mrs. Porter, you must be frank with us."

"Of course, I guessed it might be real once I felt it, but I didn't know in advance, I swear."

"Why did you visit your brother Nick the weekend before your big show?"

Viv licked her lips. "He's my brother. Do I need a reason to visit him?"

"Yes, when you never visited him before."

Omondi stood and began pacing up and down the terrace flagstones behind the couch Viv was sitting in.

"An odd moment to leave town, your busiest time of the year." He turned and headed back the other way. "It's because Nick found out about Mutani's pelt business during his visit to the northeast."

"I know nothing about that," Viv protested.

"Nick also knew you were renting animals for your fashion show."

Viv swiveled to follow Omondi's pacing with her eyes. "Yes, but I promised him I would drop the idea. It wasn't important. It had nothing to do with the pelts." She swiveled the other way as Omondi turned. Her voice became shrill. "How could Nick find out about the cheetah stole when I didn't even know myself?"

"Then how can you explain your decidedly unusual visit to Nick—the first time you saw his house in Samburu, even though he's lived there several years."

"It had nothing to do with my show. We weren't on bad terms. The rented monkey wasn't important. It was already forgotten."

"The real reason, Mrs. Porter?"

She put a hand to her throat and fiddled with a gold pendant she was wearing. "Roger had some business to conduct with him." Omondi gestured for her to continue. "Some legal business."

Omondi walked to the end of the terrace, turned and bore straight down on her. "I am losing patience, Mrs. Porter. If this is all the information you have—"

Viv's face crumpled. "Roger approached Nick a month ago about selling his land to Mutani." She pulled a cotton hankie from her pocket and dabbed at her eyes and nose with little, ladylike sniffs. "Mutani had plans for a golf course on his adjacent parcel and needed the marsh on Nick's land as a source of water."

"And Nick told Roger to go to hell." I blurted out.

Viv turned her limpid blue eyes on me. "No, not at all. Nick agreed."

I was so surprised I goggled at her, speechless. Nick agreed to sell his land to Mutani? "I find that hard to believe," I finally got out.

"We went up that weekend to pass papers. Mutani was supposed to drive over to sign them." She burst into tears. "The morning Nick was stung."

"I apologize for upsetting you, Mrs. Porter." Omondi crossed to the chair opposite her and rested his hands on its back. "I have only one more question."

Viv collected herself, daintily blowing her nose.

"Given that Wynn and Nick were not legally married, will you be inheriting that land?"

"Not married?" Viv's eyebrows rose in surprise. "Of course they were married."

"Most people assumed so, but you, of course, knew the truth." Omondi looked at her fixedly.

Viv denied it again.

"Look, Viv, if Nick and Wynn were married, then she would have had to sign the papers, also," I butted in. "You can't tell me Wynn is planning on selling the land. I know she isn't."

Viv tossed off the rest of her wine and stared into the empty glass as if looking for the right answer. "No one has approached her yet." She looked up defiantly. "All right, they weren't married."

Omondi leaned toward her. "And you expect to inherit the land."

"I assume so. What are you trying to imply?" She fiddled with the gold pendant at her throat. I looked at it closely for the first time. It looked like an Egyptian scarab with hieroglyphics. Every tourist to Egypt comes back with one.

"Now it is you who will be able to sell it to Mutani," Omondi said in his gentlest voice.

Viv looked outraged. "Are you implying I'm glad my brother is dead? What an awful thing to say!"

"Did you buy that pendant in Cairo?" I asked.

"What?" She fingered it. "This? Why, yes. What does that have to do with anything?"

"Recently?"

"This spring. We were there on a holiday. Really," she put a hand to her head, "you've got me so upset with all these questions. My head is whirling. I need to lie down. Roger will be able to help you so much better than I."

"Thank you. You've been most helpful." Omondi picked up the check from the table and slipped it into his pockets, and returned the cheetah stole to the bag. He turned to Viv. "We shan't wait for Mr. Porter, this time."

Viv suddenly switched into gracious hostess mode. She stood and extended her hand. "I'm glad I could help clear up some of your questions. None of this need go any further than this room?" She tipped her head to one side coquettishly.

"To the extent that I am able, this will remain between us." Omondi shook her hand.

"Why did you ask about our trip to Egypt?" she asked me.

I looked at Omondi, and he nodded for me to answer.

"Nick was killed by a Sahara scorpion," I told Viv. I watched for her reaction, and saw none.

"Yes?" She prompted me.

"They're not native to Kenya, but they are common in Egypt."

"You mean it was sort of a stray? How odd."

"It's more than odd. Scorpions don't stray from one side of the Sahara to the other—at least, not without help."

She went pale. "What are you saying?"

"I'm saying someone brought a Middle Eastern scorpion to your brother's home."

"I don't understand."

"Nick was murdered."

Viv uttered a small sound and sat down abruptly, her face pinched and scared. "It can't be," she whispered. "I don't believe you."

It was obvious she did believe me, all too readily. Did she suspect Roger did it?

Omondi stood over Viv. "If Nick agreed to sell to Mutani, as you told us, Mutani had no reason to kill him. The only people who would profit from Nick's death are you—and Roger. Did you plan to use his land as leverage to get a piece of the Samburu casino? Or was is to get out of debt, free yourself from Mutani, so he couldn't pressure you anymore into doing his smuggling for him?"

Viv twisted her hands. "No, no. It wasn't . . . How dare you suggest Roger. . . . He couldn't."

"There were only five people who could have done it, Mrs. Porter." Viv stared at Omondi with a mesmerized look of fear. "We can eliminate Jazz." He paused, letting her fear grow. "That leaves Wynn and Kaji, who have no motive and no access to a Middle Eastern scorpion—and yourself and your husband, who recently visited Egypt and will inherit a valuable piece of property from your brother."

"No! I mean, we didn't think of that."

"It was your last chance. Once Nick sold the land to Mutani, he'd spend the money, and your hope of inheriting anything would be gone. You had to act quickly."

"What are you talking about?" Viv put her hands to her ears, trying to blot out Omondi's implacable voice.

"As Mutani's lawyer, Roger knew about each step of the deal being made. You and Roger were the only people who knew of the impending sale. Nick never told Wynn, because he hated scenes and knew she would be against it. Since they weren't married, he didn't need her signature."

"That proves nothing. So what if we knew! It was good for everyone. Roger was earning a handsome commission. You might as well accuse every lawyer—"

Omondi lifted the bag he was carrying. "This cheetah stole is further proof of your need for money and willingness to stoop to illegal means to obtain it. Your brother was barely in the ground when you held a big party in your house: not the actions of a bereaved sister, but of someone who cares only for money. The jury will have little trouble deciding this one."

"Inspector, I swear, I swear to you neither Roger nor I had anything to do with Nick's death." Viv lifted her chin, visibly pulling herself together. "Mutani said he'd cancel my debt if Roger lined up the sheikh as an investor and got Nick to sell. And Roger did it! I went up with him to Nick's so we could all celebrate together. We weren't greedy. I was glad Nick was getting all that money, I swear!" She clutched Omondi's hand. "Ask Mutani. He'll back up everything I say. We were out of the woods. And now everything's ruined."

"You have the land now yourself. You get all the money."

"What money?" Viv sounded bitter. "The sheikh has backed out because of that damn Wynn and Jazz taking photos of his hunting trophies." She shot me a venomous glance. "With no capital, the project is dead. All I've inherited is a worthless piece of Samburu desert."

28

O MONDI RELUCTANTLY AGREED it would be too dangerous for him to confront William Mutani. Mutani would not look with favor on a police inspector who dared bother him with questions, however innocuous. The questions we had for Mutani were far from innocuous. Omondi's demotion would be swift and final.

I was vulnerable, too, of course. At the moment, Jazz Jasper Safaris was so deep in a hole, there was little room for Mutani to push it down further. What he could do was arrange for my residency permit to be revoked and have me booted out of Kenya. The very thought made me clench my jaw until my teeth ached. I had to take the risk. We couldn't tiptoe around Mutani forever.

And so I went alone to see the lion in his lair. Omondi stayed with Viv to make sure she didn't telephone Roger or Mutani, while I took the bag with the cheetah stole and drove into town. I found a parking spot near Mutani's office, and hired the same fellow with a club as car minder that I'd used before.

Mutani's secretary remembered me; at least I assume she did from her disdainful frown. Today she was in emerald-green with peach lipstick and nails. This time I had the satisfaction of handing her Mutani's card and having her page him immediately.

"Ms. Jazz Jasper. About Nick Hunter's land," she repeated into the phone. She hung up and told me to go right in.

Mutani's desk was huge, of some space-age black laminate, not the mahogany I'd expected. A handsome oil painting of an African woman—was it Mrs. Mutani twenty years younger?—hung on one wall, and a big photo of Kenya's president hung on the other. There was a seating area off to one side with black leather couches and chairs and a large, low table.

Mutani was on the phone. He gestured me into a chair opposite him while he nodded and took notes on a yellow legal pad. "Tell them next week is too late, it must be Friday at the latest." He listened, looking at a spot over my shoulder as if I were invisible. He wore a pin-striped gray suit and presumably custom-tailored shirt, but either his tailor couldn't measure or Mutani was putting on weight, because his neck bulged over the collar. He wore a red-and-gray-striped tie with the same diamond clip I'd noticed the first time we met. Another large diamond flashed on his pinkie.

"Remind him there's a penalty clause in the contract. Ten percent for every day late." The person on the other end of the line seemed to be arguing. "The word no is not in my vocabulary. If he can't deliver, we'll find someone else who can. Tell him that." The response was shorter this time, and Mutani signed off with a gruff, "Don't do your best. Do it. You're expendable, too."

He hung up and smiled at me, showing even capped teeth. "I am so pleased you followed through on my invitation to see me. Tell me about the financing of this safari company of yours."

A chill went over me. Keep away from my business, I thought to myself. Aloud I said, "I didn't come to talk about my business, but about yours."

"Ha, ha! You're a direct young lady. I like that." He crossed his hands and leaned toward me. "Tell me what's on your mind."

I pulled out the stole and flung it across his desk. Mutani didn't even blink. He kept his eyes on me. The silence lengthened.

I stared back, trying to look unfazed while my mind raced. "Perhaps you don't recognize this stole, Mr. Mutani. Despite the outlandish color, it's an authentic cheetah pelt. You would know the black market value better than I."

Mutani leaned back in his chair and crossed his hands over his paunch. "Are you trying to sell it to me?"

"Let's not play games. I know too much. I know exactly where your cousin Louis buys illegal furs for you, when and where he delivered this supposedly fake fur, where it was heading afterward."

Mutani smirked at me. I hadn't worried him yet.

"Poaching endangered animals and smuggling their skins out of the country is a serious offense." I lifted one end of the pelt and shook it. "You may be immune to prosecution in Kenya, but this is an international crime, and it will create a stink smelled around the world when it appears in the papers."

"Oooh. You're scaring me." Mutani laughed, but his eyes remained cool and measuring.

"You may find it hard to find foreign backers for your next real estate projects, Mr. Mutani. In fact, you may find current backers less willing to extend your credit beyond the projected dates for completion." At last I saw fear flicker in his eyes. "Your entire empire could collapse like a house of cards."

"How much money do you want for the fur?"

"I'm not for sale. I'm investigating Nick Hunter's murder."

"Murder?" Mutani cocked his head. "Murder? You're fantasizing."

"You may remember I caught Emmet Laird's killer earlier this year, and cleared up those tourist murders on one of my safaris last year. I'm not a daydreamer. I have proof Nick Hunter was murdered. And you're implicated, Mr. Mutani."

"Impossible." He gave an impatient flick of his hand. "I had a brief and cordial business relationship with the man and that's all. His death has been very inconvenient for me."

"More inconvenient than his life? It was Nick Hunter who discovered a Dorobo has been selling big cat pelts to you via your cousin Louis. It was Nick who discovered you'd helped Sheikh Farid set up an illegal hunting camp in the northeast." This wasn't a complete lie: Nick *may*

271

have known it. Besides, it was only because of Nick that Wynn and I discovered the sheikh's hunting. "I have two witnesses who are prepared to testify that they saw you personally hunting leopard in the company of the sheikh."

"You think you can threaten me with witnesses?" he blustered. "You think this will ever come to court? You know Africa even less well than I'd have expected."

I had finally gotten to him. I watched his eyes to see if he knew the witnesses were Wynn and myself, if he knew of our escape from the sheikh's camp, knew we had photos of the hunting trophies, if he knew of the attempt to kill us in the desert. Just how deep was Mutani into the sheikh's doings? How far was he prepared to go to protect himself? As far as murder? The look in his eyes was that of a schemer, calculating odds and opportunities, not the narcissistic entitlement and contempt of a cold-blooded killer like Sheikh Farid. My sense was that Mutani was into power, but it hadn't yet corrupted him into thinking he was a little god. He was a man I could make a deal with.

"The court I'd aim for is the court of international opinion, but I hope it won't come to that."

"What do you want, Ms. Jasper?" Mutani's voice had grown frighteningly cold.

"Your help in identifying Nick's killer."

"In exchange for your keeping silent about Sheikh Farid's hunting. And you leave without the stole."

"You're in no position to bargain. What you get out of it is not having your name mixed up in a murder investigation as a primary suspect."

"Suspect?" He gave a mirthless laugh. "Why would I kill a man who was selling me his land at a much lower price than I was prepared to pay?"

"Because Nick was also a journalist, and he was about to expose your illegal doings and blow down your house of cards."

"Nonsense." Mutani leaned back in his high-backed leather chair. He put his hands on the armrests, as if trying to look relaxed, but his hands were clenched. "I'm a good judge of character. In my business, I have to be. He wouldn't have sold me his land if he was planning to ruin

272

me; he didn't have that kind of a devious nature. Nick Hunter was keyed up when we signed the letter of agreement, but only like a man making a major life change, not like a man with a nasty surprise up his sleeve."

"I'm not saying you killed him. I'm merely talking about appearances. After all, Nick didn't go through with the sale, did he?"

"Because he was dead."

"No one knows whether or not he changed his mind at the last minute, after his visit to the northeast, when he discovered your pelt business."

"Where is this getting us?"

"Can you show me a copy of your purchase and sale agreement with Nick?" I still found it hard to believe Nick had decided to sell his land. I wanted proof.

Mutani unlocked a file drawer in his desk and pulled out a Penda-flex file. The paper he wanted was right on top. He handed it over to me. Despite the legalese, the contract was clear beyond dispute, dated and signed by Nick. There was even a map of the property, with the marsh—that life-giving source of water—clearly marked. No way around it: Nick had signed the agreement almost a full week after his return from the northeast.

So it was true. Why hadn't Nick told Wynn? Sure, she'd be upset about leaving that beloved spot, but as she'd told me, with more money, they could buy a bigger piece of land, do a more ambitious cheetah rehab scheme. Something was funny here, but I couldn't put my finger on it. I handed the paper back to Mutani and he locked it away again.

"I'd like to hear about your business arrangements with Viv and Roger Porter."

"Viv and Roger?" Mutani thrust out his lower lip and nodded thoughtfully. I could see his lightning-fast mind working. How expendable were the Porters? What would be more useful to get me off his back, lies or the truth?

"I know most of the story, so don't think you can lie to me."

Mutani's lids closed halfway over his cold eyes. "Roger Porter has been one of my lawyers for years. He's a good

273

deal maker, not like most lawyers. His wife Viv owns a nice little boutique in one of my hotels. She ran into some bad luck last year with her annual fashion show, and I advanced her some money interest-free. In exchange, I had a half interest in this year's show. All completely aboveboard. I'd have done the same for any longtime friend and colleague like Roger."

"Now tell me the belowboard part."

Mutani's slitted eyes bored into me and I felt a cold shiver go down my back. I pointed to the pelt, still lying across his desk.

He smiled thinly and remained silent.

"How much money did Viv owe you, after your projected proceeds from the fashion show were deducted?"

"Nothing. I told Roger if he found an investor for the Samburu project and convinced his brother-in-law to sell me his land, I'd consider their debt canceled."

So Viv had been telling the truth about Mutani releasing them from debt.

"Why were you driving on Nick's land the day he was killed?"

"We had a meeting planned to sign the final papers. That's why Roger and Viv were up there. We were going to drink a toast over the deal."

"Why not do it in Roger's office downtown? Wouldn't that be more usual?"

Mutani shrugged. "Maybe Nick wanted it that way. Roger asked me if I'd mind, and I said no. I wanted to look over the property, anyway, and check how the surveyors were doing. I like to keep a direct eye on my projects."

Again he'd corroborated Viv's version of her visit north.

"And what about Gerry Weller?"

"What about him?"

"What was his role in the deal?"

"That day? He was along for the ride. He's a smart man and knows how to keep his mouth shut. I'd asked him to come out and look over the land with me."

"Why?"

"He works for Kenarabia Oil; the sheikh had him check out my original piece of land for water. That's how we knew we had to acquire the Hunter property if we were to develop a golf course. We're going to need a lot of water."

I pulled the stole off his desk and put it in the bag. There was nothing more to accomplish here, except to protect my back.

"Thank you for your cooperation." I stood up. "I'll be keeping this stole and Nick's notes in a secure place, as assurance that you won't harm me, or anyone associated with me, in any way. I trust you will find Louis another job that does not take him into the bush. I'll be watching. If I learn that your pelt business is continuing, the notes and the pelt will be released to the *International Trib* the next day."

"Ha, ha!" Mutani shook his head with pretend admiration. "You're a hard woman." He stood and offered me his hand. "I've closed multimillion dollar deals with this handshake. I accept your offer."

I thought of it more as a threat than an offer, but he could call it what he wanted. The important thing was that his fur smuggling would stop. I shook his hand and swept out of the office, feeling horrible. I had to agree with Mutani's statement: Nick wouldn't have signed a purchase and sale agreement if he was planning to expose Mutani. Mutani had also corroborated everything Viv said. Her compelling need for money had disappeared when Roger delivered the sheikh as an investor, and Mutani canceled their debt.

I'd been trying to ignore a nagging thought all afternoon, and as long as Viv and then Mutani were center stage, it was easy to do. Now I couldn't hide from my own thoughts any longer: the motive of moving quickly to kill, and stop the land from being sold, applied to one other person perhaps even more strongly than to Viv and Roger. A person who had no other options at all, no future, no other resources. A person who loved the land like her own soul. Someone I couldn't imagine killing Nick in a million years: Kaji.

29

"**K**AJI." OMONDI ECHOED my conclusion. I'd picked him up at Viv's and filled him in on my meeting with Mutani on the way back into town.

"She had the motive and the opportunity. I don't know how she got hold of a Sahara scorpion, but I know she majored in biology at the university, plus being so immersed in nature. A scorpion is the kind of murder weapon she'd think of, more than any of our other suspects." I pulled up at the curb in front of his apartment building and left the motor running. "We have to find out if she knew she was inheriting the land."

"Hard to prove, but not hard to imagine." Omondi thrummed his fingers on the dashboard. "She might have overheard a discussion, or snooped among Nick's papers."

"It was kept in a locked box."

"Those little locks mean nothing. We will have to think about this." He put a long, elegant hand on my knee. Its warmth glowed through the fabric of my pants. "For now, my dear Jazz, we have done a good day's work. Time to let the mind rest and work on its own in the back room. Would you like to come in for a drink?"

"Thanks, but not tonight. I'd like to get home." I'd never been in Omondi's apartment. It was a symbolic line I was reluctant to cross—perhaps for fear it wouldn't remain symbolic.

"What's your hurry?" Omondi held my hand in his. "Does some pleasure await you at home?"

I laughed.

"What are you afraid of? You tiptoe around me as if I'm candy and you're on a diet."

"That's because you're always trying to tempt me."

"It could be wonderful." Omondi's eyes were full of promise and affection.

I shook my head. "You don't want a relationship with me, Omondi. I'm not easy. I fight too much."

"You think my feelings are so fragile they would be broken in a fight?"

I looked at him speculatively. "I can't imagine you fighting."

"Ah, that is my trouble." Omondi threw his head back and laughed.

We left it at that. I drove home wondering why I hadn't told Omondi yet that Striker was leaving. Striker. I gave a big sigh. Life had been simpler those first two years after my divorce, when I was avoiding men. Yeah, and it's simplest of all when you're dead. I thought of Nick. Simple, except for those left behind.

A message from Helen Wakaba at the National Museum was waiting on my answering machine. I called back, but the museum was closed for the night. She'd left her home number, too, and I dialed that, wondering if she'd found out more about the scorpion that stung Nick.

"Jazz, hello." Helen had a soft voice. "I called because Dr. Oticno is back. He returned a few days ago, and yesterday I had a chance to show him your specimen." She sounded embarrassed. "He would like to talk to you about it himself. Can you come to the museum tomorrow afternoon?" I could hear papers rustling. "He has some time free after lunch, say, around two?"

"What did he say?"

"That is what he wants to talk with you about. You can ask him that directly when you see him."

It was definitely embarrassment. I had a sinking feeling that she had misidentified the scorpion and that Nick hadn't been murdered after all. I realized with dread that I'd pinned an awful lot on the word of one post-doc who'd warned me scorpions weren't her specialty. "It *is* a Sahara scorpion?"

She laughed awkwardly. "Oh, yes, it's most definitely *Androctonus australis*. That's not the problem."

277

And that's all she would say.

When I awoke the next morning, the two interviews with Viv and Mutani came flooding back before I'd even opened my eyes, and in their wake a new thought that had me bolt upright in bed. If Kaji had killed Nick on an impulse, to stop him from selling the land, that was one thing. But if she'd done it to get the land, there was still an obstacle between her and her goal: Wynn.

The two of them were all alone up there. I jumped out of bed and started flinging on my clothes like a madwoman. I had to get up to Samburu and get Wynn out of danger. By the time I got my shoes on, I was a bit more awake and sanity returned. The danger was not as imminent as all that. Even if she wanted to, Wynn couldn't sell the land until Nick's will cleared, which would be months, so there was no time pressure on Kaji to act. Also, two sudden deaths in quick succession would be far too suspicious. Nick's murder had certainly been planned to appear totally natural. Still, I had to warn Wynn immediately. I didn't want her life depending on my logic.

I radioed and Kaji answered.

Sound normal, I told myself, my throat immediately drying up. "How is everything?"

"Just fine."

"Wynn there?"

"No, she went out on a game drive at dawn. Took Comet, packed breakfast and lunch, and plans to spend the whole day. Is it something important?"

Relief flooded through me. "I can catch her tonight. What are your plans today?"

"The pregnant cheetah I've been observing has been nosing around, as if scouting out den sites. I don't expect to be back till dark. Gin and Tonic are going to be on their own the longest time ever."

We chatted a moment longer and signed off. There was no cause for alarm, I told myself, but I called the airport to reserve an afternoon flight to Isiolo, and rent a car at the Isiolo airport. I had no illusions about being Wynn's bodyguard. She could protect herself a lot better than I could. But I wanted to warn her without Kaji knowing, and the radio afforded no privacy. Besides, if I got there early enough to poke around on my own, I might be able to pick up some more evidence, now that I had a better idea of what I was looking for. I wanted to look in Kaji's room, and in the cheetah barn.

The morning's mail brought me some happier messages in the form of two checks with the deposit for my November safari. I went immediately to the bank to deposit them. As soon as they cleared, I would be able to pay my two months' back rent. That would leave me back at square one, sweating out the rent due for next month. Was this any way to live? No wonder Striker wanted me to give up.

I'm not a quitter, I told myself defiantly. I was looking forward to my next safari group: a half-dozen friends, most of whom had been on traditional safaris before and this time wanted to see things in more depth. Find a family of cheetahs, for example, and follow them for a few days, get to know the pattern of their lives. I'd been planning to take them to one of the private game ranches between the Abedare Mountains and Mount Kenya. Now I wondered if Wynn would be interested in letting me set up a camp on her land. It could be a nice bit of extra income for her, and more profitable for me. If it worked out well, we might make it into a permanent arrangement.

Back at the apartment, I called Omondi and let him know about my conversation with Kaji and my plan to go north and warn Wynn. He agreed it was the sensible thing to do. I did a few other errands for Jazz Jasper Safaris, grabbed lunch, and headed over to the National Museum at two to see professor Otieno. I figured it would take an hour at the most, the outside limit for getting to Wilson and catching my plane north.

This time I went to the staff entrance, gave the professor's name, and was ushered into a cool, high-ceilinged entry to wait for Helen.

"Hi, Jazz." Helen's bright eyes were partly hidden by her horn-rim glasses, and she didn't meet my gaze directly. Something was wrong. She led me through the maze of halls to Dr. Otieno's glass-walled office in the bowels of the Invertebrate Biology Department, pointing out items of interest along the way, talking about everything but scorpions. By the time we got to the office, I was definitely uneasy.

"Dr. Otieno, Jazz Jasper to see you." She mumbled my name all in a fluster, and retreated to her desk and microscope.

Dr. Otieno was a stout man of middle height, with a big, open face, and broad triangular nose. "My pleasure." He shook my hand firmly and gestured to a chair crowded next to his paper-covered desk.

I sat, but my eyes were immediately drawn to a magnificent head-dress of enormous white ostrich plumes and curving hippo tusks mounted on the wall above the desk. Next to it was a full-length robe of flamboyant black and white colobus monkey skins.

Dr. Otieno beamed. "You are familiar with the Luo tribe? We come from near Lake Victoria. If a man's name begins with an O, like mine, you can tell he is Luo. We are known for being big talkers and theorizers. That is why so many academics are Luo."

"I have a close Luo friend whose name is Omondi. And he does like to lecture!" Omondi rarely mentioned his tribe, perhaps because his mother was Kikuyu, and he preferred to think of himself as Kenyan. I'd have to ask him more about his mixed ethnic background sometime.

Otieno beamed. "You see?" He gestured at the wall. "We had the most colorful costumes in all of Kenya. Now, the only place you can find one is in a museum, or a tourist show. My father's generation was the last to see such things, but even they had stopped making them." He shook his head, but didn't look a bit depressed. He pointed. "This is a Luo warrior's headdress, and this robe, a dancing costume. I cadged them from the Anthropology Department." He gazed up at the wall dreamily, as if imagining himself a dancing warrior of a hundred years before. "But that is not what you came for." He leaned toward me across the desk and linked his fingers.

I opened my mouth to ask about the scorpion, but before I could get a word out, he kept on talking. "I know another friend of yours, I believe. Marianne Kanja."

"Of course. How do you know her?"

"She was a student in my taxonomy course." Dr. Otieno tipped his chair back and folded his hands across his stomach. "Did an excellent senior paper on dung beetles, using our collection here at the museum."

"Did you cover scorpions, too?" I asked. My feeling of unease, set off by Helen's weird embarrassment, was completely forgotten. This was proving more useful than I could have dreamed. Dr. Otieno was a supremely credible witness who could testify that Kaji knew something about collecting scorpions!

"We skimmed the surface. In a general course like that, there's no time for in-depth treatment."

"Does it include fieldwork, too?"

"It might, depending on the student's ambition and topic." Dr. Otieno rocked his chair on its back legs. "I like to give everyone a flavor of live collecting at least, so I usually manage to take them out on an evening expedition."

"Collecting scorpions?"

"Scorpion collecting is among the most interesting." He leaned forward again and his face shone with enthusiasm. "Scorpions have an interesting property that makes collecting surprisingly easy for an animal that likes to hide in rock crevices during the day and emerge at night." He waited for a reaction.

"It certainly sounds like it would be difficult."

"Tremendously difficult, except for one thing: they fluoresce in ultraviolet light."

"Really!" I was starting to feel like a sweet little student buttering up the professor for a good grade.

"Yes. All you have to do is go out into a good rocky bit of desert at night with a UV lantern, and they shine like glow worms. You simply go around picking them up."

"What's a UV lantern?"

"You can take any fluorescent camping lantern and adapt it by removing the glass and sticking in a UV bulb. It looks black to us: we don't see UV, but we sure see the effect on scorpions." He chuckled. "On a dark night, with a new moon or at least a quarter moon, they show up for almost fifteen meters—approximately forty-five feet. In a good habitat, you can find a thousand in an evening's work."

"A thousand scorpions!" This time my reaction was genuine. "Did Kaji, I mean, Marianne, go on one of these scorpion expeditions?"

"Hmm. I can't say I remember exactly. You'll have to ask her. But I do take most of my seniors, especially avid students like Marianne."

He asked me how she was doing, and I told him about her work with rehabbing Gin and Tonic, and the field study she was doing on her own with breeding wild cheetahs. He was happy to hear she'd maintained her interest in science.

"Bringing it back to scorpions for the moment," I said. "When you collect them, do you kill them first, or how do you do it?" I asked.

Dr. Otieno's eyes twinkled. "You grab them by the tail, very, very quickly."

"No!"

"Yes, but only for the nonpoisonous ones. For those with nasty stings, a forceps is recommended. You paint the tip with fluorescent paint so you can see what you're doing. Wouldn't want to miss."

"You're joking."

"Not at all. And you thought working in a museum was a musty, safe profession."

"So you collect them live."

"In the field you pop them in a sandwich bag." He smiled broadly.

"You wouldn't want to mistake it for your midnight snack."

"No, indeed."

"How do you take care of a scorpion? Keep it alive, I mean."

"All you need is a little box with air holes. A bottle cap holds all the water they need for fourteen days or so. They can live for many weeks with no food, although they'd be happier with the occasional live cricket or moth, or a roach if you happen to have any around." He chuckled.

"So someone could easily have collected this Sahara scorpion in the Middle East and brought it alive into Kenya."

"Oh, yes. No problem at all. Easy to sneak through Customs. But that's not what happened with your specimen."

My God, was he going to tell me where my scorpion actually came from! "What happened?"

"This is the scorpion you brought to show me, that Helen identified for you." He picked up a jar from his desk, which I recognized as the jam jar I'd brought, with the crushed body of Nick's killer floating alone at the bottom.

"Yes, I recognize it."

Dr. Otieno rummaged in his desk and pulled out a tweezers. He fished out the scorpion and placed it on a petri dish. He held it out toward me. "Touch it."

"Touch it?"

"Yes, go ahead. Pinch the abdomen."

I gingerly pinched the abdomen.

"How does it feel?"

"Stiff and rubbery."

"Yes. That is how a specimen feels that has been in preservative for a good long time. Not overnight. Not a mere week."

My fear about Helen's embarrassment came flooding back. I could hardly bear to take in what he was saying.

"Your hypothesis that a man was stung by this scorpion last week and died as a result is false. This scorpion has been in a bottle for a long, long time." Dr. Otieno leaned back with a satisfied smile. He thought he'd just done a clever and useful piece of detective work.

I stared at the petri dish with loathing. My murder weapon had just been wiped out.

30

I LEFT THE museum and sat for a while in my car without turning on the engine. The bit of shade I'd parked under had moved, and the seat was hot. I barely noticed. Slowly, a few thoughts stirred in my head. My weapon might be dead, but the reality of murder was now easier to prove than before. Wasn't it? I tried to grab on to the facts a court would respect. The coroner's report asserted with certainty that Nick had died of a scorpion's sting. You might argue he was stung by a freakishly venomous local scorpion, but you'd still have to explain how the preserved specimen of a Sahara scorpion got into the loo.

My head started to whirl. Take it from the top again, I told myself. The coroner's report did not prove that Nick died of a scorpion's sting, only that he died of scorpion venom. Nick was not stung by the Sahara scorpion found in the loo. A Kenyan scorpion couldn't kill him. Therefore the venom must have been introduced by the killer in some other way. I reviewed the coroner's report again in my mind. Nothing in it contradicted this conclusion. Although Nick's hand was swollen as if the venom entered his body there, the coroner didn't find any sign of a puncture from the scorpion's sting.

The killer must have poisoned Nick with scorpion venom, and then staged it to look like he was stung. How? I racked my brain, staring unseeing through the windshield. Nick had a bandaged cut on his finger. Could a concentrated dose of venom have been introduced into his cut? How?

And where did the venom come from? Not from a local

scorpion. I held my forehead, as if my hand could extract thoughts from my brain. One Kenyan scorpion couldn't kill a man, but if Nick wasn't actually stung, why assume he'd been poisoned with venom from a single animal? Two factors combined to make the sting fatal: the virulence of the venom and the dosage. That's why children were more at risk. The killer could have collected a number of scorpions, removed their stingers with their venom sacs, and produced a concentrated dose.

My mind was finally clicking into gear. I remembered the Dorobo's herbs. Lodogia said he'd given Nick herbs for a poultice to stop infection in his finger. It would have been easy for someone in the house to doctor his poultice, watch when he used it, then slip the Sahara scorpion near wherever he collapsed. Roger could have planted it in the outhouse when he was supposedly discovering it. Or someone else could have put it in there and hastily retreated so as not to arrive first on the scene.

I reviewed all the candidates for murder in light of this new theory. Strangers like Mutani or Gerry Weller wouldn't know that Nick used traditional healing remedies, wouldn't have been on the spot to do the split-second timing necessary to plant the scorpion. Wynn, Viv, and Roger fit those conditions, but how would any of them have procured scorpion venom?

I was back to Kaji as my prime candidate, even more than before. She alone had knowledge of scorpions and knew how to collect them. I had to get up to Samburu and warn Wynn. I looked at my watch with alarm. Why was I sitting in the museum parking lot when I had a plane to catch in fifteen minutes? If I missed it, I'd have no chance of arriving at Wynn's before Kaji. I threw the car into gear and sped out of there.

It was four-thirty by the time I got to Isiolo, rented the car, and did the long drive to Wynn's, but I still had a good hour and a half before dusk, which is when I expected the two women to return. More than enough time to search the couple of places where I figured I might find some evidence. Gin and Tonic were lying on the shady verandah. They were overjoyed to see me, bouncing around, jumping on me, then getting overexcited and racing around in a game of tag.

The front door was unlocked. I'd picked up Wynn's and Kaji's mail at Isiolo, and dropped the stack on the hall table. It hit the table with an unexpectedly loud slap that made me jump. The house was totally silent, as only a house without electricity can be. There was not even the hum of a refrigerator to riffle the air. For some reason, it got on my nerves, and I found myself tiptoeing into Nick and Wynn's bedroom. Cut it out, Jazz, I told myself. Relax.

I checked the bureau and bed tables for the Dorobo herbs, on the off chance that Wynn hadn't been able to throw away anything of Nick's. Nothing. Down the hall to Kaji's room, not expecting anything there, but checking. Her bed was pushed against one wall to make room for a writing table and bookshelf. There was an old manual typewriter on the table with paper in it. I looked at what was written: field notes on her observation of the pregnant cheetah. Nothing suspicious in that.

I walked over to the cheetah barn. Here, I really was hoping to find evidence, something indicating scorpion collecting. There was a large storage closet, a small room really, that was full of the most incredible miscellany of stuff: camping equipment, a badminton set, an inflatable dinghy, the first box that Gin and Tonic slept in when they were tiny cubs, a cabinet of medicines and diet supplements for them, other shelves stacked high with all sorts of junk, from salt-encrusted old flowerpots to parts for the pump.

I found a pair of gardening gloves and put them on, thinking of fingerprints. An hour later, hot, sweaty, and dirty, I peeled them off, defeated. I went to the outdoor pump, drank long and deep, and stuck my head under the faucet for good measure. That felt better. The sun was getting low, casting long shadows of Gin and Tonic as they sat side by side and watched me be wet and frustrated.

"There's got to be something, somewhere!" I told them. Kaji might have thrown out whatever she used, probably had. I trotted around to the garbage midden, screened from the house by a mat fence. The vultures and jackals took care of all the kitchen scraps, and a weekly burning took care of paper. What was left was cans and bottles. Not really a good place to chuck out something secret, because everyone used it, and the animals tended to dig in the pile and scatter stuff about. I poked around. Nothing.

A big shadow moved over me, there was a whoosh of air, and I ducked. A Nubian vulture landed on the other side of the midden, folded its eight feet of wings, and stared at me with unblinking eyes. The folds of skin on its neck and head were a raw red, like the newly dead meat they liked to scavenge. I've heard vultures make affectionate pets, but this one wasn't looking very affectionate. I got out of there fast.

I still had some time, although I was beginning to cut it short. I didn't want to be caught snooping in here if Kaji returned early. It could be dangerous.

I reentered the cheetah barn and cast my eyes and mind around. I ran my hand through my hair. There weren't a whole lot of places to look. There was the space with the cheetah cages—for when they had to be transported, an area used as a garage, the storeroom I'd already searched. I realized I hadn't come across a hardware closet, a place where used tools were often kept. There was a low metal cabinet in the garage section. I opened it with a sense of anticipation. Damn. Nothing but innocent wrenches, spare spark plugs and the like.

Where? Where would I put collecting equipment where it wouldn't be noticed? Along with all the other forgotten junk. I went back to the damned storage closet. Ignoring a growing sense of claustrophobia, I began more systematically at one end and worked my way around. I was getting dirtier, more tired, and more grumpy by the minute. The thought of being caught in here unawares by Kaji didn't add much to the experience. I doggedly kept going.

The highest shelves held a bunch of half-used cans of stain, waterproofing, paint, and turpentine. Was there room for something to be stuck behind them? Not behind the big cans, but there could be room behind some of the half-gallon and smaller ones. I pulled over a ladder, moved about seventeen things to make room for it, and climbed up.

There it was.

I'd found the smoking gun: an oversize flashlight with its glass shade removed and an odd-looking light bulb. I picked it up in my gloved hands, trying not to smudge things. Yes, the bulb was labeled UV. Farther along, pushed way into the corner, was a thick white crockery bowl with a stubby pestle sticking out of it. Little gold specks that could have been ground-up bits of scorpion tail adhered to the working end of the pestle. My heart started to pound dully in my chest. I'd done it.

I tried not to think about Kaji standing trial as I emptied a cardboard box holding a few jars of the cheetahs' food supplements. I put in my finds and stuck the box in the back of my car. The sun was approaching the western hills, turning them an ethereal blue. I headed to the kitchen for a beer and to wait for Wynn's return. I could feel myself beginning to unwind, and realized I'd been coiled tight as a spring. Even if Kaji returned now, I'd be in no danger.

I washed the grime off my hands, opened a beer, and headed out to the porch, when my eyes fell on a hook by the kitchen door. I'd seen it a hundred times, so I hadn't registered its possible significance. Nick had a bad habit of forgetting his keys in odd places, so he'd put up this hook and gotten into the routine of hanging his key chain there whenever he wasn't using it, which was most of the time. It had keys to the front door, and the barn, but also small keys. I pulled it off the hook. Two were luggage keys, but there was a tiny gunmetal-gray key that looked like the sort that came with fireproof boxes.

I looked out the window. No dust plume from an approaching car. Besides, if Kaji caught me searching the desk, she wouldn't guess I was testing to see if she'd been able to get into Nick's private papers. I headed for his little office with its beat-up old roll-top with a million cubbyholes. I was glad I didn't have to go through them.

Setting my beer down, I quickly peeped in the drawers. A file drawer on the bottom right had a wooden divider. In the back section sat a gray metal box. I lifted it out. It was full of file cards. Shit.

As I started to put it back in the bottom drawer, I noticed that below it was a stack of glossy brochures of sailing yachts. It caught my attention because in the mail I'd picked up in Isiolo, there'd been a registered letter that I'd had to sign for that had a sailboat logo on the return address. I'd noticed it because of Nick telling Striker he should go on a round-the-world cruise. It was obviously Nick's own fantasy.

I lifted out the top brochure. It was from the same boatyard, Hutchinson and Hinckley. Stuck inside the front cover was a letter congratulating Nick on his judgment and taste in requesting information about a custom-built yacht. They requested a ten-percent deposit: fifty thousand dollars. Even with rusty arithmetic I could figure out the boat cost a half-million dollars. Expensive daydreams. I put the brochure back, feeling sad at the thought of all of Nick's unlived dreams.

I took another gulp of my beer. Back to work. Concentrate. Where would Nick keep his important documents? The box wouldn't be too large. I went to his bedroom and checked out the closet. Not on the floor. I brought in a kitchen chair so I could search the top shelf. This was getting to be repetitious. Behind a pile of sweaters was a fireproof box the size of a large shoe box. Fitting the tiny key into the lock took only a second.

I sat down on the chair and opened the box. It was crammed with papers. Passports on top, the deed to the land, stock certificates, other financial papers, and yes, a will. I pulled it out and started to read. The legalese was heavy going, so I skimmed the pages, looking for Kaji's name. There it was: from what I could make out, it said that if Wynn died without leaving a new will, the land and house were to go to Kaji.

I must have had my head in the closet when the car returned. I was concentrating so hard I didn't even hear footsteps on the porch, or the front door open. The first thing I heard was someone in the hall, tearing through the mail. I hurriedly stuck the will back in the box when the steps approached the bedroom. I shoved the box under the chair, then pulled it out again. Trying to hide it would be more suspicious than brazening it out. My heart was in my throat.

The person entered.

"Wynn! Hi. I'm so glad it's you."

"Hello. This is a nice surprise." Wynn took in what I had in my lap. "What in the world are you up to?"

"I have some upsetting news, Wynn." I gestured at the box and showed her the keys I'd used to open it. "I was testing to see if Kaji could have learned about the will in her favor."

Wynn's eyes narrowed and the lines in her face deepened. "Kaji? You're not suspecting Kaji? No! Absolutely not her. Impossible."

"Wynn, I—"

The sound of a Land Cruiser approaching quickly drew our attention.

"That's her." Wynn turned on her heel and left. I hurried after.

"You're not going to say a word to Kaji, are you?" Wynn asked over her shoulder.

"No, of course not. I came up to warn you to be careful, that's all. Not all the evidence is checked out yet, anyway."

"Careful of Kaji?" Wynn turned an angry face toward me. "Don't say that to me again, okay?"

God, this was going more badly than I could have imagined. I shouldn't have underestimated the impact on Wynn. She prided herself on being a strong person, thanks to all the traumas she'd survived, but they'd left deep fault lines. Wynn tended to see the world in black and white, bad guys and good guys. Kaji was definitely a good guy, and having to admit otherwise would be painfully difficult for Wynn. I should have been more sensitive. Still, I had to warn her, I comforted myself. I'd leave the rest until tomorrow, when she'd be calmer and readier to listen.

I stopped in the front door, allowing Wynn to get ahead of me. I could see Kaji's Land Cruiser on the next slope. She was driving much faster than usual. I needed to collect myself before facing her. I realized I looked like a mess, hot, dirty, discombobulated, with dust and cobwebs in my hair from the storage closet.

My eye fell on a ripped envelope on the floor, probably because of the sailboat next to the return address. It was the registered letter from Hutchinson and Hinckley. Still in snooping mode, I pulled a crumpled piece of stationery out of the wastepaper basket and smoothed it out. The letter was short and to the point. Wynn had obviously written to them, telling them that Nick was deceased. The next sentence explained why: "We are most sorry to inform you that the deadline for a full refund of the deposit was July 30. Enclosed please find a check for the fifty-percent refundable portion in the amount of twenty-five thousand dollars."

Twenty-five thousand dollars?

"Jazz! Hurry!" It was Wynn's voice. She sounded ebullient. I rushed out to where she stood with Kaji, next to Kaji's dusty Land Cruiser.

"Gin and Tonic have made their first kill!" Kaji shouted.

Wynn was practically jumping up and down with excitement. "Let's go!"

Kaji ran toward the house. "I want to get a camera. I'll be right there."

"We'll take my car!" Wynn had already jumped in and had the engine going. "C'mon, Jazz."

I climbed into the passenger seat. Wynn roared out of the parking area.

"What about Kaji?"

"That's okay, she'll take her own car. The cubs are in that rocky area, past the humpbacked hill. You know where I mean?"

"Yeah."

"If we don't hurry, the sun's going to be down before we get there. Besides," she took a quick sidelong glance at me, "I thought you'd be happier if we weren't with her."

"Oh, if there's two of us—" I started to say.

There was something off, something that was making me uneasy. It was that letter from the boat company. Nick had sent them a fifty-thousand-dollar deposit. That meant he wasn't just daydreaming about a round-the-world cruise. Or about a half-million-dollar sailboat. Paying the deposit must have used up all of Nick's life savings. How could he afford a half-million-dollar boat?

The answer was obvious: sell the land. Everything fell into place. Sell the land, buy a boat. That's why Nick hadn't been fastidious about who he sold to: he was giving up on Kenya, like Striker was, selling out on the animals and everything else. I knew he'd been burned-out from covering the Somali civil war, but I hadn't realized it had got to the point where he wanted to leave and burn his bridges behind him. Where did Wynn fit in? Was he leaving her, too?

I could see Wynn agreeing to sell this land in order to buy a bigger piece with even better cheetah habitat. I did not see Wynn leaving Kenya for the cramped world of a boat, no matter how fancy and swift.

Why hadn't she told me about Nick's bombshell, for bombshell it must have been? It would have been the natural thing to do when I confided to her that Striker had decided to leave. Maybe she didn't know until she got the letter from the boatyard just now? No, that was ridiculous. They were answering a letter from her, a letter than must have been written immediately after Nick's death, to judge from the speed of the response.

There was only one reason I could think of for Wynn hiding Nick's plans. She'd killed him. The killer wasn't Kaji, it was Wynn. My mind idiotically repeated this new thought, wanting to find a reason it was false, wanting to declare "Impossible!" But it was all too possible.

Rescuing and working to free Gin and Tonic was a lifeline to Wynn, a lifeline to happiness, to mental stability. She would no more abandon the cubs than cut out her own heart. Which is what she did, anyway. How else could she have held together when Nick died so painfully in her arms? Had Nick's betrayal already ripped her heart out? How could she live with what she had done? Done to someone she loved! She must have turned him into a figure of evil by then, a traitor who deserved no quarter. Maybe she got satisfaction from the murder, as if she was finally getting back at the man who tortured and killed her sister. I was afraid to look at her, to move, to breathe, afraid that anything I did would betray my realization of the monstrosity that Wynn had committed.

I looked behind us. No sign of Kaji following. For a moment I feared that Wynn was driving me into the desert in the opposite direction from Gin and Tonic's kill. She meant to kill me and dump my body. . . . My pulse sounded loud and erratic in my ears. Calm down, a panicky voice inside me yelled. I took a deep breath. As long as Wynn thought it was Kaji I suspected, there was nothing to fear from her. She couldn't read my mind.

The sun was an angry red blob balancing precariously on the line of the horizon. I shivered. The temperature was already plunging. There's no prolonged dusk on the equator. One minute it's day, and the next it's night. Wynn put on the headlights and speeded up.

I grabbed onto the dashboard to keep from being bounced into the ceiling, door, windshield, and back again. "Hey! Slow down a bit. Let's make sure we get there."

She slowed fractionally. "Kaji shouldn't have left them, even to get us. What if those lions show up to steal the kill?"

Why hadn't it struck me before how overprotective Wynn was toward the cubs? They didn't need us to tell them to run away from lions.

It was that shadowy moment before full darkness when we rounded the foot of a rock-strewn hill, and there were the cubs, looking washed out and mysterious in the headlights. From the size of the carcass, they'd caught a full-grown gazelle. The animal must have been lame or sick. Now there was nothing left of it but the skin and shreds of meat still attached to the bones, but they were still working away at it. Predators don't succeed often enough to squander food when they do get it. The cubs' stomachs were as distended as a pregnant female's. Maybe I'd been too quick to criticize Wynn: they looked like they could hardly walk, let alone run.

They looked up briefly when we approached. Wynn stopped and cut the engine about thirty feet away. "I know it's far, but I don't want to interfere," she explained, "or block their view of uninvited guests."

"Mind if I turn on the spotlight?" Without waiting for an answer, I reached up and flicked the switch of the roof-mounted light used for night game drives.

"Don't bother. It's broken," Wynn said quickly, but it was already too late.

There was no beam of light, and for a moment I believed her. Then I noticed the eerie spots glowing in the sand around us. I saw one, two, a dozen, fifty. Little greeny purple lights, scurrying about. Scurrying about, looking for something to sting. Scorpions. We'd hit a hot spot, as Dr. Otieno would say.

"So it is." I reached up to turn off the switch, hoping my voice sounded natural. Hoping Wynn wouldn't notice that I'd noticed the UV, wouldn't guess that I knew what we were seeing: she'd put a UV bulb in the car's spotlight when she went collecting, and forgotten to remove it.

"Leave it." She blocked my hand from reaching the switch.

I darted a look toward her. She was gripping the steering wheel with two clawlike hands. My only hope was to convince her that it was Kaji I still suspected.

"The light isn't broken, Wynn, it's a UV light. Used for collecting scorpions. Kaji learned how to do it at the university. I learned it this morning, and came straight up to warn you. If she did kill Nick—which seems more and more likely—it was to get the land. That means you're the next victim."

"You had to come snooping in my house without asking permission." Her voice was calm and cold.

She knew. My throat went dry.

"I wasn't snooping, I was looking for evidence that Kaji killed Nick. You weren't here to ask, and I didn't think it should wait."

"It's no good, Jazz." She didn't look at me. "I glanced inside your rented car to see who'd arrived. It was stupid to leave that box from the cheetahs' food supplements in plain view. I knew there was no reason for you to have it there, so I checked what was in it." She turned toward me.

Her face was shadowy and bland, free of all emotion, like her voice. "Kaji told me about how they collected scorpions. It's too bad you found the flashlight and the mortar I used. They're covered with my fingerprints."

Then she lunged for me. We grappled. I managed to grab her arms and stop her from getting at my throat, but only for an instant. She jammed my hand backward at the wrist. Excruciating pain flashed up my arm and my hand let go on its own. The next moment she pulled her other hand free, clutched a handful of hair on each side of my head and began to twist my head as if it were a jar top she was trying to open.

I struggled, I punched, I tried to kick, but in the confined space, with her on top of me, I couldn't land an effective blow.

"You bitch," she spat in my face. "You had to mess everything up."

I started to black out from the pain. My neck was going to snap at any moment. She was like an animal. She had no mercy in her. A tremendous bubble of outrage and refusal grew in my chest. I refused to let her kill me.

She was pressing my back against the door with her full weight so that I couldn't roll with the attack, couldn't relieve the agonizing twisting of my neck. She pressed my head backward. The door handle cut painfully into my scalp. There was a gush of hot blood on my neck. I shoved my head down against the handle, ignoring the pain. Open! Open, damn it! I screamed inside. I might fall on my head and break my neck anyway, but at least it would have been through my own action.

The door lock released and the door flew open under our combined weight. We tumbled onto the rocky desert floor. Her hands flew off my head. I tucked my chin under and curled into my shoulder. I landed on my upper back, sustaining only a jolt, kept rolling and got to my feet.

Wynn was even faster. When I straightened, there she was in a crouch, her knife blade gleaming in the headlights. I flung myself at her legs as she lunged forward, tumbling her to the ground. Before she could scramble to her feet, I jumped onto her back, pinning her down. She still gripped the knife, and twisted like a cat. I couldn't keep her face down. She was as strong as I was, and better trained. The knife slashed my chest. My arm. I let go and started to scramble away as she rolled onto her haunches. I almost put my hand on a scorpion, noticed the glow and flinched away.

Tonic, distended stomach and all, couldn't resist the invitation to wrestle. He loped over, and as Wynn leaped for me, he threw himself against her. The knife meant to rip out my guts sliced into him. He twisted in midair and yelped with pain.

Wynn was distracted for a vital moment, and I ran around the car, out of reach of her knife. If I stopped long enough to climb behind the wheel, she'd be back on top of me. I watched her through the windows, and kept moving, keeping the car between us. We circled the car. I was panting with the exertion. The loss of blood from my scalp wound and the cuts on my chest and arm didn't help, either. Wynn had the same eerily calm look on her face she'd worn since I turned on the UV light.

How was this going to end? Play ring around the rosie until one of us dropped? I was going to slow quicker than she was. Where the hell was Kaji?

I wasn't going to get out of this by running. I had to go for her. The next time I rounded the hood of the car, I scrambled onto the front bumper, across the hood, onto the roof, and in one swift, unstoppable rush threw myself on top of her.

We crashed to the ground in a roiling mass of struggling arms and legs. The knife was gone. She must have lost her grip on it. The small rocks the scorpions love bit into my back and legs. I managed to get on top again.

Wynn drew her arm back and smacked my head, hard, while at the same time snaking her other hand up my chest and face, her fingers in a V, going for my eyes. She'd taught Kariankei and me the technique during our street fighting lesson in his desert cave. It was the best way to blind your opponent. I felt her fingertips on my eyelashes. In a rush of terror and adrenaline, I jerked backward, falling away from her. Instead of rushing me, she turned and scrambled for her knife.

She never reached it. Suddenly she recoiled with a wild scream. The cheetahs chirped in alarm and scattered. "I've been stung!" Her voice had a hysterical edge. She got the knife and slashed at her hand in an attempt to wash out the poison.

I kept a wary eye on that knife hand. "One sting won't kill you."

"It stung me twice!" She cradled her right arm. It was swelling by the second. I breathed easier, but I still kept my distance.

"Jazz. I'm sorry. I don't know what came over me. Get me the antivenin kit from the glove compartment, would you? I promise not to attack you again." She raised her arm slightly, and gave a startled grunt of pain. "I couldn't, even if I wanted to. You've got me now."

I went to the car, and still keeping my eye on her, fished the kit from the glove compartment and threw it to her. She caught it in her left hand and fumbled awkwardly to open it. "Give me a hand getting this open, would you?"

"I don't think so."

"Fuck you to hell, then." Grimacing with pain, she used both hands, got the thing open, and managed to fill the hypodermic. "I made sure to get scorpion antivenin before I went collecting." She injected herself above the sting. "I had to order it from Egypt; the same place that sold me the scorpion specimen. I assumed anything called the Sahara scorpion would be endemic here." She refilled the hypodermic. "That was my one mistake."

I started toward her. "Don't overdo it. That stuff is dangerous."

"Oh, really?" She plunged the hypodermic into her arm a second time. "I want to make sure this works." She smiled ghoulishly. "An overdose is gonna hurt worse than jail, but it doesn't last as long."

"Wynn!"

"I'm glad I killed him! He betrayed everything we lived for! Not just me. No, not just me! The cheetahs. The land. Kaji's work. He was destroying everything!" Suddenly she

297

vomited explosively. A look of terror came over her face. "Even hope," she whispered. She vomited again, and again. Her entire body started to twitch and jump. She struggled to breathe, and froth bubbled at her mouth and nostrils.

There was nothing I could do for her. I half dragged her to the car and got her into the backseat. Somehow that felt better than letting her die in the sand. It didn't take long.

31

WHEN I GOT back to the house, Kaji was waiting for me in the yard. Before I could find the words to tell her what had happened, she burst out, "Where's Wynn? She took the keys from my car so I couldn't go out again! What's going on here? I'm so mad!" She looked behind the car. "Gin and Tonic didn't come back with you? Were they run off the kill?"

"Gin and Tonic are on their way home. They're fine, but Wynn isn't." I got out of the car, and Kaji saw the slashes on my arm and chest. They were still oozing blood, and my clothes were coated in blood and sand. I felt woozy and stood still until my balance got steady.

"Oh, my God! Let's get you inside and cleaned up." She took my arm gently to lead me to the house. "Was it the lions? Where's Wynn?"

"A terrible thing has happened."

"Don't tell me . . . ?"

"She's dead."

Kaji put her hand against her mouth and began to cry. "I can't believe it," she said in a choked voice. "How . . . ? Dead?"

"She killed herself, Kaji." A weight of sadness descended on my shoulders. "She confessed to poisoning Nick. His death wasn't an accident."

"What!" At that Kaji broke down, crying hysterically.

She set me off, and I began to cry also. We fell into each other's arms, and for a long time there was only the sound of crying, and muffled expressions of disbelief, horror, and sorrow. Finally we pulled ourselves together. I locked up the car, went in the house, and radioed the police.

Omondi had already left for the day, but they promised to get the message to him right away. Kaji insisted I clean up, dress my wounds, and lie down for a while before trying to tell her what had happened. Putting antibiotic on the cuts made me think of Nick, and I was almost afraid to do it. I had to force myself to be rational. Wynn had not poisoned the tube of first-aid cream. She was not going to reach from the grave to harm me. I lay down, and Kaji brought me a cup of tea and some toast. It was comforting to eat it. The radio beeped. It was Omondi. He listened to my terse account without interruption.

"Are you injured?"

"A couple of knife wounds. Not deep. They've already stopped bleeding."

He urged me to call the flying doctors, but I refused, saying it wasn't an emergency, and the thing I wanted more than anything was simply to go to sleep. Omondi understood, and we made arrangements for returning to Nairobi the next morning with Wynn's body. An ambulance would take her to the morgue, and I agreed to make an appointment with my own doctor to look at my wounds. Omondi quietly congratulated me on my quick thinking and bravery. I didn't feel smart or brave, just lucky. Lucky to be alive.

Kaji had heard me tell Omondi the gist of what happened, but she asked me to go over it again more slowly, and asked a lot of questions. The idea that Wynn killed Nick was unbelievable to her, and I don't think she took in half of what I said, including the part about the land going to her now. I had another piece of toast as the rest of my dinner, and went to bed, where I fell into a deep, dreamless sleep.

The effects of Nick's murder and Wynn's suicide, and of the earlier parts of the investigation, continued to unfold for several weeks. *The Nairobi Star* played up the story, of course, covering every angle, including a banner headline on Sheikh Farid hunting cheetah. He was already safely back in Saudi Arabia by then, and the Kenyan government declared there was insufficient evidence to press charges, as Omondi predicted.

The sheikh didn't get off scot-free, however. The story of his illegal hunting got a lot of play in the international press, with spinoffs on how the top Saudi aristocracy were slaughtering endangered birds by the tens of thousands in their search for greater sexual potency. I'd been impressed by the hunting camp I saw, but it came out that in Pakistan they were actually building entire palaces as temporary lodging in the desert. The stink embarrassed even King ibn-Saud, and he was not pleased. Farid was stripped of his role in Kenarabia Oil and pressured to contribute three million dollars to the East African Wildlife Foundation. I expect he'll be ashamed to show his face in Europe or Africa for a while.

I upheld my agreement with William Mutani and did not reveal his involvement in the hunting, or his nasty little business in cat pelts. It was frustrating not to go after him, but I had to bow to the reality that I wouldn't succeed. At least, by holding on to the evidence I had a way to pressure him into closing down his trade in furs.

The Limuru Road casino is unfinished and has run out of money, and Mutani's been kept pretty busy staving off his creditors. He couldn't find any new backers for the Samburu golf hotel, and the project was abandoned. He donated the land to Kaji's newly established Cheetah Foundation. It brought him a lot of great publicity as a philanthropist and friend of wildlife, including a front page photo in *The Star* of him handing Kaji the deed.

Kaji is still waiting for the probate court to process the will before she can get title to the land she's inheriting. But all the publicity led the African Wildlife Foundation to issue her a grant for her fieldwork, which should provide her with enough money to live modestly for a few years. Comet also got his picture in the *International Trib*, and enough donations flooded into Kaji's Cheetah Foundation to hire a top-notch young Ph.D. in animal behavior. That way Kaji will learn about scientific research methods while they do the work together, and she'll have someone living with her in that isolated house.

She also received a large anonymous donation to the foundation. From me. Yes, I temporarily had buckets of money, and I gave most of it away. Omondi didn't see any point in registering the princess's diamond bracelet as evidence when there was no case, so he passed it back to me. I paid myself well for my time and expenses in pursuing the case. As for the remainder, returning it to the princess didn't seem as moral a solution as donating it to Comet. On his behalf, I split it between Kaji's fieldwork on cheetah fertility, the African Wildlife Foundation, and the Humane Society for their fight against the trade in wild pets and furs.

As for Viv's fashion show, the cheetah stole of course simply disappeared, and her name was never connected with anything illegal. The show barely broke even financially, and I heard on good authority, from my rich friend Alicia, that Viv was telling everyone it was the last show she'd ever do.

With the rotten economy, Striker couldn't find a buyer for his cabin on Mount Kenya. He ended up renting it out as a weekend house to a Nairobi couple who love its location next to the conference center facilities. They're thrilled to have a pool, nightclub, and restaurants a few minutes' drive away. As a result, Striker was able to charge them a lordly sum. He's planning to return to the States to visit old friends for a couple of months while deciding his next move.

As for me, business is looking up. Gerry Weller's friend Gabriella has booked my safari company for a week's tour at the end of the month. She's expecting a houseful of relatives from Italy, and says I'm saving her life. She's also promised to pass my name on to her wide circle of friends in Nairobi and Rome, the sort of people who can afford a custom safari. I can't wait to get back to work and back into the parks. I'm going to take them to the lakes and mountain parks and skip Samburu.

Gerry has also promised to line up some clients for me. The American oil company families living in their compounds in the Middle East always travel on their vacations, and Kenya is a short plane ride away for them. Most of them take cheap group tours, but some of the higher-up executives could afford me. Ford Motor Company in Europe has been flying all their executives to Kenya in batches for one-week training seminars and team building. How they justify the expense is beyond me, but they're doing it. Gerry says he's going to talk to the personnel department at Kenarabia and see if they have anything similar in the works. One contract like that, and my money problems would be over—but I've said that before.

My other big news is that I'm leaving my apartment. Gabriella has a big airy room on the top floor of her house, with its own kitchen, that she's used in the past for a caretaker. All she really wants is someone living in the house year-round, especially the months when she's in Europe. The rent she's asking is a quarter of what I pay now, and although it's only a studio instead of a one-bedroom, the space is actually larger than my current apartment. It'll be a great relief to me not to have to worry about bills piling up and scrounging for each month's rent. My landlord, Mr. Matua, is salivating at the prospect of getting my apartment. I suspect he's going to move in a family of refugees and triple the rent. Wars are always good for some people.

Wynn's family wanted her body flown back to the States for burial, but Kaji arranged to have a memorial service at her family's church. She said it was important that we bury her ourselves, at least spiritually. I think she was right. We decided a eulogy would be inappropriate, but the minister picked a nice passage out of the Bible about acceptance. It would probably be easier for me if I held her innocent, and blamed her actions on the man who'd tortured and killed her sister, but it was Wynn who chose to join his ranks.

I've been having a bad time with nightmares. I wake up several times a night to escape Wynn's hands twisting my neck, the crunching of vertebrae about to snap, her contorted face staring into mine without one shred of human decency left in it. The only thing that helps is Striker holding me.

I've been staying at Striker's a lot, soaking up his company before his departure. We both feel more in love than ever, like the glory of an Indian summer when you can taste the coming winter in the crisp night air. I know it's stupid, but I'm nursing a secret hope that he'll try out a new place, realize Kenya is better, warts and all, and come back.

As for Gin and Tonic, after the triumph of their fist kill, they started spending more and more time away from the house. Sometimes they came home after a day or two with their ribs showing and beg for food, but more and more often they seem well-fed, and are only passing through to say hello to Kaji and Comet. Comet has fully recovered his health—with sleek pelt, shining eyes, and nonstop energy. Kaji is following the new regime and not touching him, so he'll keep more of his wild nature. She's hoping that by the time he's ready to learn to hunt, Tonic will adopt him as a coalition partner and be his model. Being partners would increase both their chances of survival.

FOR INFORMATION ON PROTECTION OF CHEETAH

African Wildlife Foundation
1717 Massachusetts Avenue NW
Washington, D.C. 20036
Tel.: 202-265-8393

AWF supports numerous programs in Africa that help protect endangered species, including the cheetah. The Foundation also works to educate its membership on the plight of this beautiful animal through its newsletter and mailings.

Cheetah Conservation Fund c/o Humane Society
   International
Humane Society of the United States
2100 L Street NW
Washington, D.C. 20037
Tel.: 202-452-1100

The Cheetah Conservation Fund was founded by Laurie Marker-Kraus and Daniel Kraus, two scientists studying cheetah in Namibia. Namibia is the only country in the world that still has a sizable population of cheetah, and is vital for conserving an adequate gene pool for their long-term survival. The Krauses are working with ranchers to solve the problem of cheetah being shot as vermin; these ranches provide the last habitat for free-ranging cheetah.

Friends of the National Zoo
30001 Connecticut Avenue NW
Washington, D.C. 20008-2598
Tel.: 202-673-4956

The National Zoo in Washington, D.C., has a model cheetah program. They are studying behavioral patterns (with
the help of volunteers) and developing strategies that
mimic natural conditions in order to stimulate breeding.
You may visit the cheetahs at the Cheetah Conservation
Station; call in advance to learn the hours of their interesting exercise program.